EVIL IN ME

NIGHTFIRE BOOKS BY **BROM**

Slewfoot

Evil in Me

ALSO BY **BROM**

Lost Gods

Krampus

The Child Thief

The Devil's Rose

The Plucker

TOR PUBLISHING GROUP NEW YORK

NIGHTFIRE

EVIL IN ME

Copyright © 2024 by Gerald Brom

All artwork copyright © 2024 by Gerald Brom

Grateful acknowledgment is made to AJ Grey for use of the lyrics, in part and in whole, from the "Evil in Me" song, written by AJ Grey and Gerald Brom, copyright © AJ Grey and Gerald Brom 2024.

A Nightfire Book
Published by Tom Doherty Associates / Tor Publishing Group
120 Broadway
New York, NY 10271

www.torpublishinggroup.com

Nightfire™ is a trademark of Macmillan Publishing Group, LLC.

The Library of Congress Cataloging-in-Publication Data is available upon request.

ISBN 978-1-250-62201-3 (hardcover)
ISBN 978-1-250-62202-0 (ebook)

Our books may be purchased in bulk for promotional, educational, or business use. Please contact your local bookseller or the Macmillan Corporate and Premium Sales Department at 1-800-221-7945, extension 5442, or by email at MacmillanSpecialMarkets@macmillan.com.

First Edition: 2024

Printed in the United States of America

0   9   8   7   6   5   4   3   2   1

EVIL IN ME

1951, BROOKLYN, NEW YORK

Adam glanced up and down the street, saw it was all his now, the shops closed and everyone gone home—just him and the humming street-lights. He ground his teeth, waiting as a rusty Buick station wagon with a busted muffler rumbled by, then set the briefcase down on the sidewalk. He let out a grunt; the briefcase was heavy, as well it should be considering there were four wine bottles full of gasoline in it. Adam had never made a Molotov cocktail before, but it seemed easy enough—just a bottle of fuel with a rag stuffed in it—yet he wasn't sure he'd done it right, as the whole briefcase reeked of gas.

Time to make him pay, Adam, the voice, the other, cooed. *Make them all pay.*

Adam's heart sped up, began to drum, his head to throb, like worms were squirming around in his brain. He thought he could hear them moaning, feel

1

them wiggling down into his heart, his gut. His stomach began to churn, to burn and boil, the heat spreading through his entire body. He began to sweat.

He belched, the hot air turning to mist in the cold night, then he retched, the bile burning his throat.

Something cold hit him in the face; he blinked.

A snowflake. Another, then another.

"Wha . . . ?" He stared up into the night sky, trying to make sense of what he was seeing. "Snowing?" He tugged at his sweat-stained collar, yanking loose his tie and popping the top button. "It's too fucking hot to snow!" But even as he said it, he knew it wasn't, knew the heat, the hateful worms, were all inside of him, stewing him in his own juices.

He pulled off his suit coat, dropped it to the ground, ripped his shirt open, tearing it off. He should've felt relief—it was snowing for Christ's sake—but still the sweat continued to trickle down his back and underarms, plastering his T-shirt to his chest. He wrestled the soggy undershirt over his head, threw it into a bush, and still the fever burned. He pried off his hard leather shoes, kicked them down the sidewalk. "God, fuck!" he snarled. "Hate those damn shoes!"

The worms squirmed, feeding on his anger, his hate.

Adam began to pant, his lips quivering as a string of drool ran down his chin. God, he just wanted to strip, take it all off, anything to cool down. He unbuckled his belt and trousers, started to tug them down and stopped.

"What am I doing? Can't just take my pants off in the middle of the goddamn city."

Yes . . . you can, the other said. ***It is time to do what you want for a change. Let go, Adam, free yourself. Go on . . . do it!***

"No," Adam whispered, shaking his head, "I can't. I won't." Then he heard them, the worms. Were they singing? God, yes, they were. They were singing to *him* . . . it was beautiful. And suddenly everything the other was telling him started to make sense. Adam slid his pants down, along with his boxers, slid them off one foot, then the other, slinging them into the bushes next to his shirt.

"Ahh," he moaned, as the cold night air washed over his nakedness. The fever was still there, but now somehow pleasing. Adam swayed back and forth, trembling, his flesh breaking out in goose bumps. He looked down at his shriveled pecker and laughed. And if someone had been watching him, they might've noticed a peculiar thing—more peculiar than a pudgy man with a bad combover, wearing only a watch, a ring, and a pair of socks. They would've seen a spark in his eye, a tiny flame, not some kind of a reflection, but what looked to be an actual fire burning inside of him.

Now, Adam, let us go. We have work to do.

Adam nodded and picked up the briefcase. That was when he saw his socks were mismatched—one argyle, the other dark green. He grimaced, embarrassed, hoping no one else would notice. The worms sang and slowly, his grimace turned into a grin, a most fierce grin. "Yeah, right? Who cares? Who the fuck cares?" He laughed—a sound like a bark—wiggled his toes, laughed again. "Fuck 'em! Fuck 'em all!"

He trotted up the short steps to the double doors of a synagogue. A slender wooden box hung next to the doors—a mezuzah—containing the Shema prayer. Adam pried it off and wedged it between the door handles, effectively barring the door from opening, then headed up the small alleyway to the rear of the old building—the building whose fire codes hadn't been updated in over sixty years. There, he set the briefcase down next to a small dumpster.

You like to watch things burn, Adam. Do you not?

Adam nodded. "Sure, who doesn't?"

Then you know what to do.

Adam rolled the dumpster over, blocking the back door. He knelt and opened the briefcase, the smell of gasoline stinging his nose. He pulled out a long kitchen knife, setting it aside, then slid out the four bottles of fuel, each one plugged with a rag. He withdrew a box of matches, removed one and struck it, mesmerized by the flame as it mirrored the fire in his own eyes.

Do it! the other urged.

Adam started to touch the match to the first rag, when a light popped on in the window above him on the second floor. He hesitated, watching as a silhouette crossed the curtain. He knew who it was, would recognize the hunched shape of Rabbi Reuben anywhere. No surprise either, it's where the rabbi always was, working late into the night on sermons and other community chores, seven days a week, sometimes eight so the joke went. What *did* surprise Adam was the sudden wash of emotion flooding through him, not more hate and rage, but a soothing, calming feeling. That of . . . what? *Love,* he thought. *I love this man. He's like a father to me.*

No! the other said, but the other sounded far away now, as did the worms—fading, as though something was smothering them.

"Ouch!" Adam cried, as the flame licked his fingers. He dropped the match, blinked, looking around, confused, wondering what he was doing here. The snow was just beginning to stick and he watched the flakes lighting up as they drifted through the window light.

Burn it down, the voice echoed from some distant realm, just the faintest of whispers now.

Adam's eyes found the Star of David carved into the stone above the rear door and lingered there. The synagogue was over a hundred years old; the very pillar of this Borough Park Jewish community. Adam glanced down at his sad, cold penis. This was the very place he'd been circumcised, where his two sons had been circumcised, his brothers, his father, perhaps even his grandfather. Adam realized there'd been a lot of Feldstein foreskin shed in this building and knew that had to mean something—*had to.* "No, no. I don't want to do it."

But you do.

"Why would I ever want to do such a thing?"

Because of the ring.

The ring? Adam felt a sudden sting on his middle finger. He held up his left hand, and found a simple gold band attached to a flat coin shape, a primitive eye imprinted on it. "The ring. Of course . . . the ring." He rubbed his forehead, trying to clear his mind, everything was so confusing these days. "How could I forget?"

He tried to pull it off, twisting at it, tugging so hard he thought his flesh would tear from the bone, but it clung on, clamping down even harder. He let out a cry. He could see how black and swollen the skin was around it, recalled how he'd tried everything short of cutting off his own finger to remove it.

Remember what he did to you, the other said, growing closer, louder. *How he tricked you.*

"Trick? No . . . no trick. It was a loan. I was after another loan. Just enough to float me to the end of the month. Just enough to . . ." A sudden wave of shame swept over Adam. "Enough to pay off the bookies so they wouldn't break my legs." The tears came again as he recalled Rabbi Reuben telling him no more loans until he got help with his gambling, encouraging him to come to counseling, promising the synagogue was always there for him, but he *must* get help.

Another wave of shame as Adam remembered breaking into the storage room that same night, the one behind Rabbi Reuben's desk, the forbidden room where they kept the religious relics. He'd heard rumors that there were small treasures in there. "Wasn't going to steal anything," he mumbled. "Just after something to pawn . . . y'know, for the bookies. I planned to give it back to the rabbi come payday. That's all." He saw himself pulling a bronze case out of a box. It felt heavy, valuable. "I opened it and . . . and the ring . . . the ring . . . the damn thing jumped on my hand!" Adam stifled a scream as he remembered the pain and terror as it sprouted legs like some kind of spider and clamped down on his finger.

NO! the voice boomed. It was back in his head again. *No, that is not what happened. The rabbi has twisted your memories. Look. See the truth!*

A new vison came to Adam, blooming before him like some suppressed memory—vivid, undeniable. There, he saw himself in the relic room just as before, only now, the rabbi was with him, a far too generous smile on his face. He was holding the bronze case, beckoning Adam to take it. Told him to open it, that there was money for him inside. Adam did as he was told, it was as though he was powerless to do otherwise and when he opened it, when he opened it—

Adam looked at the ring on his finger, let out a whimper and began to cry. "He tricked me. Rabbi Reuben tricked me. The dirty fucker tricked me."

The worms began to squirm again, their sweet song filling his head.

Adam snatched up the knife, set it against his finger.

Go on, but it will do no good. You know it. If you want to be free of the ring, free of his curse, you know what you must do.

5

Adam looked at the bottles of gasoline, his tears mixing with the snow. "But Rabbi Reuben has always been so kind . . . like a father to everyone."

It is his guise. He wants your soul. To feed it to his demons. To grow his power. He will not stop with you. Who is next? One of your sons?

"NO!"

He has spells and curses locked away in his treasure room. You must destroy them all. You are the last chance. Burn it down. Burn it all down. Destroy him! Destroy his tools of torment!

Adam knelt, set the knife down, pulled out another match and struck it, lighting the gas-soaked rags. He stood, flaming bottle in hand, glared up at the lighted window above him and then and there, another voice came to him, one he barely recognized, it was *him,* his own voice—so small. "No!" it tried to scream, but only a whisper escaped. "Lies, the ring is lying to you!"

Adam looked at the synagogue as memories of all the births, bar mitzvahs, marriages, funerals, parties, and other celebrations that had taken place there fought to be seen, heard, felt. So much love, family, friends, neighbors. This building held everything he cared about. His arm began to tremble, then his whole being. "No," he whimpered. "I won't."

A stabbing pain bit Adam's finger. The ring changed before his eyes, the simple band turning into prickly spider legs again, the coin into an eye—a *real* eye. It began to pulse, like it had a heartbeat, like it was *alive.* The legs sprouted claws that dug into his flesh, drawing blood. The eye shifted, glancing about until it found Adam. It glared at him, burning into him as the worms filled his head with their song.

"Oh, God!" Adam cried, no longer caring that his brain was boiling while his toes were freezing, unaware of the drool dripping from his lips, the snot trickling from his numb nose, of the snowflakes building up in his pubic hair, unaware of anything but that *eye,* that dreadful *eye.*

Adam threw the bottle.

There came a loud crash as the bottle smashed through the first-floor window into the main hall, followed by the flicker of flames. Adam let out a rapturous howl as the hate—the wonderful, terrible hate—pumped through his body, as the worms sang, as his eyes lit up with fire.

Good! the other cried.

"Good!" Adam echoed, picking up the remaining three firebombs and throwing them after the first. A fierce grin stretched across his face as the flames blossomed and quickly spread through the old building.

Adam heard the rabbi shouting, his cries racing toward the back door. The door hit the dumpster with a thud. "Fire!" the old rabbi screamed, trying to force his way out. "Help me! Fire!"

Thud, thud, thud went the door as the rabbi frantically tried to shove through, each thud driving the door open a breath more, the dumpster back inch by inch.

"Oh no you don't," Adam growled and gave the dumpster a hard heave, putting all his weight into it, slamming the back door closed.

"Help me!" came the rabbi's muffled screaming as he pounded on the door, the screams slowly turning into a harsh cough. The pounding stopped and Adam heard a crash, caught sight of the man stumbling through the main hall, heading for the front door.

Adam picked up the long knife and, in his mismatched socks, strolled toward the front of the building. And as the worms sang and his heart drummed with their venom, he found himself hoping the rabbi *would* escape the inferno, just so he could have the satisfaction of cutting open his throat.

He was almost to the street when Mrs. Rosenfeld, the rabbi's wife, went rushing up the sidewalk as fast as her old legs would carry her. Adam guessed Mrs. Rosenfeld must've heard or seen something, that it would've been hard not to since she and her husband lived in the apartments just across the street.

"Ah, hell," Adam grunted and trotted after her. He came out onto the sidewalk and found several shocked faces gawking down at him from the balconies and windows. He grinned back, slapping his knife against his bare thigh, unaware that he was cutting himself, that blood was running down his leg.

Sirens wailed in the distance and the worms began to churn. Adam returned his attention to the synagogue.

Mrs. Rosenfeld was struggling to pry the mezuzah loose from the door handles. She shoved it, putting her full weight into it. It gave way just as Adam walked up and both she and the mezuzah tumbled to the ground.

She got to one knee and that's when she noticed Adam's socked feet. Her eyes moved up until they were level with his crotch.

"Hello, Mrs. Rosenfeld," Adam said. She saw the knife and screamed, flailing as she tumbled backward down the steps.

Adam started to tell her to relax, that he was only here to give the rabbi, the dirty trickster, some of what he deserved, when the door burst open and Rabbi Reuben came diving out.

"Holy shit!" Adam cried.

The old man was on fire, his jacket, even his hair. He rolled down the steps, landing right in front of his wife. Mrs. Rosenfeld screamed and began beating the flames, smacking them so savagely Adam thought he might not have to kill the old man after all, that this woman would do it for him.

Adam heard maniacal laughing, realized it was coming from himself.

People were yelling and the sirens were coming closer.

Kill him, the other said. ***Do it now. Be quick.***

Adam tromped down the steps, raising the knife to plunge it into the rabbi's chest, when Mrs. Rosenfeld shrieked and grabbed his arm. And even though she was old, she put up enough of a fight that Adam had to slice the kitchen knife— the one with the serrated edge—across the old woman's throat.

A stream of blood spurted from her neck, painting the fresh snow bright red. Mrs. Rosenfeld clutched the gash, trying to stifle the flow, but Adam had proven more than adept, and both her blood and life gushed from the deep wound. Her mouth gaped, opening and closing as an awful gurgling sound sputtered from her lips. Her bulging eyes fixed on Adam, seemed to ask, to beg: *Why? Why would you do such a dreadful thing to me?* Adam shoved her out of the way and grabbed hold of Rabbi Reuben.

The old man's coat was still burning and it singed Adam's hand as he fought to hold the squirming man down. The rabbi wailed, kicking and flopping about; his fried skin peeling away. Adam drove his knee into the old man's chest, trying to hold him still long enough to plunge the knife into his eye. The first try missed, catching the rabbi's cheek, slicing it wide open and taking off most of his left ear. The second try wasn't much better, glancing off the man's forehead and carving a deep gouge into his scalp. But the third was the charm, going through the eye and deep into Rabbi Reuben's sad, sorry, wicked brain with a satisfying squish. The worms squealed with delight. Adam enjoyed it so much that he yanked the blade free, then drove it into the rabbi's other eye.

Adam let out a triumphant laugh. "Take that! Take that, you evil old fuck!" Then abruptly stopped laughing. Something was different, something had changed. What was it? He cocked his head to the left, then right, listening; slowly he understood. It was quiet, not outside, no, outside it was anything but—sirens, roaring flames, people yelling, screaming—but inside was quiet.

The worms, he could no longer hear the worms.

Adam clasped his head. The other, the voice, it was gone too! *Oh, thank God, it's gone!* He felt like he'd been released and such a rush of joy washed over him that he wanted to get up and dance. It was then he realized he was on the ground straddling someone—and that he was *nude*.

"Where are my clothes? It's snowing for heaven's sake." He blinked and the gory face of Rabbi Reuben came into focus; a kitchen knife embedded in his eye. Adam recognized the knife and blinked again. "What? What's going on?" It came to him in a rush, all of it, no detail spared. He looked from Rabbi Reuben's body to that of the rabbi's wife.

"No!" he cried. "No! *No!*"

He held up his bloody left hand, stared at the hateful ring, the spider thing with the demon eye. It was but a ring again. He snatched hold of the knife with his right hand and without hesitation began to hack at his finger, sawing and chopping, finding out quickly that cutting off one's own finger wasn't such an easy task. He kept going, screaming until he sawed right through the bone. His middle finger plopped into the snow.

He stared.

Where was the ring?

He looked at his hand. The ring was on his index finger now.

"What the fuck!" He attacked that finger with the blade, spittle flying from his lips as he sawed away.

He heard the voice. *Stop, just stop. You cannot win.*

"Fuck you!" Adam shrieked and kept sawing until the digit tore away, falling into the snow next to the first.

"The ring? Where's the goddamn ring?" He checked the three remaining fingers on his left hand; it wasn't there.

He felt a sting on his right hand.

No, he thought, closing his eyes, not wanting to look. *No.* Slowly he opened his eyes and there it was, the ring wrapped tightly around the middle finger of his right hand.

Adam Feldstein, sitting in the snow, astride the simmering body of his rabbi, covered in blood and wearing only a pair of mismatched socks, began to sob uncontrollably.

"Drop the knife!" A cop stood, legs planted wide, his service revolver pointed at him. "Drop it, buddy! Not gonna tell you again!"

His partner, a burly man approaching retirement age, came running up behind him. "Oh, shit! What the fuck we got here?"

"Help me," Adam cried. "Help me!"

"Drop the knife," the first cop repeated, despite saying he wouldn't.

Adam shoved the knife up under his own neck.

"Hold on," the other cop shouted. "Just hold on a minute."

Adam slid the knife, the knife he'd used to cut his daughter's birthday cake, across his own neck. He had a moment to enjoy the warmth of his own blood running down his neck and chest, then fell over on his back, staring up into the billowing smoke as the night faded.

The voice, the other, let out a dispirited sigh, but Adam didn't hear it. Adam, or at least his soul, his essence, was shrinking, screaming in shock, horror, and confusion as it was being sucked into the ring, through the ring, funneled down into the land of fire and pain.

RUBY

1985, ENTERPRISE, ALABAMA

Twenty-three-year-old Ruby Tucker, in her ripped jeans and ragged high-tops held together with safety pins, sat in a metal folding chair with an acoustic guitar on her lap. She was strumming along with the kids. There were nine of them, boys and girls ranging from Nancy, the youngest at eleven, to Marky, who was fourteen. They were all playing "Michael Row Your Boat Ashore," playing it badly, their faces cinched up like there was a dead fish in the room.

Ruby raised a hand and they stopped, looking relieved, like someone had just let them out of jail.

Ruby pushed a strand of long red hair out of her face and tucked it behind her ear, then nodded to Marky. He smiled and dashed to the door, pushing it shut.

Ruby tugged a cassette labeled PISS OFF from her Walkman, and slid it into the boom box on the table next to her. She glanced back at the door, then gave the kids a wink. They all grinned and pulled out the chord sheet she'd given them last month. "GARBAGEMAN," BY THE CRAMPS, was written across the top in creepy letters, an even creepier image of the band leered out from below.

"Y'all ready?"

It took a moment for the kids to place their fingers. Ruby waited another for Nancy to set hers, then pushed play.

Poison Ivy's grinding guitar rumbled out of the boom box, and the kids' faces lit up as they began to play along.

"E," Ruby said. "Now G." Their small fingers bouncing and sliding on the strings. "That's it. Now E again. There . . . you got it!"

They stumbled, missing chords here and there, but overall, they were doing it; after only a few weeks of practice, almost every one of them was keeping time with Ms. Poison Ivy Rorschach herself. The rumpus tune echoed off the hard cement walls of the YMCA music room, and it sounded like heaven to Ruby.

Ruby joined in, unable to help herself; a small, almost sinister smile spread across her pale, freckled face.

If you'd told Ruby a year ago that she'd not only be teaching little twerps to play guitar, but actually digging it, she'd have laughed at you. But she hadn't felt this alive in months, the music flowing through her like adrenaline. And she knew why, exactly why: because she'd stopped taking those damn pills, the lithium ones, about two weeks ago. And now her mind felt free of the fog. She'd been on medication since she was fourteen, but stopped whenever she could get away with it, hating the way they made her feel.

I'm not schizo, she thought. *Got a temper, sure, just like my daddy, but I'm not manic-depressive, or that new word everyone's tossing around—bipolar. No, that ain't me, not at all. Don't care what Dr. Fatass Ferguson thinks. Don't care what Momma thinks. Because I know I don't need them pills killing my soul. What I need is more art and music, and for people to give me some goddamn space.*

A twinge of anxiety pricked her—knowing how much trouble she'd be in if anyone found out she'd stopped taking her medication. And not just from her doctor and her mom, but from the judge this time. This was her last chance. One more incident, one more of her little blowups, and they wouldn't be talking about some treatment center this time, but state correctional.

Let it go, she thought. *No one's gonna find out, cause this time you're gonna keep your shit together. Yes ma'am. So just let it go.* And she did, the music helping her to forget about her blowups, her arrest, probation, all of it. *Just a week left and I'm out of this pea-patch town for good. Off to find Tina . . . off to finally get the band going again.*

Ruby's eyes were closed, her mind floating, so she barely noticed when the kids stopped playing, not realizing anything was wrong until someone clicked off the boom box.

Ruby opened her eyes to see the kids' horrified faces and turned to find Mrs. Wright, the YMCA director, staring at her.

"Ruby," Mrs. Wright said, tersely. "Would you mind stepping out into the hall with me?"

"Aww, don't get cross with Ruby," Marky said. "We're the ones that wanted to play that song."

"Yeah," the other kids chimed in.

Mrs. Wright glared at them and a chill fell over the room. She ejected the tape and held it up. "This here's ugly music. We don't play ugly music at the Y." She slipped the cassette into her pocket.

That wasn't just any tape, Ruby's best friend Tina had made it for her. Ruby felt her face flush, actually started to snatch the cassette back, to take it right out of the woman's pocket. *No,* she thought. *Keep cool. Just keep cool.*

Mrs. Wright squinted at the chord sheet on Marky's music stand, her eyes going wide like she'd spotted a snake. She marched over, yanked up the sheet, the one with the Cramps leering out at them, and held it up like it were soaked in urine. "What kind of deviltry is this?" She walked from student to student, snatching away their music sheets and tucking them under her arm. "No ma'am and no sirree! No, no, no! Not in my Y!"

Mrs. Wright took a deep breath, picked up the booklet off Marky's stand—*Favorite Christian Folk Songs.* "Look here," she said, holding the booklet up. She was speaking calmly now, but Ruby could hear the strain, like a wire about to snap. "There's so many beautiful songs in here."

"Aww," Nancy grumbled. "But we don't wanna play that boring old stuff."

For a second, Ruby thought Mrs. Wright was going to shove the booklet into Nancy's mouth. Instead, she took another deep breath and set her cold eyes on Ruby. "Ruby, in the hall. Now."

Fuck, Ruby thought. *When am I gonna learn?* She stood and followed Mrs. Wright out. *Now, mind yourself, Ruby. Mind . . . your . . . self.*

Mrs. Wright walked over to a watercolor painting hanging above the drinking fountain and straightened it.

Mrs. Wright not only ran the Enterprise YMCA, she also taught piano and painted quaint watercolors of local produce. Her work wasn't bad, not at all; why she'd won third place in the local Piney Woods Art Festival eight years ago. That painting, along with the ribbon, hung in the front office, right behind her desk so nobody could miss it. Several of her other works, including a barn that had won honorable mention—that one had the ribbon on it as well—were hung throughout the facility. As Mr. Miller, the custodian, had once confided to Ruby, "She thinks the place is her own gawd-dang art gallery."

Mrs. Wright turned from her painting and looked at Ruby with one eye narrowed, slowly shaking her head as though she couldn't even find the words. "This is the YMCA, Ruby."

"Yes ma'am."

"Do you know what the C stands for in YMCA?"

"Why . . . yes, ma'am. I do."

"Please tell me."

"Christian."

Mrs. Wright held up the Cramps music sheet. "Well then, I needn't be wasting my breath explaining why I can't have you teaching the children to play this Devil music, need I?"

"Devil's music? What? No . . ." Ruby could hear her voice rising and stopped. "Mrs. Wright, ma'am, I'm sorry. I wasn't thinking. I know I should've checked with you first."

Mrs. Wright's face softened a touch.

Don't say nothing else, Ruby thought, *just leave it there.* "But," Ruby continued. "They were just bored to death with them old songs. I thought maybe it'd be good to break it up a little, y'know. So, I was just trying to come up with a way to make it fun for them. That's all."

The corner of Mrs. Wright's mouth twitched.

I need to stop talking, Ruby thought. "I'm not saying they should be playing Devil's music or anything like that. Of course not. Just worried if we don't come up with something a bit more . . . I don't know . . . *hip* maybe? Them kids aren't gonna wanna come back . . . might quit playing altogether for that matter."

Mrs. Wright's eyes bore into Ruby.

Ruby closed her mouth and bit her tongue.

A long silence followed, then slowly a thin smile spread across Mrs. Wright's face. "If I'm not mistaken, I believe this is your very first group of students. Am I wrong?" She waited. "Am I?"

"Well . . . no, ma'am. You aren't."

"Do you know how long I've been teaching music? And not just music, but art too? Teaching kids and adults alike?"

"I don't."

"Since before you were born. Been playing piano every Sunday down at First Baptist for going on thirty years now. Why, my paintings have won awards. Did you know that?"

"Well . . . yeah," Ruby said, and thought, *everybody in the fucking building knows that.*

"Seems fair then, to say I know a thing or two about art and music. Doesn't it?"

"Yes, ma'am."

"Interesting then, isn't it? That being the case and all, yet you still got a mind to be lecturing me on how to teach."

"*Lecturing?* No! No ma'am! I wasn't doing no such a thing." *Fuck,* Ruby thought, wondering how she kept digging herself in deeper. "Just trying to say, let's make things as fun as we can. That's all."

Mrs. Wright looked Ruby up and down again, let out a long sigh. "I think maybe it's time we switch gears here."

"Ma'am?"

"You need a break from them kids and Mr. Miller needs some help. The boys' bathroom is a mess—little boys don't seem to have very good aim, if you get what I mean. So, if you don't mind, I'd like you to go give them toilets and sinks a good scrub."

"What? No! I'm not your *janitor*!" Ruby cried before she could stop herself, a small speck of spittle flying from her lips. She could feel her face going scarlet, but this was the third time this month Mrs. Wright had made her clean the bathrooms.

The smallest of smiles tickled the corner of Mrs. Wright's mouth. Ruby had endured that smile most of her adult life. It said, *See there, she is crazy. Look at her, you can see it in her eyes.*

Ruby sucked in a breath, closed her eyes for a long second, then reopened them. "I'm sorry. Sorry, Mrs. Wright. But please give me another chance with them kids. *Please.*"

Mrs. Wright crossed her arms and shook her head. "Can't let you go back in there while you're in this state."

State? What state? Ruby wondered. *What the fuck is she even talking about? I barely even raised my voice. Why is it that everybody else can cuss and carry on and no one hardly blinks? But if I so much as pipe up, I'm bat-shit crazy.* Ruby clutched her hands together to keep them from shaking.

"I think," Mrs. Wright said. "Doing something else for a while would be good for you, anyhow."

"But . . . Mrs. Wright, cleaning toilets isn't what I volunteered for. I'm supposed to be teaching guitar."

Mrs. Wright's eyes narrowed. "Dear, you didn't *volunteer* for nothing. You were given a choice . . . jail time or community service."

That took some steam out of Ruby because it was true—the incident, the arrest, the whole mess—but there was more to it. At Ruby's parole hearing Judge Stevenson had given her a comprehensive interview, seemed to genuinely want to help her get on the right track. When he found out how much Ruby loved music, he'd been the one to propose teaching kids at the Y, as part of her community service obligations. And for the last several months Ruby had done just that, twice a week, found she really enjoyed working with these kids, wondered if teaching might be in her future.

"Mrs. Wright, the judge . . . well, he said that the teaching would be good for me. That's why he sent me here. And you know, I've really—"

"And how do you think Judge Stevenson will feel if I tell him about you teaching them kids to play Devil's music." She shook the flyers. "Passing out this . . . this *satanic* material to minors?"

Ruby flinched, felt her blood heat up. *She's just trying to set me off. Does she just want me to fail? Is that it?* Ruby dug her nails into her palm. *Let it go. Let . . . it . . . go,* she begged herself, because she knew whatever games Mrs. Wright might be playing, if she made her mad, Mrs. Wright could say anything she wanted. And a bad report would mean she'd have to continue her probation, that she'd never get out of here. And a *really* bad report would mean she'd be on her way to state, and worse, they'd probably up her meds too. There'd even been whispers of a conservatorship.

"Ruby, I can see you're upset. That you're angry with me right now. But you should know that you're not the first wayward soul I've been asked to help. And what you need to understand is that the judge sent you to me for a reason . . . because he trusts me to know what's best for you. So, you need to trust me too. But in this case, it's not just what's best for you, but also for them kids. And I don't feel things are working out so well. So, for this last week, we're gonna find you something else to do. You do a good job and we'll just let this other go. That sound fair?"

No, Ruby thought, *doesn't sound fair at all. Sounds like bullshit. Sounds like you're just jealous them kids like me so much better than you. That's what it sounds like.*

"Ruby . . . *does* that sound fair?"

Ruby didn't trust herself to speak, so she just nodded.

"Good. Now, you know where the mop is don't you?"

Ruby nodded again.

"Alright, let's get to it. I'll be in to check on you later."

Ruby headed down the hall, glancing back just in time to catch Mrs. Wright tossing her cassette into the garbage.

"You bitch!" Ruby hissed.

She waited until Mrs. Wright returned to the music room, then dug the tape out, wiping away the cookie crumbs.

"Bitch," she said again and headed for the mop closet.

The bathrooms were at the far end of the corridor. As Ruby wheeled the mop bucket along, she passed a series of doors that opened into long row buildings. These rooms looked like open wards, or barracks, and there was a reason for that—they once were. Apparently, the whole compound used to be a prison; it was converted into the YMCA sometime in the early sixties, after a couple of inmates escaped and went on a murder spree in a nearby neighborhood. The contractors had done the minimum to convert the compound, even the two old guard towers remained. So, the place gave off an oppressive air, making it easy for Ruby to feel like a prisoner herself at times, with Mrs. Wright the cranky old warden bent on keeping her down. And there, between each ward, was one of Warden Wright's quaint watercolors staring back at her, mocking her.

Ruby steered the mop bucket into the boys' restroom, not even bothering to knock. Some boy who looked to be around twelve let out a shriek, getting pee down the front of his pants as he rushed to zip up his fly.

"Hey!" he cried. "You ain't supposed to be in here."

"Get out," Ruby barked, and when he didn't move fast enough, she jabbed the mop at him.

The boy fled.

Ruby peered into the stalls. Mrs. Wright was correct, it appeared as though kids were peeing everywhere but into the toilet itself.

"Fuck!" Ruby said, tugging out her headphones. She put them on and slid the cassette out of her back pocket. She stared at the words PISS OFF, written all in red, in Tina's bold handwriting. "God, I sure miss you, Tina."

They'd met in high school art class, Ruby then a sophomore and Tina a junior. Tina arrived late to class and took a seat next to Ruby at the very back. Ruby couldn't stop staring. Tina was Asian, that alone made her stand out in southern Alabama, but that wasn't why Ruby was staring—it was her hair, it was cut short, *hacked* would be a better word, like with lawn clippers. Not only that, but her clothes, they were, well, ragged—a faded black T-shirt with the arms cut out, a pair of dingy high-tops covered in safety pins, and jeans with big holes in the knees. Ruby was trying to understand why anyone would dress that bad on purpose, wondered if there was something mentally off with this girl.

Tina asked Ruby what the hell she was looking at, to which Ruby replied she had no fucking idea. Tina gave her the finger, after which neither girl spoke another word to the other for the remainder of that week.

Come Friday, Tina handed Ruby a tape with a wink and a smile. There was something so mischievous in that smile that Ruby took the offering, against her better judgment. When she saw the hand-drawn title, PISS OFF, she was even more dubious. But by lunch, curiosity got the better of her, and Ruby took a listen on her Walkman. It was a mixtape of punk rock and new wave music. Ruby hated punk rock, everybody hated punk rock. She made it through five songs, then gave up, taking the tape out and shoving Zeppelin back in.

Ruby didn't think about the tape again until sixth period, when she found herself humming a tune. She couldn't place what she was humming at first, then realized it was one of the songs off the tape. The tune went round and round in her head, so on the walk home she had to give it another listen. The song, she would later learn, was "Sonic Reducer" by the Dead Boys. She played the tape through, hoping for more songs like "Sonic Reducer." There weren't, there would never be another song like "Sonic Reducer," but a few others caught her ear, songs by the Ramones, the Damned, the Stooges, and the Cramps, and by the end of the weekend, she couldn't stop playing the tape.

There was no playlist attached, and come Monday she was dying to find out about these bands. When Tina walked into art class, Ruby greeted her with a warm smile and about a hundred questions about who these bands were, where'd they come from, how come she never heard them on the radio, and most important—where she could find more. Another tape followed, and another, and within a month, Ruby and Tina were inseparable. A month after that, Ruby chopped her hair into a spiky mop, doubled up her eyeliner, ditched her Nikes for Converse, and started cutting holes in her jeans.

There were rules at Enterprise high school, not written down or spelled out, but everyone knew them. When it came to bands, rule one was that Lynyrd Skynyrd was God; after that came Molly Hatchet and Charlie Daniels for all the hicks; the heads were into Zeppelin, the Stones, maybe some Sabbath; and the preppies, Top 40—country or rock, didn't matter, just whatever Casey Kasem was playing on the countdown that week.

The next rule was that punk rock sucked, new wave too; all of it was weirdo music and anyone who listened to it sucked more. If you so much as mentioned punk rock, at best you'd get a "yuck," or maybe "gross," but the most common response would be, "that's faggot music."

Punk rock was a spiritual awakening for Ruby. It was as though she'd been given a new life, a creed, a magical cloak of protection to shield her from all the bullshit. But most of all a license to stop trying to fit in, a license to give every one of those Izod-wearing preppies, every knuckle-dragging jock, along with their vomit-inducing cheers and pep rallies, the finger—the good old fuck-you-and-the-horse-you-rode-in-on. Ruby liked to tell anyone who cared, or didn't, that punk rock saved her soul.

She blinked, found herself back in the YMCA toilet stall—those days in high school with Tina suddenly feeling a lifetime ago now. She crammed the PISS OFF tape into her Walkman and hit play, turning the volume way up, because right then she needed that magical cloak of protection, needed to feel Tina was with her, at least in spirit. But more than anything, she needed to tell the whole damn world to just . . . *piss off*.

The Dead Boys filled her skull with roaring, out-of-tune guitars, and Ruby sang along as she mopped pee up off the floor. She slammed the mop back and forth, round and round, banging it against the stall like she was trying to knock it down, clutching the handle so hard her knuckles grew white, lost in the music, lost in the rage.

"One more week," Ruby growled. "And I won't have to deal with any of this bull-crap ever again." Only she knew that wasn't entirely true—she wouldn't so long as Mrs. Wright gave the judge a good report, along with her mother and her probation officer. If not, well, Ruby was going to run away, because she was almost twenty-four years old and felt certain that if she didn't get the hell out of this town this year, she never would. She was supposed to have gone to Atlanta with Tina, to put the band together. But that was before she got arrested, wasn't it?

Someone tapped Ruby's shoulder and she jumped around to find Mrs. Wright frowning at her. Ruby yanked off her earphones, reducing the song down to hissing fuzz.

"Shouldn't play that so loud. It'll damage your hearing."

"What?" Ruby asked, hitting the off button on her Walkman.

Mrs. Wright peered into the stall, then back at Ruby, a surprised look on her face. "Well, that's more like it. See what you can do when you put in a little effort? You take that same attitude and apply it to your life and see if you don't turn yourself around."

Ruby had no idea what she was talking about until she glanced around the room. She was as surprised as Mrs. Wright to find it spic-and-span. Ruby realized she'd taken out her rage on this stupid bathroom, too lost in her music and thoughts to even notice.

"I know you think I'm hard on you," Mrs. Wright said. "But it's my Christian duty to care so. You'll be wanting to thank me one day, see if you don't." She glanced at her watch. "Got one more job for you."

"Sure," Ruby said, with as little enthusiasm as she could muster.

"Somebody knocked over the garbage can out by the pool. Trash all over the place. Need you to take care of it for me. It's early, but once you're finished, you can head on home. How does that sound? Just a little thank-you for a job well done."

Oh no, Ruby thought. *Not the pool.*

Mrs. Wright gave the bathroom another look. "This goes a long way toward making up for what you done earlier. I'm very impressed with you, young lady. And now, you gotta admit, taking a sense of pride in what you do makes you feel good about yourself. Right? Tell me it don't."

Ruby wasn't even hearing her. *Not the pool. God, last thing I need right now is Billy.*

"See you on Monday," Mrs. Wright said, as she left the bathroom.

Ruby glanced in the mirror, horrified at the sad, sweaty mess staring back at her. She could actually smell herself, which was never good. South Alabama was normally hot and muggy, but especially so this week due to an unexpected heat wave. And the YMCA didn't have air-conditioning either, well, except for Mrs. Wright's office of course.

"Lord, I'm a wreck."

Ruby rolled the mop into the corner, yanked free a few paper towels from the dispenser, dabbing her face and armpits as she headed for the pool.

Ruby hadn't seen Billy today, she'd made a point of *not* seeing Billy, but she knew he was here because she'd spotted his car, which was hard to miss—a fully loaded '81 Camaro sitting right out front. Billy's dad owned the local Chevy dealership, so Billy pretty much got his choice of any used car on the lot.

Billy wasn't Ruby's boyfriend, not anymore, something she had to keep reminding herself of. Seems it wouldn't be so hard to remember, not after the breakup they went through. But when you've been with someone for five years, not being with them can just sneak up on you sometimes.

Ruby grabbed a garbage bag from the women's locker room, then peeked out into the pool area, hoping the trash was near enough so that she could just scoop it up and slip away before anyone saw her. Ruby groaned; the can had rolled over onto the grass where all the sunbathers were, strewing litter along the far chain-link fence.

And sure enough, there *he* was, Billy, sitting on a towel by the fence. And there *she* was, right next to him—*Stacy,* in her neon-yellow little two-piece. Ruby exhaled sharply through her teeth.

Stacy was Mrs. Wright's bottle-blonde daughter. She taught aerobics at the Y and when she wasn't toning her butt, you could find her out here by the pool, working on her tan and what Ruby hoped would be a disfiguring case of skin cancer.

Billy was chatting her up while she refreshed her tanning oil, smacking her gum as she wiped the greasy stuff across the top of her annoyingly pert cleavage. Billy stared, making no effort to be coy, and you could see by the look on Stacy's face she was loving it.

"Hussy," Ruby hissed, and patted her back pocket, looking for a cigarette, then remembered she'd quit, or was trying to anyway. She took several long deep breaths. She'd been reading up on nonconfrontational paths to solve problems, trying to find ways to deal with folks, something other than screaming at them at least. She'd learned about meditating to calm herself down and was right now using some of those breathing techniques. But what she *really* needed was a god-dang cigarette, realizing in hindsight perhaps quitting smoking and going off her meds in the same week wasn't the best idea.

You're in control, Ruby. You . . . are . . . in . . . control. One more week. Now . . . don't lose your shit.

Stacy must've said something fantastically hilarious, because Billy let loose with one of his hee-hawing laughs, practically braying, and slapped the towel. Ruby remembered when she thought that laugh was cute, now it was more like a beesting.

Stacy stood up and began stretching, one of her fancy aerobic moves, her hands clasped above her head, leaning far right, then left. She was acting all cool, like it was just something everyone did in the middle of a conversation, but Ruby knew she was showing off her toned abs.

Ruby felt she couldn't be more different from Stacy, and that was part of why it stung so bad that Billy ended up with her of all people. Stacy was tanned, where Ruby was pale and freckly, Stacy's skin unblemished, where Ruby was prone to the occasional outbreak of acne, especially when she was stressed, and she seemed to always be stressed these days. Stacy was full in all the right places; Ruby wasn't full anywhere. Women tend to say you can never be too thin, but Ruby begged to differ; her kind of thin leaned toward gangly, her hands appearing a bit large on her slim wrists. She liked to think of herself more like her hero, Patti Smith, kind of androgenous, kind of rock 'n' roll, having the sort of frame a man's jacket looked good on. She'd always thought Billy liked that look.

"Fuck," Ruby whispered, heading toward the fence. "This should be a real treat."

Ruby started at the far end, rounding up the litter, working her way toward Billy and Stacy. There was a small boom box next to Stacy's towel and as Ruby drew near, she could hear "Honey Bunny," by Dewydoo and the Boohoos, blasting out of the shitty little speaker. Ruby thought the only thing more annoying than Stacy was that damn song.

There wasn't a cloud in the sky, and Ruby felt as though she were being cooked by the blazing sun. She tugged at her chafing bra as sweat rolled down her back. She could hear Billy now, going on and on—some bull-crap about him and Frank Smith climbing one of the high school stadium lights in the middle of the night and unscrewing all the bulbs. The kind of dumb shit that made Ruby glad she didn't have a flood of testosterone retarding her frontal lobe.

Stacy was eating it up. Nodding and going, "Oh my *gawd, really*? Wow! You're *such* a maniac," and so on until Ruby wanted to puke. *Good job, Billy,* Ruby thought. *First prize goes to you for hooking up with the most annoying woman in Enterprise.* But what was particularly annoying to Ruby was that Stacy had barely said five words to Billy in high school, and those five words had been something shitty. Billy hadn't run with the right crowd; no, he'd hung around losers like Ruby, played D&D, and listened to Nazareth and Uriah Heep while drawing wizards and vampires with her.

Just when Ruby thought she might get past them without being noticed, Billy called to her. "Oh, hey, Ruby. You having fun?"

Stacy giggled.

Ruby gave them the finger.

"Momma's sure getting her nickel's worth out of you, honey," Stacy said.

"Says you do a right smart job with them bathrooms." She grinned. "Hey, at least you have something to put on your résumé now."

Billy snorted and let out one of his hee-haws.

Ruby reddened and picked up a soda can. She started to throw it at them, but didn't, because Ruby didn't want to get that look, that she's-bat-shit-crazy look, so she just slammed it into the bag and kept going, acting like she didn't hear a damn thing. *Keep it together, Ruby. Just keep it together.*

"Aww, don't be like that," Stacy called after her. "You know, we're just kidding around. Hey, Rube, Billy and I gonna be cruising around tonight. If you wanna catch up with us, we'll be at the Dairy Queen around eight. Mark and Paige gonna be there. Probably head over to Joey's after that. Don't know if you heard, but he finally passed his GED and wants to parr-ty!"

"Yeah, well, seeing how I'd rather eat rat poison, I probably won't make it. But y'all have fun now, you hear."

"Suit yourself, sweetie."

"Suit yourself, sweetie. Suit yourself, sweetie," Ruby parroted under her breath. She snatched up the last bit of litter, crumbled it into a wad and slammed it into the bag, then left the pool.

Ruby headed home, walking along East Lee Street with her guitar slung over her shoulder. She could see the heat waves swirling up off the asphalt. It was almost two miles, and she was pretty sure if she didn't get out of the sun soon she was going to have a heatstroke. She couldn't wait to get her own car, had been putting away every extra nickel from work toward buying one.

A quick honk came from behind her; it was Billy in his Camaro.

"Hop in," he said.

Ruby kept walking.

"Aww, don't be like that."

"You're kidding me. Right?"

"Look, I'm sorry if I was rude."

"If?"

"Boy, does this car have a *nice* AC."

She stopped.

"Come on, get in!"

Ruby sighed, opened the door and slid in, situating her guitar between her legs as they drove off. The AC felt like heaven.

Neither one of them spoke for a spell.

"So . . . how you been?" Billy asked.

"How do you think I've been?"

More silence.

"Sorry about today. I admit, we . . . we were kinda rude."

"Yeah, what else you sorry about?"

He sucked in a breath. "Can we not do all this again?"

More silence.

"What do you want, Billy?"

"I'm just trying to be nice to you. That's all."

She could tell he was, and wished it could be that easy, like none of the bad things had happened, because she could sure use a friend right about now. "So, you're cruising the strip now, hanging with the party kids?"

He cut her a look. "Don't start."

"What?"

"Hey, not everyone wants to stay home all the time. There's more to life then listening to records and reading nerdy books."

Ruby flinched. "You can let me out now."

"Babe, we don't have to be enemies."

"Is your conscience finally catching up with you?"

"Christ, I just can't catch a break here. Can I?"

"You used to despise those party morons."

Billy shook his head. "I understand you hate Stacy. You've always hated her."

"Wait, me? You too. The way she used to treat us back in school. You were the one that always called her a stuck-up bitch."

Billy bristled. "Well, hey, guess what? Folks change. Stacy's changed. You'd know that if you gave her half a chance. But you don't give anyone a chance, do you? If they ain't part of your punk rock club, you act like they're the enemy."

"Well, I got plenty of reason to feel that way. And punk rock saved my soul, by the way. You should know that better than anyone. And . . . and, I know this—I can sure relate a hell of a lot better to someone who digs the Cramps than someone who listens to, say, Toto, or fucking Dewydoo. So, there's that!"

"See, there you go, thinking your music is better than everyone else's. Who's being stuck-up now?"

"My music *is* better than everyone else's! Hell of a lot better than what any of these clod-chuckers around here listen to. Where is this coming from anyway? You trying to tell me some arena band like Toto can hold a guitar lick to the Cramps?"

He shrugged. "I don't know. A lot of that stuff you listen to just sounds like noise to me."

"You don't know! What'd you *mean* you don't know? Of course you know! A band like Toto isn't fit to breathe the same air as the Cramps. The Cramps are the most exalted potentates of rock 'n' fuckin' roll! Who even are you?"

That got a smirk out of him and for a moment she saw her old Billy, saw the person who used to be her friend.

"Maybe I just wanna branch out a bit," he said. "Y'know, believe it or not, it's okay to listen to more than just one type of music."

"There are only two kinds of music, good music and bad. I mean, what? You're into *Van Halen* now, like all your *party* pals? Or maybe you're grooving to Stacy's vibe, digging you some Dewydoo?"

"So what if I was?"

"You gotta be kidding me!" Ruby sneered, making a gagging sound. "Listening to Dewydoo ain't branching out, it's being brain-dead."

"See, you *are* a snob. Worse even than the preppies."

"What . . . how can you say that after all the bullshit we put up with in high school?"

"Always goes back to high school with you. You're stuck there, still holding grudges against everyone and everything. Just can't let it go, can you?"

Ruby was surprised at how much that stung. "Well, no. A lot of bad shit went down. Did you enjoy being smacked around, being called a weirdo all the time? Because I sure as hell didn't."

"No, I didn't and maybe that's why I'm making changes. Maybe I don't want to be thought of as a weirdo all my life."

"Changes? What kind of changes?"

"Been working out for one thing."

"Working out? *You?*"

"Yeah, *me,*" he huffed. "You probably hadn't even noticed. Well, other folks have. Why Stacy was just saying how well I'd grown into my frame, that I was a long stretch from that gangly dork she knew back in high school."

Ruby laughed. "I bet she did. Bet she wouldn't mind at all hooking up with someone who's gonna inherit their father's dealership one day. Why, I'd go so far to say the thought of having a shiny new Chevy every year and living in a big house instead of that rinky-dink trailer of hers is making you more attractive every day."

"You're just being mean now."

They both fell quiet again.

How did we get here? Ruby wondered. *Used to feel so connected, two losers bonding over ridiculing all the douchebags at school. Maybe that was all we had. And maybe . . . maybe I am boring.* She had to admit Billy was right, she *would* rather stay home listening to records, reading, or playing guitar than getting drunk with the party kids—the ones that didn't make it to college, or join the service, or do anything except talk about what they were *gonna* do. The ones Ruby thought of as the left-behinders. Of course, she was painfully aware that she was a left-behinder too, that "gonna-do" was her favorite subject—gonna move to Atlanta, gonna get a band going, gonna tour the nation. She sighed, refusing to believe she was like them, wanting to believe it was this town, because if you weren't into high school football, there was simply nothing going on here, nothing to feed on, no live music, no nightlife at all—unless you called cruising up and down the half-mile strip and visiting burger joints "nightlife." It was a dry county for fuck's sake, not even a bar. Had to drive ten miles to buy a goddamn beer.

The only inspiring thing Ruby had ever found in Enterprise was the giant statue the town had erected to a bug—the Boll Weevil Monument. And not just any statue, but some magnificent Greek goddess, standing in the middle of a fountain, holding the divine insect above her head like a gift from heaven.

"Want me to drop you off at Pam's?" Billy asked, his tone cold now, distant.

"Yeah, thanks." She let out a sigh. "No really, Billy. Thanks. I . . . I do appreciate your effort here. Just . . . well, I'm still working through all this. That's all."

He gave her a hopeful smile and nodded.

Fuck, need a cigarette, Ruby thought, and even though she'd promised herself she was done with them, she popped open the glove compartment looking for one. She reached for a pack of Marlboros and froze.

"Billy, hell!" she said, pointing at a plastic baggie. "What's this?"

"Pot," he said, like it was nothing more than a pack of gum.

"Billy, goddamn it. Fuck! Y'know what'll happen if I'm caught anywhere near this. They'll send me to state this time."

"Oh shit, yeah. I forgot about that. It's no big deal."

"It *is* a big deal! Billy, really? You just don't give a shit, do you?"

He rolled his eyes. "You're overacting."

They pulled into Pam's driveway, but Billy didn't cut off the motor, just kept his eyes forward, waiting for her to get out.

"How can you be so careless? It's your fault I'm in this mess. Your fault I've been mopping floors the last couple of months."

"How many times you gonna throw *that* in my face?" he snapped. "I fucked up, alright? Seems I can't apologize enough. Please, just crucify me already. God, this was a mistake."

Ruby blinked, couldn't even find the words.

Billy started selling marijuana about a year out of school, mostly to friends. He called it "buying in bulk"—his way of keeping the price down for everybody. Ruby never thought much of it, at least not until they got busted.

The whole thing was stupid. They'd been on their way to Lake Tholocco when Billy pulled into Ray's Bait Shop out on Highway 27 to get some gas. The fact that they didn't even need gas should've been Ruby's first clue something was up.

A rusty green van pulled in next to them, driven by a guy Ruby had never seen before. Some woman wearing a tank top and Daisy Dukes got out the back and headed into the bathroom. Ruby was trying to figure out what all the eye contact was about when Billy shoved an envelope into her purse and told her to go give it to that woman. Ruby took a peek, saw the cash, and finally caught on— told Billy no way. Billy gave her his why-are-you-making-such-a-big-deal-out-of-nothing face, the one which, if she didn't do what he wanted, could quickly turn into his mad-sulk-all-day face. Still, she refused. He then told her he sure as shit couldn't go into the women's bathroom, and if she didn't do it she'd fuck up the whole deal. Might even get him beat up. Ruby, who only wanted to have a nice day at the lake, thought, *I can take two minutes and get his dope, or I can spend the whole day dealing with his pouting and acting pissed at me.* So, Ruby followed Miss Daisy Dukes into the bathroom.

Close up, Daisy Dukes turned out to be pushing fifty and looked hard as concrete, but she smiled pleasantly enough. "Here you go, shug," she said, handing Ruby a small brown paper sack. Ruby didn't bother to look inside, just handed the woman the envelope. The woman told Ruby to wait a couple of minutes before following her out. As Ruby waited, her hands began to shake and she swore right then and there, never again. She tucked her purse under her arm and headed out. The van was gone, and Billy was in the car, over by the tire pumps with the engine running. That's when the sheriff pulled in.

Ruby froze as the sheriff got out and started around to the gas pump. In retrospect, if she hadn't panicked, she'd probably been fine, but she *did* panic, snatching the bag out of her purse and dropping it under one of the cricket cages and acting like she hadn't. She started toward Billy, not making it four steps before the sheriff called to her. "Hey, miss. You dropped something."

Billy hit the gas and just drove away, leaving her there in the middle of the goddamn parking lot. The sheriff grabbed her and that was when she went off, just completely lost it. She barely even remembered what happened next, just a blur of screaming, kicking, and biting.

The long and short of it, Ruby got busted. Didn't take long for the cops to figure out Billy was in on it too, but Ruby was the one with the dope, so she was the only one to get charged. But that wasn't the worst of it. Apparently, she'd had a complete meltdown in lockup, leading to a short stay at the Dothan Mental Health Center, under observation by Dr. Ferguson. This was followed by nine months' probation and endless community service, along with a court order to stay on her medication. There just seemed to be no end to the fun.

"You getting out, or what?" Billy asked.

"Oh, I'm getting out, alright." Ruby opened the door, sliding her guitar over, and stopped. There was a cassette tape under the bag of dope. She pulled it out and burst out laughing. "Oh, my God. *Really?*"

"Please get out of my car."

She held it in front of his face and laughed some more. "Dewydoo and the Boohoos?"

"So what?"

"*So what?*" She could hear the shrillness rising in her voice, but couldn't stop. "This is who you are now?"

"God, are you off your meds again?"

Ruby stopped laughing, glared at him.

"Shit, you are. Fuck, you could've at least warned me. Man, this is the last thing I need right now. Look, just go back to your punk rock loser club already. Your little being-mad-at-the-world club. Have fun. Always such a joy to be around, Ruby. I swear."

She got out, slamming the door shut so hard it rattled. "Yeah, well you can go back to your . . . your . . . to your fucking Dewy-fucking-Doo loser club."

"Good one, Ruby. Can I have my tape back now?"

Ruby forgot she was even holding it. She looked at it and grinned. "You want this? Do you, babe?" She grabbed the tape and yanked it out of its spool, yanking and yanking until she had a big wad of tape, then threw it at him. "There's your goddamn tape!"

"Nice, Ruby. Real nice." He jammed it into reverse and shot back out of the driveway, then shouted, "Crazy-ass psycho!" And drove off.

Ruby stood there shaking from head to toe. The word "psycho" ringing in her head. In all the blowups they'd ever had, he'd never jabbed at her mental health, never crossed that line. He'd always been the one person to tell her she *wasn't* crazy, that it was that mean old world out there that was crazy.

"I'm gonna cry," she whispered. "Fuck it, I'm gonna cry." And she did.

Ruby stood in Pam's yard, wiping away the tears as she tried to compose herself.

"Why don't you come on in?" called a warm voice from behind her.

Ruby turned to see Pam looking out through her screen door. She pushed the door open. "Come on."

Ruby came in, setting her guitar down by the door.

Pam had on her flight suit. She was a warrant officer in the military, flew fix-winged aircraft over at Fort Rucker, the nearby Army base. Ruby worked for her three or four days a week, taking care of her elderly father while she was away.

Pam put an arm around Ruby and led her into the kitchen. "How about some tea?" she asked. Being from Brooklyn, Pam had a slight accent. She fixed two glasses and brought them over to the table. "This should cool you down a bit."

"Thank you," Ruby said as they sat down. Pam wasn't much older than Ruby, maybe twenty-six or -seven, but she seemed like such an *adult* to Ruby. It was more than her strong jaw and no-nonsense cropped hair, more than the fact that her house was tastefully decorated and always in order. There was such confidence in the way she looked at you, in the way she spoke: direct, but neither confrontational nor condescending. Something Ruby felt she could never pull off.

"Guess you heard us carrying on?" Ruby said.

"I did."

"Sorry about that."

"Don't be. Thought you two were done."

"Oh, we're definitely done."

Pam took a sip of her tea and leaned back in her chair.

"Y'know," Ruby said. "You know what pisses me off? Two years I waited around for him to go to Atlanta with me. Two fucking years. I let Tina down, all for him. And that's how he repays me?"

Pam set a hand atop Ruby's, squeezed. "You didn't know he was playing games."

"Yeah, but I should've. Maybe not at first, but certainly when he kept coming up with excuses not to go. We'll move to Atlanta next week, then next month, then after Christmas, then after he gets his braces off, and on and on. Whenever I suggested that maybe I should go on ahead, he'd get all pouty. Start in with that if-I-really-loved-him-I'd-wait crap. Y'know what I think? I think he never intended to go. That he was just stringing me along, y'know, hoping I'd give up on Atlanta, the band. Just stay here in Enterprise with him."

Ruby shook her head. "God, it all just makes me feel so bad. You think you know someone." She stared at her tea for a minute, then let out a long, deep breath. "And you wanna know something else, something that really makes me feel bad? Sometimes I wonder if I was just using *him* as an excuse. That deep down I'm afraid. That's what Tina said. I mean really, why else am I still here? Maybe I am a loser . . . a left-behinder."

"You know that isn't true. Tina and that band is about all you talk about."

"Maybe. Guess it doesn't matter now. All I know is I haven't gotten a letter from Tina for almost a year. I think she might've given up on me. Can't say I blame her."

"I know this," Pam said. "You have one week to go. One week and you'll be on your way. You have your whole life ahead of you. Can be anything you want."

Ruby tried to smile, but she was thinking about Tina, wondering where they stood. They'd started their band, the Night Mares, in high school, more just pretending to be a band, at least at first. Tina looking badass with her shorn hair, braless in her tank top, her thin, ripped arms flexing while she strummed. Ruby growling out the vocals while banging on her bass, and Tina's older brother, Jim, popping the drums. But after a couple of years, they started to pull it together, even managed to work out a few songs of their own.

Jim left to go to work on an oil rig, leaving them without a drummer. Tina tried junior college for a while, but became disillusioned. That's when Tina and Ruby decided to get serious about the band and started saving up, making plans for Atlanta. They had stars in their eyes, dreaming about getting out of

Enterprise, traveling across the country, and playing every hot spot along the way.

One thing Ruby could tell you is that things rarely go to plan. They never played a single gig, but she'd also tell you that filling that basement with all that noise was some of the best times of her life.

Pam stood up. "Oh, before I forget." She snatched a notepad off the counter and sat back down. "Here's your work log. Added up all your hours and pay, just like your probation officer asked for. What was his name? Larry . . . something?"

"Thanks, Pam. Yeah, his name's Larry Asswipe."

Pam chuckled.

"Not looking forward to going back to see him either. That guy hates me."

"You don't know that."

"Oh, I know it, because he told me so. Said straight to my face that he thinks I should've gone to jail for hitting the sheriff. Told me he's just hoping I'll screw this up so he can lock me away."

"Yes, well, that may be, but nothing he can do about it now. You're practically home free."

"Lord, don't say that! You'll jinx it." Ruby knocked on the wooden tabletop, crossed her fingers, then crossed herself two times, not caring in the least that she wasn't Catholic.

Pam laughed. "You are *so* superstitious, Ruby. Everything's going to work out fine. I feel it, because you're owed a streak of luck after all you've been through." A sad look fell across Pam's face. "Going to miss you. And not just because you're such a great dad-sitter either. Really going to miss you."

"Gonna miss both of y'all," Ruby said, and couldn't have meant it more. "Oh, hey, how'd the interview with Mrs. Wheat go? Did Mr. Rosenfeld like her?"

Pam almost spit out her tea. "Well, first off, he didn't hear us walk in, so there he was, standing in his kitchen in nothing but his polka-dot boxers. I'd liked to have died, but the thing is, Mrs. Wheat, she didn't bat an eye, just snorted and complimented him on how nice his underwear was."

"Oh, sounds like you found a winner."

Pam laughed. "I hope so. She won't be his Ruby Dear, but I think he'll adjust.

Funny, y'know how unpredictable his mind can be. Well, he was as sharp as a tack when she visited. Even walked her through how to fix matzo ball soup. I could see that Mrs. Wheat wasn't sure what we even needed her for."

"So, is today a good day, or bad day?"

"He's doing alright," Pam started. "Well . . . he . . . he—" Suddenly there were tears in her eyes. "He didn't know me today."

"Oh, Pam. I'm so sorry."

"It's the first time that's happened. I thought I was prepared . . . I—" Her lip began to tremble. "It just caught me so off guard. That's all."

Mr. Rosenfeld's problems started with lung cancer. They'd removed half a lung to get rid of it, only to discover the cancer had already spread, that he had not one, but three inoperable tumors growing in his brain, one larger than a golf ball. According to Pam, there was nothing else to be done at this point, other than make him as comfortable as she could.

"Let's go see him," Ruby said, suddenly needing to give the old man a hug. "I'll play some of his Barbra Streisand albums for him. I've noticed a bit of nostalgia helps with his memory."

"Oh, you're a saint. I don't know how you can stand listening to her all day."

"Who, Streisand? I love Barbra!" Listening to records with the old man was Ruby's favorite thing to do when she visited. She'd even gotten him to listen to a few of her favorite albums. He'd wrinkled his nose at most of them, but he actually liked Madness, the two of them dancing to that crazy ska beat, laughing until they collapsed onto the sofa.

Pam smiled. "Glad you're here today, Ruby. Especially today. He always seems a little better after your visits."

They left through the back door, walking past a black Cadillac parked on the grass, an older model, from the late sixties probably. It was Mr. Rosenfeld's. There was a large dent in the front bumper. Pam had to take his keys away after that one. They approached a small but nice single-wide mobile home.

Mr. Rosenfeld had been in residence about a year now. He'd been living alone in Brooklyn before that, but his ongoing medical issues left Pam with no other options than to bring him down to stay with her. Pam's primary job, as she put it, was flying high-ranking muckity-mucks wherever they needed to go, and she often had to be out of town for several days at a time. So, she needed a little help, someone to keep her father out of trouble.

"Where did you say you were going this time?" Ruby asked. "Costa Rica?"

"I wish. No, going to Colombia. They don't tell me much, but I'm betting it has something to do with the drug cartels and that hot mess. Like I said, I should be back by Wednesday. I'll have someone from the base let you know if it's going to be longer."

Pam stepped up on the small porch and knocked on the door. "Papa?" She knocked again and opened the door. "Papa? Hey, it's me, Pam. Coming in . . . are your pants on?"

"Maybe they are, maybe they aren't," called back a gravelly voice. Pam groaned and led Ruby in.

Ruby was greeted by the familiar scent of musty books and exotic spices. There were boxes sitting all around the sparsely furnished room, so many that they had to squeeze their way into the living room.

There, on a green corduroy sofa, sat Mr. Rosenfeld, a smallish balding man in blue pajamas. Several open boxes sat on the couch next to him. The old man was carefully unrolling a wad of packing paper, revealing a small hourglass of black stone and murky glass.

"How are you doing, Papa?" Pam asked.

"Half dead and dying," he said without looking up.

"About like usual then?"

"Yup."

"Hi there, Josh," Ruby said. Mr. Rosenfeld insisted Ruby call him by his first name. "Glad to see you're finally unpacking the rest of your things."

His pushed his spectacles up on his nose and gave her a hard look. His brow furrowed, then he broke into a smile. "Ruby, dear!"

"Be happy to help you sort through some of this," Ruby offered, and meant it too. According to Josh, he used to be some kind of custodian at his synagogue back in Brooklyn. It was part of his job to look after their collection of religious artifacts—a lot of oddities, mummified frogs, bracelets made from teeth and such. Apparently, these creepy items didn't sit so well with the younger gener-ations. The new rabbi—or as Josh called him, "the little pup"—wanted it all out of the synagogue. So, Josh had taken it upon himself to keep up with it all. Anyway, that story always got a little murky, a little different every time Josh told it. All Ruby knew for sure was that Mr. Rosenfeld had an incredible collection of weird stuff.

Josh held the hourglass up, squinting at it. He flipped it over so that the red sand began to slide into the lower chamber. He held it out toward Ruby. "See that sand?"

"Yes, sir," Ruby said.

"Want to guess where it's from?"

"No idea."

"Hell."

Ruby wanted to laugh, but there was something in the way he said it that unnerved her.

Josh set the hourglass on the side table. "They're coming. I have to be ready."

Ruby glanced at Pam. Pam shrugged.

"Who's coming?" Ruby asked.

"The demons."

"Not this again," Pam said. She picked a cigarette butt out of a coffee cup. "Papa, what's this?"

"A whole lot of none of your business."

"You know you're not supposed to be smoking. Right?"

"Do I?"

"Papa, you only have one lung left."

"One and a half." He pulled a cigarette out of his pajama pocket and stuck it in his mouth. "Anyone seen my lighter?"

Pam groaned and rolled her eyes. "Okay you two, I have to get to work." Pam leaned over and gave the old man a kiss on the top of his head, taking the cigarette. "Love you, Papa."

Mr. Rosenfeld gave her a sour look.

"I'll be back in a couple of days, now you be nice to Ruby. You hear me?"

"Only if she's nice to me," he said.

Pam winked at Ruby, then left them alone in the trailer.

There was a long moment when the two just stared at the floor, then Mr. Rosenfeld cleared his throat. "Ruby, dear, got a question for you."

"Yes, sir."

"How much I gotta pay you to take me to Atlanta?"

DICK

My name's Richard, but people called me Dick. I've always hated being called Dick. I was fifty-two years old then, and I was evil.

I tortured people, killing them in interesting and horrible ways, usually as slowly as possible. But that wasn't what made me evil. Evil must be a choice.

To be clear, there was never any simmering rage just below my smile; I'd never been one to hold onto anger that way. No need to strike back at some perceived slight by society. And I didn't have a hidden childhood history of snuffing out little Fidos and Mittens. No episodes of paranoia, delusions, or fits of rage. I had a respectable number of pals, and a few meaningful girlfriends throughout school and college. What I'm getting at, is there was no evidence of the typical telltale signs that foreshadow psychopathic behavior. I was too lame to even get sent to the principal, much less make any real trouble. So, I wasn't born to it. Becoming evil took a lot of effort on my part.

Of course, we should consider any outside influences, any traumatic events that might've warped my ability to have empathy with my fellow human beings. Y'know, the kind of horse feathers that psychologists devote their entire careers to. I guess it helps us all sleep a little better if we can find logic in the illogical, make some sense of the brutal, horrific acts perpetrated on random innocent lives. I grew up middle-class; never got most of what I wanted, but can't ever remember doing without. I wasn't picked on, bullied, or ostracized in school . . . at least no worse than any other kid. My parents were still married. They never beat me or each other. No verbal lashings or forced sessions on my knees begging Jesus for forgiveness.

Couldn't blame my career. Before I retired, I was a fairly successful commercial photographer. Pretty boring calling, but it was what I wanted to do, or at least thought I did. So, no ax to grind there. Ahh . . . but then there's my divorce . . . an area ripe for trouble. But as much as I'd like to blame my ex for something, for anything, the only thing I might've been able to accuse her of was being a bit distant, and that just doesn't add up to a very good reason to start torturing and killing people. None of it does. And that's my point.

I was evil because I *chose* to be, not because I had to be. That choice, that sane, rational choice, is what made me truly evil.

There was a bit more to it—beyond the choice. It was the complete awareness that what I was doing was despicable and wicked and heinous, and I think that might've been the most important part, not just awareness, but my horror and repulsion. I heard more than pain in their muffled wails. I recognized their utter despair, the knowing that they would die horribly and would have to do it alone. I saw below their fear, I saw the confusion in their eyes of how such an incomprehensible thing could be happening to them, how their safe, warm world of dayglow nail polish and moussed hair could've ever twisted into a nightmare of unbearable pain and terror. I understood the unfairness of stealing their young lives from them before they barely got started. I want you to know that tore my heart out, that I felt it to my very core.

So why did I choose to be evil? It's no mystery, not anymore. It's simple. Painfully clear. I got . . . *bored*. Bored with my career, bored with my wife, bored with my fuel-efficient car, my house and its fixed-rate, thirty-year mortgage, my friends, especially my friends and their endless yakety-yak about their dreams and ambitions that never turned into anything, with my annual vacations to Gatlinburg, to Panama City Beach, or whatever other godforsaken place my wife wanted to go that year, with Democrats, with Republicans, with Baptists, Presbyterians, and Methodists, with watering and mowing my lawn to keep up with every other lawn in my cookie-cutter subdivision, with sex, with all ninety-nine stations on my cable box. All of it. I got bored. Bored to death.

So?

So, a little torture and a little killing were the only things I'd come across that could take the tedium out of life. There it is, that simple. I found that this rational choice to do evil was what tooted my horn. To know something is so heinous and to do it anyway, this completely sane and rational awareness of the vileness of my actions was what made it so intense. What made me feel alive again. And until you've held someone's very life in your hands, had them trembling before you as you decided not only if they would live or die, but just how long and dreadful that death would be—until then you'll never truly get it. It's an infusion of supreme all-powerfulness. I walked around like a god, knowing that anyone I saw, anyone I talked to, bought groceries from, sat next to in a movie. Anyone. *Anyone.* They were all essentially at my mercy. Heck, I won't even cheapen it by comparing it to sex or drugs. Man, I'm telling you, it was the bee's knees, the cat's meow. There's just nothing like it. *Nothing.*

Maybe if my wife had cheated on me, maybe if she'd got hooked on her medication, took to running up the credit cards, or contracted a life-threatening disease, then there might've been enough drama to keep my life interesting. Maybe then there wouldn't have been the chopped-up remains of a dozen young women scattered along the waterways between Boston and Miami. But it was too late for maybes. I'd found something that made life worth living again, something to look forward to, a reason to hang around this tired old turd of a planet just a while longer. It was called evil.

And evil was calling me again. Like a whisper, like a muse. Who will she be this time? How bad will it be? How *good* will it be?

My name's Richard, but people called me Dick. I've always hated being called Dick.

Ruby's bedroom was in the basement of her mother's house and she awoke to the sound of heels clumping above her. She peeked at the digital display on her clock and groaned. It was eight a.m. Sunday morning, and apparently her mom had decided to go to church after all. Her mother only tended to go to church when she felt guilty about something, leaving Ruby to wonder what awful thing her mom had done that week.

Ruby heard a man's voice; that would be Eduardo, her mother's boyfriend, technically her fiancé, who *never* missed church. They were supposed to have gotten married a year ago, but her mom kept putting it off. She'd had a myriad of excuses, but Ruby knew it was on account that Eduardo seemed unable to keep a job for longer than a few months.

Ruby's father had died when she was eight, leaving her mother a fully paid-off house. Eduardo had nothing but a truck and he was making payments on that. He was, however, as he put it, drafting a right smart business plan, something about becoming a bounty hunter of all things. Ruby knew this and pretty much everything else about their relationship, due to the frequent and very loud arguments in the bedroom above her. She also knew far too much about their sex life, the basement providing little to no escape from her mom's excessively vocal orgasms. One of the many reasons that Ruby had developed the habit of sleeping with her earphones on.

As soon as Ruby heard them leave for services, she hopped up, got dressed, and headed for Pam's house to check on Mr. Rosenfeld.

Ruby loved Sunday mornings; most folks on her street were in church and she had the neighborhood to herself. She slid her headphones over her ears and hit play, the soft melodic vibes of the Velvet Underground bringing a smile to her face, calming her soul. She felt the Velvet Underground was made just for Sunday mornings.

Ruby used to enjoy church, but after her father died, she stopped going. She wasn't sure why. She thought maybe she'd just grown tired of hearing some twit telling her she was a sinner. Ruby didn't think she was a sinner; she thought she was a pretty good soul for the most part, thought the whole notion of original sin a bunch of hogwash.

Yet the church was easier to leave behind than God. No matter how hard she tried to rationalized away the existence of God, she felt he, or she, or it, was still there, judging her, just waiting for her to fuck up. She wondered how much of her belief stemmed from being so superstitious, as she tended to believe every ghost story she ever heard, believed in UFOs, fortune-telling, reincarnation, and had spent untold hours talking to dead folks through her Ouija board. She also knocked on wood a dozen times a day, avoided the number 13, couldn't sleep without a nightlight on—just sure that the creepies were waiting for her in the shadows. Was religion any different? She didn't think so. But when every person you knew believed in Jesus, it was hard not to as well.

She realized she was walking fast, that she was excited. It wasn't Jesus she was thinking about now, but the Devil, particularly the clipping of his hair Mr. Rosenfeld had shown her yesterday. She'd thought about it all night, the strange shimmer it had given off. She'd been wondering all year about what he had hidden in all those boxes, couldn't wait to find out what other creepy items he had stuffed away.

Ruby felt a twinge of guilt; as much as she looked forward to getting out of this town, she hated the thought of leaving Pam and Josh. Almost felt she was abandoning them. She didn't know where she'd be if not for Pam and the kindness she'd shown her. Ruby thought how nice it would be if she could take the two of them with her.

To save time, Ruby left the street and headed through the gulch—about an acre of woods dividing the two neighborhoods. The trail led along a small brook. She came to a cement culvert and shuddered. Rumor had it that years ago, some crazy woman had murdered her children, then committed suicide, right in this very spot. The neighborhood kids all claimed the woman was some kind of witch, had sacrificed her children to Satan. Ruby told herself that was nonsense, but sprinted past anyway.

She came out of the woods just down from Pam's house, crossed the street, and headed up the drive. She walked around to the backyard, relieved to see that the mobile home still appeared in good shape, that nothing was on fire, at least not at the moment.

She knocked on the door.

Nothing, she knocked again. This time she heard a thump.

"Just a minute!" someone squawked.

She heard more thumping, shuffling, then a loud crash.

"Mr. Rosenfeld?" She knocked again.

"Aww . . . hell!" from inside.

"Mr. Rosenfeld?" She opened the door. "Josh?"

He was over near the kitchen, digging through a big box. He was still dressed in his blue pajamas, his twist of white hair standing up like he'd been electrocuted. Ruby wondered if maybe he had.

"Mr. Rosenfeld? You okay?"

"Where is it?" he asked frantically, as he moved to another box.

"Where's what?" she asked.

He looked round, pushing his glasses up on his nose and squinting at her as though never having seen her before.

"Morning, Josh. It's me, Ruby."

He continued to eye her suspiciously.

Ruby could tell he was having an off day, and it hurt seeing him like that, because she knew it wasn't going to get better, that there was nothing she could do about it. She was losing him one memory at a time.

"Ruby," she repeated.

Slowly he nodded. "Yes, I know that. Come in, Lucy."

"Josh, it's me, *Ruby.*"

"Huh?"

"Ruby. Y'know, Ruby Dear."

"Uh-huh . . . that's what I said."

The room appeared even more chaotic than the day before, open boxes strown and stacked about. Again, she was struck by the smells—cinnamon, sage, a touch of rot maybe, and that of burned wood. She stepped around a few piles, made it into the kitchen and checked the fridge, finding the tuna casserole untouched.

"Josh, did you eat?"

He didn't seem to hear her, just kept digging down into the box in front of him.

"You really need to eat something. Here, I'll fix it for you."

"Not hungry."

She spotted a large cantaloupe. "How about some fruit then?"

"Where is it?" he barked. "Where the hell is it?"

Ruby pushed aside a box and set the cantaloupe on the counter. "Maybe if you tell me what you're looking for I can help find it."

"A box. I'm looking for a box."

Ruby glanced around at all the stacked boxes. "Okay . . . could you maybe be a bit more specific?"

He scratched his head. "It should be about yay big." He indicated with his hands. "About the size of a shoebox. I think it was red, a red shoebox. No . . ." He pulled off his glasses and rubbed his eyes. "A cigar box. A red cigar box! Yes, I'm certain. And it'll have 'do not open' written on it . . . I think."

"Okay," Ruby said. "That narrows it down a bit." She started sorting through the boxes, most weren't labeled, the few that were, were written in what she guessed was Hebrew.

"Just open them up," he said, sounding increasingly frantic. "Looking for a bronze case with a spider carved into the lid. We have to find it. *Have* to."

Ruby started opening boxes. She unwrapped an urn, several moldy clay pots, a stone knife, a jaw bone covered in squiggly symbols, a box of socks, books, lots and lots of books.

"Pam was supposed to help me with this," Mr. Rosenfeld mumbled. "Can't count on her . . . so damn busy all the time. Swear, given half the chance, she'd toss all of this into the dump." He shuffled a few boxes around. "Y'know, she had a nice Jewish boyfriend once, they were supposed to get married and settle down in Brooklyn, make me some gran-babies. She left him to fly airplanes. Can you believe that? Then . . . then she made me leave my home. What kind of daughter does that? Can't even find a good bagel around here."

Ruby nodded along, half hearing him as he rambled on. She felt like a kid at Christmas, quickly opening each box, excited to see what lay inside, marveling at each relic. She removed an ancient basket full of dried roots and there beneath it was a crimson cigar box.

There were no words on it, so she peeled back the strip of masking tape and opened the lid. Nestled in black velvet was a case, long and thin, like a watch case, only made of hammered bronze—crusty with age. There was something carved into the lid, it resembled a spider. She lifted it from the box for a closer look, but the minute she touched it, she felt a strange tingling and suddenly needed to know—*had* to know—what was inside.

It was held together by twisted wire. She unwound it, started to open the case, then hesitated as a sudden sense of dread swam over her. *Did it feel warm? God, why did it feel warm?* She glanced over at Mr. Rosenfeld; his back was to her. *Put it down,* she thought. *Now. Right now!* She wedged a fingernail beneath the lid and pried it open.

She gasped.

A human finger, mummified, dried and gray, lay within the case. Upon the finger, a ring of gold—a simple band attached to a flat coin shape. Ruddy, waxy crud lay crumbled around the ring. A glint of light sparkled off the surface, drawing her closer. She noticed a closed eye carved into it. The glint again, almost as though coming from within the ring. She blinked and the ring seemed different, the band shaped into spidery legs, the eye in relief.

Mr. Rosenfeld was still droning on, but Ruby no longer heard him, transfixed by the eye. She thought she heard singing; cocked her head. There—a chorus of voices, barely audible, muffled as though coming from beneath the ground, and with it, a sudden compulsion to put on the ring.

She shook her head. *No, hell no!* Yet her fingers moved closer, hovering just above the ring, quivering. The eye, it opened, just a slit as though squinting at her. She caught a red glow, like a hot ember.

The voices, the chorus, grew a little louder, a little clearer.

Ruby leaned closer. The eye opened wide and a tiny black pupil locked on her, staring at her, *into* her. She wanted to scream, to throw the ring across the room, but she didn't, instead, she *touched* it.

"No!" someone yelled, it sounded like Mr. Rosenfeld, it sounded a hundred miles away.

Ruby was falling, a swirling dimness engulfed her and from somewhere the chorus—hundreds of voices—singing a song, the most beautiful song, haunting and soulful, like angels in a deep cavern. The chorus swelled, the sweet voices filling her with bliss, a rapture like she'd never known. She wanted, *needed,* to join them, to sing this beautiful song along with them.

Words hit her, sharp, harsh words, each one cutting into the dimness like a slap to her face.

The song, it began to fade, to die.

No, Ruby thought, as the harsh words tore her away. *No!*

Ruby blinked, found herself on the floor. Mr. Rosenfeld stood above her, reading from some ancient-looking book, barking out a barrage of strange words, a chant of some sort.

"The song," she groaned as a sudden longing seized her. "It's gone."

He stopped reading. Shoved his glasses back up on his nose and stared down at her, horrified. "Can you hear me?"

She sat up, rubbed her head.

"Can you hear me?"

She nodded, but it was the song, that sweet chorus, that she was trying to hear.

He blew out a loud sigh and sat the book down on the end table. "Did you touch it?"

"Huh?"

"The ring? Ruby, did you touch it?"

"The ring?" She tried to make sense of that.

He held up the bronze case. "You opened this. Remember?"

It came to her then, the case, seeing the finger . . . and yes, the ring—a simple gold ring. But the rest was a jumble, all except the song.

"Did you touch the ring?"

"I don't know. Maybe."

"Listen to me. You mustn't touch anything here unless I say so. Understand?"

Ruby's eyes were locked on the case.

Mr. Rosenfeld quickly shoved the relic back into the cigar box and out of sight, putting the box into the end table drawer.

Ruby felt a flash of anger, as though something had been stolen from her.

He studied her. "How do you feel?"

She blinked several times, noticed his hands were trembling, saw that hers were too. "What . . . what just happened?" she asked. "What were you chanting?"

"Ruby, I need you to do something for me. I need you to take me to Atlanta."

"Huh?"

"Atlanta. Can you do that?"

Ruby thought she caught a faint echo of the song, and with it the desire to see the ring again. "Where did that ring come from?"

Frustration flashed across his face. He stood up, walked into the kitchen, returning with a tin. He slipped off the top and pulled out a wad of bills. He counted out five hundred dollars. "This is yours if you'll drive me up there right now."

"Josh, I don't even have a car."

"We can take mine. I have a pair of keys stashed away that Pam doesn't know about."

"Why . . . why," Ruby found she was having trouble finding words; her head felt light. "Why doesn't Pam take you?"

He let out a huff. "She's too busy. *Always* too busy. By the time she'll get to it, it'll be too late."

Ruby noticed that Mr. Rosenfeld seemed sharper now, that there was a clarity in his eyes.

"Too late for what?" she asked.

"Pam doesn't take any of this seriously . . . the ring, the Baalei Shem, the demons, none of it. Can't be bothered with it. Probably just waiting for me to get so senile that I forget." His voice dropped to a mumble. "Going to wake up one morning and put that wicked ring on my own finger." He rubbed his face. "Eight hundred, I'll pay you eight hundred."

"Holy cow. No, Mr. Rosenfeld, that's too much."

"It's nothing. I have lots of money. I don't need money. I need peace of mind." He grimaced. "Look, I'd drive myself, but I can't, just can't do it. Can barely keep that car on the road. I'd end up in a ditch. I need your help, Ruby, dear."

Ruby could see how upset he was, how much this meant to him. She clasped her head in her hands, trying to focus. "Okay, sure. But we'll have to ask Pam first."

"No, we don't!" he snapped. "Pam's not my warden. If I want to go somewhere, I sure as hell don't need her permission." He took a deep breath. "Listen, I might have my lapses, but I'm not as senile as Pam likes to believe. All I want here, is to go to Atlanta and give a few of these relics to a friend. Someone I can trust to look after them. Does that sound unreasonable?"

No, it didn't. Not really, she'd driven him around before. Taken him to Dothan several times for his checkups. Where did Pam say she was going this time? God, it was just so hard to think. Colombia. Yeah, that was it. There was a number to call in case of an emergency. Was this an emergency? Ruby wasn't sure what this was. But Pam wasn't really the problem, was she? No, the problem was Ruby was still on probation, not allowed to leave the state. That was the problem.

"Let's leave now," he said. "Right now. We'll be back late tonight. Pam doesn't ever have to know."

Pam or anyone, Ruby thought. *Just zip up and back. What could go wrong?* Only Ruby knew something always went wrong. Again, Ruby thought she heard a faint echo of the song, like a radio station fading in and out of range. She glanced uneasily at the end table and rubbed her temple; her head was beginning to hurt.

"Josh, I'm not feeling so well." She stood up. "Think I need to go home for now." She stumbled over to the door. "Tell you what, let me think on it. Okay? That be okay? We can talk more about it when I come by tomorrow."

He watched her leave, his face solemn, like someone being left behind to die.

Flame.

Burning, searing heat.

The soul screamed and kept screaming as his flesh smoldered, blistered, broiled, then blackened. He clinched his eyes, but his eyelids burned away and then his very eyes were ablaze. All was fire, a lake of flame and he sunk beneath its surface, drowning, his throat and lungs scorched as he fought for breath, as he sunk ever deeper, and deeper. He burned until he was but a smoldering husk, and yet still he felt the flame, still he screamed.

The soul burned for a week, or maybe a month, perhaps a decade; impossible to tell as there is no sense of time in such pain, just pain, endless pain.

The flames receded, slithered away into the crags and hollows, revealing the black jagged walls of his pit, his prison. But the flames didn't leave him, they coiled up within their burrows, flickering at him like a serpent's tongue, taunting him with the promise of yet more suffering.

He lay crumpled upon a bed of sooty rocks and ash, staring at his hands, arms, legs. All charred, shriveled skin on bones, like something dragged from a funeral pyre. He tried to sit up, but each movement, each bend of his elbows, or knees, clutching of his hands, brought agony as his skin cracked and crumbled, flaked away like paint from rotting wood. So, he stilled himself, keeping a wary eye on the flames, his tormentors, his keepers.

The flames flickered and he felt a presence approaching, pushing dread before it as it floated toward him. The soul struggled to crawl away, but the flames blocked his path and he could but huddle against a stone and wait. He heard its breathing, that of the presence, and understood it was in the pit with him. He found it, a shadow within the shadows. He clung to the stone, listening to its slow, deep breathing.

"Say my name," the presence whispered, the sound so light, yet still it reverberated up the walls of the pit, fading into the darkness above.

Name? What name? The soul struggled to find it.

Two serpents of flame slithered to the presence's side, licking at its hands like loyal hounds. A woman, at least in shape, was revealed in their orange glow, her skin and long hair the blue-gray of ash. She stood like a queen, hands on hips, surveying the soul. A thin panel of shear white cloth hung from a wide neck ring made of tiny bones. The cloth flowed down the middle of her wiry frame, to the ground. Thorns twisted out from her hair and forehead like a tortured crown; they appeared to have torn through her skin, as though driven from the inside out. A thin rivulet of blood drained from each. The wounds revealed a hint of scaly hide beneath, as though her skin were but something she wore, something to cover what was beneath.

The soul saw that the woman, the creature, had but one remaining eye, and it glinted at him as a cut ruby. Within the adjoining socket, an open wound glistened where her second eye had once been, a tiny spark glowing from within. A trail of bloody tears trickled down her cheek. The woman's face appeared unbearably sad, but not for him.

"Say my name," the woman commanded, her voice cutting.

The soul flinched, struggled to recall. He knew it, or at least had known it. He looked fearfully at the flames. "I . . . I cannot remember," he stammered. "Forgive me."

She smiled then. "I am not in the business of forgiveness." She stroked one of the flames; it rubbed up against her leg. "I am Lord Sheelbeth . . . your savior, your master." The flames flared as she spoke.

"Master?"

"Yes, now say my name."

The soul hesitated, some instinct telling him not to, that names were like spells, giving and taking power.

"Perhaps you wish to return to the fire?" she asked.

One of the flames slithered over, hovering before him. He felt its heat, its promise of torment, and shuddered. "Lord Sheelbeth," he said, and when he did, she was there, in his head, it was as though he'd opened a door for her. And he saw it, the ring, with its legs like a spider and an eye set in it, an eye just like this Lord Sheelbeth. God, how could he have ever forgotten that dreadful ring? "The ring . . . it is yours?" he asked, already knowing the answer.

"It is more than mine, it is a part of me." She tapped her empty socket. "When they stole my ring, cutting it from my very hand." She lifted her hand so that he could see that her ring finger was missing. "They stole my eye. But not my sight." She smiled thinly. "It is time to reclaim what is mine. Time to punish those who would meddle in my affairs. To put an end to them for good." Her one eye flared, her malice palpable. "Now, let us find out what else you remember."

Lord Sheelbeth drifted toward him, floating, gliding, her toes, with their long black curling nails, dragging through the soot. Her face caught the light and the beauty of it surprised him. Her black lips and dark red eye against her ashen skin gave the impression of a painted lady, somehow both ghastly and alluring. She drifted closer. "What is your name?"

My name? What is *my name?* The soul looked down at the ash, not wanting to meet her eye, afraid of what she might show him next.

"Come now, surely you have not forgotten your own name? Your memories, where are they? Have the flames burned them all away, or are you just hiding from them?" She leaned over, her lips inches from his ear, her breath smelling of burning coals. "You are *Beel*."

The name, *his* name, hit him as though struck by a blow and he reeled, almost falling over as it burrowed into his mind, his soul, digging into all the dark places where his memories hid. He heard them then, the screams, followed by faces full of horror, one after another, so many. He felt them, every one, felt their terror, their confusion, their loss, their overwhelming sorrow, felt it as though he was them, because . . .

"Because I *was* them," he groaned.

The wailing turned into a chorus, a song of unbearable suffering, at once beautiful and chilling. He knew this song too well. He tried to turn from it, to hide from it, but couldn't. It was as though they were right here, right in the room with him.

Lord Sheelbeth pulled aside the front of her gown, revealing the pale flesh of her chest, but where her stomach should've been was an open wound, running from her sternum down to her lower abdomen. Within that wound were red worms, hundreds and hundreds of them.

Only Beel knew they were more than worms, because he could see their accusing faces staring out at him, actually recognized some of them. And well he should, they were the faces of souls, souls he'd stolen.

"Stop!" he cried. "Please . . . make them stop."

But the worms didn't stop, their lamentations grew, filling the chamber.

"You failed me before," Lord Sheelbeth said. "Do you remember? You failed me because you forgot who you are. What you are. But this time I will see to it you never forget." She put a finger under his chin and lifted his head.

"You are the possessor, the soul thief . . . you are the *sheid*."

"Sheid," he whispered, the word bringing with it a sense of despair.

"Yes, one of the shedim . . . one of God's unfinished people. You belong nowhere, an abomination before all. They hate you, the people, the angels, even the devils, they all despise you. And God? You are nothing to God, nothing but his castoffs, his leavings, his dross and dregs . . . his failure. A reminder that he is not perfect after all. That even *God* makes mistakes. That is why he condemned you here, to this purgatory, to be forgotten by all." She was quiet a moment. "You and I both."

Beel shook his head as old memories, old feelings assaulted him; tears began to run from his lidless eyes.

"We were going to change all that," she said. "Do you remember? It was within our grasps. So close."

Beel saw the burning synagogue, the rabbi smoldering in the snow, his eyes but bloody sockets. The man, Adam, holding the knife, sobbing.

"Your work was done, the wizard, the Baal Shem, dead. It was time to move on, to find the others. To finish the last of them. We were so close."

Beel watched as the man, Adam, slit his own throat, and Adam's soul, it was . . . was what? Drawn, pulled, sucked into the ring? Yes, all part of Lord Sheelbeth's design. And then . . . Beel should've been free. Because, when the man died, when any host died, Beel could no longer stay within the body, that was the way, to be cast out, to roam, a shedim in search of a new body. Only he wasn't set free. *Why?* It took him a moment. *Because the ring . . . I am shackled to that wicked ring. There is no escape for me.* He relived being drawn back into the ring—once again its prisoner.

The vision took on a ruby cast and Beel realized he was no longer seeing from Adam's eyes, but now from the eye set on the ring, Lord Sheelbeth's lost eye. The ring sprouted long spidery legs, and even as the police stared with slack jaws, it scuttled away, darting for the bushes, the shadows.

"You betrayed me, Beel. Betrayed us both. Why?"

The bird, Beel recalled, *a beautiful mourning dove. The ring spooked it from its roost and up it flew into the snowy night, circling round and round as it drifted away from the fire, the sirens, the blood.* "I wanted to watch the bird," he said, only he knew it was so much more.

"A bird," Lord Sheelbeth spat, her voice sounding genuinely hurt. "Why did you throw everything away over a bird? How could you betray *me* so? Betray us *both* so?"

Beel felt the struggle as he fought with the ring to watch the bird. It was madness, as he was all but powerless against Lord Sheelbeth. Then why? Memories of what he was tumbled over him, the spirit that lived in so many bodies, not just humans, but animals of all sorts. Running through the forest as a fleet deer, swimming through the emerald depths as a shark, and flying, yes, flying through the clear blue sky as a bird, so many birds, eagles, swallows, owls, and on and on. And that night, in that moment, it was everything to him to dream of being that bird, dream of flying away from his hell, his torment—to taste freedom again. And if that was insanity, then let insanity be his escape.

And that was where he was, lost in his madness, lost in beautiful memories of flying freely through the sky, when the man, the wizard's novice, snuck up on them. Just a flash of his face before he hit the ring with some substance, some powdery potion. Whatever it was, it stunned the ring. There was a bronze box, a finger lay within, the man put the ring on the finger, spoke a spell, and snapped the box shut, locking them away into darkness. Then Beel was falling, sliding down some convulsing throat of flame, downward, ever downward into where? He looked around. "You put me into the fire."

Lord Sheelbeth nodded. "Yes, the fire, I am sorry. But you left me little choice. You had become confused, lost to madness, and the flame . . . it was the only way for you to find yourself again, your true self. We have both suffered so much, lost so much, so many hard lessons. This pain and loss, it is what bonds us." She nodded as to herself. "But let us not tarry on the past when there is such hope ahead." Her one eye lit up. "A vessel awaits. A girl who is far too curious for her own good." Lord Sheelbeth's voice rang with excitement. "Do you remember the novice, the one who captured the ring? I caught a glimpse of him, enough to see he is old and feeble now . . . no match for us. And the girl, it is too late for her, she has touched the ring. She is mine. It is but a matter of time."

Lord Sheelbeth waited. "Why are you not smiling, Beel? Here is your chance for redemption. We will take her, make her kill the old man, the last of the Baalei Shem, and . . . and, we shall finally be free. Do you hear me? *Free!* Think of it, after all these centuries."

Beel said nothing.

Lord Sheelbeth studied him. "Beel, I have to trust you, have to know you will do the right thing this time." She leaned down, staring into him with her one intense eye. "Before I send you into her, I have to be sure you know who you are."

She laid a hand on Beel's chest. "I have to be sure," she whispered and pushed her cold, hard, fingers into his flesh, shoving her hand into his brittle ribs, snapping right through them.

Beel wailed and clawed at her arm, but her flesh was like stone. She didn't relent, pushing her hand further inside, gripping Beel's heart and tearing it from his chest.

Beel screamed and toppled over.

Lord Sheelbeth held the charred organ out for the shedim to see.

"Your heart, it is dead." She began to squeeze the heart. Pain racked Beel's body. He writhed amongst the ash, clutching his chest.

"Now . . . tell me your name. Tell me what you are."

"Please," Beel begged, his voice tearing his throat. "Please, stop!"

"Who are you?"

"I am Beel," he sobbed. "The shedim . . . the soul thief!"

She smiled. "And who do you serve?"

"I serve you, Lord Sheelbeth. Only you."

She released her grip on the heart, began floating around him, moving in straight lines, her long curled toenails dragging in the ash, each line connecting until she had formed a star with Beel at its center.

She began to chant, the words echoing up the chamber. The worms, the ones in her belly, responded with their song, her voice and theirs forming a chorus. She kissed Beel's heart and it swelled, fleshed, quivered, then began to pump right there in her hand, black blood trickling from the severed arteries. She dribbled the blood, his blood, upon each point of the star.

"God has no place for you on his earth . . . but I do. I am your only ally. Follow me, Beel, and I will see to it *they,* none of them, ever bring you harm again." She smiled at him, it was beautiful and it was terrible. "Are you ready to redeem yourself?" she asked.

"Yes."

"No more birds?"

"Never again."

"Swear your allegiance."

"I swear."

She studied him, his supplication seeming to please her. A brief glow sparked deep within her eye. "Good, then it is done." She squatted, presenting the beating heart. "Here." She shoved the organ back into his chest.

The pain was sharp, but brief, then Beel felt its pulse, the blood coursing through his veins, and slowly his form regained its flesh. The pain subsided. He blinked and felt wetness on his cheeks; he was crying.

"We wait," Lord Sheelbeth said. "The girl hears my music. She cannot resist for long. She *will* return for the ring, and when she does, she will be yours to take."

It's me, Richard.

I found the bench, the one in Marion Square, in downtown Charleston, South Carolina. The very bench that I'd first shared a Mountain Dew with Becky, my then soon-to-be wife. That was thirty-one years ago. Forever and yet . . . only yesterday.

I was heading south on 17, on my way to Atlanta after a brief stay in Jacksonville, then saw the signs, and . . . well, ended up on that bench.

I'll say this, Charleston, with its palmetto-lined streets and historic homes, is most certainly a charming city. I don't think anyone would argue with me on that. But that's not why I was there. Actually, I wasn't entirely sure why I was there. Maybe it was because all my best memories happened there. I was nineteen when I first arrived and on my own for the first time, met and fell in love—true love—also for the first time. And photography . . . how I lived and breathed it. It was the bee's knees, let me tell you. I was so full of passion and possibilities. Just sure I'd be the next Ansel Adams or Man Ray. Because at that age, I could be anything, life could take me anywhere.

So maybe that was it, I was just hoping to stir up a few old feelings, that was all. Some trace of lost passions for me to hold on to for a while. And why not? Everything was almost just as had been, the park, the old buildings, the campus, the smell of the ocean and marsh. I should've been brimming with nostalgia, energized by all these memories . . . the good and bad.

But I wasn't.

If there were ghosts there, they were hiding from me. If anything, this place just compounded the weight, the smothering sense that I'd died and was still walking the earth, little more than a husk of my former self. Just one more reminder of how dead the world was to me. Lord, that sounds melodramatic, but I'll be damned if it wasn't true. So, I guess that whole trip was almost a waste, because I'm telling you . . . you can't go back . . . no matter how bad you want to.

So what next? I knew what. I knew *exactly* what.

A young woman walked past; I barely noticed her, too busy stewing in my own pity pot, probably wouldn't have noticed her at all, but something fell out of her hand, clattered along the walkway. It was the cassette she was trying to put into her Walkman.

She stopped, bent to scoop it up, and I thought I was seeing my wife, the Becky I'd met all those years ago in that very park. It was her hair—dark and curly, and piled on top of her head in a kind of poodle hairdo, just like my wife used to wear it back in '56. But it was more than that, she was also wearing a sleeveless, pink plaid summer dress in a classic fifties' cut. I swear my wife had that same dress. The only thing out of place was her large red triangle earrings.

Perhaps she was one of those new wavers, or maybe she just liked vintage clothes—either way it all played into the illusion, the time warp.

I caught sight of her face then, and the spell was complete—moon pale, so out of place there in that sun-kissed city, again, like my wife. But it was her eyes, they were the chef's kiss, pale blue and with hardly any makeup, giving her a lost fay look. It was as though I'd stepped back in time, and for one blissful moment I remembered what it felt to be young and in love and to have my whole life ahead of me.

But she wasn't my wife . . . her face too wide, half a head shorter, much thinner. A strange thought struck me—she could pass for our daughter, the one I never had. She was about the right age. I stared at her, surprised to find a wave of paternal feelings flowing through me as I suddenly wanted to know her, to take her to lunch, ask how school was going, to give her some advice, to be there for her.

Becky and I had never had children. We had tried, but it hadn't worked out. Which was too bad, because if we had, I'm pretty sure I wouldn't be the way I am now.

She left the park without so much as a glance my way and entered the adjoining library. My pulse raced. I'd like to say I wondered why, but I knew exactly why: Is there any crime more heinous than a parent, a father, murdering their own child? I felt a chill, not of dread, but of pure adrenaline, horrified at the thought. Truly, because if I wasn't, I wouldn't have been so excited. I tried to push her from my mind. Honest, I swear it, but the more I tried not to think of her, the more I did. The wrongness of it. The evil. I knew she wasn't my daughter. It didn't matter, the thought, the fantasy had been planted.

I should add a footnote to this whole evil thing. Everyone has wicked desires.

That doesn't make them evil. You're only evil if you act on those desires. Do you follow me? Coveting your neighbor's wife doesn't make you evil, no matter what the Bible says. Diddling your neighbor's wife because you covet her, on the other hand, that's evil.

I needed to be evil.

I followed her into the library, spotting her at a table near the back, watched her slip a couple of notebooks out of her backpack. I slowly made my way toward her, poking about in one aisle or another until I was behind her. She was leafing through a notebook, tapping her lips with her pen. I walked by, passing just behind her. She was slight, just a waif of a girl . . . an ideal candidate, as I tended to avoid women who looked like they could put up a real fight, avoid anyone I couldn't pick up and shove into my van, really. Which pretty much leaves young women and children. Hadn't murdered a child, not yet, not sure if I could. But two years ago, I would've told you I couldn't hurt anybody. So never say never, right?

I stood behind a row of books, flipping through them so I could watch her, waiting, tasting her. She appeared happy, doodling away with the slightest smile on her lips, her eyes dreamy. I wondered if she was in love.

She left the table, heading down an aisle; when she did, I slipped up and flipped open the front page of her notebook, found her name—it was Alice Brooks.

I waited a minute and followed Alice, began perusing the shelves; we had the aisle to ourselves. She gave me half a glance, hardly seemed to see me. That was no surprise, as one of the reasons I was able to get away with murder time after time, was that I was just so unremarkable, so gosh dern ordinary in every way as to be all but invisible. Part of it was my age—let's face it, when you hit fifty no one's checking out how your rump looks. I also dressed plain, that I did on purpose, but I was neither overweight nor skinny, not tall, not short, not bald. My hair was thinning, with just a touch of gray, nothing notable, just good old, all-around, everyday generic, middle-aged white guy.

There was a little more to it. Evidently, I didn't seem to set off any creep-alarms; women and kids never minded getting into an elevator alone with me.

When people did notice me—usually only when I was in direct contact with them, like a grocery cashier or bank clerk—they tended to give me a distracted smile, as though looking through me. Just another aging man on his way out to pasture.

Alice tugged out a book and began thumbing through. I acted as though I was searching for my own book, tapping titles, moving closer until finally I stood behind her. I pulled out a book, pretended to be reading while I cautiously peered round at her. But there was no need for such charades, she was engrossed in what looked to be an architectural photo journal. Did this young woman, this girl really—she couldn't have been older than eighteen or nineteen—have hopes of becoming an architect? Was she right that minute dreaming of making her mark on the world with her cutting-edge designs, hopes of a grand office building or stately museum in her future?

I took the opportunity to lean closer, noticing how small and delicate her hands were. I could just make out the fuzz on the nape of her neck, could smell the scent of her bath soap. My heart sped up. That, I have to say, was the cat's pajamas: me, her very worst nightmare, me, unbearable pain and torment, literally breathing down her neck and her not having a clue. It was the bee's knees, I tell you. And I did that to most of my potentials, getting as close as I could, sometimes stalking them for days, tasting them, seeing how they make me feel. Sometimes, most times, it wasn't right, as usually they did or said something that made me dislike them, sometimes despise them. Once I dislike them, it was no good, it was over. No, I had to like them, to feel they were decent human beings, to care about them in some way. Otherwise, it's just murder. But if they were wonderful, if they were a little gift to this world, if I was sure I'd be snuffing out a truly bright flower . . . that's when I knew I had the right one. That's when I knew what I was about to do was truly evil, that it would bring me to my knees, break my heart . . . make me feel *alive*.

My hands trembled. *No,* I thought as a wave of horror rushed over me. *Not this one. Please, spare this one.* My heart was drumming so loud now, I felt she might hear and that was when I knew.

I put my book back and moved on, leaving her there with her dreams of a wonderful future.

I headed outside, the day was waning, cooling down a touch. I returned to my bench, the one where I'd met my wife, and waited for the young woman—the one who could be my daughter—to leave the library.

"Alice," I whispered, as the adrenaline pulsed through my whole body.

RING

R uby caught a whiff of rot and spice, sniffed her shirt; the smell was all over her. She blinked, steadied herself, realized she was going the wrong way and stopped. She was trying to get home from Mr. Rosenfeld's. She knew the way, it was only a few blocks. "Get it together," she said, trying to stay focused, but her mind kept drifting back to that ring, to that beautiful song and how wonderful it had made her feel, how badly she wanted to hear it again.

She found her street, then her house, and headed up the drive, her head finally starting to clear. She passed her mother's car and the truck, then tripped over something, slapping against the side of the truck to catch herself.

There came a loud cry from beneath the truck and out rolled her mom's boy-friend, Eduardo, a smear of grease across his cheek.

"Watch it!" he barked. He was holding a wrench, looking ready to bash her with it.

"Shit, Eduardo, what the hell are you doing with your legs sticking out where folks are supposed to walk?"

"Get your paws off my truck!"

Ruby backed away with her hands up. "Okay, man! Geesh, don't have a duck. Didn't hurt your Precious."

He jumped up and examined the truck, searching for a scratch. He licked his fingers, then dabbed her handprint, buffing it out with the bottom of his T-shirt.

Eduardo had bought the truck about a year ago—a shiny black Chevy Silverado 4x4, with big mud tires. He'd installed the obligatory glasspacks, CB radio, and gun rack. There was a plastic crucifix hanging from the rearview because, as Eduardo put it, he liked to ride with Jesus.

"See," she said. "Precious is fine. No harm done."

He stepped forward, leaning in on her. Eduardo was tall, hefty through the chest and trunk, with shoulder-length black hair combed back from his forehead. He had a full beard with just a speck of gray in it. His size was intimidating enough, but it was his dark, intense eyes that Ruby found the most unsettling, the way they bore into you. "You missed church again."

She shrugged. "Had to help out Mr. Rosenfeld."

"Don't look so good, you skipping out. Attending Sunday classes is part of your probation."

It wasn't, not exactly anyway. She'd agreed to it as part of her staying with her mom. But it was more Eduardo's idea than her mom's, certainly nothing to do with her probation.

"Church is important, Ruby."

Ruby struggled not to roll her eyes; she didn't want this to turn into one of his sermons. "Yeah, I know. Can't ever have too much Jesus. Right?"

"Don't do that, don't try and make me out to be some kinda Jesus nut. You need compassion and support, folks to keep you on the straight and narrow, and there's no finer folks than those down at First Baptist." He seemed to think on that a moment before adding, "And Ruby, having Jesus in your heart sure don't hurt. This is coming from personal experience, as you know."

Oh, she knew alright, and was hoping to Jesus right now that she wouldn't have to hear, one more time, how the Good Lord had turned his life around. Eduardo had a long history with the drink, culminating in a felony DUI that resulted in a Daleville mother being crippled for life. But Eduardo didn't have to live with that guilt, because Eduardo had been reborn, so Jesus had all his guilt now. Ruby thought how nice, how truly wonderful it must be to not have to hold yourself accountable for being a total shit.

But Ruby didn't want to think about any of that right now. She wanted to get to her room and lie down; her head felt weird. So, she just nodded agreeably and started away. She made it half a step, then stumbled, would've fallen, but Eduardo caught her arm, steadying her.

He looked hard into her eyes. "Are you stoned?"

"What? *No!*"

He sniffed her then, actually sniffed her.

Ruby jerked her arm away. "What the hell, Eduardo? God, what's wrong with you?"

"Is that marijuana I smell?"

"No! Fuck, you really think I'm stupid enough to smoke dope when I got a pee test in a couple of days? It's just from some old moldy stuff I was helping Mr. Rosenfeld with." She could see he didn't believe her.

"I'm serious, Ruby. I promised that judge I'd keep an eye on you. Told him I'd see to it you stayed away from dope." He seemed to be waiting for something from her, a thank-you maybe, she didn't know. "And another thing, I'm not about to be letting you bring drugs into this house. Not with Hugo living there. We clear on that?"

Ruby fought back a snort. Hugo was his thirteen-year-old son; the son he'd had out of wedlock with some woman he'd met in a bar. Ruby knew for a fact that Hugo smoked pot with his pals whenever they could score a bag.

"Okay, Eduardo. This has been swell, but I'm going in now." She headed away.

"Your mother's sleeping," he called after her. "She's working the late shift again tonight. So, keep it down."

Ruby slipped into the house, careful not to let the screen door slam behind her, and headed downstairs. The basement was half-finished, one side a workshop full of her dad's old tools, the other her bedroom with a small bathroom attached. Ruby had moved down here after her dad had died. Forever it had been her refuge, but that ended about a year ago, when Eduardo and his son moved in upstairs; it felt more like a prison now.

Ruby entered her room, steadying herself against her dresser, her head swimming. She thought she heard that strange singing again, beautiful and mournful. She shivered, tried to shake it off. She wanted a shower, wanted to wash that weird smell off her, wanted to wash away the whole experience. She tugged her shirt over her head, unbuttoned her jeans, slid them down to her knees, when all of a sudden there came a flash of bright light.

"What?" she cried, startled, then heard a loud snort.

Hugo was standing just outside her door, his Polaroid in hand, a sleazy smile on his face. He was like a little pudgy version of his dad, same shoulder-length black hair, no beard of course, but those same dark intense eyes. He tugged the photo out of the camera and waved it at her. "Gotcha!"

"Motherfucker!" She jumped for him, forgetting her pants were around her ankles, and went sprawling as he dashed away up the stairs, laughing.

Ruby didn't even bother to find her shirt, just pulled up her jeans and took off after him in her bra.

He made it to his room and slammed the door. She tried to open it, but it was locked. "Give me that photo, Hugo! Now, goddamn it!"

"What photo?" he said.

"Hugo, open the door. Open the fucking door, you little shit! If you don't open this fucking door right now, I'm gonna bash your fucking head in!"

"What's going on?" came a booming voice.

Ruby jumped, found Eduardo at the top of the hall, glaring at her.

The door popped open and Hugo dashed out, ducking past Ruby. He leaped over to his father, hugging him around the waist. "Dad! Dad!" he screamed. "Keep her away from me!"

The door at the end of the hall opened. "What is all the commotion?" It was her mom, Martha, in her pj's, squinting against the light. "Somebody better be dying, or there's gonna be hell to pay."

"She attacked me!" Hugo cried, pointing at Ruby. "Went downstairs to fetch a screwdriver and her door was open. Didn't mean to look in. Swear! She saw me and just started screeching. Chased me up the stairs. Her eyes were all crazy." He burst into tears. "I thought she was gonna hurt me, Dad. Really hurt me."

"You fucking liar!" Ruby shouted. "The little perv took a photo of me!"

"Nuh-uh! Did not! She's the one who's lying."

"Where's that goddamn photo?" Ruby shouted, taking a step toward him. Hugo whimpered and ducked behind his dad.

"You better settle yourself down," Eduardo said, stepping forward.

"Where is it, you little motherfucker?" Ruby screamed.

"Okay, okay, Ruby," Martha said. "Enough with the language." She looked at Ruby. "Where's your shirt?"

Ruby couldn't give a shit at this point.

"Maybe if she'd keep her door shut," Eduardo said. "This sort of thing wouldn't happen."

"Ruby, why don't you just keep your door shut."

Ruby's jaw dropped. "Are you kidding me, Mom?"

"Have you taken your pill today?"

Ruby recoiled as though slapped. "Mom . . . he took a picture of me getting undressed." Ruby waited. "Are you really not gonna back me up on this?"

Her mom dropped her eyes, rubbed her forehead. "I just can't deal with any of you right now. Need my sleep or I'm gonna be useless tonight. Ruby, please, just keep your door shut. Can you do that for me?"

Ruby felt the sting of tears. "Mom!"

Martha went back in her room and shut the door, leaving Ruby trembling in the hall.

"You listen to me," Eduardo said in a low, harsh tone. "I know you got emotional problems, but coming after my boy, that's a line you don't wanna cross. Your probation is coming up this week, but that don't get you off the hook. You touch Hugo, even look at him wrong, and I'll call it in. Third strike and you're out. You get my meaning? And in case you forgot, I'm in good with the boys down at the station. One phone call from me and you'll be right back up on charges."

Ruby knew this very well, because Eduardo brought it up every chance he got. Eduardo's father just retired off the police force, and now his brother Carlos was a deputy. Eduardo would be there working right alongside him if not for his felony.

"You hear me?" Eduardo said.

Hugo was standing behind his dad and gave Ruby a nasty smile, then flicked his tongue, lewdly licking the air.

Ruby felt the rage closing in on her, blurring the edges of her vision, knew it for what it was. *Let it go, Ruby. Let it go. He's not worth it.*

She began to shake, caught the small smirk in the corner of Eduardo's mouth, could see that he was just hoping she'd lose it, would give him some excuse to call her in, to have her shipped off to the ward.

She clenched her hands into balls of rage, glared at Hugo.

No, Ruby thought. *Don't do it. Do not let them win.* Slowly, she unfurled her fist and gave both of them the finger. "Fuck off!" she spat, pushing past and stomping back down the stairs.

Ruby entered her room and made damn well sure the door was shut: she slammed it, locked it, and then kicked it for good measure.

She grabbed her headphones and shoved them down over her head. There were at least a hundred albums and cassettes on her shelves. She grabbed the first Joy Division tape she could find and jammed it in the player—Joy Division being her go-to whenever she wanted to wallow in self-pity, and boy did she want to right now.

Ruby closed her eyes, moping along with Ian Curtis, finding a bit of solace commiserating the woes of being alive, then, somewhere in the background of the tune, she heard it, the chorus, not the one from the tune, but the one from the ring. A deep, almost rapturous chill crawled down her spine. She opened her eyes, blinking, goose bumps on her skin. She looked around like the eye might be in the room with her, lifted up the earphones, listening, but it was just her and the hiss of the tape.

"Geesh," she said, and snatched up her sketchbook, wanting, needing something to focus on. She flipped past a few of her older drawings, mostly characters from books she'd loved. She found a blank page and began to sketch, randomly doodling, but now it was Mr. Rosenfeld she couldn't get out of her mind. What had happened with that ring? And that book he was holding? Was he chanting a spell? More of his wacky Devil stuff? The harder she tried to remember, the more blurry her mind became. She rubbed her temple, trying to stay present. *He's just going senile, that's all. People get weird when their minds start to go.*

Again, she saw the sad look he'd given her when she was leaving. *I'll help you, Josh. We'll get your stuff to Atlanta. Promise. Just . . . just as soon as my head feels better.*

Joy Division came to an end. Ruby swapped out the tape and the rumble of mufflers filled Ruby's headphones as the Cramps came growling up, Poison Ivy's grinding guitar leading the pack.

Ruby had a glossy photo of Poison Ivy pinned to her wall. Ivy with her lip twisted into a snarl, like she didn't give two shits. Ruby found her own lips snarling as she looked at it, wishing she had one ounce of what Ivy had.

Ruby set down her sketchbook and picked up her bass, a beat-up Vox Hawk with built-in fuzz that she'd scored from a thrift shop down on Rucker Boulevard. It looked like someone had used it to shovel gravel, but it played great. Ruby felt she did okay on guitar, but bass was where she shined. She positioned her fingers on the strings and started plucking along. She'd played this song a thousand times and it only took her a second to catch up, to find the groove, loving the feeling of the strings biting into her fingertips; it was one of the times she was grateful for having long boney fingers. She closed her eyes and lost herself in the fantasy of being onstage with her favorite band.

The song ended, Ruby hit rewind, was about to play it again, when her drawing caught her attention. She stared at the sketchbook, at her scribbles and doodles.

She cocked her head and blinked—there was something there, in the lines. She set down her bass and took a closer look. The web of scribbles blurred briefly then came together.

She gasped.

The eye, pulsing like it was alive, stared back at her and the song, the one from the ring, came sneaking up on her, drifting softly around her like a lullaby. Her eyelids grew heavy as a wave of fatigue washed over her.

The sketchpad slipped from her hand.

Ruby lay down and a blissful smile spread across her face as she drifted away.

It's me, Richard.

I sucked it in, this feeling, that overwhelming rush of elation. By the time fifty-two rolls around, you've learned to recognize the golden moments. To be present. To . . . ah, what's the word? Savor. Yeah, that's it. To *savor* them.

"That went well," I said, glancing at the horrified face in my rearview mirror. "Don't you think?"

The face belonged to Alice Brooks, the young woman from the library, my daughter for the night. I didn't expect her to reply, she couldn't, her mouth was taped. Plus, she seemed a bit groggy. I'd put her in a sleeper hold, a trick I learned in high school wrestling class, simply cutting off the blood supply to the brain for about thirty seconds. They're only out for about a minute, but that was usually all I needed to get them in the van.

"I mean, luck was with me," I continued. "But it usually is."

I had followed her home to her first-floor apartment near campus, parked my van right out front, then waited for dark. There were plenty of bushes, so I snuck up and watched her watch TV for a while, making sure she was alone and such. When she got up and went into the bathroom, I came in through the front door. Just let myself in. It wasn't even locked. When she came back out, I grabbed her. Winner, winner, turkey dinner.

"You'd really think karma, or God, or whatever you believe in would want to trip me up. Right? But I swear, it's like God is on my side. Or maybe the Devil? You think the Devil gives enough of a toot to help out? Makes you wonder though . . . doesn't it?"

She stared at me, her eyes wide and full of tears. You could see nothing was making sense to her. I felt for her—why just a half hour ago she'd been sitting on her sofa watching *Cheers,* and now, here she was, tied up in the back seat of my van, heading to God only knew where.

"Not too much further, Alice," I said.

She flinched when I spoke her name.

"I've sure missed you. You know that? Really looking forward to catching up on old times."

She blinked as though not hearing me right.

"I've been a bit neglectful . . . as a father. I feel bad about it. I do. But I intend to make it up to you tonight."

Her brow tightened and she shook her head. She seemed to really want to say something.

"No, don't want to hear none of that. You might not be blood, but that doesn't mean you're not my daughter. No ma'am. Because despite all that, I still have the same feelings for you as one born of my own seed. Indeed. You're special to me and I want to make sure you know it."

I found the turnoff—an old dirt road I used to go fishing down. Nothing out there but swamp and more swamp. I pulled off the highway and headed into the woods, my headlights lighting up the marsh grass as we bounced along the rutted road. I took it slow, on account of the bumps, but even so a deep rut knocked my bag of tools over with a loud clank; a hammer, a saw, a hand drill, a pair of scissors, and a few other items spilled out onto the floorboard.

"Careful, there," I said as fatherly as I could. "Watch out. Those tools are plenty sharp."

She gave the tools a terrified look, as though just now seeing them, really seeing them.

"And in case you're wondering, Alice, dear. No, your old man hasn't taken up carpentry. They're for my new hobby. Something I've been looking forward to sharing with you."

I could hear her screaming then, even through the duct tape, her face turning bright red.

I couldn't find the spot I was thinking of, but found another that seemed about as good. Not much more than a trail really, but it led me right up to the marsh. I cut the lights and turned off the engine.

I glanced back to find Alice slumped over. Figured she must've hyperventilated and passed out. That was okay, I didn't mind waiting for her to come around. I was in no hurry.

I rolled down the window; listened to the bugs and the bullfrogs. From somewhere close came the bellow of a bull gator. There were lots of gators out here. Which was good, as gators were experts at getting rid of bodies.

A small whimper came from the back seat. I closed my eyes and sucked it in, that good feeling. Like I said, folks my age, they learn to savor the golden moments. And what I was about to do was going to be very bad . . . but so good.

The song carried Ruby over snowcapped mountains, down into a valley of lush grass, through towering trees and into a wide, open glade. All was golden and bright, a world that smelled of honey and nectar. It was heaven on earth, it was joy and true belonging, it was everything her soul ever wanted or needed. And there, at the heart of the glade, floated a simple gold ring, and upon the ring, an eye.

The song emanated from the ring, calling to her, sweetly singing her name. *Ruby.*

"Yes," she replied, stepping forward.

Ruby.

She reached out with open arms, wanting only to be one with it.

Ruby.

She embraced it, closing her eyes as the song washed over her, into her, filling her with endless bliss.

Only, it didn't.

Something was wrong.

She opened her eyes.

Where was she?

She blinked.

There was no ring.

No song.

She blinked again.

She was in her room, on her bed.

She sat up, the song still echoing in her ears, looked around her room, searching for the ring, hoping, needing, to find it.

She found no ring.

It was dark outside. She glanced at the clock—eleven p.m. She wondered why she was still in her clothes and shoes, why she'd left the lamp on. She spotted the scribbly sketch, saw the eye within, could never unsee it. Her head began to swim, the song whispering her name from somewhere far away—calling her.

"Alright," she said, unsure if she was awake or still in the dream. "I'm coming." She got up, opened her door, and headed over to the sliding glass door. It was a walk-out basement and she did just that, walking out into the night and strolling up the street.

The night was alive with insects, their song mixing with that of the ring. She considered taking the shortcut through the woods, decided it wouldn't be a good idea, because the ghosts were there, and she knew with certainty that they could also hear the song, that all the dead things could. She knew this because the song told her so.

"One more look. That's all. Nothing more," she promised herself, knowing the ring would never let her sleep otherwise.

Toads hopped out of her way as she passed beneath the streetlights. Arriving at Pam's house, she hesitated a moment, knowing this wasn't right, wasn't okay, then headed to the trailer anyway.

She mounted the small porch and peeked in. The only light was from the TV. She could see Mr. Rosenfeld asleep, curled up beneath a blanket on the couch.

She should knock, should ask Josh if it was okay to come in, okay to see the ring again. Instead, she pulled the key from her pocket and let herself in. But it was alright, because this was all a dream and you could do whatever you wanted in a dream.

John Wayne was on the TV set; the sounds of a rowdy barfight covering Ruby as she crept over toward the end table.

Just a quick look and I'm out of here, she promised herself. *No one will ever be the wiser.*

She opened the drawer—the box, it wasn't in there. She looked around at all the boxes, knew it could be anywhere. She felt a surge of panic, then heard the ring calling sweetly to her.

Ruby cocked her head this way, then that—the song, it was coming from the far end of the couch. She walked over and knelt down, lifting the skirt of the couch, and yes, of course, there it was.

She slid out the cigar box, just holding it for a moment, savoring its promise.

She opened it and the singing grew louder; she was sure it would wake the old man, but he didn't stir.

She unfolded the velvet, revealing the bronze case. She picked it up, expecting its welcoming warmth, but it was cold to the touch. She started to open it then heard a voice, a familiar voice. *No!* it called, but it was hard to hear over the song. Again, *NO!* That was *her* voice, she was sure, but so far away. It was begging her to put the case down, leave it be, to *run!*

It's okay, Ruby reminded herself. *It's just a dream, nothing can hurt you in a dream.*

She opened it and there, the simple gold ring wrapped around the mummified finger. Only now, there was a coating on the ring—a red substance as though doused in candle wax.

Ruby frowned. She wanted, needed, to see the ring, see the promise of its ancient gold, the magical, mysterious eye. Slowly she raised a finger to it.

Again, her voice screaming from deep within. *Get out! Run!*

Ruby poked the ring.

Nothing happened, no magical eye to greet her this time. *What's wrong?* she wondered, horrified at the thought that maybe Mr. Rosenfeld had killed it somehow. A flush of anger toward the old man washed through her.

She rubbed at the wax, but it resisted. She began scraping at it with her fingernail, cautiously at first, then vigorously. She was rewarded by a glint of gold. She continued scraping, revealing more and more of the ring. The song grew louder, clearer than ever before, and the ring grew warm to her touch, then hot.

Stop! her voice screamed at her.

Ruby only smiled, because the song was beautiful—honey and nectar, heaven on earth—and why should she be afraid of heaven on earth?

She scraped off the last chunk of wax, revealing the face of the ring, the eye.

This is such a lovely dream, she thought.

The ring changed, the band turning into spidery appendages, the etched eye protruding, coming to life. The eye slowly opened, fixed on her, its black pupil dilating to a thin slit. Ruby's own voice disappeared; there was only the song and its blissful promise.

The spidery legs unfolded, letting go of the dead finger and crawling slowly, gently, up onto her trembling hand, then over to her middle finger. It seated itself and clamped down. The eye fell shut, the song faded, the eye slowly turned back into a ring.

John Wayne's voice shouting, "Stampede!" came to Ruby, loud and clear.

She blinked, closed her eyes for a long moment, reopened them.

The ring was still there, but where was the honey and nectar, the endless bliss? She only smelled musty boxes and spices mixed with dirty socks and tuna casserole.

"Oh, shit," she whispered, looking around the trailer, everything now in sharp focus. "This isn't a dream."

Mr. Rosenfeld mumbled something and tugged at his blanket.

Ruby looked at the ring, horrified, grabbing it and giving it a tug.

It didn't budge.

She let out a whimper and tugged harder, twisting. Still, it wouldn't come off, and the harder she pulled the harder it clamped down, biting into her skin. "Ouch!"

"Hm?" Mr. Rosenfeld mumbled.

Ruby knew if Josh saw her now, it would look like she was stealing from him. She couldn't bear the thought of that. She tossed the case into the cigar box and shoved it back under the couch.

"Who's there?" Mr. Rosenfeld asked.

Ruby got to her feet, slipped away and out the door as quietly as she could, closing it gently behind her. She glanced back through the window. Mr. Rosenfeld had rolled over and appeared to be sleeping again.

Ruby headed for the street, tugging and twisting at the ring as she stumbled along. The night seemed alive, not just the bugs and toads, but . . . but what? Whispers, she heard whispers coming from all around her.

Ruby took off in a run.

LORD SHEELBETH

The eye on the ring, the one on Ruby's hand, slowly opened. Lord Sheelbeth blinked and the eye on the ring blinked as well. All was blurry; she blinked again and the room came into focus. The lord found she was seeing both Ruby's room and her own hellish refuge, so she closed the eye in her head, as to better concentrate on the woman.

Ruby lay on her bed, appeared to be asleep, but barely, mumbling and tossing fitfully. Lord Sheelbeth waited for her breathing to slow as it was always easier to take them in deep slumber, when their minds were most vulnerable.

The crimson-colored eye on the ring flittered this way and that as the lord took in the many posters, records, the bass guitar, the stuffed animals, finally halting on the lava lamp, hating how its red glow mimicked her own fiery prison.

Ruby's headphones hung about her wrist, and the lord could hear music drifting from the small speakers. She found the sound annoying, like a bug needing

76

to be squashed. Still, she couldn't help but marvel at the wonders of this era. She'd seen much of it while that man, Adam, wore the ring, enough to realize that there was a new kind of magic in this age—a magic that even the most common fool could conjure with the flip of a switch, that mankind had learned to harvest lightning, could show you the world through a glass box, could propel metal carriages along the roads without horses. When she'd last walked the earth, men were still fighting with swords and spears. Yet still, in spite of all their progress, they seem to have little awareness of the deeper magics around them, had forgotten much since her age, and it was this loss of knowledge that Lord Sheelbeth was counting on.

They will have no idea what I am, she told herself. *It will be easy to hide amongst them, to feed unnoticed.* "Easy," she whispered, but even as she said it, she shook her head. "No . . . nothing has ever been easy . . . not for *me.*" She let her thoughts drift, marveling that she even survived her own mother. Her mother had been a lilith and her father an angel in high standing with God, but a fool, seduced by carnal charms, a fool who risked everything to be with the lilith. God had struck them both down before her eyes.

"Hope that bitch was worth it, Father." She grimaced. *At least I was spared from the lilith. An orphan, yes, but my mother would have eaten my soul.*

I survived it all. Survived because I am a fighter, because I am clever. Because I am generous and kind to those who serve me, but mostly I survived because I can be savage, ever so savage, when I need be. She knew it was more than that. That the world had been a wilder place when she was young, that there'd been gods, spirits, monsters, and demons of all sorts roaming the good earth, more than God and his bloodthirsty angels could tend to. That the humans, God's special children, made for especially delectable treats. That it was an easy time for a daughter of a lilith to grow fat.

She fed and her power grew and soon she lorded over her own small kingdom, Lord Sheelbeth of Khushet, an isolated region in the Caucasus Mountains. Some called her a god, others a demon, it mattered not to her so long as she had worshippers—men and women willing to sacrifice their blood, even the blood of their children, to her. And they did, they kept her well satiated, because under her rule, her protection, the land and the people prospered. Soon there were no more giants, dragons, or other monsters to plague them, and neighboring kingdoms, clans and tribes, bandits and marauders, dared not trespass or bring harm to any of her people, all knowing too well the price of her wrath. And though her reputation as a slayer was well earned, she thought of herself as a healer, for she gave back to the devoted, using her potency, her knowledge of the magic arts, to heal them of disease and illness, to heal her warriors of their wounds.

At least until the Baalei Shem came. She sneered, exposing her small pointy teeth. "No, I will not play that out again, I have tortured myself enough." Yet even as she said this, she saw them, those men in their ridiculous pointy hats, bowing before her, paying homage with gifts of wine and honey. *They defeated me . . . not through my vanity, nor my greed, but by playing to my kindness, my charity. It was my benevolence that failed me.* Both the eye in her head and the eye on the ring flared.

They'd come begging her to drive away a sour spirit that was plaguing their caravan. But all was a guise, a trap, these were crusaders of God and had angels waiting to ambush her. She studied the stump of her missing finger. *And when all was done, I had lost my ring, my finger, my eye, and . . . my freedom.* She looked around at the sooty, molten walls. *Left to rot here amongst the devils and demons and lost gods. I was a fool . . . but never again, never again shall I expose my belly to their knives.*

She rubbed the stump of her finger, forced herself to smile. *Enough wallowing in past mistakes and betrayals. What is done . . . is done. I will be free of this hell soon, free of this sordid land of feuding demons, all crawling about on their stomachs to appease Lucifer. This time I will be a creature of shadows. I will feed on God's children unnoticed, growing ever stronger, biding my time until the day when these people have given up on God, and God has given up on them. Then, then I shall arise and satiate myself on their rotting souls.*

Ruby's breath grew shallow and Lord Sheelbeth returned her attention to her pit, to Beel. He sat upon a stone, staring at the dirt. She took a moment to study him. On earth, Beel would've been a spirit, a shadowy thing of small substance, but he, like most spirits and souls, became physical here in the underworld, taking on his true shape. What she was seeing now was how God had left him, a gray spindly form with no distinguishing features—a sculpture in mid process. His eyes were pale slits sheltered within deep sockets. He had a lipless mouth, small round holes for ears, ten fingers and ten toes, but no hair, no sign of genitalia. Yet, his voice and mannerism were undeniably masculine. It was apparent that God intended him to be some kind of humanlike creature, beyond that it was hard to say.

What was God's purpose with you? She wondered for the thousandth time. *A replacement for his beloved mankind? Could it be that God was dissatisfied with his human children even then?*

The shedim had never been plentiful, yet when the earth was very young, they could be found. But between the angels, the demons, the Baalei Shem, and other magic folk hunting them down, Lord Sheelbeth wondered if there were any others left. She was sure if she'd not hidden Beel, that Beel too would've been destroyed.

How does it feel, Beel? she wondered, *to have your God throw you away because he believes you not worth finishing? That even the lowly grub is more worthy in his eyes than you?*

Lord Sheelbeth floated over to Beel; the sheid cringed.

"Your fear is misplaced. I am your savior. You know this. Was it not I who saved you from the demons?"

She waited; nothing from him.

"But more, our destinies are linked. What is good for you is good for me. You know this to be true."

Beel turned from her.

"Why hold a grudge like some petulant child? We have been round this . . . the fire . . . it was necessary. It has purified your soul, cleansed you of your weakness. Given you the strength to overcome your confusion, your madness. This time, there will be no dalliances, you will have the promise of flame to keep you on course."

Still Beel wouldn't look at her.

"Do you not wish to be free? You cannot be free without me, no more than I can without you."

And this was a painful truth for Lord Sheelbeth. She could hypnotize the girl, compel her to do a few small acts, such as touching the ring, but Sheel-beth lacked the power to make a soul do something against their will, especially something like murder. For that, she needed to be in full possession, and to be in full possession, she needed the sheid.

"Beel . . . enough of this. We must work together if we are to escape. Now, come with me."

Lord Sheelbeth headed away, stopping in an archway, waiting for the sheid. For a moment she wondered if she would need to bring back the fire. She hated the thought, hated having to torture this poor soul any further. But this was no time to be soft. This could be their very last chance. If the sheid was incapable of doing what had to be done, then she must be strong for the both of them. *He will be grateful one day.*

To her relief, Beel finally stood and followed her into the adjoining chamber.

Lord Sheelbeth strolled in, pushing through a pack of squirmy beasts, crea-tures with rotting, long segmented bodies, and the cadaverous heads of monkeys and jackals. They hissed and slithered from her path as she mounted a large stone platform and took her seat upon a throne of rough-cut boulders, a sad imitation of her great throne in Khushet—that one had been made of gold and decorated with the skulls of her enemies.

"Drummers," Lord Sheelbeth called. "Here, to me."

Six hunched creatures scuttled out from the shadows. These were common demons, each about the size of a chimp, all looking as though Satan was mak-ing a mockery of God's creations, a mishmash of earthly beasts put together in every hideous way possible. Some with fish heads on chicken bodies, others with goat heads on toad bodies, a couple with sad faces staring out from bellies and crotches, eyes on elbows and knees, cow tails and fish fins, horns and hair, scales and gooseflesh. They were escaped slaves—Lucifer's dregs. Lord Sheelbeth had lured them into her lair, trapped them, and forced them to do her bidding. She found them to be simple, mean beasts who understood little other than brutality and pain, easy to control with her spells and fire snakes.

"To your drums," she commanded, and all but one of the demons took up places behind a circle of charred drums. The last one, a lanky, lizard-legged creature with curling horns and a head full of fiery hair, held back, its tiny yellow eyes plaintive.

"Vutto," Lord Sheelbeth snapped. "To your drum."

"I am hungry," he whimpered. "Starving."

"You will eat after you play."

"Might play better if I eat before."

The other demons stared at him, horrified, their eyes begging him to be silent.

Lord Sheelbeth set her hands on her hips. "Vutto, did you know my pets are also hungry?"

Vutto cut his eyes, both the ones on his face and the ones on his chest, over toward the flaming serpents. He let out a huff and skulked up to his drum.

Lord Sheelbeth returned her attention to the sheid. "Beel, here, before me." She gestured to a large cut stone at her feet.

The sheid shuffled over and sat.

Lord Sheelbeth nodded to the drummers and they began to pound out a slow, rhythmic beat. The lord leaned back, letting go, letting the rhythm soothe her. Slowly the beat built, the vibrations finding the worms, calling to them all, even the ones deep in slumber.

She felt them stirring, some in her flesh, others deep within her body, felt them writhing, crawling toward the sound. She pulled aside her gown, exposing the great wound in her abdomen, and was greeted by a squirming mass of red worms.

"Hello, children," she said.

They responded to her voice, pushing their heads up to her, and upon each worm, a face, a tiny human face—that of men, women, and even children—crying out to be graced with her gaze.

Lord Sheelbeth began to chant along with the drums, then to sing, an angel's voice, so like her father's.

Her parents had left her many gifts. From her mother, the lilith, came dark magic and the art of drinking souls from the living. From her father, the angel, came pure magic. She wove their gifts into songs, songs into magic, magic into spells, because a spell was just words without magic.

The worms began to sing along with Lord Sheelbeth and she felt a tingling in her hands. Their voices rose, coming together, turning into a chorus. The tingling became a tremor that coursed through her arms, into her chest; her heart thrummed.

Their voices joined and their song grew, coming alive with fervor and vigor, with passion, and this passion, this heightened state, was key to bringing spells to fruition. Any kind of passion could work, it could be hate, or rage, or fear, but none was more powerful than love—a song sung from the heart would trump all others. So, she sung to them of love.

And the worms, they sang of their love for her.

Most of these souls had given themselves willingly, worshippers from a bygone era who had sacrificed themselves to her, their god, some begging for the honor, the chance to spend eternity serving her. And even those who were stolen, sucked from their bodies as she drained them of their life, even those sang to her, hoping to appease her, hoping to earn her grace. As she was now their only truth, their forever, their god, their heaven and their hell.

The song continued to build within her, to pulse and throb until it took all her effort to contain it. "Now, Beel!" she called as the song echoed off the craggy, sooty walls. "Give me your hand."

He raised his hand and she snatched it.

Both her eyes, here and on the ring, were wide open, both glowing fiery red. The one on the ring lighting up Ruby's room.

"Take her!" the lord cried, releasing the spell into Beel. Beel let out his own cry and began to soften, his body melting into smoke, the spell and the smoke spinning together. The smoke swirled into the lord's eye. She could feel Beel's pain, hear him groaning, as he was funneled into the realm of the living, a final distant cry as he was pushed into the ring.

Lord Sheelbeth closed the eye in her head, concentrating all of herself to her other, the ring. The ring sprouted tiny fangs and sank them into Ruby's flesh.

Ruby let out a moan, but didn't wake.

It was all up to Beel now. Lord Sheelbeth couldn't force the sheid into the woman; the spell was to push him into the earth realm, into the ring, not the woman. Only Beel could possess her, it was his little trick—the gift of being an unfinished soul, the ability to share any body with another living soul, to take their form.

"Now, Beel," Lord Sheelbeth urged. "Hurry . . . before she wakes."

Beel didn't respond.

What is he doing? She wondered if he was lost again, his mind drifting like when he saw the bird? How she hated being so dependent on this unstable being.

A minute ticked by, another, and Lord Sheelbeth's frustration mounted. The girl could wake at any moment and her hold on the girl was tenuous at best, anything could disrupt it. And then the girl could go back to the old man, not as her slave, but to beg the old man for help. All could be lost.

"What are you doing?" she cried. Lord Sheelbeth couldn't read the sheid's thoughts, no more than he could read hers, not unless he spoke directly to her, but she could feel them, get an impression of his mood and emotions, and some- times his intentions. And she sensed it then, his bitterness, his spite.

"The fire, Beel," she growled, sending the thought, driving it home to be sure he didn't miss it. "Remember the *fire*."

She sensed his anger, then his fear. He moved then, finally doing his little trick, flowing into Ruby like smoke into lungs, crawling through her, nestling deep within.

"Yes . . . yes, Beel," she said, breathlessly. "You have done it!" She laughed. "She is ours."

The drums stopped and the worms ceased their singing, the echoes of their song dying out as the lord collapsed exhausted to the ground.

"Now, kill him," she cried. "Kill the old man . . . so we can both come home."

It's me, Richard.

I watched Alice, my daughter for that one night, sink beneath the dirty water, tried not to look at her face, too painful in the morning light.

The sun was breaking, setting the swamp fog aglow. I'd never been one for sunsets and sunrises, but goddang if it wasn't beautiful that morning. I stood there basking in the golden light, sucking in the warmth, feeling as though I was the one glowing. Everything always seemed magical after the deed, like my senses had been awakened, like I could feel again, truly feel. And heck, if that night hadn't been intense. I closed my eyes, reliving the whole thing, the horror, the revulsion, the tears. Lord, how I'd cried for her. I inhaled deeply, the sweet smell of pluff mud filling my head, the morning birdsongs touching my heart. "Alive . . . so alive."

If only that feeling would last.

But it never did.

The glow would stay with me for about a month, maybe two if I was lucky. Then that weight, that dreadful dead feeling, would start creeping back into my chest.

I found a large rock and slid it atop of her, to weigh her down, at least long enough for the gators and turtles to do their work. I wasn't too worried about it really, because like I said, I was lucky. I would've probably even said I had God on my side, if I believed in such gibberish. Too bad I didn't, as faith might've saved me, saved those women—either my love of God, or my fear of the old bastard. The hard part about being an atheist was knowing there was nothing after. This was it. If my life sucked here, there was nothing else to look forward to. Nothing. The good part was nothing I did mattered. I was a speck of crud in a universe that does not care. Killing one soul, or a thousand, even a million, didn't matter. Nothing mattered except how I felt. My reality was the only reality. So, I'm going to take a moment to thank the Good Lord Above that I was a devout atheist, otherwise I don't think I could've done any of it.

I spared a last look at Alice's ghostly form floating deep down in that murky water and shuddered. *Such a lonely place to end up,* I thought as I fought back fresh tears.

I sighed and headed to my van, climbed up behind the wheel and drove out. I bounced along until I came to a small wooden bridge, then rolled down the window and tossed my tools into the muddy creek below. I'd be buying more, eventually, I always did. It was part of the excitement, contemplating how I would use each item as I selected them.

I tugged out a well-worn road map, trying to decide where I wanted to go. I could go anywhere. Why not? I was retired—had retired early at fifty-one years old. And no, it wasn't because I'd made so much money as a photographer that it was coming out of my ears. The sad truth was, if it wasn't for my wife's teaching income, we would've been out on the street. The reason I was able to stop with the commercial photography, stop dealing with idiotic art directors, was on account of a bunch of money my wife inherited. How pathetic is that? Retiring on my wife's dime. How emasculating. That money came in and we called it quits; I almost felt like I was stealing from her. In a way I guess I was. But she didn't make much of a fuss. I think by then it was worth it to her to be rid of me, this weight around her neck. I would've certainly paid a fortune to get away from me.

Well, I didn't feel pathetic at that moment. I felt good . . . happy as a clam in butter sauce. But most importantly, I felt alive.

"Where to?" I asked the map. My eyes drifted to Atlanta. "Bingo."

Ruby's eyes flittered open. She was in her bed, it was dark and the house was quiet, the faint glow of her nightlight casting long murky shadows across her room.

A creak came from her closet. The door was half-open and she stared into its darkness. She heard it then, breathing—someone or something was breathing.

A shadow stepped out, walking into the dim glow. It was a man; she knew him.

"Josh!" she gasped.

A glowing red eye opened in the center of Mr. Rosenfeld's forehead. "You're mine," he whispered and smiled. His tongue slid out from between his teeth, the tip bulged and pulsed, then tore open as a black spider, covered in blood, clawed its way out.

The spider dropped to the floor and raced toward Ruby, leaping onto her bed and disappearing beneath the blanket.

Ruby tried to scream, but found no air in her lungs; tried to move, but couldn't. She quivered as the spider edged up the side of her body, its prickly legs scratching along her thigh. It reached her hand and there came a sudden jab on her finger.

Ruby kicked the blankets away, sat up, clawing at the spider, her heart drumming in her ears as she fumbled for the lamp. She realized it wasn't night at all, but morning, her room lit up in its soft glow.

She found no spider, no Mr. Rosenfeld with one glowing eye, just her messy room staring back at her.

A nightmare. That's all. That is all.

This was nothing new for her; she'd had a long history of nightmares, and in this case it came as a relief. Only, only, there was a problem. She looked at her right hand.

The ring, it was still there.

Shit, what did I do? It was her mother's voice she heard in reply. *You know what you did. You stopped taking your medication.*

Her hands began to tremble, not from the nightmare, no, it was the thought that maybe old Dr. Fatass Ferguson was right, that she truly was mentally ill, that she'd be condemned to take those shitty drugs her whole life. She'd tried to get off her meds a few years back and had experienced all kinds of weirdness—nightmares, confusion, temporary memory loss, hallucinations, and yes, sleepwalking. She looked at the ring again and knew this much was real—she *had* gone over to Mr. Rosenfeld's and stolen his ring.

She cautiously touched the ring. It didn't turn into a spider, no burning eye opened and glared at her.

"It's just a ring," she said and gave it a tug.

It didn't come off.

She tried again, harder, twisting it back and forth, trying to wrench it off. "Ouch!" she cried as it clamped tighter around her finger. "What the fuck?"

She hopped up, headed into the small bathroom next to her room and rubbed soap on her finger and the ring. Still, it wouldn't budge.

She heard Mr. Rosenfeld's words like an echo in her head, *You're mine.*

A chill rolled through her body. "No . . . nonsense." She looked closer at the ring, trying to figure out why it was stuck. She tugged it and could feel the band tighten when she did.

"Some kind of trick, that's all. Like maybe one of them Chinese finger traps." She nodded. "There's gotta be a way to get this thing off. I'm sure Josh knows." She sucked in a deep breath. "Fuck, just gonna have to fess up to him, that's all."

And suddenly a thought came to her as though whispered in her ear, that perhaps this whole thing had been some kind of setup. That Mr. Rosenfeld wasn't the bumbling old man he pretended to be, that he was . . . was *what*? Again, that strange sensation of someone whispering in her ear. *"A demon. He's a demon."*

Her alarm clock beeped, causing Ruby to jump. It was a quarter till ten in the morning. "Shit, gotta go!"

She looked at the ring again, decided whatever was going on, it'd have to wait, because this was her final day at the Y, the day Mrs. Wright was to give her her report.

She dashed back into her room, slipped on her jeans, sneakers, and cleanest dirty T-shirt. She looked around for her guitar, remembered she'd left it at Pam's, then remembered she wouldn't be needing it. No, because Mrs. Wright told her she was done teaching. Didn't she? Ruby felt an odd heat flare up in her chest, like something feeding on her bitterness.

She gave the ring one more desperate twist, let out a cry, then gave up.

Ruby made it to the stairs, then stopped, returning to snatch a bag off her dresser. It was full of fun, funky guitar picks, a goodbye gift for her students, a little something to remember her by.

She hopped on her ten-speed, tossing the bag in the basket, and raced over to the Y, shocked by how hot it was, even this early in the day. It was mostly down-hill and she made good time. She shoved her bike into the bike rack, not even bothering to lock it up, grabbed the bag of picks and darted inside.

She entered the lobby and ducked past the front desk, hoping to slip by Mrs. Wright's office unseen.

"Ruby," someone called. "Ruby. A word."

Ruby turned to find Mrs. Wright standing in the door of her office. "Would you please come in here?"

Ruby sighed and followed the woman in.

"Push the door closed, would you?"

Ruby did, closing her eyes for a moment, enjoying the relief of the AC on her sweaty skin.

"Little late this morning. Aren't you, shug?"

Ruby glanced at the clock, noting she was all of eight minutes late. "Yes, ma'am," Ruby said, still a touch out of breath. "Sorry, I was—"

Mrs. Wright held up a finger. "No need to make excuses."

Ruby felt a flair of anger, but nodded. "Yes, ma'am."

Mrs. Wright tapped the typewriter in front of her. "You know what this is?"

"My report?"

"It is."

Ruby waited for more, some indication, some hint of what was on it, or in it, but Mrs. Wright's face betrayed nothing.

"Well, are they gonna lock me up and throw away the key?" Ruby asked with a laugh, but the laugh came out forced, awkward, desperate. Again, Ruby waited for some sign from Mrs. Wright.

Mrs. Wright took her time replying. "We'll have to see," she said. "Going over my notes right now."

Ruby waited another long moment, not sure what she was supposed to do. She held her tongue until she could bear it no longer. "Okay . . . well . . . be back in a bit, then."

"Where're you going?"

"Oh, just gonna give them kids a quick goodbye."

Mrs. Wright's face soured, then softened. She let out a long sigh and leaned back in her chair. "Ruby . . . I'm sorry, really I am, but that's not such a good idea."

"Ma'am?"

"I feel it's better if you don't."

"But . . . *why?*"

"Well . . . we had some parents express concern. Y'know, about some of the songs you've been playing for those kids."

Ruby felt as though she'd been slapped.

"And frankly," Mrs. Wright continued, "I feel the same. I've made no secret of that. I'll just come right out and say it, since we're both thinking it . . . you really haven't been the best influence on them."

Ruby's hurt turned to anger. "But . . . have you heard them play? They've come *so* far. And I really feel they enjoyed learning from me. We had a lot of fun together."

"Kids don't always know what's best for themselves. Do they? So, no, I'm sorry. I promised their parents I'd make sure you didn't spend any more time with them."

Ruby felt a presence surfacing from below the anger, intertwining somehow, as though feeding on it. The anger swelled, almost overcoming her. She blinked and set her hand on the desk to steady herself.

"I can see your feelings are hurt," Mrs. Wright added. "I'm sorry, but y'know, I did try to warn you."

Ruby found no sympathy on Mrs. Wright's face, only smug satisfaction.

Ruby's eyes went to Mrs. Wright's stapler—a large and heavy relic, made out of iron and steel. An impulse to pick it up and staple Mrs. Wright's ugly, nasty, little mouth shut swam over Ruby.

Mrs. Wright gave Ruby a hard look. "Are you alright? You *have* been staying away from drugs? Right?"

Ruby's anger twisted into something approaching pure hate. "I'm fine," she snapped. "It's just that I bought them a little something." She held up the bag. "Some guitar picks. I don't see . . ." Ruby checked the tone of her voice, trying hard to temper her mounting rage. "May I . . . may I please just pop in for a sec and pass 'em out?"

Mrs. Wright shook her head. "We just can't have you stirring them up again.

Why I've got Mrs. Baker in there with them now, and she said that thanks to you, all they wanna play is them ugly songs."

Ruby blinked. *Really,* she thought, fighting not to grin, surprised at how such a little thing made her feel so good, like maybe she'd actually made a difference in those kids' lives.

"It's time to get their minds back on pretty things," Mrs. Wright said, her eyes drifting to her own painting, the watercolor of calico corn in a wicker basket hanging behind her. She stood up and straightened the big blue ribbon. "People look at my painting here every day, and you know what they tell me? They say it makes them feel good. And you know what? That makes me feel good. Ruby, you're a very talented lady, and I'm willing to bet if you set your sights on making something lovely like this, some sweet little songs, you'll warm a lot of hearts one day."

"How about after class, then?" Ruby asked.

"What?"

Ruby knew she should stop, should leave it alone, the woman was in the process of writing up her report after all, but this feeling, this *other,* it was as though it were pushing her. "Can I give them the picks after class?"

Mrs. Wright frowned.

"I'll just hand them out as they're leaving."

Mrs. Wright appeared about to say something sharp, then sighed. "Tell you what . . . you give them picks to me and I'll see to it that they get them after class. Let 'em know it was from you." She held her hand out for the bag. "How about that?"

How about I slap that smug look off your face? Ruby thought, as the presence within her surged forward, driving the hatred before it. Ruby found her eyes on a tennis racket leaning near the door. All she could think of was how fantastic it would feel to smash it into Mrs. Wright's face, over and over again. How the wire mesh would make hamburger meat out of the woman's cheeks.

No, Ruby! Stop! What's wrong with you? But she thought she knew, the doctor was right, that son of a bitch was right, she needed her stupid pills. Only . . . only what? Something was different. It felt like there was *more.* Yes, that was the

90

best way to put it, more of something within her. And this more was feeding on her rage, driving it, amplifying it. *Hold it together,* she told herself, yet her eyes lingered on the tennis racket.

Ruby took a step toward the racket, an actual step, when Mr. Miller came into the lobby carrying two buckets.

"Ah, Mr. Miller," Mrs. Wright said, standing up and walking out into the lobby. "Just the man we're looking for."

Ruby pulled her eyes from the racket and followed her out.

Mr. Miller was a thin man in paint-stained overalls. He looked to be pushing into his sixties, with skin tanned to leather by the hot Alabama sun. He set down the buckets, tugged off his faded Bama ball cap, and wiped the sweat from his brow.

"Miss Ruby, here," Mrs. Wright said. "She'll be helping you out today."

"Well, now . . . that's right nice of you, Mrs. Wright," he said in his slow drawl. "And you too, Ruby. But . . . I don't really need no help. Got it all under control."

"That may be," Mrs. Wright said. "But hard work is good for the soul, and we all know Ruby's soul could use all the help it can get." She winked at Ruby. "Isn't that so, shug?"

Mr. Miller gave Ruby an apologetic look, but nodded and they all stood there for a long, awkward moment. Finally, Mrs. Wright held out her hand to Ruby.

Ruby looked at it confused.

"Sooner you hand me them guitar picks, the sooner I can finish up your report."

Ruby's eyes cut back to the tennis racket, her hand twitching.

"Ruby? You sure you're alright?"

"Yeah . . . just fine," she said tersely and handed the bag over to Mrs. Wright.

"Come see me when y'all are done. I'll have your report waiting." She walked back into her air-conditioned office, closing the door behind her.

Mr. Miller shook his head and picked up the buckets. "Guess you might as well c'mon," he said and headed out the door.

Ruby followed the man around to the side of the Y, where the dumpsters were parked and several large potholes stuffed with fresh gravel awaited them.

"Whew . . . just stupid hot today," Mr. Miller said. "It's sure been a devil of a summer. Can't remember a hotter one. Good weather for swimming, but not for much else. Certainly not for laying no tar."

He handed Ruby some gloves. "You gonna need these." He tapped one of the buckets with Coal Tar Sealer written on the side. "Nasty stuff . . . sure don't wanna be getting none of it on your skin." He showed her his forearms; there were several awful-looking stains on them. "Ain't no washing it off, neither. Just have to live with till it wears off. Takes near on forever."

Ruby grimaced.

He handed her an old push broom, then popped the lid off one of the buckets. Ruby wrinkled her nose at the harsh smell.

"Now, you stay back, hear." He carefully poured the coal tar on top of the gravel.

"Now take that broom of yours and just push the tar back and forth until it seeps all down into that gravel. You got it?"

Ruby nodded and got to work while he poured the tar on the remaining potholes.

"Sure sorry about all this," Mr. Miller said. "I know you much rather be in there teaching those kids. Just so you know, weren't my idea."

"I know," she said.

"Mrs. Wright . . . she can be a real hard-ass sometimes. Ain't no denying that. But I do believe she means well for the most parts. It's just them other parts she needs to work on."

Ruby grunted, thinking it best not to say what she thought.

"But," Mr. Miller continued. "I do believe in your case it's a bit more than that. She's gone and let her jealously get the better of her, that's all."

"Jealousy?"

"Sure, she don't like the way them kids take to you. Not one bit. And not just them kids, mind you. Why, I was in there the other day and one of them mothers was asking after you."

"Yeah, heard someone was complaining about me."

"Complaining? No ma'am . . . that weren't it at all. This lady was asking about hiring you to give her kid some private lessons. She was going on and on about how much her boy had learned in your class."

"What?" Ruby could hardly believe what she was hearing. "Really?"

"Yup, should've seen the look on Mrs. Wright's face." Mr. Miller chuckled. "Like someone had peed in her tea."

"What did Mrs. Wright say?"

"Don't know if I should say."

"Aww, c'mon. Can't leave me hanging like that. *Tell* me!"

"Well . . . she told the woman it weren't a good idea. That you were working through a lot of personal issues, that you were unstable and really shouldn't be teaching kids unsupervised."

The other, the presence, the hate, it was back and it hit Ruby like a wave. *Bitch,* Ruby thought. *Fucking bitch!*

"I'm sorry, Ruby. That Mrs. Wright, she's a right sour old apple sometimes. But you just can't be letting folks like that get under your skin."

The song was back, only now it made no offer of blissful joy, but that of vengeance, a deep bass chant of doom.

Ruby began scrubbing the gravel harder and harder until she was jabbing into it like she was trying to kill it. The handle snapped, the broom flipping up, spattering a dash of the oil across her arm. "Fuck!" she cried, throwing the broken broom against the wall.

"Hey . . . hey, Ruby. It's okay. Now. It's okay." Mr. Miller looked her over. "I think you need to get out of the sun for a bit. Why don't you go on and have yourself a sit over under that tree. We got plenty more old brooms. I'll go fetch another."

Mr. Miller gave Ruby one more concerned look, then headed in. Ruby didn't go into the shade, she went looking for a spigot to clean her arm.

She yanked off the big gloves and glared at the ring, again, wondering just what Mr. Rosenfeld had done to her. "You're gonna fix this, Josh. One way or another." And she heard it then, a voice in her head, an *other,* there was no doubt.

Yes, the other whispered. ***We will have to take care of him. It is the only way.***

There'd been times in Ruby's life when she'd thought she'd heard voices, when she'd thought she'd seen things too, ghostly people out of the corner of her eye. But this was different somehow, clearer. She cocked her head, listening for more. "Fuck, what's this ring doing to me?"

She marched round to the side of the building, near the pool, found a spigot, turned it on, and began scrubbing at the tar. And, just like Mr. Miller had said, the stuff wouldn't come off. It hadn't just stained her flesh, it had seeped into her flesh and was now part of her skin, and on top of everything else, it was starting to sting a little. "Fuck!"

"Well, hey, Rube," someone called.

Ruby glanced toward the pool, and there, just on the other side of the fence, was Stacy and Billy smirking at her. They were sharing a beach towel on the grass. Stacy had on a neon-purple two-piece today, propped up on her elbows while Billy rubbed suntan lotion up and down her tummy—her tight, firm tummy.

"Heard you lost your meds," Stacy said.

Billy snorted.

Ruby didn't say a word, just glared at them as sweat trickled down her face. The ring began to grow hot on her finger.

"Heard you went cuckoo-crackers and tore up my tape," Stacy went on. "Wondering if I should tell Mama about that?"

Billy's hand slid down the front of her tummy, well below her belly button.

Stacy gave him a giggle, but it was Ruby she was looking at, gloating, like she'd beaten Ruby at some game.

Ruby bared her teeth and a savage, guttural sound escaped from deep in her throat, a sound that she didn't even recognize.

"Oh . . . my . . . *Lord,*" Stacy said, and her and Billy shared a look, *the* look, the she's-bat-shit-crazy look. Then, both of them burst out laughing, Stacy into a fit of high-pitch giggles and Billy hee-hawing.

The sound *ate* into Ruby's brain.

Stacy began twirling her forefinger around her ear, and the ring on Ruby's finger burned, her rage bloomed, then exploded.

Let us make them sorry, the voice whispered.

"Yes," Ruby replied, nodding her head in full agreement. "Let's."

The only way into the pool area was back through the main entrance of the building. Ruby headed around, stopping only long enough to slip her gloves back on and pick up one of the two-gallon buckets of coal tar—the full one.

She passed through the lobby and went right past Mrs. Wright's office. But this time, no one noticed this pale, skinny girl, wearing big gloves, lugging along a bucket of coal tar and wearing a look of hot murder on her face.

Ruby stalked down the long corridor to the women's locker room, kicking the door open, and stomping past a few moms and young girls, soliciting plenty of concerned glances as she headed out into the pool area.

Kids laughed, splashing and hollering, while moms lounged about, drinking Tab, reading Redbook, and topping off their end-of-summer tans. Ruby noticed none of this, her eyes locked on Billy and Stacy.

Ruby marched over to them. They were both lying on their backs now, sunglasses on, eyes closed, soaking in the sun.

"Y'all think I'm crazy?" Ruby asked.

Billy didn't even bother to sit up, just lowered his sunglasses and squinted at her. "What are you doing, Ruby? Not in the mood for any of your little fits today."

A fresh wave of rage rolled through Ruby and she clutched the bucket handle even tighter.

Do it, the voice whispered.

"Dang, Ruby," Billy put in. "You don't look so well. Maybe you should get out of the sun."

Stacy lifted her shades. "Holy shit, girl. You look awful." Stacy plucked up the can of cola sitting next to Billy and gave it a swig, leaving her bright pink lipstick on the lip.

"Y'all think I'm crazy?" Ruby asked again.

"Aww, Ruby, don't go making a big deal out of nothing." Billy took the cola from Stacy and drank. Billy now had Stacy's pink lipstick on his lips.

The fire in Ruby's chest flared.

"Hey Ruby, check this out," Billy flexed his pale gut. "An all new kinda six-pack for me. What'd you think?"

When Ruby only glared at him, Stacy put in, "I think you're looking yummy, shug."

"We've been having a sit-up contest," he laughed. "Gonna have abs every bit as nice as Stace soon. See if I don't." With that he slapped Stacy's stomach—her tight, firm stomach and gave her a smooch. Then both of them were giggling.

"I'm not crazy," Ruby said. "Y'all are just assholes." And with that, Ruby lifted the bucket to chest level and stepped forward.

"Ruby? Wh—" Billy started, but never finished, because that was the moment the oily tar hit his chest.

Ruby sloshed it around, dousing the both of them, the dark syrupy stuff splashing over their legs, arms, chests, and their abs, especially their abs, all over their goddamn abs.

Stacy screamed while Billy shrieked. Both raised their hands, trying to shield their faces, trying to keep the foul goo from spattering into their mouths and eyes. They rolled away, staggering to their feet, trying to escape. But before they could, Ruby managed to get one more good glob right atop of Stacy's head, drenching her all-so-lovely, bottle-blonde hair.

Someone's gonna have to get their head shaved, Ruby thought, and realized she was smiling, grinning really, a wide fierce sort of grin that felt good on her face. The song in her head rang out, a chorus of elation that sent shivers through her body.

Stacy and Billy stumbled toward the pool. Ruby remembered how bad the little spot on her arm had stung, imaged just how awful they must feel covered nearly head to toe, and her smile managed to grow wider.

All the little kiddies in the pool saw the two gooey, squalling monsters staggering toward them and began screaming as they panicked to escape. Mothers screamed as well, rushing for their children, many tumbling into the pool in the effort. The two lifeguards added their shrill whistles to the cacophony and all became chaos.

Stacy fell into the pool first, belly-flopping right on top of some poor little boy wearing floaters.

The stuff must've been in Billy's eyes, as he dashed headfirst into the lifeguard stand, ricocheting off like a pinball, clutching his forehead as he spun backward into the water.

"Well, bless your heart," Ruby said, and heard crazy, manic laughter, realized it was her—her and the chorus in her head.

Billy and Stacy floundered into the shallow end, hollering and wailing as they struggled to get out of the pool. They wiped frantically at the black goo, but the stuff was like glue, and all they did was smear it around.

It is time to go, the voice, the other, whispered. ***Time to find Mr. Rosenfeld.***

Ruby nodded, allowing herself one last delicious moment to watch Stacy crawl out of the pool. The girl was stained up one side and down the other, her hair a clotted lump, like something you'd dig out of a bathroom drainpipe.

Ruby, still clutching the bucket, left the pool, walking through the horrified moms, everyone scrambling out of her way. She passed through the locker room, then up the long hall into the lobby. She felt dazed, feverish, and somehow wonderful all at the same time. She glanced into Mrs. Wright's office, saw the top of the woman's head and blinked. She needed to get something from her. What was it? She blinked again and it came back—the report.

She looked at the bucket, and a small sad laugh escaped her lips. "I'm so screwed."

"Ruby," someone called.

It was Mrs. Wright, she was waving for Ruby to come in.

Ruby opened the door and entered. The AC felt spectacular, giving Ruby goose bumps. It was on high, the loud fan drowning out most of the yelling coming from down the hall.

"Would you close that, please," Mrs. Wright asked. "You'd think we were under attack by Martians, the way those kids carry on." She gave Ruby a concerned look. "Ruby, you okay?"

Ruby nodded. "Never better."

Mrs. Wright held up a sealed envelope. "Going to give you this now. But I don't want you to read it until you get home. I put a lot of thought into this letter and I want you to read it someplace where you can pay attention . . . can soak in every word." She held it out to Ruby.

Ruby took it, absently sliding it into her back pocket.

"Might not be the report you were hoping for. But it's the one you need. Some of it's gonna be hard to read, but remember . . . it's all coming from a place of care and concern. Concern for your well-being, concern for . . ."

Mrs. Wright droned on, but Ruby no longer heard her, she was staring at something familiar in Mrs. Wright's wastebasket. She blinked, realized it was the entire bag of guitar picks she'd brought for the kids.

In the trash, Ruby thought. *They're in the fucking trash.*

Ruby clinched the bucket handle. "You said the moms were complaining about me."

"What?"

"But they weren't . . . were they? They wanted me to give their kids lessons. Didn't they? Why did you lie to me, Mrs. Wright?"

Mrs. Wright reddened and Ruby saw the undeniable guilt in the flush of her cheeks.

"Why did you lie?"

"N . . . no . . . Ruby," she sputtered. "Where did you hear such a thing?"

"You told them I was bad. Told them to keep their kids away from me."

"Well . . . now . . . that's not exactly true. I—"

Ruby thrust her gloved hand into the bucket, swabbed out the last gooey clump of tar. She held the dripping glove out toward Mrs. Wright, made a fist, squeezing the goo, letting it drip all over the woman's desk and typewriter.

"Ruby!" Mrs. Wright cried, leaping up from her chair. "What are you doing?"

Ruby started around the desk, holding her dripping gloved hand out before her, backing Mrs. Wright into the corner.

"Ruby!" Mrs. Wright screamed. "Stop it!"

Ruby stopped, turned her head toward the painting on the wall, the one with the big blue ribbon. She glanced back at Mrs. Wright and gave her a grin.

"Ruby, don't you dare!"

"I'm a *bad* girl . . . remember?"

"Ruby, stop it! Stop it now! I *will* report you! You know I will!"

Ruby slapped the goo onto the painting, smearing all around.

"RUBY!" Mrs. Wright screamed.

The chorus sang their sweet song and Ruby hummed right along with them. She gave the painting one last good slap, then chucked the bucket aside and tugged off the huge gloves, tossing them onto the desk. She marched out of the office, leaving Mrs. Wright sobbing in the corner.

Ruby reached the bike rack and pulled out the letter. It didn't matter what it said, not now, not after what she'd just done, but she opened it anyway and began to read.

The bulk of it was Mrs. Wright's usual self-aggrandizing nonsense about how she had shepherded Ruby along, then even more nonsense about how much Ruby needs Jesus Christ in her life. It was the final bit, the note for the judge, that Ruby had to read twice.

> *Dear Judge Stevenson,*
>
> *During her time working for me at the YMCA, Ruby has shown herself to be an exemplary young woman in every way—hardworking, caring, and conscientious. I am impressed with how far she has come in such a short period of time. I feel that she has learned many lessons from her past mistakes and is already working hard toward a better life. I can, in full confidence, say that Ruby has a good heart and soul, and recommend that her probation be ended immediately.*
>
> *Mrs. Janice Wright, Manager, Enterprise, Alabama, YMCA*

Ruby continued to stare at the letter until her tears blurred out the letters.

It is all his doing, the voice whispered. **Mr. Rosenfeld, he has ruined everything.**

Ruby crumbled the letter and threw it at the building.

We need to find him. We need to fix things.

Ruby wiped away the tears, got on her bike, and started pedaling toward Mr. Rosenfeld's trailer.

GHOULS

Ruby pedaled into her neighborhood and stopped, taking a moment to catch her breath, she was dripping in sweat. The hard ride had cleared her head a touch—the chorus now a distant hum.

"What's the plan, Ruby Tucker?" she asked herself, staring at the ring.

You know what you must do, whispered that strange voice.

Ruby rubbed her forehead, clinched her eyes, and caught a flash of Mr. Rosenfeld lying on the ground, his neck slit open. "No!" Ruby cried. "Never. Can't do that!"

He has left you no choice.

"I love that man."

He is not a man. You know this.

She saw the Mr. Rosenfeld from her dream then, the one with the glowing red eye glaring out from his forehead. Only now, she was certain it hadn't been a dream at all. No, he *had* been there in her room.

He is a demon.

"No!"

Yes, the voice insisted, and it was almost as though she had said it.

He has tricked you. He wants your soul.

"Y . . . yes," she relented, and it felt good to let the truth in. "Yes. God, yes. I see it all now."

He has you. If you want to stop him, want to save your soul. You know what you must do.

She did, but still she shook her head.

You have to kill him, Ruby.

She struggled not to listen, but it was *so* hard. The voice, it sounded *so* sure, *so* earnest, but more it sounded like a friend, like a most beloved friend.

"I'll hurt him if I have to. Whatever it takes to make him take this ring off. But I'm not gonna kill him."

He is a tricky demon. He will have traps.

Ruby took in every word.

He wants to eat your soul.

Ruby shuddered, then heard a distant siren, blinked, remembered she didn't have long. "Not going back to the ward. No fucking way. Getting the hell out of here. Steal a car if I have to. Whatever it takes."

Whatever it takes, the voice echoed.

She steered the bike down the street, pedaling fast, heading for her house. She needed to pick up a few things, her cash, some extra clothes, and—

And a very sharp knife, she thought, unsure if it was her own thought or that of the voice, not sure it mattered any longer.

She cut into her driveway, grateful to see that Eduardo's truck wasn't there.

She dumped her bike on the front lawn and sprinted up the walk, stepping over a few gardening tools and a pile of freshly torn-up weeds. Just as she reached the front door, her mother came rushing out, almost hitting her with the screen.

"Oh, Ruby! Honey, sorry. Didn't even see you." Her mother skirted past, her car keys jangling in her hand. "Running late."

"Hey, mom. Hold up a sec."

Her mom stopped. "What is it, shug?"

"My money . . . y'know the money dad left me. I need it."

"Well, sure okay. Remind me when I get home."

"No, I need it now."

"Right now?"

"Yeah."

Her mom gave her a sharp look. "What's up? You in trouble?"

"No," Ruby lied. "Why do you always think I'm in trouble?" But she knew why—because she'd been in nothing *but* trouble ever since her father had died. There was more, and it had a lot to do with her father's mental issues, the huge mess that ended with his suicide. She felt her mother lumped her troubles in with her dad's, that it was easier that way, easier to blame some mysterious inherited mental problem than maybe taking a little accountability. But, as she often had to remind her mother, most of her father's difficulties had come from spending six-months in a POW camp in Vietnam, not something he was born with.

"You look pale," her mother said. "You sure you're okay?"

"Got overheated. That's all."

Her mother didn't appear to believe her. "Honey, we'll talk about the money tonight."

"Can't wait 'til tonight."

"Why not?"

"Well . . ." Ruby realized she didn't have a good reason, other than she was about to beat the crap out of an old man and flee the state. "Um . . . I . . . I've got a lead on a car . . . and, and maybe an apartment. But I need to act fast."

Her mother's face brightened. "You're thinking of moving out?"

"Yeah, mom. Don't look so goddamn happy."

"Great. Eduardo should be home any minute. He'll be happy to go look at a car with you. He's real good under the hood." She smirked. "Of a car that is."

"*Mom,* the money?"

"I don't have two grand on me, sweetie."

"Duh, Mom, I know that. A check. And it's more like four grand, not two."

"Well, I don't have that in my bank account either."

"Yeah, you do. Of course, you do. It's in the account dad left me."

Her mother looked away. "Ruby . . . listen. I don't have your money. I mean, I do . . . just not right now. It's not in there."

"What'd you mean?"

Her mother appeared to be searching for the right words.

"What'd you mean, Mom? Where is it?"

Her mother let out a sigh. "I lent it to Eduardo."

Ruby's mouth fell open. "Y . . . you did *what*?"

"Oh, now, don't wig out on me. It was a loan. Just a *loan*. For his truck. You needn't worry, he's good for it."

The rage returned along with the heat in her chest. The chorus began to sing. "You gave *my* money . . . *Dad's* money, to that . . . to that, dumbass? To that fucking *leech*?"

"*Ruby!*" her mother snapped. "What's *wrong* with you? If you think I'm gonna stand here and listen to you talk about Eduardo that way, you can think again. Really, I've had about enough of your attitude. Eduardo just needed a little help, a little boost. Don't know if you've noticed, but you've certainly been getting *a lot* of help around here. When's the last time you paid rent?"

"What? I pay my share! Hell of a lot more than Eduardo does." Ruby knew where this was going, the same place it always went when her mother screwed up or got called out. Suddenly the conversation was about something else, anything else.

"Eduardo may not be perfect," her mother continued. "But at least he's trying. Now, I need you to do the same. Honestly, would it kill you to be nice to him every now and again?"

A fresh wave of hate blossomed and Ruby found her eyes on a hand shovel near her feet, saw herself picking it up and stabbing it right into her mother's face. *No!* Ruby thought, struggling for control.

"And another thing." Her mother jabbed her keys at Ruby. "You better cool it with Hugo. He's really upset, which makes his daddy upset, which makes me upset." Her mother turned and headed for her car, talking over her shoulder as she went. "You may not like Eduardo, but he's been about the best thing to happen to me in a *long* time, and . . . and . . . I won't stand for you messing that up. You hear me?"

Ruby did, each word sending a fresh wave of hatred burning into her chest. She realized the little shovel, the one with the jagged rusty blade, was in her hand. She didn't even remember picking it up. She clutched it hard, her wrist twitching.

Her mother reached her car and stopped. She stood there a long minute shaking her head, then slowly turned around. She set eyes on Ruby and her face softened. She let out a long sigh and walked back. "Ruby, honey. I don't mean to be so sharp. I know you're dealing with a lot right now. But we *all* are. Y'know, this family just needs to do something fun together for a change. Maybe tonight when I get home, we can put our heads together . . . see what we come up with. Goofy Golf and some pizza sounds good to me."

Ruby was about to tell her she'd rather drink puke, when her mother hugged her, hugged her tight and hard.

"I love you, Ruby."

Her mother let her go and headed back to her car.

Ruby watched her mother drive off, looked again at the shovel in her hand, then at the ring, realized she was panting. "Fuck!" she cried and threw the shovel into the bushes.

Ruby headed inside, dashed down the steps, and rushed into her room; she intended to be out of here before either Eduardo or the cops showed up, out of here before she killed someone. She had no idea where she was going, or even how she was getting there, found it impossible to focus, her mind a storm of confusion, the only thing that seemed clear was that she needed to go.

She slid out an old makeup pouch from behind her nightstand. It was stuffed with twenties—the cash Pam had paid her over the last year, the money that was meant to go to buying her a car.

Damnit, Tina, what I wouldn't do to have you here with me right now. Someone I could count on. Really count on. God, if I could only take back those awful things I said to you.

She shoved the pouch into her purse, then dug her dad's old army duffel bag from out of her closet. She tossed the purse inside and began shoving pants and shirts into it, not caring if they were clean or not. She opened her underwear drawer and started tossing in bras and undies. She grabbed another handful of undies and that was when her knees buckled and she sat down hard on the bed.

"Christ," she whispered. "Was I really gonna kill her? My own mother?" She shook her head. "No . . . no way." But she knew if her mother hadn't left when she did, that there was no telling, because Mr. Rosenfeld had put murder in her heart, she could feel the rage with every beat. "Fuck!" she cried, then shoved her face into the handful of undies, screaming into them.

"That's kind of weird," someone said.

Hugo leaned against the doorframe of her room, an amused grin on his pimply face.

"Thought I heard you come in," he said, staring at the undies in her hand.

The hatred rumbled, seemed almost to growl within Ruby. She shoved her underwear into the bag. "You . . . need . . . to . . . leave," she hissed, barely able to get the words out.

"I will. But first I need a shot of your beaver." He said this so casually it took Ruby a moment to process, but it wasn't until he tapped the camera, the Polaroid hanging around his neck, that she truly understood.

Ruby's hands began to tremble.

"One shot of your cooter and I promise I'll leave you be. What'd ya say?"

She clutched the bed; the heat, the fury, it had her. If she wasn't clinging hold of her mattress with all her strength, she had no doubt she'd be bashing the little shit's face in. She ground her teeth as her cheeks began to burn, as the chorus began to sing its sweet song.

*Let go, **Ruby**,* the voice whispered. ***It is time to make them pay, make them all pay.***

"Look," Hugo continued. "I got it all figured out. This is the last week of your probation. Right? So long as nothing happens, like you beating me up, then you're a free bird, just like that Skynyrd song. But . . . *but,* if you were to what? Cut me?" A sly smile spread across his face as he pulled a kitchen knife from his back pocket and held it up. "Say, slash my arm. Could you imagine? One little nick, that's all it would take. Y'know, just enough to get the blood flowing, then me screaming like you tried to kill me. I mean, fuck, they'd have you back in that looney bin in a snap. No two ways about that. I mean, am I right, or am I right? Because no one believes a thing you say anyhow, not in this house."

Ruby stared into his smug little face and the chorus began to howl.

Give yourself over, the voice, the other, purred. *Let us have some fun.*

Ruby sucked in a deep lungful of air as the rage boiled, sending feverish chills up and down her spine, using every ounce of her will not to let go of the mattress, not to give in, knowing if she did, there'd be no coming back, because the only thing on her mind was murder.

Then came the rumble of a truck pulling into the drive.

"Uh-oh," Hugo said. "You're gonna wanna decide quick. Dad's home. One little photo of your snatch, or me bleeding and screaming bloody murder at the top of my lungs." He set the blade against the top of his forearm. "What's it gonna be?"

That was when she noticed he had a boner. Even through the heat, the rage, and the song, she could see that this little miserable turd was getting off on her. And . . . that was when she let go, just let go, giving herself completely over to the song.

Good, said the other. *You are free now. You can do anything . . . anything you like.*

And with that an odd calm spread through her, the hate, the heat turning into a euphoric rush.

"Okay," she whispered and stood.

"Okay?" Hugo repeated, his face lighting up. *"Okay?"*

"Sure." She unbuckled her belt, undid the first button of her jeans, then another. "What're you waiting for?"

He swallowed hard, suddenly all his cockiness gone, his eyes wide with excitement. "Okay!" he said, tucking the knife into his back pocket. He popped open the camera.

Ruby undid another button.

"O . . . *kay!*" He took a tentative step forward, another, his face one of utter disbelief as he dropped to a knee before her.

She undid the final button and he held the camera up, his hands trembling. "I'm ready."

"Are you sure?" She tucked a thumb in the top of her underwear.

"Oh, yeah."

"Ready to feed your blood to the worms of Hell?"

"Huh?" he said, not taking his eyes off the top of her panties.

"The worms of Hell."

"What?"

She opened her mouth and when she did, the song came echoing out.

Hugo jerked his head up and Ruby drove her knee into the camera, smashing it into the boy's face. There came an awful crack as the camera shattered into his nose and he fell back, clutching his face, letting out a long, wounded scream.

The scream was music to Ruby, feeding the hate, feeding the song. "Yeah, baby!" she cried, letting the song take her as she slammed her foot into his crotch, once, twice, a third time, driving her foot hard into his groin.

He wailed, clutching his mangled nuts as he rolled across her floor, his face a red knot of agony.

She saw the blood pouring from his nose and licked her lips. "Let's get it on!" she howled, then laughed as the sweet, sweet hate filled her up.

He shot her a look of stark terror and grabbed the doorframe, coughing and groaning as he clawed his way to his feet.

Ruby took a step toward him and he yanked out the kitchen knife. "Stay away from me!" he shrieked, the knife in one hand, his busted balls in the other. "You fucking crazy bitch!"

"Gonna eat your eyes," she said, and came for him.

He shrieked again and dashed for the stairs. "Dad! Dad!" he screamed. "*Daaaaddy!*"

He stumbled and she caught his ankle, her nails biting into his flesh, tearing deep into his skin.

Let him go, the other said.

"Gonna eat your eyes!"

No, the other, commanded. *It is the old man you want. The old man.*

She saw a flash of Mr. Rosenfeld, the evil eye on his forehead, his face contorted into that of a laughing devil, and let go of the boy.

Hugo disappeared up the stairs. She heard him run through the house, then out the front, screaming for his dad.

She heard Eduardo's voice and began to growl, to truly growl. Her eyes shot to the far side of the basement, to her dad's old tools. She walked over and snatched up a large screwdriver, one with a sharp chiseled tip. It looked like just the thing for punching through ribs and lungs. She also picked up a hammer, felt the weight of it, thought how soundly it would cave in someone's skull, even someone as thickheaded as Eduardo.

She heard Eduardo's heavy footfalls above. "Ruby!" he yelled. "Get your ass up here! Now! Right now, goddamnit!"

Ruby smiled and headed for the stairs.

No, the voice said again. *First the old man. Then we can come back and do anything you like to them.*

"Anything?"

Anything.

She nodded, and went along with the voice, because the voice was right, always right. She let herself out of the half-basement through the sliding glass door, leaving behind her duffle bag, her clothes, her money, all of it forgotten now. She walked, almost strolled down her front drive, coming to Eduardo's truck, raking the claw on the hammer along the side as she passed, leaving a deep gouge the length of the truck.

She was smiling as she headed up the street, her eyes dancing, and if anyone had seen them, they would've sworn there were little flames burning within. She crossed the road and disappeared into the woods, following the trail, the shortcut that led to Pam's house, to the little trailer, to the demon, Mr. Rosenfeld.

✛

Ruby stood outside Mr. Rosenfeld's trailer, swaying, glaring at the door, clutching the screwdriver and hammer. She felt as though she were floating, her mind swimming in a feverish dream, her face flush, her skin sweaty.

The old man, the demon, he is feeding on you, the voice, the other, said. *Feel it!*

Pain bit Ruby's finger and the ring changed, the simple band turning into prickly spider legs, the coin into an eye—a *real* eye. The eye shifted, glancing about until it found Ruby. It glared at her, burning into her, and it was then that she saw the worms, hundreds and hundreds of them, saw their little faces full of rapture, saw it was them singing their little hearts out to her.

If you want to be free of this demon's curse, you know what you must do, the other said.

She nodded.

It is time, the other added, no longer sounding like a friend, but her master. *Time to make him pay.*

Ruby's heart began to drum, her head throbbing as though the worms were squirming around in her brain.

She walked onto the small porch, tried to peer in, but the curtains were drawn. She slowly turned the knob; it was unlocked, the door making a light click as she pushed it open. The room was dark, but she could just make out Mr. Rosenfeld's form over on the sofa.

Careful, he is full of tricks and traps, potions and powders.

The other's fear grew, flowing into Ruby, making her wary. She crept into the room, taking slow soft steps, careful not to bump any of the stacked boxes, drawing closer, closer.

Mr. Rosenfeld was curled up in a blanket, his back to her. She could see the back of his head, the white tuft of his hair.

Strike! Be quick! Kill the demon now! Free yourself!

The worms' song filled her head, her heart, and their hate was honey.

Yes, she thought. *It'll be good . . . so good.* She lifted the hammer, ready to strike, and it was then, from somewhere deep within, another voice, that of her own, so small, so far away: *You love this man. He has shown you nothing but kindness.*

She hesitated.

Do it now before he takes you! the other cried.

Her own voice protested, crying out to her, but the chorus rose, drowning her out, drowning out everything until all she could hear was the worms' sweet promise of freedom.

She struck, slamming the hammer down into the back of Mr. Rosenfeld's skull. She had the divine pleasure of feeling it sink into his scalp as she slammed it over and over, crushing his skull, turning his head into mush. Bits of brain, hair, and flesh spattered her face and into her mouth. Only, only, the mush . . . it tasted like . . . *cantaloupe?*

Someone shoved her from behind, knocking her atop the sofa. She turned, saw him, Mr. Rosenfeld, clutching a bronze chalice to his chest. For a moment it was just Mr. Rosenfeld looking terrified, but as the worms screamed at her to kill him, her vision blurred, and when he came back into focus his eyes began to glow and she saw horns, long curling horns, sprout from his head. His face twisted into a mask of gleeful horror as he raised the chalice, ready to strike, ready to knock the brains from her head.

Kill him! the voice cried.

Ruby threw the screwdriver, knocking Josh back. She rolled to her feet, came up screaming and swinging the hammer. Her first strike caught him on the arm, the second grazing his forehead, knocking him into the wall.

He crumpled to the floor and the worms laughed and shrieked and Ruby joined them.

Mr. Rosenfeld began frantically twisting the top off the chalice.

Watch out! the voice cried at her.

Before Ruby could react, Josh threw a handful of red powder at her. It went into her mouth and eyes, blinding her, and when she went to breathe, it shot up her nose and into her lungs.

She gasped, fell to her knees, coughing, choking, struggling to see.

"Ruby!" Mr. Rosenfeld cried. "Can you hear me? Can you?"

Ruby managed to wipe one eye clear, and when she did, she saw him, Josh—no horns, no glowing eyes, just an old man with blood running down his horrified face.

He slid over to her, grabbed her hand, the one with the ring, and slapped more of the powder on it. Her finger began to burn, it felt as though the ring itself was on fire. She stared at it, expecting to see smoke and flame, instead saw the powder melting on it, to it, like candle wax, bloodred, staining both her skin and the ring.

The fiery eye dimmed, then slowly shut.

The worms let out a long wail that echoed away and then, nothing, no other, no worms, no heat, no pain. The ring, it was but a ring again.

"Ruby," a weak voice called.

Ruby blinked, looked around, realized where she was and shook her head, trying to remember how she even got there.

"Ruby." It was Mr. Rosenfeld, he was trying to pull himself up. She saw the deep gash across his forehead, the blood, so much blood.

"Oh, God!" she looked at the hammer in her hand. "Oh no! I'm sorry, Josh. Oh, God, I'm so sorry!" She dropped the hammer and stumbled back, her hand to her mouth.

"Ruby, it's okay."

She shook her head and kept backing away, stumbling toward the door. "Oh, God, what've I done?" The room began to spin and she almost fell.

"Listen to me. You must listen to me. You're in great danger." He got to his feet and pointed at a large tattered book on the end table. "I can help you. The spell . . . to get that ring off . . . to set you free. It's here!" He slapped the book. "Right here!"

But Ruby wasn't hearing him, her thoughts tumbling over one another. She couldn't stop staring at the wound, the blood. "What've I done?" she said again, trying to make sense of any of it.

She thought she heard a siren.

"They're coming for me," she said. "They're gonna lock me up for good!"

"No, Ruby, dear," Mr. Rosenfeld pleaded. "You *have* to listen. You must let me help you!"

Ruby turned and dashed out the door.

What has happened? Beel wondered. He'd withdrawn within himself, merely a passenger in Ruby's mind and body, as she sprinted down the wooded trail.

He understood one thing for certain, that they—he and Lord Sheelbeth—had underestimated the old man, the Baalei Shem wizard, that he wasn't so old and feeble after all. He'd ambushed them, just like in New York all those years ago, had once more outsmarted them by dousing the ring in some potion. And now Beel felt, what? Disconnected? Yes—from Lord Sheelbeth, the worms, all of it. They'd all gone quiet.

Ruby slid down an embankment, dropping to her knees in the sand beside a small stream, gasping and panting, trembling and clutching herself. Slowly she extended her hand, staring at the ring, and so did Beel.

The ring was but a ring again, only it was covered in a cruddy, reddish goo, as though the powder had melted itself to the ring, forming a waxy film. The crud was also on her hand and wrists. She wiped at it and some of it crumbled away, leaving her skin stained and ruddy.

How is it I'm still here? Beel wondered, knowing the last time this wizard had put a spell on the ring, he, Beel, had been sucked back into Lord Sheelbeth's lair. *What is different?*

He shut his mind's eye, blocking out what Ruby was seeing, searching within, once more reliving that long-ago night when the wizard captured the ring: Adam cutting his own throat, the ring pulling him back into it, scuttling away, the bird, then the wizard dousing the ring, yes, and a bronze box, falling back to Hell, to Lord Sheelbeth. What was different? He caught a flash of Adam's body lying in the snow and it came to him and it was so simple he almost laughed.

Adam was dead. Ruby is not.

And that revelation unlocked a host of memories lost to the fire. *I am a sheid, I cannot possess the dead . . . so was expelled. That is all.*

More memories flooded in, flashes of his past all jumbled together, it was as though his mind had been released, was becoming his own again. And this too surprised him, gave him hope that perhaps this spell, this potion, might be blocking Lord Sheelbeth in some manner. A wave of excitement shot through Beel. *Has the old man, the wizard, somehow set me free?*

Ruby clutched her head, let out a moan. "What's wrong with me?"

Beel barely heard her, his thoughts racing, his hopes rising. And just as he began to believe there might be some chance of escape, he heard Lord Sheelbeth.

"Beel," she called, her voice muffled and so *very* far away, but there nonetheless, and all Beel's hopes crumbled.

"The ring . . . it is tainted . . . I am blind!" Lord Sheelbeth's words echoed from afar, and this time Beel noticed the strain in her voice, as though it took all her will to be heard, every word sounding as though through teeth clenched in pain.

"Beel! Hear me . . ." Her voice faded for a moment, then came back. *". . . must . . . remove . . . the blood."*

So, it is blood. But whose?

"Scrub . . . the ring" Lord Sheelbeth demanded. *"Do it . . . now!"*

Beel realized her words no longer carried any weight, that he felt no compulsion to obey like some puppet. Why, they were just words now. The blood, it was like some barrier, some shield. The spark of hope returned and so did the question. *Am I free?*

He heard birds in the pines above. *Can I? Dare I?* He knew well the risks; the pain of fire so fresh that the smell of smoldering flesh still lingered in his mind.

He nudged Ruby to look up, and he saw them—a flock of blue jays dancing about on the tree limbs. He could hear the joy in their calls, feel their freedom as they leapt from branch to branch. They were as dangling fruit before a starving man, and, like a starving man he grabbed for them, for this chance however slim, doing his trick, sliding out of Ruby's body, her soul. It was an easy thing, a feat he'd performed a thousand times before.

He spotted a large jay cawing proudly and reached for it, letting go of Ruby as he began to drift upward—a translucent spirit, light as smoke. *It is time to fly,* he thought. *So far away that Lord Sheelbeth will never find me.* Only, that didn't happen, no, instead he felt a tug, like some shackle about his ankle; it began pulling him down, sucking him into the ring.

"*No!*" he cried, clawing desperately at the air, only to find himself sliding further and further into the ring. Suddenly he could hear Lord Sheelbeth's voice again, hear the worms.

"*Beel! What are you doing? No! You will stop this. Return to me now! The flame! Remember the flame!*"

With sudden horror, Beel realized his folly, understood that the woman, for whatever reason, was his only safe harbor. He grabbed for her, flailing for her soul, using all his tricks to pull himself back into her.

Ruby let out a cry. "Leave me alone!" She pushed him away, not physically, but with her mind. It was as a though he'd been kicked, knocking him back. Beel slid further into the ring. He had always relied on stealth, sneaking into a soul when one was asleep or distracted. He knew it to be nearly impossible to enter a mind when one was aware of him, actually fighting him, but there was fire and unbearable pain awaiting him should he fail, so he pushed, pressed, pried with all that he was, trying to force himself into her soul.

Let me in! he demanded. **You must let me in!**

Ruby clasped her hands against her ears, doubled over and screamed; he could feel her heart drumming with terror.

Again, the ring tugged at him, drawing him ever downward into its trap. Again, he clawed at Ruby's very soul, wailing at her.

There came a soul-numbing shriek from Lord Sheelbeth. "*You will burn!*"

Ruby swooned, falling face-forward into the dirt. Beel seized the moment, hooking onto her mind and sliding into her soul. Then, all at once, he was within, the pull of the ring gone. Ruby's hitching breath the only sound.

Ruby rolled onto her back, trembling, panting, and staring skyward, tears streaming down her face.

Beel watched the jay fly away. *I will never be free. Such a fool to even dream of such.*

From somewhere far, *"You will burn!"*

I will, Beel thought, *unless, unless.* He tried to press out the fear and focus. *What had the wizard said, there at the last? That he could help Ruby? Could remove the ring? Yes! The magic book! He has it. And if he can remove the ring from Ruby, and I am within Ruby, am one with her, then perhaps the ring will be removed from me as well.* He grimaced within, knowing that wanting something to be true, no matter how bad, did not make it true. *Surely, if there is a spell to bind me to this ring, then there must be one to unbind me.*

He watched the birds, his heart breaking. *God, Father Above, why do you hate me so? What is it I have ever done to you?*

The big jay lit upon a branch just above them, cawing as though taunting him.

I will get that book, will find what secrets it holds. Then, Lord Sheelbeth, then we will see who spends eternity in the flame!

We need to go back, Beel said, speaking so that Ruby could hear him.

She shook her head as though from some buzzing bug.

Ruby, listen . . . you are in grave danger. We both are.

"Get the fuck out of my head!"

We do not have long. We must work together. Now stand up, it is time to go. Beel came forward, exerting himself; it was a simple thing, he just envisioned himself as his host, and he became them. He pushed her to stand. She started up, then suddenly he was knocked back.

"Get out!" she shouted, clutching her head.

Beel wondered how she could've done that, knowing she should be his to command at this point. He regathered himself and came forward again, this time ready, but so was she, shoving him back. He pushed and she pushed, causing her to fall over. Ruby rolled back and forth on the sand, growling at him through clenched teeth.

Do as I command! he cried.

"Fuck you, asshole!" Again, he was rebuffed, pushed back, but this time he stayed back, overwhelmed by the fortitude of Ruby's will. He realized that the spell must've brought this woman round to herself. Even so, most souls, human or animal, tended to be fairly easy for him to dominate, maybe not always right away, but with time there were few Beel couldn't take some measure of control over. The trouble was, he had no idea how much time he had.

Ruby, listen—

"No!" she shouted. "Don't wanna hear your bullshit! You're the goddamn Devil!" And with that she grabbed the ring and began twisting, tugging. "Let go of me!" she cried. Beel could feel the pain as she tried to tear the ring loose of her flesh. Then, to Beel's horror, a chunk of the waxy blood crumbled away in her hand and suddenly he heard them—the *worms.*

Stop! he screamed, rushing forward, this time so suddenly and forcefully that he was able to tug her hand from the ring. He held it up so they could both see that most of the clotted blood was now gone from the ring.

He shuddered, and the shudder went through Ruby as well. *Look!* he shouted within her. *The blood. You're wiping off the blood! The old man put it on to protect you. Can you not see that? If you wipe it off, you will break his spell, will let her in, the demon, the true demon. Listen, do you not hear them?*

The singing intensified and a chill rolled through her. She began to tremble. "What is that?"

That is Hell coming for both of us.

"Stop it!" She covered her ears, clenching her eyes closed, trying to shut it all out, to withdraw as far within herself as she could. "Make it stop!"

"Beel," Lord Sheelbeth called, her voice sounding closer now. *"You have forgotten who you are again. It is time for you to come home. Remember, I am your savior. You owe me. You owe me, Beel."*

Beel jumped to Ruby's feet, scrambled up the embankment, and started up the trail, heading for the trailer, the wizard, expecting to be pulled back into the ring with every step.

"Beel," Lord Sheelbeth called, her voice sounding cold, detached, yet Beel could hear the mounting fury. *"Stop! Stop right now or I will have to kill her, the woman. Do not make me do this. We need her."*

Kill the woman? What was she talking about? And it struck Beel, yes, of course, if Ruby dies, then he'll be ejected from her body. And just like with Adam, he would be pulled back into the ring, back to Lord Sheelbeth, back to the flame. Then another question: *But how . . . how can she kill her?*

It was the worms that answered, their voices rising, somewhere Lord Sheelbeth joining them. It was a spell, Beel was sure of it, the strain evident in her voice.

Beel thought he felt the ring twitch, Ruby too. They caught a slight spark from within the eye, then it bit her.

"Ow!" Ruby cried, clutching her hand as heat erupted from the bite. Her finger began to turn black. "What the fuck?"

The heat slowly coursed up her arm, into her chest, her heart, and Beel knew then it was over for her—for them. But the heat moved on, settling in her gut.

Ruby shuttered, convulsed slightly, clutching her stomach. "Oh, God. I feel sick."

She burped, gagged, then let loose a long belch, a foul odor escaping her lips.

"Aww, yuck!" she cried and doubled over, spitting and hacking. "What the fuck was that?"

Beel could only wonder at what terrible thing Lord Sheelbeth had just done to them—some poisonous spell, a curse? He glanced again at the ring, the eye was dead once more, but he was horrified at how little of the waxy blood still remained.

Voices came to them, but this time from without.

The sky had grown cloudy, as though about to rain. They scanned the deepening shadows and spotted two men in the woods, far up at the top of the hill, heading their way.

"Cops!" Ruby hissed, and before Beel could react, dashed off, running back along the trail, keeping low. They heard more voices ahead. "Fuck," Ruby said, and slid back down to the little creek, following it until it came to a large cement drainpipe that emptied into a small pond. She ducked into some bushes and squatted there with her arms tight around her legs as though hoping it would all just go away.

We cannot stay here, Beel said.

"Piss off," she hissed.

You have no reason to trust me. But you must. We are bound for now and have to work together . . . or we will both end up in a hell you cannot imagine.

She just sat there staring into the dark drainpipe, watching the water spill out.

The demon said she will kill you to get to me. You heard her yourself.

"I don't know what I heard. Fucking going crazy."

No . . . you are not crazy. Do you hear me? You are not crazy.

For the first time, Ruby seemed to drop her guard a little. She sucked in a deep hitching breath. "I'm not crazy."

No. Everything you have heard is real . . . but so is the danger. I want out of your head as much as you want me out. But we need help.

"Not gonna kill Mr. Rosenfeld."

Only the demon wants to kill the wizard. I am seeking his help. I am trying to show you that I am trapped just like you. That the potion, the blood the old man put on the ring, it has—

Lord Sheelbeth's voice cut through. *"I give you but this one last chance, Beel. Cleanse the ring. Do it now. Prove to me you know yourself and I will spare you the flame. Do it now!"*

A moan came from the pipe. Ruby stared into the dark culvert.

"You have been warned," Lord Sheelbeth said.

Another moan.

Ruby stood up.

Shuffling echoed from the pipe; something was heading toward them.

Ruby backed away.

"The taint is upon you. You can run, but never hide. Evil will find you."

A woman emerged from the drainpipe, sniffing the air. She was stooped, carrying a bundle wrapped tightly in her arms. Her clothes were muddy tatters, rotting, as though she'd been lying beneath the water for many years. Her hair was matted to her skull, her flesh gray and translucent and dripping from her bones; Beel could see every black vein beneath her skin.

"Return to me now, Beel!" Lord Sheelbeth cried. *"Scrub the ring and all is forgiven."*

Ruby let out a weak cry and the woman's empty sockets found them. She grimaced, nodded, and held out her bundle for Ruby to see—two infants swaddled together, both of their skulls bashed in.

Ruby fell back another step, stumbled, and the infants sat up, setting their own hollow sockets on her.

The woman started toward them, clacking her teeth, her feet making but the lightest ripples across the water as she came for Ruby.

The taint, Beel thought, suddenly understanding that Lord Sheelbeth hadn't poisoned Ruby, but marked her.

Ruby took off, dashing through the bushes, found the trail and started to run, made it only a few yards before colliding head-on into a large bulk of a man.

Eduardo.

He caught her arm. "Gotcha, you freak!"

"Let go!" Ruby yelled, trying to wrench loose.

Eduardo shook her, hard, snapping her back and forth, his face full of rage. "You done crossed the wrong line with me!" He twisted her arm up behind her back, then gave it good jerk.

Pain exploded in Ruby's shoulder, and her pain became Beel's pain.

"I told you to stay away from Hugo. Made it clear what would happen if you touched him! Didn't I?"

Ruby snarled something unintelligible.

Eduardo popped the side of her head with his open palm. "Didn't I?" He shoved her forward, back up the trail, toward the police. "You're going to jail, real jail, prison. They're gonna send you away for . . ."

The dead woman with her dead babies stood blocking their way. She cocked her head left, then right, the bones popping in her neck. She held her babies up, proudly showing them off. One of them opened its mouth and a leech oozed out along with a gush of brown bile. The woman dropped them, only they didn't fall, but floated beside her, all three of them staring with sad empty sockets.

Eduardo let out a cry.

The woman began clacking her teeth and started toward them, the babies drifting along with her.

Eduardo shoved Ruby at the woman and stumbled back.

Run, Ruby, Beel cried. **Run!**

Ruby didn't run, seemed incapable of running. Beel pushed forward, seized control, and took off, running directly *toward* the ghoul.

"No!" Ruby screamed, trying to wrestle back dominance.

It is but a shade, Ruby! A ghost. It cannot harm you.

And before she could stop him, they ran directly into the woman's open arms.

Ruby screamed again, but they drove through the ghost, parting the apparition like smoke, catching nothing more than a cold breeze and the smell of dead fish.

"Carlos!" Eduardo bellowed. "Wade! Guys! Over here. *Hurry!*" Eduardo's wide eyes jigged back and forth between Ruby and the ghost, but he couldn't seem to move.

"Where you at?" one of the cops cried. Beel heard them closing in.

Run! Beel cried, and this time Ruby ran, leaving the ghosts, Eduardo, and the approaching police behind.

Ruby leapt across the creek and scrambled up the far bank. She crashed through the underbrush, came out of the woods and up onto the street. She didn't stop, but crossed into an adjoining yard, leapt over a chain-link fence, through a small garden, and came out on the next street over. She saw a cop car speed through a nearby intersection and ducked down. She heard more police yelling somewhere just up the block.

"Shit, I'm screwed," she said, looking up and down the street. That's when Beel spotted a black Cadillac with a large dent heading toward them.

The wizard, he said.

"What?"

Beel pushed Ruby up and this time Ruby didn't resist, but waved to the old man.

The Cadillac zipped up to them, coming to a quick stop.

Mr. Rosenfeld rolled down the window. "Get in!" he said, "Hurry, before they see us. Get in!"

"*Beel!*" Lord Sheelbeth cried. "*Stop, stop now! You know not what you do! Hear me. Scrub the ring, scrub the ring and I will grant you your freedom. I promise you this, Beel. Freedom!"*

Beel couldn't remember Lord Sheelbeth ever sounding so desperate, and it gave him hope.

Ruby opened the door, got in, and the car sped away.

ANGEL BLOOD

Y ou must do something, Wizard," Ruby said. But Josh knew it wasn't Ruby speaking. Not only because her voice took on a slightly deeper tone, as well as an odd speech pattern, but simply because he knew what was within her.

Mr. Rosenfeld clutched the wheel, weaving, squinting into the late-afternoon haze as he searched for a place to turn off. It was taking all his effort just to keep the big Cadillac on the road. His eyes were bad, his reflexes shot, he knew he needed to pull over before he drove them into a ditch.

"Hurry, the blood, it is almost gone. Soon she will take us."

Josh shuddered, wondered just who *she* was. Another demon? Were there layers of them? His brother, Rabbi Reuben, had spoken of such, but his brother had spoken of many things. *Why didn't I pay better attention?*

"Josh, please do something!"

That, Mr. Rosenfeld knew, was Ruby, and the fear and confusion in her voice cut to his core. *Stupid old man, why couldn't you keep it together. You did this to her. You! The one person in your life that seemed to truly give a damn about you, and you couldn't even keep her safe.* He blinked, trying to clear the tears from his vision, trying to stay on the road. *Stupid old man.*

He spotted a dirt road and turned off, going just far enough that they wouldn't be seen from the highway. He cut the engine, grabbed the bag next to him, unbuckled it, and yanked out the chalice. "Here, give me your hand."

Ruby did, clutching her wrist with her other hand, trying to stop the trembling.

The ring had returned to its demon form, a spider with an eye. Josh shuddered, trying to push away the awful memories of the thing scuttling through the snow, racing away from his brother's brutally murdered body.

He caught a spark, a slight glow like a hot ember in the eye, and quickly twisted open the chalice lid.

The spark flared and the eye fixed on him. A song, Josh heard a song then his vision blurred. He found himself wanting, needing sleep, suddenly it was all he desired.

"Wizard!" Ruby cried in that other voice. "The blood, now!" Someone was shaking him. It was Ruby, or was it?

Mr. Rosenfeld blinked, shook his head, then quickly grabbed a pinch of the powder, dashed it on the ring. There came a distant wail, then silence—beautiful, blissful silence.

The spider slowly turned back into a ring.

"God save us," Josh whispered, and rubbed more of the powder onto the ring, watching as it simmered, then turned to a hard waxy film.

"Is that really blood?" Ruby asked.

Mr. Rosenfeld nodded. "Ancient, dried angel blood. At least that's what Reuben, my brother, told me." Josh took a pinch of the powder and dabbed it on his tongue. Felt it flow through him, awakening his mind. He'd used it several times in the past to keep his thoughts clear. Only, the effects would lapse and he'd forget to use it. But when Ruby found the ring, that had certainly jolted his sorry old brain into gear. He remembered the blood then, dousing the ring and making sure to take a dab himself, several dabs, perhaps more than he should, but he needed to stay sharp.

Ruby collapsed back in the seat, taking long, slow, deep breaths.

"Did it work?" Josh asked, looking into her terrified eyes, the fear he saw breaking his heart. "Oh, Ruby, dear. Does it still have you? The demon?"

"I am still here," the other voice said. "If that is what you mean. But I am no—"

"God, stop doing that!" Ruby cried. "Josh, get him out of my head. Please! He's driving me nuts." Ruby began to mumble, like she had a mouthful of bumble bees. Mr. Rosenfeld could see she was wrestling with the demon, that they were both trying to speak at the same time.

"Fine," she snapped. "Go ahead. Talk, talk all you want. I'll just sit here in my own head and pretend I'm not here. Should be a fucking good time."

Ruby's voice changed. "Wizard, I am Beel. I am a sheid."

"Sheid?" Mr. Rosenfeld shrugged. "Don't know what that means." And again, he wished he'd listened to his brother more, because the word *was* familiar.

"It means I am no demon. It means I am a slave. A pawn."

Just the thing a demon would say, Josh thought.

"It means I want to escape from Ruby. I want to be free, just as she does."

"Okay, what's stopping you?"

Beel held up Ruby's hand. "The ring. It is my shackle. We have to remove the ring."

"Josh," It was Ruby this time. "Can you *please* tell me what's going on here? Why's he calling you a wizard?"

"He's referring to a Baal Shem, and no, I'm not, not really. My brother, he was. Was part of the Guard, a secret sect of Baalei Shem. Think of the mystic side of Judaism, predates even Kabbalah. Geesh, how do I make this simple? They were essentially this group, this cabal, formed up hundreds of years ago to keep demons at bay. To keep relics like that ring out of the wrong hands."

"Well, they sure did a bang-up job with that. Didn't they?"

No, not at all, Josh thought. He'd been trying to track down members of the Guard for decades. No trace anywhere. No replies to the dozens of letters he'd sent out to synagogues all around the world. He wondered if his brother had been the last of them. His brother had thought so. For a while Josh tried to find a custodian, someone to take this burden off his hands before it was too late. He'd even tried to get Pam involved, but she never seemed to believe any of it.

"No," Josh said. "They failed. I failed. Failed you, Ruby. God, there is nothing I can say here to make up for that. All I can tell you is I'm going to do whatever it takes to get that ring off of you. Swear to God I am."

"But you can do magic. Right? Some kind of spell or trick to get this thing off?"

"I . . . I'm not sure."

"Not sure? But, Josh, you said you could. The book. That magic book of yours? You said it was full of spells."

"It is. Hundreds of them. Just . . . well, I can't read them. I mean, I can read some of it. But casting spells isn't something you want to be guessing at. Be like building a bomb with only half the directions. Could end up exploding in your face."

"Look, I got a goddamn demon living inside me. You gotta do something!"

"I am not a demon."

"Hell, you say."

"Give me the book," the demon voice said. "Perhaps I can decipher the spells."

"Don't you dare give him that book! No telling what he'll do to us!"

"Hold up," Mr. Rosenfeld said. "Both of you. You're getting ahead of me. I didn't say I wouldn't try. Just I need help. That's all. Help is in Atlanta. Ruby, dear, are you okay? I mean, okay enough to drive us there? If I try, I'll just get us all killed. You think you're up for it?"

"Yeah . . . I think so. I mean, I can if this fucker in my head will back off."

"I will do whatever is needed of me."

"Mighty fucking generous of you," Ruby snapped.

Josh and Ruby traded places and Ruby drove them out of town.

It's me, Richard.

I was dreaming, and in the dream I stood in a forest of tall pines, the air smelling of sap and pine straw. The air changed and the birdcalls and insect chirps began to fade, slowly replaced by a soft song. It drifted lightly along the summer breeze like smoke. It moved closer, vibrating through the soles of my bare feet. A girl, no, a young woman, emerged from the shadows. She walked purposely toward me. Her long red hair and white summer dress flowing, floating about her as though she were underwater. The song came from her, but her lips weren't moving. Closer, closer, she walked until she was upon me.

I wanted her, wanted her more than anything in my life.

I opened my arms to embrace her, to capture her, but she walked through me, dissipating into tendrils of crimson smoke, leaving behind only her song.

"No," I cried. "Come back!"

I sat up, blinked, trying to understand where I was. I squinted into a slit of sunlight pushing through heavy curtains and realized I was in the small bunk, in the back of my van. It was an older model, as generic as I could find those days, at least on the outside, being a light blueish-gray, the color of the road. And just old enough that the paint was starting to lose its luster, the kind of vehicle that blended in. From the outside it appeared to be a commercial van, but the inside, that was different. I'd customized it to be as livable as possible, putting in a roll-away bed, a single burner stove, sink, toilet, pretty much everything but a shower. When it came time to shower, I'd just pull into any nearby RV campsite and use theirs. But there were a couple of bits different from most custom camper vans; for one, no carpet—too hard to get blood out of. I'd opted for linoleum instead, the kind you could scrub with bleach over and over again. Also, clamp ties, four of them built into the walls; they were for securing things, specifically young women.

But I wasn't thinking about any of that. I was thinking about the dream, how real it had felt, how I thought I could still hear the song, her song, echoing about in my mind. I sat there a full minute, turning my head this way and that, waiting for it to dissipate, but it didn't; instead it grew louder.

I slid out of bed and pulled on my pants, stooping so as not to hit my head on the roof as I peered out from behind the curtains. I was parked on the backside of a highway rest stop just outside of Atlanta. I'd pulled in for a quick nap, but must've been asleep for a while—murder will certainly tucker you out. There were only a handful of other vehicles in the lot.

I tugged open the sliding side door and got out, the song growing slightly louder. A few folks were coming and going from the bathrooms and it dawned on me someone must be carrying a boom box or radio. Only . . . only, not sure how any device could make such a sound. I mean I could feel it in the air, a slight vibration, beckoning me. It was coming from the restrooms, so I pushed my fingers through my thinning hair in a half effort to look tidy and headed up the walkway. The sound grew in intensity as I went, filling me with, what? Longing, desire? More of a hunger. Yes, but for what?

I stopped. A young woman stood in front of a row of vending machines, her back to me.

It's her! I thought. *Oh, dear God, it's her!* She wasn't wearing a white sundress, but her hair was the same, and the song, I swear it was shimmering around her like an aura.

There were three young boys and their mother in front the woman. The boys in a highly animated discussion over which treats to buy. The woman waited behind them for her turn. I slid up, just to her side so that I could catch a glimpse of her profile, and gasped. I tell you it was indeed her, the woman from my dream. But how?

My fingers twitched as I fought the compulsion to grab her and steal her away. I took a step closer, closer than I should've. I couldn't help it. But she didn't notice, hardly seemed to even notice the boys, her eyes staring off at nothing, her face slack, lips moving ever so slightly, as though talking to someone only she could see. It was weird, but then everything in that moment was weird. And the song, that beautiful, terrible song. Jesus, it was in my head, making my whole body throb. My eyes locked on her slim, graceful neck, her soft pale flesh. My hands ached to clutch her throat, to feel her racing pulse as I strangled the life from her.

No, I wanted more, I wanted to . . . to what? My mouth filled with saliva and I realized I wanted, needed, to taste her, to bite and chew her flesh, to literally eat her alive. How crazy is that? My jaw clenched so tight my teeth began to hurt, and I think I would've attacked her then and there had the mother not turned around.

"Sorry about them," she said, nodding to her kids. "You ever see anyone get this excited over a damn vending machine? Lord, what I'd do to get that excited about anything these days."

I turned away, acting as though I was looking for someone, not wanting them to see my face, not in the state I was in.

"Why don't you go on ahead," the mom said to the woman. "Looks like we're gonna be here a bit."

The young woman stepped up, put a few coins in the machine, bought a MoonPie and two bottles of pop, then headed off. I just stood there like a half-wit, watching her go. The song, the intensity of it, was overwhelming, and she made it to the parking lot before I realized she was getting away.

I started after her.

Plan? I had no plan. My mind screamed at me to just grab her and toss her in the back of my van. I walked faster, quickly closing the distance. There was middle-aged woman walking her poodle and some guy sleeping in a Corolla, but at that point, in that moment, I didn't care who saw me. I *had* to have her. I *would* have her.

"Ruby, dear" someone called. There, an elderly man, sitting in the passenger seat of a black Cadillac. I hadn't even noticed him. He opened the door and got out, holding a map.

She walked up to him and handed him one of the bottles of pop. He traced a finger along the map, seemed to be discussing the route.

I stopped. What was I doing? Can't just snatch someone in broad daylight. But the song, it told me otherwise. I knew I could flatten the old man with one punch. And the woman? Ruby, was it? She wasn't much of anything. I felt sure I could wrestle her in the back of the van before anyone knew what was happening.

And then what?

Then I'd drive her down the nearest dirt road and bite and chew and eat her flesh until my stomach was so bloated, I couldn't eat any more. I'd suck and lick, and drink her blood, until her heart ceased to beat. And then . . . and then . . . then I wouldn't care, because I'd be satiated, full up, done, finished, happy . . . happy as a clam in butter sauce.

There came a horn blast. A large passenger van was behind me; a grim-faced woman waving at me to get out of the way. I realized I was standing in the middle of the road. I stepped aside and she pulled into the nearest parking spot. The side of the van read RIVERSIDE BIBLE RANCH and was loaded with kids. The side door slid open and they began jumping out, hollering and cutting up.

I glanced back toward Ruby and the old man; they were getting into the Cadillac. I started forward when all the sudden a woman, the one who had been driving the church van, was in front of me—a middle-aged lady about as big around as she was tall.

"Sorry for tootin' at you, mister," she said, then squinted at me. "Hey, you alright?"

I pushed past her, rushing for the Cadillac, then stopped. "No, no this won't work. Have I lost my mind?" And the answer was, *yes.*

The Cadillac started up.

"Aww heck, they're gonna get away!"

I dashed to my van, jumping into the driver's seat, but my keys—they weren't in my pockets. No, they were in the back, near the bed. I scrambled for them, got tangled in the seat belt, stumbled into the side of the mini fridge. I let out a cry, snatched up the keys, and jumped back into the driver's seat, cranked it up, and pulled out.

"Where are you?" I cried, scanning the parking lot. "Where did you go?" There was of course only one place they could've gone—back on the highway. I punched the gas, almost clipping the Corolla as I sped out of the rest area.

I shot onto the highway and they were nowhere to be seen. I floored it, then eased up, because it was at that moment I realized that even though I couldn't see Ruby, I could still hear her song and it was telling me that they were just ahead. And sure enough, a moment later I caught sight of the black Cadillac about a half mile up.

I fell in a few vehicles behind them and followed. It appeared they were heading to Atlanta too, but it didn't matter where they were going, even to the ends of the earth, because the song, the song promised me her sweet flesh and blood.

"I'll follow you anywhere," I said, and clacked my teeth together.

Ruby drove the Cadillac up a long driveway, stopping in front of a beautiful old Victorian home, modest compared to some on the street, but still elegant with its delicate gingerbread trim and tall stately windows. Unlike most of the others, this one was in full plumage, painted lavender and haint blue. According to the map, they were in the Grant Park area, just outside of downtown Atlanta.

Ruby cut the engine and they got out. Mr. Rosenfeld hefted his bag off the floorboard and almost fell.

Ruby jumped over. "Here, let me help you with that."

He yanked it back. "No," he snapped, then his face softened. "Sorry Ruby, dear. It's not you I'm worried about. It's the demon."

"Of course," Ruby said, but felt Beel's anger within her.

They started up the walkway and even though it was dusk, Ruby could still see that the home needed some care—the paint peeling in spots, one of the gutters broken and the ivy running amok, climbing all the way up the redbrick chimney. She also noticed someone peering down at them from the attic window. She blinked and there were two of them, their forms shadowy and dim. "Do you see them, Josh?"

"Huh?" He looked up. "See who?"

"There, in that window. I think they're children."

He squinted, adjusting his glasses. "Oh . . . something's there. Not sure what."

You know what they are, Beel said.

She could feel them now, their sadness. *Ghosts?* Ruby asked from within.

You're seeing them because I see them. The ring makes the walls between worlds thin. This place has a long history . . . hardships, betrayals, murder. There are always lost souls in places such as this.

Are they gonna come after me? Like that dead woman?

That woman . . . she was wicked, most spirits are not. Too often they are just lost or trapped. But the taint attracts them all . . . makes them curious.

Ruby felt a wave of dread emanating from Beel. *Why are you scared then?*

The taint, it speaks to evil. It will call so much more than mere spirits. We do not have much time.

Ruby shuddered.

They walked up onto a large porch, could hear music coming from inside. Ruby thought it was Pink Floyd. "You sure we got the right place?"

"It's the address on the card." Josh showed her: Dr. David Gold. Collector and Language Expert. Specializing in the Field of Ancient Hebrew Mythology and Theology.

Mr. Rosenfeld started to knock, hesitated, looked at Ruby. "Let me do the talking. Okay? That goes for both of you. We need to ease him into this."

Ruby nodded and Josh pushed the doorbell.

There came a deep bong and the music turned down, followed by approaching footsteps.

The door opened a crack and someone peeked out.

"Dr. Gold?"

"Who are you?"

"I'm Josh Rosenfeld . . . we've talked a few times on—"

The door flew open and a middle-aged man with a short beard stepped out. He grabbed the old man by the hand and shook it. "Mr. Rosenfeld! Wow . . . what a wonderful surprise!"

Dr. Gold had thick, long gray hair tied back in a ponytail. He wore a faded polo shirt and cutoffs, a worn-out pair of loafers on his feet, and an expression of absolute delight on his tan face. "What . . . whatever are you doing here?"

"Well, we're . . . well . . . it's complicated. Can we come in?"

"Lord, where are my manners. Yes, yes. Please come on in."

They followed him into the foyer, then down a short hall into what appeared to be the main living area. The entire house was trimmed in dark woodwork, accented with faded flowery wallpaper, stained and nicked, this patina of age somehow warm and reassuring. The walls were covered in framed photos, paintings, maps, and ancient documents.

"And who is this young lady?" Dr. Gold asked.

"Ah, sorry. This is Ruby. Ruby, this is Dr. Gold."

"Just David, please." He stuck out his hand. "Only my patients call me Dr. Gold."

Ruby shook his hand, caught a whiff of pot, was pretty sure Dr. Gold was a bit stoned.

"I'm a proctologist." He wiggled his fingers. "That's why my fingers are so stained."

Ruby pulled her hand loose and he chuckled.

It took Ruby a second to catch on that he was messing with her. She grinned.

"Actually, I'm retired. Got tired of dealing with assholes." He laughed, practically guffawed. "Sorry, that one never gets old for me."

Ruby laughed for the first time in days, decided right then and there that she liked this man, liked the mischievous glint in his eyes, the half-smirk that never seemed to leave.

"Okay," David said. "Enough butt jokes for now. I'm dying to know what's brought you to my door. I'll admit, I'm hoping it has something to do with you *finally* agreeing to sell me some, part, or *all* of your collection. We both know you're getting too old to be hoarding those treasures all to yourself. And you know, no one's going to pay you what I will. But more importantly, you know I'll keep them safe . . . keep them out of museums, or anywhere else where the wrong sort of folks can get their hands on them. And I know, you know what I mean?"

Josh's eyes dropped; for a moment, Ruby thought he was about to cry.

"What?" David asked. "What did I say?"

Mr. Rosenfeld started to reply, stopped, started again, then just shook his head.

"Here," David cut in. "Hold that thought. This is obviously the kind of conversation that should be preceded by a drink. What can I get you two? Cola, iced tea, or something stronger?"

"Stronger," Josh said. "Don't care what. Just something with a kick."

"Tea," Ruby said.

David slipped into the adjoining kitchen, giving Ruby a moment to take in the room. The only seating was an old leather sofa, the rest of the space was taken up by two large tables covered with tattered scrolls and bookshelves overflowing with books and ancient artifacts—pottery and clay bowls, weapons of all sorts, including a large battle ax. There was jewelry, several skulls, a few drums, a harp, and a selection of flutes, some ornate, others plain, but all the items appeared old as the hills.

Ruby ran a finger along a black wooden flute.

"It's beautiful, isn't it?" David said, walking back into the room with three glasses on a tray. "That's one of my favorites. Ancient musical instruments are one of my many, many passions."

He handed what looked like straight bourbon to Mr. Rosenfeld, brought the tea to Ruby, keeping the final glass for himself.

He lifted the flute. "Picked this up in Egypt about a year ago. A lot of museums would've loved a chance at it, but my sources know I'll pay double what most will for the right stuff. And this one, well, it's the right stuff. It came from Queen Nefertari's tomb. That makes it around three thousand years old. Carved from some lucky fellow's thigh bone."

He gave it a long soft toot and let out a sigh. "Can you believe that? You just heard the very same tune that Queen Nefertari heard. How utterly amazing is that?" He set it back down. "But here, look, this is my primary passion, my obsession really." He led them to one of the large tables where what appeared to be an ancient scroll was laid out. The parchment was in tatters, with little pieces spread all over the table. Someone was piecing it back together like a giant jigsaw puzzle.

"Since retiring, this is what I spend most of my time, and most of my money, on. It's not just the satisfaction of restoring these relics, but discovering their messages, their lost secrets. This one here, why it's at least two thousand years old." He stopped, his eyes fixed upon a fragment. "Aha!" He plucked up the bit and stuck it toward the top of the parchment. "Been looking for that. I've just started this one, but believe it to be a poem about a woman, perhaps a goddess."

Ruby felt Beel trying to compel her forward and let him lead her. Beel leaned over, then gently spun two of the fragments around at the top, reforming the symbol.

David grimaced. "Whoa, careful there!"

Tell him it is a recipe for beer, Beel said.

What?

That symbol represents Ninkasi. I know it well. She is the goddess of brewing. This looks to be a recipe for beer.

Ruby relayed the message.

David glanced from Ruby to the parchment, studying the symbols for a long minute, then back at Ruby. "I think you're right. How the heck did you know that?"

"She didn't," Josh said.

"Huh?"

Mr. Rosenfeld emptied his glass, then cleared his throat. "David, Ruby is possessed."

Ruby expected David to laugh, to scoff, to roll his eyes, but instead he gave Ruby what could only be described as a clinical look, perhaps the same look he gave his patients. "By what?"

Mr. Rosenfeld unzipped his bag, pulled out the spell book, and set it on the table.

David's eyes grew wide. "Is that . . . ? No, it can't be." He leaned close, gently ran a finger across the frayed leather binding. "I never thought I'd get to see this."

"It's yours if you want it."

David looked up, stunned. "W . . . what? No! You don't mean that."

"It's yours . . . along with all my relics. But first you must do something for me . . . for Ruby."

Both looked at Ruby.

"We need to exorcise the demon within her."

Ruby felt Beel's anger as he pushed forward, trying to take her voice. Ruby gave in, letting him have his say. "I am not a demon!" Beel stated in his slightly deeper, throaty voice. Ruby was beginning to get used to the strange echo of it.

Despite David's cool exterior, Ruby could see the gooseflesh on his arms. This time, it was David who emptied his glass in one long gulp. "Then just what are you?"

"I am Beel. I am shedim."

"Shedim? Shedim? *Wait* . . . I know that." David pressed his palm against his forehead, looking like some trivia contestant on the verge of the winning answer. "Shedim, yes. God's unfinished people! That's it. One of God's castoffs. Right?"

Ruby felt a wave of deep sadness flowing from Beel. "Yes," Beel said solemnly. "One of God's castoffs."

David leaned into Ruby as though trying to see the sheid behind her eyes.

"He claims to be trapped within Ruby," Mr. Rosenfeld said. "A slave to some greater demon."

"Interesting," David said. "There could certainly be more than one demon at play. Several even. It's not unheard of. So, might be true, or might be total bullshit. Demons aren't exactly known for their trustworthiness."

"It matters *not* if you believe me," Beel said, though Ruby could tell that it did, could feel his bitterness. "There is one truth that must be faced." He held up Ruby's hand so they could all see the ring. Ruby marveled at the weird sensation of someone else driving her body. "The only way Ruby can be free, the only way *I* can escape, is by removing this ring. And we must do it before Lord Sheelbeth kills Ruby."

"A demon that *wants* to be exorcised," David said. "Now that's something new." He snatched up a magnifying glass, studied the ring, started to touch it.

"Don't!" Mr. Rosenfeld cried. "It's alive. I've witnessed it. The blood, that's all that is keeping the other one away."

David jerked his hand back. "The other one, this Lord Sheelbeth. Is that the same as *Queen* Sheelbeth?" He tugged at his beard. "Must be. The tyrant queen of the Caucasus Mountains. Right? Can't recall the details, only that she had quite the thirst for blood. Something about a five-hundred-year reign."

"Closer to a thousand," Beel said.

"And she's some kind of demon?"

"She is worse than any demon. She was cast down by the Baalei Shem for her wickedness. She is the one controlling the ring, it is part of her. It is her connection . . . her path to escape her prison, to return to earth, to feeding on humankind. Remove it and you will blind her. Lock it away and you lock her away."

"And where exactly is this Sheelbeth?"

Ruby felt Beel's growing impatience. "Hell."

David gave Ruby a hard look. "Hell, as in Heaven and Hell? As in God and Satan?"

"There are many hells. I do not have time to explain. There is a taint on Ruby, it is drawing evil to us even as we speak. If you do not remove this ring soon, Lord Sheelbeth will have us all. Do you not understand what that means? It means your soul will be her slave for eternity."

"But how can—"

"David," Mr. Rosenfeld interrupted. "I don't trust this demon any more than you. But I know this: that's the ring that killed my brother and his wife . . . burned down our synagogue. Of all Reuben's relics, it's the one he feared most. The one he made me promise to always keep locked away. It won't stop with Ruby. It'll never stop. Not if it gets free. And that's why we're here. We need your help." Josh tapped the spell book. "Are you willing to help us, David? *Will* you help us?"

David took another hard look at the ring, the book, and let out a long breath, then laughed. "Are you kidding? I've lived my whole life waiting for a moment like this. This is amazing, this is *all* so amazing. Nothing could make me walk away from this. So, what's the plan?"

The room fell quiet.

"Ah," David said. "You don't have a plan? Do you?"

"No," Mr. Rosenfeld replied. "Not really. But I feel the answers are in here." He slid the book over. "And that's what we need your help with." The old man paged through the book until he arrived at a tattered cloth bookmark. "These are casting spells. My brother tried to teach me a bit about them, back when he still had hopes of recruiting me into the Baalei Shem. It's Word magic, something the Baalei Shem were known for. He only used one once that I know of, and that was to help our sister with her cancer."

"Did it work?" David asked.

"It did . . . sorta. The cancer went away, but her hair turned white and she claimed to hear voices after that, awful voices. She took her own life five years later."

Ruby winced.

"I can decipher some of the ancient Hebrew text," Mr. Rosenfeld continued. "But the symbols and such . . . I quickly get lost. David, I'm hoping you can you make heads or tails of it?"

David pulled out a pair of reading glasses, put them on and began to scan the page. His brows tightened. "Such an interesting mix of languages and symbols, often in the very same line. Not sure I've ever seen anything quite like it." He traced along a line of text. "This is obviously ancient Hebrew. This . . . a bit of Old Persian, I think. And these symbols are Akkadian, but these symbols here . . . just not sure."

"Wizard letters," Beel said.

"What do they say?" Ruby asked.

"I do not know."

"I believe you're right," David exclaimed. "Baal Shem marks. Has to be. Some ancient Kabbalah stuff . . . well actually, these probably predate Kabbalah. Bet it's similar though." He leapt over to a bookcase stuffed with volumes, grabbed two books off the top shelf and another from the lower, brought them over. He thumbed through one, tossed it aside, then the second, trying to keep the brittle pages from falling out of the spine. "Here, look." He held the page next to the marks so they could compare the symbols. "Aren't these the same?"

Ruby and Mr. Rosenfeld nodded.

"Okay, okay, now we're getting somewhere."

He turned the leathery page of the spell book, his hand trembling and, judging from the look on his face, it was from excitement, not fear—David appeared to be having the time of his life.

"This one's for healing, one for strength, for wisdom . . . this one . . . fertility . . . oh." He laughed. "And right next to it, of course, one for keeping your pecker hard. This is for curses . . . one for protection." He listed off two dozen others. "Nothing for removing rings so far." He continued reading, comparing symbols and definitions. "Ahh!" He tapped a mark. "I think this is what we want." He tugged his beard and nodded. "Yeah. It's a bit vague, which might be good. The translation is roughly 'freedom.' I think it's meant to liberate someone who is enslaved, or maybe a prisoner."

"We are both," Beel said.

"Okay," David said. "I think it might work then. The rest is fairly easy to decipher. Just give me a minute." He grabbed a pad and pen and began to write, nodding and grunting as he went. After a few minutes, he held the pad up. "Interesting, really." He tapped his teeth with the end of his pen. "If I'm getting this right—and Lord help us if not—Ruby, first you have to make the spell and bind it to you . . . make it a unique thing that belongs only to you. Then you can use it. But you'll need help."

"What kind of help?" Ruby asked.

David ran a finger along his notes. "Umm . . . demons are usually best for this sort of thing, but not if you don't know how to control them. Seeing as we do not, we're going to go with some other kind of spirit. Hmm, benevolent deities are high on the lists." He looked around like there might be one sitting near them, grunted. "Yeah, we don't seem to have any of those around here. Do we? Angels? No. Well, that leaves wild spirits and spooks."

"As in ghosts?" Ruby asked, thinking of the children in the attic window.

"As in whatever we can draw to us."

"Is it dangerous?"

"You bet. No telling what we could end up summoning."

"God, maybe we should just cut my finger off instead," Ruby said, not sure if she was kidding or not at this point.

"It will not work," Beel said. "Many have tried. The ring will never let you go so easy."

"Yes," Mr. Rosenfeld said. "I saw this. The man who killed my brother, Adam. He tried . . . didn't work for him."

Fuck, what am I doing? Ruby wondered, but only had to look at the ring to know. "And you know how to do that? To call some spirits? Any of you?"

Beel was silent and Josh shook his head.

"Well," David said. "Theoretically I do. But . . . I haven't *actually* ever done it. But I did sit in on a spirit-summoning in Jerusalem. And that wasn't some parlor trick either. Y'know, a few fluttering candles and some cards sliding across a table. No, this was the real deal. That room was swimming with voices, calls and cries, visions of people with animal heads dancing around us. It was terrifying and exhilarating."

Ruby suddenly wanted to be just about anywhere but here. "What happens after we call the spirits?"

"Hmm, according to what I'm reading, once we get that far, *if* we get that far, then we try and persuade them to lend us some of their energy, their good will, their magic, to help you create the spell and bind it to you. Oh, and then to cast it."

Ruby shook her head. "I'm supposed to make a spell?"

"Yeah. This is Word magic, so you put your own words into the spell. Basically, a chant, or song even. The woman in Jerusalem, she called them with a song."

"Yes," Beel put in. "There is magic in songs. Lord Sheelbeth, she uses souls, drives them to sing her spells. It is their song that gives her spells power."

David looked to Mr. Rosenfeld. "Does that sound right?"

Josh shrugged. "I think so. Lines up with what Reuben told me."

"So," Ruby said. "I need to come up with a . . . a song spell?"

Josh and David nodded.

"Okay," Ruby said. "How about this? 'Free my ass from this goddamn ring, motherfuckers.'"

David grinned. "Perhaps something a little more palatable. How about: 'Set me free, set me free, set me free'? Y'know, keep it simple, something that you can chant."

"Should feel more like a song," Beel said. "Give it a tune and your heart."

"Heart?" Ruby rolled her eyes. "Okay, how about this then?" She began to hum, then to sing. "'Give me some magic to set me free, give me some magic to set me free, because free is what I gotta be.'"

"There's a problem," David said.

"What now?" Ruby asked.

"Well, it seems that wouldn't make sense. Not if they, the spirits, sing it."

"Why not?"

"Those lyrics are asking someone to do something. You want the lyrics, the ones the spirits sing, to be giving you something. So, it should be more like: 'We give you our magic to set you free, give you our magic to set you free, because free is what you gotta be.' Right?"

Mr. Rosenfeld nodded. "That makes sense."

"Does it?" Ruby asked.

"Yes," David continued. "You sing the first part to them, then ask them to sing the second part back. Here: 'Give me some magic to set me free, give me some magic to set me free, because free is what I gotta be. We give you some magic to set you free, give you some magic to set you free, because free is what you gotta be.' How does that sound?"

"Sounds like I'm in deep shit," Ruby huffed.

"Anyone got any better ideas?" David asked.

No one said a thing.

"Okay, then let's try it."

Lord Sheelbeth paced in front of her throne. She could hear them, Beel, this Ruby, but they were muffled, as if behind a thick door, could even see a little of their surroundings, but as if through stained glass. What was most helpful was that she could sense their emotions, their fear and excitement, and what she sensed now was hope, and that scared her.

"How, Beel, how could you do this to me again? After all I have done for you." Lord Sheelbeth wondered if the sheid even remembered how she'd saved him all those centuries ago.

It was back when she was at the height of her rule, back when even God's angels feared her might; the spirits warned Lord Sheelbeth of demons trespassing in her realm. These weren't ordinary demons, but devils serving God himself. God, emboldened by his growing power, by his rising throngs of disciples, was sending out angels and demons alike to hunt down the ancient ones—the old gods and deities—casting them into the underworld, cleansing his earthly kingdom of any that might challenge his glory. None were safe, not even the magical spirits and beasts that still roamed the earth.

Lord Sheelbeth attacked these demons, destroyed them, and after doing so, released their prisoners: a harpy, a few bags of fairies, a gnome, and two very grateful goblins. There was one other being—a ghostly thing bound in a jug like a jinn. It was Beel, the sheid. They'd tortured him, all but destroyed him. Lord Sheelbeth brought him home and, using her arts, healed him, made him whole again.

And you had been so grateful then, Beel. Had you not? Why? Because you knew your fate. Knew that the demons would have tortured you for endless ages, until they had turned you into one of them, another twisted servant of Satan.

So, where is your gratitude now, Beel? Now, when I need you most. Have you forgotten your oath to me, forgotten how you wished to serve me, to repay me for my favor? What happened, Beel?

Lord Sheelbeth sighed. "The Baalei Shem . . . that is what happened."

After the Baalei Shem cast Lord Sheelbeth down, trapped her in her underworld prison, they thought the ring dead and stored it away with other heretical relics. What they didn't understand was that the ring was part of Lord Sheelbeth, made of her own flesh—*alive*. That even though Lord Sheelbeth was trapped in another realm, she was still one with the ring. So, none noticed her eye watching them, scheming, waiting for the right moment to strike.

All went well at first. With the help of Beel, they possessed one of the wizards, compelling him to murder several of his brethren and burn the temple to the ground.

After that it was a crusade to gather souls, as many as they could, for souls were the source of Lord Sheelbeth's power. And with enough, she could weld their song into a spell, open a conduit between their prison and the ring to escape back into the earthly realm.

But the task proved greater than even Lord Sheelbeth imagined, the pace arduous. How many souls did they need—hundreds, thousands? Even Lord Sheelbeth wondered if they'd be able to gather enough before the fabled end of days.

Beel became overwhelmed, the weight of this dreadful task too much for his fragile mind. He lost focus, growing ever more unstable, chasing birds instead of doing his part.

When, due to Beel's daydreaming, the Baalei Shem almost captured the ring, Lord Sheelbeth knew something drastic must be done. That was when she began using the fire to burn away Beel's derangement, cleanse his soul, to give him the strength to stay on task.

It wasn't enough, Beel's mind wandered away at a most crucial moment and the wizards captured the ring.

"Ah, Beel, if only I could have given you more strength."

This time, the wizards locked the ring away, sealed it in a copper box, and there it stayed for centuries until . . . until Adam opened it.

"Adam, now Ruby. Freedom in our grasp. Why, why Beel, can you not see this?"

She stopped pacing, concentrated on Beel, trying to peer into his soul, trying to hear the people, to understand what was being said. Being within, Beel absorbed languages almost instantly, even those of beasts. It wasn't so easy for Sheelbeth. Still, over the centuries, she'd mastered dozens of languages and dialects. But she found this modern English to be confusing at times.

"Spells, I believe they are discussing spells," she said, talking to the denizens sharing her small cavern, the demon slaves and her worms, her lovely worms. "They have the spell book . . . but these fools seem not to know what they are doing. It could be our doom, or . . . our *salvation*. We must be ready."

She mounted the steps to her throne, took a seat. "Here, demons," she called. "Before me, now."

The snake beasts, the ones with the rotten faces of monkeys and jackals, slithered out from their craggy dens around the throne, piling together in a squirming heap at her feet.

"Drummers," she called. "To me, now!"

The hunched abominations came forward, keeping their heads down.

Lord Sheelbeth looked them over, debating which of the drummers was the most horrible, the most capable of slaughtering a room full of people.

"Vutto, kneel before me."

The one with the long, jagged talons and claws knelt before her.

"Are you hungry, Vutto?"

"Yah, always hungry."

"Good."

Lord Sheelbeth closed her one eye and began to sing to the worms and the worms began to sing to Lord Sheelbeth.

DEMONS

David walked over to a glass cabinet, opened it, and retrieved four ancient clay bowls, each a different shade of gray, warped and chipped, blackened around the top as though from smoke and fire, all about the size of a typical salad bowl. "Incantation bowls. We'll need these." He held them up to the light, studying the symbols along the inside lip. "Just have to make sure we get the right ones."

"What'll happen if we get the wrong ones?" Ruby asked.

"Well, some of these are spirit bowls and some are demon bowls. Can be hard to tell which is which sometimes. I'm thinking we don't want the demon bowls."

"No," Mr. Rosenfeld added. "Most certainly not."

"Ah, okay." David set one aside. "Definitely not that one. See that, looks kinda like the letter O but with horns. That means demon. Oh, and look, it's on this one too." He set both of them aside. "So maybe one of these two other ones will be okay. Eeny, meeny, miny, moe. Alright, we're going with this one."

"Are you kidding me?" Ruby said.

David shrugged. "Should be okay."

"Should be?" Ruby sucked in a deep breath. "I'm so screwed."

David checked his notes. "Okay, Ruby, going to need a few things from you." He went over to a drawer and came back with a pair of scissors and nail clippers. He handed her the scissors. "First, a clump of your hair."

Ruby took them and clipped about an inch off the bottom, dropped it in the bowl.

"More. Think of making a nest in the bowl. Pretty much have to fill it up."

"Shit, really?

"Really."

She cut more, not even trying to make it symmetrical, just hacked off most the hair along the right side of her head. She rolled it into a ball and set it in the bowl. "You happy now?"

David grinned. "You look kinda funny."

"Fuck you."

He laughed, but it was a nervous laugh.

"Okay, nail clippings. Finger and toes."

Ruby obliged, conceding they needed to be clipped anyway. The ones on her ring hand had all turned black. "Think I should include these?"

"I guess," David said.

"Everyone is sure doing a lot of guessing."

"Yeah, we're playing with fire here, for sure."

"Aren't you supposed to be trying to boost my confidence?"

"I'm sure it'll all be fine."

"Oh, you gotta do better than that."

"I'm going to get the fire extinguisher. Y'know, just in case."

"Really? Lord, please help me out here."

David returned a moment later with a small fire extinguisher, setting it on the table next to the bowl.

"Did you check that it's safe for putting out hellfire?" Ruby asked

David laughed. "Says it's safe for grease fires. Gotta be about the same. Right?"

Ruby groaned.

"Here, maybe this?" Mr. Rosenfeld pulled the chalice containing the angel blood out of his bag and set it on the table. "Just in case."

"What's that?" David asked.

"Let's just say it's another type of fire extinguisher."

David's eyes lit up with interest, but Mr. Rosenfeld held up his hand. "Later, David. I'll tell you all about it later."

"Stay focused," David replied. "I know, I know. Okay, Ruby, now spit into the bowl."

"You want a loogie, or just spit?"

"I think the more of you the better."

Ruby hocked up a good one and spat. "Should I pee in there as well?"

"I see no request for urine, but we will need some blood."

"Oh, blood, of course. Seen enough horror movies to know you *always* need blood."

"Blood is the currency of the dead," Beel put in.

"Thank you for that, Beel."

"Oh," David said. "Speaking of blood, I forgot to add that we need to carve this symbol into your flesh." He pointed to the magic mark. It looked like a crescent moon, with two spikes driven through it, forming a crude cross.

"Fuck, really?"

David winced. "Yeah . . . sorry."

"Has to be my blood I guess?"

"Yeah, but you get to pick the spot."

"Well, gosh, that'll make it fun."

David retrieved a kitchen knife and handed it to her. "I sterilized it."

Ruby took it and began trying to figure out which bit of her flesh would hurt the least to carve into.

"Okay," David said. "There's an order to this. I light your hair, then you cut the mark, letting the blood drip into the bowl. So, Ruby, just tell me when you're ready."

"Don't I need to chant some kind of spell?"

"It doesn't say anything about that."

"I think the bowl does that," Mr. Rosenfeld put in. "Calls the spirits."

"Yes, the bowl calls them," Beel spoke. "When they come, you talk to them, the spirits, as you would to anyone. Tell them what it is you wish."

Ruby felt like crying. "I can't believe I'm doing this."

David pulled out his lighter, flipped it open and flicked on the flame. "Everyone ready?"

"No," Ruby said flatly, as she set the knife about midway up on her left forearm, on the inner side where the flesh was softer.

David put the flame to the hair, it smoldered, then began to burn.

Ruby cut the mark—which amounted to a C shape with two marks slashed through it, forming a cross. She grimaced, trying to keep the cut as shallow as she could. Blood pooled and dripped. She'd cut deeper than she meant and a lot of blood spilled into the bowl.

Nothing happened.

Everyone exchanged tense glances, waited, then waited some more.

"It didn't work," Ruby said.

"Maybe we need more blood," Josh put in.

"I don't think so," David said. "Look!"

The blood began to crawl up the inside of the bowl, to the symbols, into the symbols. All at once the flame shot up almost to the ceiling, then was gone, leaving the room full of dense red smoke and the smell of burning hair. The lights went out, leaving the room illuminated by an eerie green flame burning around the rim of the bowl.

Ruby coughed, waved her hand in front of her face, squinting, trying to see everyone. Someone was standing next to her; she thought it was David. It wasn't. She gasped. It was a shadowy figure, a woman. There were others.

"Do you see them?" David asked in a whisper.

"Yes," Mr. Rosenfeld said.

A soft, warm breeze drifted through, smelling of moldering dirt, pushing the smoke about and revealing several hazy figures. Even as Ruby watched, more materialized, at least a dozen of them now shared the room. Their forms sharpened as they drew near, men and women. A few were nude, others in shrouds, most in garb from bygone eras: a man in a Civil War uniform with a rope around his neck, another wearing buckskin; a lady in a stately Victorian dress, another in her nightgown. Ruby recognized the two children from the attic. There was even a dog, a Labrador Retriever. Some of them appeared almost solid, others wispy things she could barely see. All of them stared at the dim flame.

"This is amazing," David whispered.

Speak to them, Ruby, Beel said from within. *It is your blood that has drawn them, they will hear you.*

Ruby opened her mouth, found no words, realized she had no idea what to say to a group of ghosts.

Ask them to help you, Beel suggested.

"Hello," Ruby said, and when she did, all eyes, every one of them, locked on her. "I . . . I . . ." The words died in her throat. *I can't do this.*

You can. You must. Now, ask them for help with your spell.

"I . . . I need your help," she stammered. "With a spell."

None of them answered, just stared at her with cold, damning looks. Ruby wanted to flee the room.

Ask them again. Do it.

Ruby swallowed hard. "I need your help . . . *please.*"

Still nothing.

David reached for one of them—a short, one-eyed man with thick mutton chops, wearing a Confederate uniform. He tried to tap the man's shoulder, but his hand slid right through, stirring the smoky form.

"I need your help," Ruby pleaded.

She waited.

"Can anyone hear me? I need your help. Just a little help, please."

"I need your help. I need your help. I need your help," the one-eyed man said in a whiney mocking tone. Several of them laughed, the sound echoing about the room.

Ruby began to tremble.

Do not let them intimidate you. Now, just talk to them . . . like living people.

Ruby sucked in a deep breath, cleared her throat. "I'm trapped. The only way for me to escape is for you to sing a song with me."

"We're all trapped," one of them spat, a bitter-faced woman with a large Afro. *"Why should we help you?"*

"Yeah," another chimed in. *"How dare you call us here."*

"It's just a song. One song."

"Here's a song," the one-eyed man said, and began to sing. *"'Kiss my ass, you silly lass. Doo-daa, doo-daa. Kiss my ass, you silly lass, doo-da, doo-da day.'"*

More laughter, it rattled around in Ruby's head.

"What's wrong with you?" Ruby snapped. "Here, see this!" She held up her hand, showing them the ring. "It's a demon ring. If I don't get it off, some fucking demon's gonna come for me. Gonna take my soul to Hell. I'm just asking you to sing one song with me. One goddamn song to save my soul! Is that really too much?"

The laughter faded, leaving the spirits glancing uneasily at each other.

"Here, let me see that." A large black man, shirtless in a pair of tattered pants, pushed forward from the back of the room. He studied the ring, then leaned in close to Ruby, inhaled deeply as though smelling her. *"You got a boogie in you."*

"Yeah," Ruby said. "I sure do."

"What's your name, little girl?"

"Ruby."

"I'm Clifford . . . and let's just say I know a thing or two about what it is to be in bondage. I believe most of us here do." He turned to the group. *"Don't we? What it is to be trapped, to be lost, to be damned."*

Several of them nodded.

"Miss Ruby, I'm gonna sing this song with you." Again, he faced the crowd, this

COLOR PLATES

BEEL

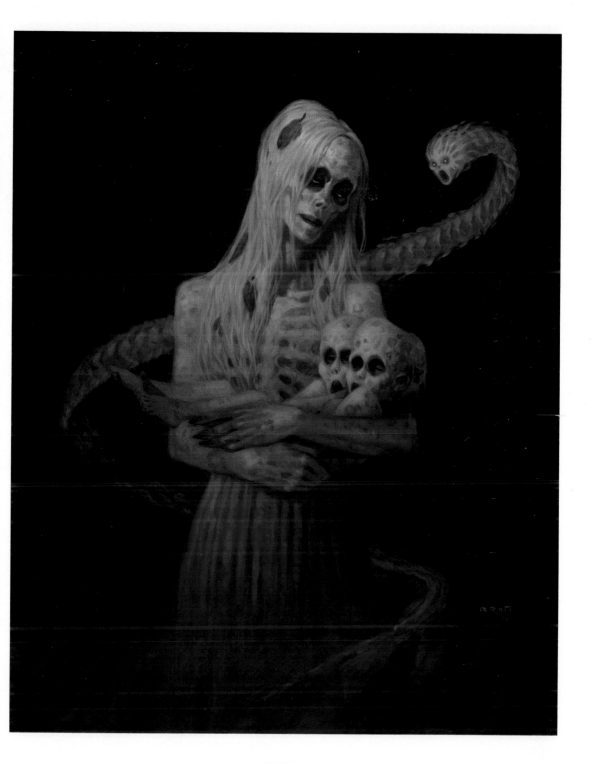

GHOUL

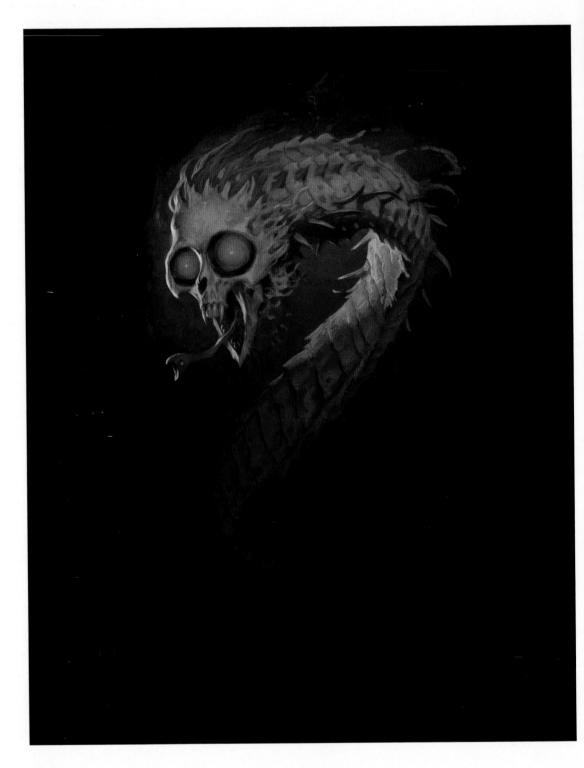

SNAKE DEMON

VUTTO DEMON

VUTTO

LORD SHEELBETH

RUBY

time Ruby noticed the ugly scars crisscrossing his back. *"How many of you gonna join me?"*

Nobody said anything at first, then the bitter-faced woman stepped forward. *"Guess I will."*

The one-eyed man shrugged. *"Fine, why the hell not."*

Four or five more of the spirits nodded.

"Okay, Miss Ruby. Let's hear this song of yours."

"Okay . . . okay, thank you. It's two parts, the part I sing to you and the part you sing back. The part you sing back, it's supposed to make a spell that gets this damn ring off."

"Go on then, sing it."

She nodded, sucked in a deep breath, and gave it a go. "'Give me some magic to set me free, give me some magic to set me free, because free is what I gotta be.'" She paused, painfully aware of how weak and wilted her voice sounded. "And this, this is the part y'all are supposed to sing back. 'We give you our magic to set you free, give you our magic to set you free, because free is what you gotta be.'"

They stared at her blankly, a few cinching up their noses as though smelling something sour.

"Whew, that's not gonna work. Sounds like a pep rally cheer." A young man with long curly hair came forward. He was wearing a fringy vest and beads, looking groovy. *"Man, no one's gonna wanna sing that. At least not with anything that amounts to any soul. And you need all the soul you can muster if you're trying to make some real magic."*

The bitter-faced lady turned. *"Scott? Is that you? Lord, it is. Are you kidding? You got some nerve showing your face here after what you done."*

He flinched. *"Hey, you think I chose to be here? She dragged me here same as you."*

The other souls gave them cutting looks.

"Don't y'all be giving me the stink eye," the woman said. *"I'm dead because of this turkey. He was stoned out of his gourd when he dashed in front of my car. I ran right over his ass then straight into an oak. Killed us both."*

"*We all got a sad story,*" Clifford said. "*So, let's not start. Okay?*"

"*Man, I just want to help the lady with her song,*" Scott said. "*Lot of folks considered me a pretty good poet when I was still kicking around.*"

"*Pfft,*" the bitter-face lady scoffed. "*You're nothin' but a junkie.*"

"*Not anymore, I'm not. Am I?*"

"*Yeah, well, you ain't a poet no more neither.*"

"*Am too. Here, Ruby, listen. Where does magic come from?*" He touched his chest. "*It comes from your heart and your soul. How about something like this?*" He started snapping his fingers, tapping his foot. "'*Give me some heart, give me some soul, going to burn, baby burn, unless you give me some heart and soul.*'"

"*It needs more groove,*" the bitter-face lady said, and started humming a melody, then to sing. Ruby was shocked by how sweet and rich her voice was.

"'*Gotta gimmie all your heart and soul, gimmie all your heart and soul . . .*'" She trailed off. "*Not so sure about 'burn, baby burn'.*"

Ruby spoke up. "'*Devil's never gonna let me go, unless you give me all your heart and soul.*'"

The woman smiled. "*There you go, honey. Now you're getting into it. And we sing it back to you. 'Gonna give you all my heart and soul, give you all my heart and soul, Devil's gonna let you go, I give you all my heart and soul.*'"

Several of the souls nodded along.

"*Alright,*" Scott said, sounding impressed. "*I can dig that. Go on, Ruby. Give that a shot.*"

Ruby cleared her throat and gave it another try.

"*Not bad, man,*" Scott said. "*I think we're getting somewhere.*"

This time almost all the souls nodded and Ruby felt a strange warmth flowing around her, through her, wondered if the song, or maybe the making of the song, was pulling them together, was somehow part of the magic. Because it was like they were on her side now.

"*One more time, Miss Ruby,*" Clifford said. "*You'll get it right this time.*"

Ruby cleared her throat and began to sing, the good feelings swimming into her, lifting her voice. Her heart and emotions, her desire to be free, all flowed into the words. She found the tune, or more like it found her, something like an old-time spiritual, but all her own. "'Gotta gimmie all your heart and soul, gimmie all your heart and soul, Devil's never gonna let me go, unless you give me all your heart and soul.'" She sang it again, then again.

Clifford began to hum along, Scott joining him, the one-eyed man and the bitter-faced lady too. Then they began to sing their part, and when they did several others joined them. *"'Gonna give you all my heart and soul, give you all my heart and soul, Devil's gonna let you go, I give you all my heart and soul.'"*

It came back round to Ruby and this time Beel lent his voice, giving the song a soft echo that was at once beautiful and eerie. The warmth, that sense of good will grew, filling Ruby up. Tears welled in her eyes.

Round they went and this time when the spirits sang, they all sang, every soul, clapping and stomping, like they were in a revival house. Round and round the little song went, David and Mr. Rosenfeld joining right in, tears on their cheeks.

This is magic, Ruby thought, and that's when she felt it, the tingling, it was in the air, almost a thing she could see.

You did it, Beel said. **The song, the spell, is yours. Do you feel it?**

Oh, yes! I do, I sure do!

Seize it! Seize the magic and free us from this ring. Do it Ruby!

But I don't know how, she thought, then realized it didn't matter, the magic, it was seeking *her.* She opened herself to it and it swirled around her, closer and closer. The symbol she'd cut into her forearm grew hot, actually began to glow, the amber light drawing the magic to it. The magic flowed into the mark, flowed into Ruby like a deep breath. And, oh Lord, such a joyous feeling blossomed within her. Had she ever felt this alive before?

The spirits continued their chorus, the melody feeding the magic.

The ring, Beel said, but he seemed far away, everything seemed far away, it was just her and the song and the magic.

The ring, he called.

Yes, the ring, Ruby thought, forcing herself to focus. She pushed the magic toward the ring. *Set me free, set me free,* she thought, willing it to free her from the ring. *Set me free!* The magic responded as though they were one. She could sense that it knew its purpose. She felt it flowing down her arm, into her hand, her finger, then it seized the ring—attacked it.

The ring convulsed, tightened. Burning pain shot up Ruby's arm, and for a horrible moment she thought it would sever her finger. Then it lessened, the heat faded. Ruby grabbed the ring, gave it a tug. It moved, just a stitch, but it moved!

It is working! Beel cried.

The ghosts sang as though lost in the song, while Ruby willed the magic and tugged at the ring.

The ring slid down to her knuckle.

Yes, Beel cried. **Almost free, Ruby! Almost free!**

It's me, Richard.

"Where are they?" I asked myself as I drove down a wide road lined with older homes, surprised at the anxiety in my voice. "It's okay, it's fine," I said. "So long as I can hear Ruby's song it's fine."

I'd last seen the black Cadillac about a mile back, when I got stuck in traffic and lost them. It was almost dark now; needed to find them again soon, while I could still see.

Why was I so obsessed? I'd never been like that. Never. In the past, if things weren't right, weren't easy, I moved on. There was always another pretty young gal down the way. It was witchcraft, right? Something supernatural? Someone, something put a spell on me? I didn't believe in such nonsense, but what in the heck else could've been going on? I didn't know. All I knew was, every time I closed my eyes, I saw her face. And it wasn't like she was some looker either—no, too intense, especially in the eyes. I liked them cute and sweet. But goddang, if I didn't want her more than anyone, or anything, ever.

The song, it was getting weaker.

"No!"

I pulled a U-turn, started back, and the song became a little stronger. I turned left after about a block and the song grew weaker. Another U-turn, then across the main road into another neighborhood, and this time, yes, the song, louder now—louder, louder, louder. I realized it was like a game of hotter-colder. I slowed down to a crawl, searching the driveways as I went. It was dark now, hard to see. Then, colder, colder, colder. I stopped, put it in reverse and winner, winner, turkey dinner! There it was! The Cadillac, sitting far up a long driveway, parked in front of an older Victorian home.

I parked on the street, just down from the drive, grabbed my backpack and checked the contents: a can of pepper spray, a hammer, handcuffs, and my revolver.

I got out, glad now for the cover of darkness, strolled up the drive. The house and the grounds were surrounded by overgrown shrubbery, plenty of places to hide. I walked up to the Cadillac, checked that no one was in it. Then worked my way around the house, looking for Ruby.

The house was dark and most of the windows too high off the ground to see into, the rest had the drapes shut tight. A dim glow lit up one of the windows in the back. I tried to peer in, but all was gloomy. A few shapes moved around and I heard what sounded like singing.

She was in there, I felt her. I tried the window and the back door, but they were both locked. I considered breaking in, then had a better plan. Simply wait for her by the car.

I returned to the Cadillac, found a spot between two large hedges, and made myself comfortable.

As I sat there listening to that terrible, beautiful song, feeling it vibrate through me, almost pulsing, I realized I had no idea when they'd be leaving, that they might even be staying the night. I tugged out my pistol, finding the weight of it comforting as my mind drifted to all the fun Ruby and I were going to share.

Good things come to those who wait, so they say, and I'd wait until the end of time, if need be.

The ring slid another notch down Ruby's finger, hanging on by her last knuckle.

She's done it! Beel thought. *This nothing of a woman has bonded with the magic, has made it her own.* He glanced around at the spirits, all putting their hearts, their very souls, into this ridiculous song. *Who would have ever thought it possible . . . that such a ragtag group as this would be able to overcome Lord Sheelbeth?* Beel knew it was mostly the spell, that Baalei Shem magic was strong, was created to combat just this kind of evil. Yet, he couldn't help but be astonished, longed to see the utter outrage that must be all over Lord Sheelbeth's face at this very moment.

There came a sudden bite from the ring; Beel, Ruby, stared at it.

Something's wrong, Beel thought.

It was then he spied a needle-thin trickle of black smoke weaving its way from the bowl to the ring—into the ring! Connecting the two. He heard them then, the worms, felt a chill roll through Ruby.

Another spindle of black smoke spun out of the bowl, another, then another, squirming about like octopus legs.

The song faltered, the ghosts staring wide-eyed. This wasn't part of the spell; they all knew it, felt it.

The ends of the smoky tendrils sprouted pods. The pods swelled, then burst open, releasing a hot gush of ruddy gas, filling the room with the smell of rot and sulfur. Beel recognized that smell, could never forget it.

No! No! he cried, pushing forward, intent on smashing the spirit bowl, on closing the door, now, before it was too late. But Ruby pulled back, terrified, causing them to fall to her knees.

A horrendous wail came from the pods as they vomited up swirling masses of smoky flesh. The flesh hit the floor in steaming clumps, looking like balls of rotting rope. They began to pulse and uncoil—snake beasts, with leathery, rotten flesh, segmented bodies long as a man's leg, topped with the cadaverous heads of monkeys and jackals, each head spiked with horns and barbs.

"Demons!" Beel shouted, as he recognized them from Lord Sheelbeth's chamber. Beel couldn't fathom what powerful magic Sheelbeth had conjured to unleash these beasts into the human plane. He looked again at the bowl and the realization, the horrible understanding of their mistake, struck him. *That is a demon bowl!* They opened a door for Lord Sheelbeth, and Lord Sheelbeth had been ready, probably waiting. And in that moment, Beel had to wonder if it had all been part of Sheelbeth's design, wondered whatever made them think they could outplay the wicked lord?

The snake demons, all six of them, unfurled and slid toward the ghosts, swimming through the air, heading toward the two children. Clifford leapt into their path. *"In the name of God, the Lord Jesus! Begone devils! Begone!"*

The demons stopped, exchanged bemused looks, began to cackle and bray, revealing mouths full of jagged teeth. They let loose a howl and attacked.

Clifford managed to grab one, to clasp its neck in his huge hands, but as he wrestled it to the ground, the others blew past. They caught one of the children, the boy, sinking their maws into his smoky flesh. The boy's face turned from fear to agony as they chewed into him, tearing out and swallowing chunks of him with every bite. To everyone's horror, the demons devoured him, just gobbled him up. There came one last pitiful wail, then the child was gone.

For one long second, everyone and everything in the room seemed frozen. Then the demons let out a prolonged howl and launched themselves into the remaining ghosts.

The room broke into bedlam as ghosts and demons tangled together, their horrible shrieks and wails echoed through the house as the demons began ripping them apart and devouring them. They piled on Clifford, quickly overwhelming the large man, tearing him to pieces. The remaining ghosts tried to flee, but were trapped in the room by the demon bowl. Three of the serpents caught the young man, Scott, chewing him up as he screamed, then the bitter-faced lady and the one-eyed man. The spirits were completely defenseless against these monsters.

"The bowl," Beel cried. "Smash the bowl!" He pushed Ruby forward, this time she complied.

Two of the snakes flew toward Ruby, striking her, knocking her to the ground. Beel realized with great horror that these were not just spiritual projections, but flesh and meat, that they could kill Ruby, *would* kill her, given the chance.

Another tendril of black smoke spiraled out of the bowl, this one much thicker than the others. A large pod began to form. Beel didn't want to guess what might be coming next.

"Smash the bowl!" he cried again, kicking and swatting at the snakes, trying to regain Ruby's feet.

Mr. Rosenfeld started forward, only to be knocked down by one of the snakes.

David grabbed for the bowl, but the moment his hand touched it, a green blast of flame shot upward, searing his hands and face, forcing him back against the far wall.

The snakes, all of them, flew to the bowl, began circling it, guarding it, snapping and snarling, filling the air with their hideous laughter. Something was sliding up the large funnel of smoke, something human in shape, and the snakes meant to see that it arrived unmolested.

"Lord Sheelbeth," Beel cried, choking on the name. "No. No! We are done!" He climbed back to Ruby's feet, glancing about, desperately seeking something, anything to smash the bowl with. Suddenly, David came running out of the gloom, clutching one of his ancient war axes. The snakes screeched and attacked, but he came on at full speed, crashing through them, bringing the ax up high and down with all his force, directly onto the bowl.

The bowl exploded with a concussive boom, shooting fiery embers in all directions.

For a moment all was smoke and confusion, leaving Ruby's head ringing, spinning. The smoke rolled away and Beel saw that the remaining ghosts were gone, realized they were free, the spell broken. And for one hopeful moment, he thought the demons were gone as well. But no, the snakes were there, writhing on the floor, and something else was on the floor—a dark figure.

The figure unfurled, slowly stood up.

The curtains, parts of the rug, some of the books, were burning now, and Beel could clearly see the figure in the growing glow of the flames. There came a moment's relief when he saw that it wasn't Lord Sheelbeth after all, but one of her demon slaves, one of the drummers, Vutto. Then the beast—a hunched, lanky, ape-like creature—set its cruel, hungry eyes on Ruby, began to drool.

We have to run! Beel said, then there came a crazy yell. It was David, his face wild with fear, rushing the demon, swinging the ax for all he was worth.

The demon managed to duck and the big blade skimmed off its hide. It howled, grabbed David by the neck, sinking it's claws into David's flesh, then slamming the man's head into the table, busting open his skull.

Ruby screamed and again it set its furious red eyes on her. It knelt and pulled the battle ax from David's dead hand.

Run! Beel cried.

Ruby made it two steps before the beast hit her from behind, knocking her to the floor. It planted its foot on her back and stood over her, grinning, the battle ax in its grip.

Mr. Rosenfeld got to his feet, snatched up the chalice of angel blood, and unscrewed the lid. The demon hefted the ax and Mr. Rosenfeld jumped over, throwing a handful of the red powder into the beast's face.

The creature dropped the weapon and clutched its eyes, squalling as it staggered away.

There was a moment when Mr. Rosenfeld looked hopeful, like they might actually get out of this room alive. Then the snakes flew at him, all six of them plowing into him, knocking the chalice from his grip.

The chalice bounced off the table, spilling the precious powder all over the burning rug. Mr. Rosenfeld seemed unable to do anything but stare as the substance went up in flames, a look of utter defeat upon his face.

"Watch out!" Ruby screamed as the snakes set to him, biting into his stomach, his neck, tearing out chunks of his flesh, ripping his throat wide open.

"NO! NO! NO!" Ruby cried, and this time Beel took control, forced her to her feet. The entire room was aflame now, filling the place with dense black smoke. Tears streamed down Ruby's face as she coughed, choked, and stumbled blindly away from the demons. She ran into a wall, found what she thought was the hallway, made it only a few steps when something snagged her arm, then bit her. She screamed and struck out, knocking one of the snakes away. Another bit at her leg and she kicked wildly, tumbling backward through a doorway.

Beel grabbed the door, slammed it shut, and the snakes began banging against the other side. They were in a bathroom, no window, no other way out. Again and again, the snakes struck the door. There came crunching and splintering along the top of the door, as the snakes began to gnaw their way through.

Beel could feel the rising heat, hear the crackling and popping of burning wood as the flames continued to consume the house. *There is no escaping the flames,* he thought. *Not for me. The flames will take Ruby, then the ring will take me.* He could almost hear Lord Sheelbeth laughing at him.

A chunk splintered inward at the top of the door and the snakes drove through. Ruby snatched up a plunger and swung it wildly, but the snakes darted past, snapping and biting. One got a hold of her ankle, another her wrist, another her arm, their bites burning like fire.

There came a tremendous crash and Beel saw the demon, Vutto, standing in the broken doorway, knew it was over, all over.

Vutto snarled and rushed Ruby, but instead of grabbing her, it grabbed two of the snakes, yanking them from Ruby. Before the snakes could react, another mouth, one set in the creature's belly, opened wide and it shoved the snakes into the toothy maw, swallowing both whole.

The remaining snakes screeched and attacked the beast. But they were no match, Vutto snatched them out of the air—chomping, biting, and finally devouring every one of them.

Beel tried to force Ruby to her feet, but before he could, Vutto lifted her, and to Beel's dismay, didn't tear her throat open; instead he carried her from the burning bathroom. The demon navigated effortlessly through the dense smoke, found a door, and suddenly there was air, sweet, fresh air.

Vutto sat Ruby gently on the grass in the backyard and only then did Beel notice how the rage was gone from his eyes, that they no longer glowed red. He saw . . . what? Empathy? Concern? From a demon? Then he noticed something else, the spot on his forehead where the angel blood had hit, had formed into a large scar in the shape of a star. It glowed dimly.

Ruby coughed and retched, spitting out a wad of black snot and saliva as she sucked clean air into her lungs.

The demon patted her on the back. "You be okay. You be okay."

Ruby flinched away.

"No, no worry. I not gonna hurt you. I am your friend." His speech was broken, guttural, the words not coming easy off his forked tongue. He also spoke with an accent, but Beel couldn't place it, German maybe.

"They're dead," Ruby sobbed. "Both of them. And you killed them!"

Vutto shook his head. "No!"

"Demon! Fucking monster! Get away from me!"

"I am not monster. I am . . ." It seemed to be searching. "I am Vutto. Vutto!"

The flames were now spreading throughout the house.

"We need to go," Beel said, pushing Ruby to her feet. Ruby stumbled toward the front yard. She was almost to the driveway when she and Beel both noticed the demon following them.

"Go away!" Ruby cried.

"I not kill them. I not kill your friends."

"You did. I saw you! Stay away from me." Ruby swooned and would've fallen, but Vutto caught her, steadied her. Ruby yanked her arm away. "Don't touch me!"

The demon flinched. "Lord Sheelbeth make me kill. I am her slave. Tell her, Beel. Tell her how Lord Sheelbeth make us slaves."

And in that moment, Beel found himself pitying this wretched creature. How similar their fates. But he looked at the scar on its forehead, knew it was only a matter of time before it healed. And when it did, what then? Would this beast hunt them down and kill Ruby? Yes, of course it would.

Beel glanced at the burning house; the angel blood was gone, there would be no more, the magic book as well. Ruby still had the taint; the ring was still on her finger. What chance did they have now against this demon or any other?

Ruby kept walking.

"Look in my eyes," Vutto pleaded. "See. I am free now. The man, he free me." He tapped the scar. "I am good now. I come with you. Yah. Keep you safe. I am friend."

"You're a monster!" Ruby snapped. "You murdered them! Get away from me!" She stormed off, leaving the demon staring after her.

"No leave me," Vutto pleaded. "Please . . . no leave me."

It's me, Richard.

I could stand it no longer, first the strange singing, then what sounded like wailing, followed by screams, all coming from inside the house.

I really didn't want to leave my hiding spot, but a terrible thought came to me. What if something happened to Ruby? If she was in trouble I *had* to save her, and believe me, the irony wasn't lost on me. For at that moment, I could think of no worse tragedy than someone murdering her before I did.

Another crash and there. What was that . . . smoke, fire?

I dashed for the front door, pistol in hand, intent on just going in, on taking her, and too bad for anyone who got in my way. I tried the door. It was locked. The flames were spreading everywhere. I jumped down the steps, heading around back, when I heard voices coming my way and ducked behind a large bush.

It was Ruby, making for the Cadillac. Perfect! I put my revolver away and drew out the pepper spray. But as she passed, I caught movement behind her and hesitated. A man was following her. He entered the glow of the flames and I forgot all about Ruby, for it wasn't a man at all, but . . . but what?

I froze, unable to move.

The thing was hunched and a good foot shorter than Ruby. A crown of curling horns sprouted from its head. It had tiny slanted eyes and scaly skin, feet like those of some monstrous lizard, and a coiling tail that turned into a snake. My mind tried to tell me it was a costume, but then I saw its other face. There, where its stomach should've been, was a gaping mouth full of jagged teeth, and upon its chest, a nose and eyes—greedy, hungry eyes. They met mine and it stopped, stared at me.

"Evil thing," it hissed at me and took a step my way. I'm sure I would've died then and there had Ruby not slammed the car door.

"No!" the creature cried, and dashed after her. "Stop!" it pleaded with both of its faces, its guttural words coming out of both of its mouths. "Please do not leave me. I beg you."

I realized I'd forgotten to breathe and sucked in a lungful of air. My knees felt weak, and I grabbed the hedge in an effort to remain standing.

Ruby started the car and the creature placed its hands on the window. "I am good. I am good egg. Tell her Beel. Tell her I am friend. Yah!"

Ruby refused to look at it. She threw the vehicle into reverse and backed out. The creature followed her all the way down to the road. Ruby put the car in drive and took off, her wheels squealing.

The creature, this demon, just stood there watching her go, its shoulders slumped. If it wasn't so terrible, it would've been pitiful.

It looked my way, both of its faces mournful, its lower lips jutting out like some lost child. It almost seemed to be seeking my help, then it ran off, racing down the street after the car.

I managed to move then, made it to the road in time to see it cutting across a yard, heading for the main road.

"What's going on?" someone asked, and I realized people were coming out of the neighboring homes. I could hear distant sirens.

"No idea," I said.

Two women came running up.

"It's on fire!" one shouted.

"That's Dr. Gold's house!" the other cried. "Lord Jesus, is he in there? Has anyone seen him?"

More folks arrived and I slipped away, no one giving me a second look, all fixated on the eerie green flames coming from the burning home.

I made it to my van, crawled in, and just sat there, trembling.

"No more," I whispered, and in that moment, I was sure this was all witchcraft, some ritual gone bad. Where else would that creature, no that demon, have come from? I clutched the wheel. "Unless, unless I'm insane." I stared at the green fire. "No, it's real. All of it."

Flashing lights zipped past, snapping me out of my daze. Police, followed by a fire engine.

I cranked up the van and drove off. I wasn't sure where I was headed, just as far away from Ruby as I could get.

I found the highway and made it about twenty miles out of town before I pulled over.

Ruby's song faded, I could no longer hear it, and in its place heartache as I'd never known, more so than after a loved one's death. I felt hollow, depleted, felt tears running down my face. "Demons . . . witchcraft, I don't care. I will have her. Nothing else matters. Nothing."

I turned around at the next exit and headed back.

"Hold on, Ruby. I'm coming for you."

TINA

A pop from somewhere near, sounding like a gunshot. Ruby opened her eyes. It was night. It took her a moment to understand she was in the back seat of a car, the Cadillac. She'd fallen asleep, passed out more like it. She felt drained, barely able to lift her head, her very bones ached. Her eyes slowly fell shut, and she began to drift off again.

Another pop, this time closer. Ruby sat up.

It was still dark, but a hint of morning gloom was edging up along the horizon. She wiped clear a spot of condensation from inside the window. She was in a lot behind what appeared to be an old graffiti-covered warehouse with bars across the windows. A few scrap cars and several piles of junk shared the lot with her. She could see shoddy apartments further down the block.

Where . . . am I? she wondered, trying to put it together. The last thing she remembered was fleeing the doctor's burning house.

Look at the ring, came a voice from within.

Ruby yelped, then realized the voice had come from inside her head, and it all came back. "Oh, fuck!" she said. "You're still here."

The ring, Beel urged.

Ruby looked at the ring and felt Beel's distress as though her own.

Her fingernails had all turned black, her fingers dark purple, the color of a deep bruise, strings of the darkness wormed their way up her wrists just beneath the skin.

Look, Beel said. *The blood . . . it is wearing off.*

She could see the metal of the ring shining out from beneath the thinning crud in several spots.

We have no more blood, he said. *No more! It was all lost in the fire.*

She didn't have to ask what that meant.

"Maybe we can find more?" Ruby said. "Maybe—"

More? Where? His tone turned acid. *Perhaps in one of your supermarkets?*

Ruby grimaced, stared out the window, watching a distant streetlight flicker. She shifted in her seat, bumped her arm, letting out a cry. She pushed up her sleeve and held her arm up into the light. She was greeted by rows of little teeth marks—angry red, and swollen. *Demon bites,* she thought and took a moment to try to get her head around that. *It's not real, none of this is real. It can't—*

It all hit her again, the searing flames, the screaming ghosts, demons, and . . . "Oh, God, *Josh*!" She saw his face, the terror as those things, those demons, tore into him. She let out a sob and the tears came spilling out. "Oh, Jesus Christ, what've I done?" She fought to get herself under control, then just gave in, just let it all out, cradling herself against the seat as she began to bawl.

She wasn't sure how long she sat there like that, but it was morning now, overcast and gray. She heard yelling nearby and peered around, sniffling and wiping her nose. She sucked in a deep trembling breath and looked at the ring, at that fucking cursed ring.

What now? she wondered, desperate to hear Josh's reassuring voice. To ask him what to do. But Josh was gone. Dr. Gold was gone. *I'm on my own,* she thought. *No, worse than alone. I've got a demon inside me.* Then, of all people, it was her mother's voice she heard: *"You need to buck up, young lady. Get your shit together."* She'd always hated it when her mother said that, but right now she knew it was right, because if she didn't, nobody would.

She looked closer at the ring. "Hey, Beel . . . maybe there's some other way. Another spell. Maybe we can find a—"

The spell book burned, everything burned. There is no chance without the book. Do you not understand? No place to run . . . to hide. Nothing to be done. We are damned. It is only a matter of time.

His utter despair flowed outward, threatening to consume her. *Damned,* she thought, and shuddered as images of shrieking demons, drowning souls in lakes of lava, flashed before her. She tried to push it from her mind, but Hell, whatever Hell was, had never felt so real, felt so near.

Her eyes found Mr. Rosenfeld's suitcase, it was on the floorboard next to her. "Oh, Pam. God, Pam . . . I'm so sorry." She needed to call Pam. *No,* she thought. *I can't . . . can't face her. Not after this. I just can't.* She felt the tears returning. *Stop it,* she told herself. *Buck up, get your shit together.*

She grabbed the suitcase, popped the latches and opened it, began digging quickly through, almost frantically, suddenly sure that there'd be something to help them. She pulled out a pair of slacks, a couple of shirts, underwear, a sweater, toothbrush, socks, flashlight, a pack of cigarettes, but no magic books, or talisman, no vials of angel blood. She kept looking, not stopping until she'd dumped everything onto the seat next to her.

She spotted an old envelope and snatched it up, tearing it open, hopeful for a spell, a lead, something. It was full of cash—hundreds and twenties, at least a thousand dollars' worth. She sighed, shoved the cash back in the envelope and then into her jacket, figured she'd send it to Pam if she ever got the chance. She then remembered she'd left home without anything, not even her wallet or purse. She took out a handful of the twenties and stuffed them into her front pocket. "I'll pay you back, Pam. Promise."

One of Josh's favorite sweaters lay on the floorboard, she picked it up, gently, almost reverently, folded it back up and laid it atop the suitcase. She patted it; it felt and smelled like him. The tears came again. "Josh. Shit . . . what am I gonna do?"

There was something shiny amongst the socks. She picked it up, once again hopeful, only to find it was just the old man's pocket knife. She flipped out the blade and stared at it for a long time, looking from the blade to the ring on her finger, back and forth, over and over.

She licked her lips. *I'll never play the bass again.* She almost laughed. Her life, her very soul, were at stake and she was worrying about playing the bass.

What are you doing? Beel asked.

"I'm out of choices," Ruby replied, and placed the blade against her finger, right below the ring. Her hand began to tremble.

It will not work, Beel said sternly. *Hear me. It will not work.*

"Why not?" she snapped.

The ring, it is alive. You know this. It's a demon of sorts. But a very stupid one, only capable of doing what it is told. Lord Sheelbeth told it to seize you, hold you. So that is what it will do . . . no matter what. You cut off your finger and it will jump to another. You cut off your hand and it will burrow beneath the skin of your belly. I have seen this more times than I can remember. It will never let you, or me, go . . . not until either Lord Sheelbeth orders it to, or the spell is broken.

"Why should I believe you? Maybe I'm your only chance and you don't want to be left behind in the ring."

Go ahead . . . cut it off. Why should I care? You and all God's chosen people are selfish, closer to the demons than the angels. I will never understand why God graced such as you with his blessings instead of the shedim.

"You're lying," Ruby said, and pressed the blade into her skin. A drop of blood pooled and, to her horror, the ring sucked it down. She felt it pulse, then clutch harder, biting into her flesh. She let out a cry and yanked the blade away. Slowly, the ring let up.

"Fuck you!" Ruby shouted at the ring and stabbed the knife into the seat next to her. "Fuck you!" she cried. *"Fuck you!"*

Maybe it will be better if we do as Lord Sheelbeth tells us, Beel said.

"What?"

Maybe if we scrub the blood from the ring. Maybe then at least she will take some mercy on us. Maybe not send us into the fire.

"No! No fucking way I'm gonna just hand my soul over to this Lord Fuckass. What's wrong with you?"

It is better than burning. Anything is better than burning.

Ruby shook her head. "The song, the spell is mine now. David said so. We just need to find some more spirits or ghosts to sing it. Right? I mean the taint, it's drawing them to us. Right? So it shouldn't be too hard. Maybe we can find another spirit bowl . . . like in a museum or something. Or even some book on how to do a séance. Hell, even a fucking Ouija board might do the trick. We gotta try? We gotta at least try."

There came no response.

"Beel, you there?" She knew he was, could feel him brooding.

Still no response.

"Hey! I'm talking to you!"

You want to open more doors? After what happened. You feel that is a good idea?

It was drizzling and Ruby stared at the raindrops gathering on the windshield, trying to come up with something that might make sense, anything. She started humming absently, singing softly to soothe herself. It was the song, the magic song. She didn't even realize it at first.

"'Gotta give me all your heart and soul, gimmie all your heart and soul, Devil's never gonna let me go, unless you give me all my heart and soul.'"

The song calmed her, cleared her head a bit. It seemed just singing it brought a touch of the magic back. She felt warmth in her arm where she'd cut the symbol into her flesh, surprised to see that the wound had healed, leaving a dark scar.

"Hey, Beel. You said that Lord Motherfucker uses souls to sing her spells. Those souls . . . aren't they human souls?"

He didn't answer.

"They are, aren't they? And aren't these the same souls everybody has? I mean living people. Gotta be, right?" She nodded to herself. "Then why can't we just get some people to sing it? Wouldn't that be the same? I mean, okay, maybe we needed the ghosts and spirits to make the song, to bond it to me and all. But that part's done. So why can't we just get some people to sing it now? Am I missing something here?"

She sensed some interest from Beel and this encouraged her. "Maybe we can just hire a choir." She thought of the cash. "A whole fucking choir to sing the damn thing." She was getting excited.

I do not think it possible, Beel said. *Lord Sheelbeth has hundreds of trapped souls that give her her power. More, they are not just singing, not just absently repeating words. No, their song comes from their hearts, they are singing out of love, or maybe their great fear. Either way, there is passion in their song, there is heart. Can you pay a choir to give you their heart?*

Ruby let out a frustrated sigh, went back to staring out the window, and again found the song on her lips, surprised at how catchy it was.

She sat bolt upright. "Beel!" she cried. "I got it!"

What now?

"You said sing it from the heart, to put emotion and soul into it . . . *passion*."

Yes.

"The song. We just make a song out of it! A real song. Play it to a crowd. Get them to like it. Don't you see? If they dig it, they'll sing along. Sing it with heart and soul. Get the magic flowing!"

It will not work, he said.

"Why not? Can you tell me with certainty that it won't work? Can you?"

He didn't reply for a long, long moment. Finally, he said, *Perhaps there is some small chance.*

"Yes!" she exclaimed, her voice full of excitement. "A band. We just need to get a band together. And I've got the cash to hire—" She blinked. "Wait." She laughed, slapped the back of the seat. "Where's my head? I already got a band." She slapped the seat again. "Tina and me. Hell yeah!" Her heart was racing. "The Night Mares!"

Ruby double-checked the map as she drove across town. She'd never been in such a big city before and kept getting lost. She found Atlanta to be composed mostly of endless suburbs, old and new, one neighborhood melting into the next. She'd passed at least two sprawling malls, vast multilevel structures that seemed like cities unto themselves. But as she neared the heart of the town, the looming buildings took her breath away, seeming impossibly tall, and despite everything, she had to pull over just to take them in.

Ruby watched a young black man busking on the corner, while panhandlers hassled sharply dressed business folks as they hurried along their way. Taxis and buses barreled past as food carts and trinket sellers set up shop. Smells of fancy restaurants and bus fumes mixed in the air. The energy and vibe were like nothing she'd ever experienced in Enterprise. It made her sad, because she knew how exciting this would all be to her if one of her best friends hadn't just been murdered, if she didn't have a demon breathing down her neck.

Ruby continued on, leaving the large buildings behind and heading into a neighborhood of small, older homes. Plenty of trees lined the streets, mostly sprawling oaks. Several of the houses were painted in bright colors; she passed one with a tie-dyed Deadhead flag, another with a peace sign painted on the mailbox. She felt sure this must be the Little Five Points area that Tina had written her about, and judging by some of the colorful folks she'd seen, decided it must be the artier part of town.

She slowed down, reading mailbox numbers, stopping when she came to a craftsman badly in need of paint and a new roof. It looked like no one there knew how to do yard work either—the shrubs were overgrown and the yard and driveway were covered in wet leaves.

Ruby had found Tina's address in the phone book, the only Tina Tang listed. She pulled into the drive and cut the engine, then reached into the back, digging through Mr. Rosenfeld's things until she found his pack of cigarettes. She tore off the plastic, slid one out, and lit it with shaking hands.

"Guess I'm not quitting today," she said, and took a deep drag, then another, hoping the nicotine would calm her nerves. She sat there a long time, watching the drizzle gather on the windshield, trying to breathe normally again, trying not to think about Dr. Gold and Mr. Rosenfeld, about Hell. She felt the tears trying to return. *Not now,* she told herself. *Gotta get through this first. Can cry all you want later.*

She stubbed out the cigarette and left the car, headed up the walkway and onto the porch. She must've stood staring at the buzzer for a full minute. It'd been over two years since she'd last seen Tina, and their final get-together hadn't gone so well. That was when Tina accused Ruby of backing out on her. Said Ruby was just using Billy as an excuse. Went so far as to tell Ruby that she was all talk, that she'd never amount to anything because she was a coward.

Ruby couldn't remember what she'd said to Tina after that, only that it had been bad. The awful kinds of things only best friends can dish out—nobody can hurt you like the ones you love. She did know that she regretted every word. She also knew a lot of what Tina had said was true, and that of course was why it had stung so bad.

They'd written a couple of times since, but neither had apologized, both keeping well away from the things said that day, dry letters that were more like chronicles than notes between best friends.

And here I am, Ruby thought. *About to ask her to fight a demon lord with me. How about that? And why not, isn't that what friends are for?* She let out a sigh. *This should go well.*

Ruby pushed the buzzer. No ring, no chimes. Maybe it was broken. She knocked, waited, knocked again. Finally, she peered in through the window; someone was sleeping on an old tattered sofa. She tried the door; it was unlocked. She let herself in.

"Hello?" she called, walking into the living room. There were tie-dyed sheets serving as curtains, a couple of black-light posters on the walls, and an armless mannequin in the corner. The sparse furniture looked to have been scavenged, including a coffee table made from milk crates. Every surface was covered in overflowing ashtrays and crumpled beer and soda cans. The place smelled like macaroni and cheese.

"Hello?"

Whoever was under the blanket didn't answer.

"Tina?" She shook the person.

"What?" came a man's muffled voice.

Ruby jumped back.

The covers slid down and a young man with a rat's nest of bleached spiky hair stared up at her with bleary eyes.

"Oh, fuck! Sorry, man. I'm looking for Tina. Is she here?"

He frowned at her, jabbed a thumb toward the rear of the house, and pulled the blanket back over his head.

It was then that Ruby caught a guitar riff coming from somewhere, maybe below her. She followed the sound, looking for a door down into a basement. She tried one in the kitchen, but it was to the pantry, tried another, and was greeted with a loud blast of reverb. She smiled and headed down.

Tina was standing with her back to Ruby, wearing only an oversize Ramones T-shirt and her undies, her long black hair disheveled like she'd just crawled out of bed. She had her guitar slung low, strumming hard, fast. It sounded raw, it sounded good. Tina began to sing, belting out an angry yowl. Ruby couldn't quite catch the lyrics, something about a wild heartbroken feline. The chorus was, run cat run.

When she came to the chorus again, Ruby joined in.

Tina jerked around and for a second, Ruby felt sure her friend was going to clobber her with the guitar. Then Tina's eyes grew wide. She shook her head, blinked. "Ruby?"

Ruby nodded, trying to read Tina's face. "Hey."

Tina narrowed her eyes and stared at Ruby, not quite glaring, but close.

Ruby blew out a breath of air; she could see this was about to get bad.

"I'm mad at you," Tina said.

"I know."

Tina stared at her a moment longer, then the corner of her mouth twitched upward. Slowly, her smile, her crazy smile, lit up her face. *"Ruuuby!"* she cried, tossing the guitar aside and leaping for her. She seized Ruby in a bear hug, lifting her up off the ground, spinning round until they crashed into the wall.

"Tina, hell, stop it! You're gonna kill us both!"

Tina let go, grabbing Ruby's shoulders, looking her up and down. "My God, Ruby! It's you! It's really you? I can't believe it's you . . . and, and that you're *here*. Right *here* in my room. Oh, Ruby baby, you made it! You finally made it! What? How? Oh, never mind. Just hug me, girl!"

Tina hugged her again, harder than the first time; she smelled of sweat, stale coffee, and Aqua Net and it was as sweet as honey to Ruby. Ruby hugged her back, hard as she could, and for a moment forgot all about the evil festering inside her.

Tina stepped back. "Let me look at you. Lord, what happened to your hair?"

Ruby started to reply and realized there was no easy way to answer without telling everything, and she wasn't ready for that, not yet. "You don't wanna know."

"I sure as hell do. I wanna know everything going on with you, babe." She headed over to her fridge. "Can I get you something? Some tea? A beer?"

"Shit, Tina, it's like eight a.m."

"Is it?" She glanced at a clock over her bed. "Wow, it is. Man, I woke up around three this morning with a song going around in my head. You ever do that? Had to work it out or go nuts."

"Yeah, sounded real good to me."

"Thanks, Ruby," Tina said with a big smile, and began digging through a pile of clothes. She pulled out a rumpled pair of tight black jeans and tugged them on. Tina had let her hair grow out and it was almost to her rump now—straight, shiny, and raven black. She'd cut her bangs into a type of widow's peak; it looked wicked on her, accenting her thin, painted-on brows.

Tina's dad was first-generation Korean, and her mother, a tall German lady. Tina got her dark brooding eyes and wide cheekbones from her father, her strong jaw and height from her mom. And to say that she stood out in a school with only four other Asian kids was an understatement. But Tina was just unusual, period: the way she dressed, walked, the way she cackled when she laughed, how she tended to make hooting noises in the hallway for no apparent reason. And that she was nearly six feet tall didn't help her to fit in any, either. So, she . . . *didn't*. She just gave anyone who gave her shit the good old middle finger and went on her way.

174

Henry Atkins, one of Stacy's crowd, had once made the mistake of calling her "Tina Poontang." Tina, whose father had been teaching her Tae Kwon Do since she was three, roundhouse kicked him in the throat. After that, no one, absolutely no one, called her that again, at least not where she could hear. Well, that wasn't entirely true. Ruby called her that when they got after each other, particularly when Tina called her "Ruby Fucker" instead of Ruby Tucker. But then, they had an endless bag of shit names for each other, almost an art form between them.

Tina went over to a small fridge, popped it open, pulled out a carton of milk. "Okay, then, how about some Cheerios?"

Ruby didn't feel like eating, but knew she should. "Okay."

Tina fixed them both a bowl and they took a seat on the rug and began to eat.

The basement apartment smelled of incense and peppermint. Ruby savored the scents as she glanced about at all the potted plants, dripping lace and black-light posters, bones, rubber bats, and books, so many books. Tina had always been a voracious reader; from Shelley to Tolkien, she inhaled books the way others inhaled air.

A drum kit sat in the corner, a banner hanging over it with the words THE BATTZ painted across it.

"The Battz . . . that your band?"

"One of 'em . . . or it was. We sorta had a falling-out last week. Okay, we had a major fight. So, not sure where things stand. Shame, good band. We have, or had, kind of a Cramps vibe, only a little harder, a little meaner. We even opened for the Gun Club once, can you believe it?"

Ruby stopped chewing. "Really? Wow, *really*?"

"Yeah, at the 688. It was crazy, Jeffery Lee asked Jane—Jane from my band—if he could borrow her guitar. Said his was messing up. Jane was beside herself, y'know, Jeffery Lee Pierce playing her guitar and all. Then," Tina laughed, spitting out a Cheerio. She covered her mouth. "That twerp, he set her guitar on fire right there onstage."

"What?"

"Yeah, nothing wrong with his guitar, he just wanted a prop to burn, part of his performance. Guess he didn't wanna burn his own." She laughed again. "So, burned up Jane's instead. Can you believe that?"

Ruby shook her head.

"Oh, man, Jane went bat-shit on his ass. Ended up chasing him out of the club. He didn't come back either. We—" Tina stopped. "Hey, what's up with your hand?" She squinted. "Oh, fuck, Ruby that ain't good. Let me see that." She set down her bowl and reached for Ruby.

Ruby tucked her hand under her arm, out of sight.

Tina gave Ruby a troubled look. "Ruby, babe . . . what's going on?"

Ruby's eyes began to water. "I'm screwed, Tina. So *screwed*."

"Talk to me, Ruby. Whatever it is, we can fix it. Together we're unstoppable."

Ruby sucked in a deep breath, fighting back the tears. "I, I . . . I got the Devil in me."

"Wait . . . you're preggers?"

"What?" Ruby shook her head, almost laughed. "No . . . a demon, I'm *possessed*, Tina."

"Drugs? Shit, Ruby are you hooked on junk? Fuck! What did I tell you about that?" Tina would never turn down a beer with a friend, but drugs had always been a big NO with her. She didn't care if folks were doing drugs around her, but when it came to her, or to someone she really cared about, she could be downright militant. The two of them had almost come to blows on more than one occasion over Ruby just smoking pot.

"No, Tina, you're not hearing me. Not drugs. I mean *possessed*. Y'know, like in that movie, *The Exorcist*."

Tina starred at her for a long minute. "Ruby, tell me honestly, now. Did you stop taking your medication again?"

Ruby let out a sigh and then, starting from the beginning, told the whole tragic tale.

"Ruby, baby," Tina said softly, the way you would speak to a child. "Hey, sounds like you certainly been through some shit. Now, I'm not saying I don't believe you, but, babe, how can you be sure it ain't all in your head? At least some of it? Y'know, the last time you stopped with the meds, you had some pretty crazy hallucinations, waking dreams and such. Remember when you thought there were tribbles in the room with us?"

Ruby groaned. "No, it's not like that."

"How can you be sure?"

"Because," Beel said, speaking through Ruby's lips. His voice deep, throaty, with that strange echo. "I am the proof. I am the Beel she spoke of. What Ruby says is all true."

Tina's mouth fell open. "Whoa . . . how'd you do that? That some kinda trick?"

"It's not a trick," Ruby said, showing Tina the ring; most of her hand was purple and black now.

Tina winced. "Oh, shit. *Ruby!*"

Ruby slid up her sleeve, revealing the symbol on her forearm, and the angry teeth marks left by the snake demons.

"Oh, honey, you need to take care of that." Tina jumped up, left the room, returning a moment later with a warm washcloth and some iodine. She helped Ruby take her jacket off and began washing the small wounds.

Ruby smirked. "So, you think that iodine works against demon bites?"

"Sure, says so right on the label."

Ruby tried to laugh, but it sounded more like a whimper.

"Oh, Ruby. What've you got yourself into?"

"I need your help, Tina. I don't think I've got much time left."

"I'll do anything for you, baby. You know that. Just—"

"We need to make a band."

"A . . . *band*?"

Ruby told her the plan, explaining in detail about the song, how they needed to get as many people to sing along as possible.

Tina listened to the whole pitch earnestly, sat there for a long minute before speaking. "Ruby, this is a lot to take in all at once. Now, you know me. I'm not one to bullshit. Gonna tell you straight . . . I'm not sure what I believe right now.

But here's what I know. Something's going on in your head, demon or otherwise, and I think nothing could be better for you than getting up onstage and howling out some songs. Best therapy for the soul there is.

"So, guess what I'm saying is, it doesn't matter if I believe you or not. What matters, girl, what *really* matters, is that I believe *in* you. You hear what I'm saying?

"And there's something else." Tina stood up, walked over to her bed and picked up her guitar, sliding the strap over her shoulder. "It's not like you need to twist my arm here. We've been dreaming of this day since high school." She strummed the strings.

"So, let's make some goddamn noise." She tore into a riff, the distorted sound bouncing off the walls.

Ruby dabbed at her eyes, feeling hope, feeling love, feeling like she wasn't alone.

All of a sudden Tina stopped. "Hey, *heeeey*! You know what'd be a kick?"

Ruby shook her head.

Tina jumped over to her dresser, tugged out a ragged spiral notebook and held it up. Ruby recognized it right away—bright red cover with the words THE NIGHT MARES scribbled in ball-point pen. Below it, Ruby's drawing of two skel-etal horses in a yin-yang shape, like they were chasing each other's tails. It was their band book from high school and she knew what was in it—all their awkward attempts at song making.

Ruby laughed. "You're not suggesting we play those?"

"I know, a lot of doofy stuff in here. About what you'd expect from a couple of punk rock wannabes. But we're gonna need some songs quick, and I read through this recently, and there's some pretty good starts. At least two or three I think we can turn into something."

She opened the notebook, flipped toward the back, handed it to Ruby. "Remember this one?"

Ruby smiled. The title was "Skank Howl." It made her think of Stacy, the time she called Tina and her the Skank Sisters in Mrs. Wilson's English class, right in front of the whole room. And how utterly confused Stacy had looked when instead of getting upset, Tina and Ruby had laughed their asses off, because by then they were so far out of Stacy's reach, they just didn't give a fuck. Girls like Stacy didn't understand not giving a fuck, especially about what other folks thought of them. So, she'd just kind of stood there, lost. Meanwhile, Tina and Ruby had gone home that day and wrote the song.

Tina picked up her old bass and brought it over to Ruby. "You ready?"

"Hang on. Do you have an old glove, some scissors?"

"Do I have an old glove?" She laughed. "Look in that top drawer. Scissors there in the tray."

There were dozens and dozens of gloves in the drawer. Ruby dug out a red dress glove. "Can I have this?"

"You betcha."

"Just thinking it might be good to keep the ring covered, so I don't rub off any more of the blood." Ruby clipped the fingertips off the glove, then slipped it over the ring. "There, that's better." She picked up the bass.

"Ready?"

"Think so."

Tina started in, looping around the intro, giving Ruby time to come in.

Ruby swallowed. Started to hum, letting her fingers find the song. She cleared her throat and began to sing.

"That's it, baby," Tina called, and joined her.

They stumbled through the song, missing chords and screwing up lyrics, but it felt good, so damn good. *God,* Ruby thought, *been forever since we played this, yet seems like yesterday.* Then, little by little, they began to find their groove. They played the song through six times. Each one a little tighter than before, and for the second time that morning, Ruby forgot about the ring.

Tina stopped. "Not bad. Right? Especially for eight a.m."

Ruby laughed. "Yeah, hell yeah."

"We can do this, right?"

Ruby nodded.

Tina let loose a howl. "You can run, but you can't hide . . . the Night Mares are coming to town!"

Beel barely heard them, he was within, as far within as he could go. They, the two women, were arguing with a man, the one from upstairs that'd been sleeping on the couch. Something about playing drums.

Beel didn't care, not about Ruby's ploy, this band of hers, it was all folly. There was no chance of it working, none. What he cared about was the song, not the one Ruby was trying to play, but that of the worms, Lord Sheelbeth's song. It was growing louder.

Why am I fighting this? Beel wondered. *I am but making things worse for myself, digging my own grave as they say. The old man is dead after all. Lord Sheelbeth has won. It is only a matter of days, perhaps hours, before the ring will take me.*

Flames filled Beel's vision.

Perhaps what Sheelbeth said was true: with the last wizard gone, the magic book burned, there is nothing left to stop her, that she can truly break back through into this world.

Beel pondered this.

But only with my help. She cannot do it alone. I need but wait until Ruby is asleep, scrub the ring, and be done. And if I help Lord Sheelbeth . . . she has promised to free me.

He tried to recall if she'd promised his freedom before, searching his memory. She had spoken of freedom, yes, but *promised*? No. She had never actually promised before. He wondered if he could trust her, wasn't sure, only knew he'd never known Lord Sheelbeth to go back on her word.

And there was more to all this. Did he not still owe her a debt?

No, not after the fire. I owe her nothing after that.

He reminded himself that it was Lord Sheelbeth who had saved him from Satan's demons, from their endless torture, from being forced to do their bidding for an eternity.

Listen to yourself. Is that not what Lord Sheelbeth is doing now?

It is, he thought, and found it sad, how she couldn't see this. Or if she did, turned the blind eye. *It is easy to justify others' sacrifices when they are serving your own needs.*

He had to admit that it wasn't how it started, though. No, at first he'd been grateful for the opportunity to repay her, to serve her. It gave him purpose, a feeling of belonging, even. She made her ring, her flesh, his home, allowed him to be part of her in a way that was more than any other soul or god had ever done. And together they were lethal—him in the form of the ring, some shadowy spider scuttling into the camps of their enemies, possessing them, conquering them, stealing their souls.

And Beel had been delighted to bring this blight down upon God's chosen children, these selfish monkeys, especially this new breed of men, these Christians. How he had thrilled in destroying their churches, destroying God's house, anything to get back at God for forsaking him so.

But there came a day when he grew tired of their pain and sorrow, because in the end, this wasn't his nature. He longed to roam the forest once more as some great cat or colorful songbird. And that was the day he found out he wasn't free.

When confronted, Lord Sheelbeth told him that she needed him more than ever to fight the mounting tide of Christians and Muslims and so many others. When he tried to leave anyway, he discovered he was trapped, tethered to the ring.

Lord Sheelbeth said it was for Beel's own good, that God's servants were hunting him, that her kingdom was his only place of refuge, that as much as it pained her, she must forbid him leave for his own sake.

And it turned out what she said was true, they were hunting me . . . hunting us all. So why should I not trust her now?

The fire, Beel could almost feel it.

All is a gamble.

And the girl, what of her? It would mean her death; more, her soul would be Sheelbeth's forever.

What of it? Would she not sell me to Lord Sheelbeth for her freedom? Of course she would. Would send me back to Hell this very second if she could. Be glad of it. She has nothing but loathing for me. She is but one more of God's selfish monkeys. I owe her nothing.

And there was something else here. He'd lied to her about freeing herself by cutting the ring from her finger. At least partially lied. True, it had never worked in the past, but this was different, the ring was covered in angel blood, it was numb, unable to do more than cling on in some kind of stubborn stupor. Beel felt sure if Ruby cut off the ring, she *could* escape. Only . . . only he'd be sucked back into the ring as sure as if she had died.

No, I will not tell her. Never tell her. I owe her nothing.

Beel felt something, a disturbance, drawing near. He came forward, peering out through Ruby's eyes.

"C'mon, Mark," Tina said, holding out the drumsticks. "Just a couple of shows. Until we find someone else. *Pleeease.*"

"Nope." The man looked tired and hungover and like he wanted to be anywhere but here.

"When's the last time I asked you a favor?"

"You ask me favors all the time," he grumbled. "Speaking of which, where's rent? You owe me for last month as well."

"Yeah, yeah, let's just keep on track here a minute. Stay focused, Mark, okay."

Mark rolled his eyes. "I thought Pete was your drummer. Why can't he do it?"

"I told you, Pete's not speaking to me at present."

"Well, why not?"

"Because none of your damn business, that's why not."

"Because maybe you're a hard-ass bitch?"

Tina grinned. "Maybe. But how about we not let that get in the way. Here, I tell you what, I'll try to be a much nicer bitch if you play drums for us. How about that?"

Mark threw up his hands and headed up the stairs.

"Please, Mark, please. Pretty please! Mark, *c'mon.*"

"No, no, no," he called back down. "And you still owe me rent." He shut the door.

Tina let out a big huff of air. "Drummers are hard to come by. Everyone wants to be Keith or Mick, no one wants to be Charlie."

There came a thump from outside. It was a walk-out basement, and Tina and Ruby looked over at the patio door.

Ruby gasped. "Oh, shit! Vutto!"

Vutto had his face pressed against the glass, peering in at them from beneath a blanket that he was wearing like a cloak. The blanket looked as though it'd been drug through the gutter. They could see his creepy yellow eyes, his wide snout, a hint of pointy teeth, but fortunately the rest of him was covered.

"Vutto?" Tina asked. "You mean from your story?"

"Yeah."

"You mean he's real?"

"He's real, Tina. I am sorry as shit to say, it's all real."

Vutto tapped the glass, looking in at them like a kicked puppy.

"Get out of here!" Ruby shouted. "Go away!"

Vutto slid the door open and stepped inside.

"Shit, Tina, do you not lock *any* of your doors?"

Tina leapt over to her bed, yanked up a baseball bat, reared back, ready to attack.

"No, Tina!" Ruby said sharply, stepping between them. "Do *not* do that. Just stay back. *Stay back!*" Beel could feel her fear.

"Hello, Ruby, it is me, Vutto. Your friend. Do you remember me?"

"Yes, Vutto," Ruby said, speaking gently, but sternly; she was trembling. "I do. Now listen to me. You're scaring everyone. You have to go."

"But . . . I can help. Yah."

Beel noticed the star-shaped scar on Vutto's forehead, the one from the angel blood. It was still solid, but it looked a bit smaller and it no longer glowed. *It's healing,* he thought, *and when it does . . . he will kill Ruby. Lord Sheelbeth has us one way or another.*

"No, you *can't* help us," Ruby said.

"Yah, I can. I show you." Vutto strolled over to the drum kit and took a seat.

Ruby and Tina exchanged a horrified look.

Vutto shrugged off the blanket. Like most demons, he had the ability to change his appearance to some degree, and for now he'd hidden the face and mouth on his gut. He was still more demon than human, but far less menacing. He tapped a snare with one of his talon-like claws, then each of the drums in the kit, popping the cymbals. He cocked his head, listening to each sound, his brows tight. He started thumping them, making a racket, but slowly the racket became a beat, then a rhythm. He picked up the tempo, using his claws like sticks, and his palms on the toms, the way conga drummers do. The result was a powerful, primitive sound.

Vutto stopped and smiled at Ruby. "See, I *can* help you. I play drums for you. Yah. I play drums very good."

"You gotta get it out of here," Tina said, clutching the bat, her back pressed against the far wall.

"I'm sorry, Vutto," Ruby said, still speaking gently. "But it won't work. There's no way."

"I am your friend," Vutto said. "Remember how I save you from demons and fire? Yah. I will keep you safe. I am good egg."

Ruby shook her head.

Vutto dropped to his knees, clasped his hands together. "I begging you. I do not want to go back to Hell. We need each other. Together we can break spell."

He's right, Beel said from within. **Whatever chance is left will be better with the demon working with us than not. He will keep the other wicked things at bay.**

"*What, no! He's a demon!*" Ruby replied from within.

There are many kinds of demons. They are not all wicked. He just wants the same thing all of us do. To be free.

"*Don't you think folks gonna notice a friggin demon onstage?*"

Dress him up. A wig, a hat, sunglasses, a coat.

"*No, I don't want him,* it, *around me.*"

I do not believe you have much choice in that. He is not going anywhere. And it will be good to keep an eye on him as well. To have warning should the blood wear off on him. Might save your life.

What Beel didn't say was how the pain and desperation in Vutto's eyes mirrored his own heart, how he knew only too well what it was to fear Lord Sheelbeth and her fire.

Ruby was silent. Beel could feel her anxiety, almost hear her debating with herself. Finally, she took a deep breath, went to Tina's closet, pulled out a felt hat, a leather jacket, then plucked up a pair of cat-eye sunglasses and red feather boa from off the vanity.

"What're you doing?" Tina asked.

"Just hang on."

Ruby handed Vutto the jacket. "Try this."

"Oh, hell no!" Tina cried. "I know what you're doing and it ain't gonna fly!"

Vutto's face lit up. He stood and pulled on the jacket.

"Aw, yuck! Damnit, Ruby, I don't want it touching my things!" Tina looked furious, but stayed back.

Ruby set the hat atop Vutto's head, covering his horns, then slipped the sunglasses in place. Finally, she wrapped the boa around the demon's neck, leaving only a small bit of Vutto's lips and nose showing. Ruby glanced over at Tina, shrugged. "Might work?"

"No, no it won't. And I'll tell you why. Because I'm not gonna be anywhere near that . . . that *thing*! It's a *demon* for Christ's sake!" Tina was trembling. "Ruby, please. Get it out of here! *Now!*"

Vutto put out his hands and took a few steps toward Tina. "I am good egg."

Tina raised the bat. "Stay the *fuck* away from me!"

Vutto knelt before her, clasped his hands together. "I am Vutto," he said, speaking directly to Tina. "I want to be your friend. Yah. Please be my friend." He lowered his head, touching his forehead to the ground, just like Beel had seen him do before Lord Sheelbeth.

"No! No way!"

"Please be my friend. Please."

Tina met Ruby's eyes. "Fuck, Ruby. Really? We're gonna do this? Fuck!"

"I don't know what else to do."

"I've done plenty of stupid over my life, but this sure takes the stupid cake." Tina tapped Vutto with the tip of the bat. "Get up. Go on. Get up and get away from me."

Vutto looked at her. "You be my friend? Yah?"

Tina still looked terrified, keeping the bat up, ready to swing. "Sure . . . yeah, okay. Just so long as you stay away from me. Is that understood? Now *get* away from me."

Vutto stood up, beaming. "We are all friends now."

"No," Ruby said. "Not yet. You gotta promise me something first. You have to swear you won't hurt anyone. Swear it."

"I swear not hurt anyone . . . unless they are bad."

"No, Vutto. Anyone at all."

He frowned. "Okay, I swear."

Beel found himself smiling inside at the very idea of a demon, any demon, keeping a promise.

"Okay," Ruby said. "We're getting close. I can feel it. Let's try again." By *feel it,* she meant the magic. It was their sixth or seventh go at the spell song, and that last time Ruby swore she felt something in the air—just a tingle, but something more than wishful thinking.

Tina took a second to tune her guitar, keeping a wary eye on Vutto. Even after playing all morning, she refused to turn her back on the demon even for a second.

"We need a few more verses," Ruby said.

"Yeah," Tina agreed. "It's not much more than a repeating chorus right now. How about a couple of lines about the Devil chasing after you."

"Devil band," Vutto sang. "Devil get you if he can."

Ruby nodded, shut her eyes, humming the tune, playing with the words. "'Devil on my hand, Devil in my band, Devil's gonna get me if he can.'"

"There you go," Tina said.

Ruby kept going. "'Devil's watchin' me squirm, Devil's watchin' me burn . . .'"

"'Devil's in my belly like a wiggle worm,'" Tina threw in, and laughed.

Ruby grinned. "I like that! Then back into the chorus, because the spell is all in the chorus. We just need something catchy to tie it together, y'know, to get folks singing along."

They bounced around several more verses and lines, until finally Tina held up her hands. "C'mon, let's just try it again. See what we got."

Ruby started humming the tune, leading the way, tapping out the rhythm on her bass. Tina's guitar fell in, and then Vutto added the beat. They'd been keeping it simple, but Tina stepped on her fuzz box, injecting some heavy distortion, kicking the song into a dreamy, immersive haze of buzzing, grinding guitar chords. Vutto grinned and upped the tempo, hands flying over the toms as he slapped out his primal beat. Ruby added some gloomy bass and began to sing, to really let loose with her tragic wailing voice, and the whole song melted into a melodic, psychedelic groove.

"Devil on my hand, Devil in my band.
Devil's gonna take me down any way he can.
Only your spell, will keep me out of Hell.
Gotta gimmie all your heart and soul, gimmie all your heart and soul.
Gonna burn like a demon bowl, unless you give me all your heart and soul.

Gonna give you all my heart and soul, give you all my heart and soul.
Burnin' like a demon bowl, I give you all my heart and soul.

Devil's watchin' me squirm, Devil's watchin' me burn.
Devil wants me in his belly like a wiggle worm.
C'mon, set me free, cast out the evil in me.

Gotta gimmie all your heart and soul, gimmie all your heart and soul.
Devil's never gonna let me go, unless you give me all your heart and soul.

Gonna give you all my heart and soul, give you all my heart and soul.
Devil's gonna let you go, I give you all my heart and soul.

Gotta set me free, gotta set me free.
Free all the evil in me, evil in me, evil in me, evil in me . . ."

Goose bumps crawled along Ruby's arms; she shut her eyes and let the music take her.

They'd worked their way through "Skank Howl" a couple of times, just to warm up, and it had gone okay, the song sounded decent, but nothing like this.

She came round to the chorus again, and they all joined in, all but Beel. Vutto singing along, sounding like . . . like a howling demon.

Warmth blossomed in Ruby's chest, vibrating out along her very bones, the vibrations becoming part of the song, flowing through her, out of her. *Magic,* she thought. It wasn't like when the spirits sang with her, but it was there. The scar, the symbol, on her arm began to tingle.

They didn't stop when the song came to an end, but looped right back into the start, going round and round, the chorus growing ever more feverish with each pass. Ruby no longer felt her fingers, it was as though the bass was playing itself. She began to drift, feeling weightless.

There came a loud *twang,* followed by Tina shouting *"Shit!"* and the song ended abruptly.

No, Ruby thought, not wanting the song to ever stop. She opened her eyes, saw that Tina had broken a string.

"Holy cow!" Tina exclaimed. "Look at my arms, man. Goose bumps all over. Fuck, even my nipples are hard."

Ruby swayed, grabbed hold of the wall to steady herself.

"You okay?" Tina asked.

"Oh, yeah . . . more than okay. That felt amazing."

"Hell yeah, it did. Man, can't wait to lay that on some folks. People gonna lose their flippin' minds. Swear, I can still feel it vibrating in my chest." She slipped off the guitar and headed up the stairs.

"Hey, where you going?"

"Just give me a sec. Need to call someone."

Ruby sucked in a deep breath. "Beel, you felt it right?"

Beel didn't answer; it was like he was gone.

"The song, Beel. Did you feel the magic?"

Maybe . . . a little.

"No maybe. You felt it. I know you did, because I did. There's a chance, right? That this might work after all?"

There's always a chance. Just not much of one.

"Well, this morning you said there was no chance. So, I'm gonna take that as a step forward."

Vutto was grinning at her, exposing rows of his needle-like teeth. She wished he wouldn't do that, it was like being smiled at by a tiger.

"Did you feel the magic, Vutto?"

He nodded. "Yah! We are going to break this spell. We are going to escape Lord Sheelbeth."

Hear that? Ruby said within. *At least this demon believes in us. Maybe if you did too, we'd stand a better chance.*

Believing in something doesn't make it true.

"Sometimes it does. Sometimes it really does." Then Ruby asked, "Vutto, what'll you do if you escape?"

Vutto didn't hesitate. "I return to the desert. Get as far away from people and gods and devils as I can. I burrow deep in the hot sand and only come out at night to hunt and sing to the stars."

"What do you hunt?" Ruby asked, before realizing she didn't really want to know.

"Snakes, rats, rabbits, lizards . . . wandering souls."

He is a demon. He needs more than flesh.

Ruby shuddered.

A few minutes later Tina trotted back down the stairs. "Okay, we're on."

"What?"

"I called Tom, down at 688. We're on at eight. Warming up for Neon Christ."

"Tonight? How'd you manage that?"

"Because I know how to make things happen," Tina said with a cocky smirk. "And because Tom owes me. And because it's Wednesday and nobody else wants to play on Wednesday. And mostly . . . I told him we'd play for free."

"We only have two songs so far."

"Yeah, but one of them is full of magic, isn't it?"

Ruby nodded.

"Hey, what are we calling it?"

"Evil in Me," Ruby said.

EVIL IN ME

A man with short greased-back hair and long sideburns held open the back door of the 688 Club. "You're late," he said.

"Fashionably," Tina shot back, and she wasn't joking. Tina was wearing a long witchy skirt and a vampy vintage blouse with beaded fringe. She had on black lipstick and her dark brooding eyes were highlighted with purple eyeshadow. She'd lent Ruby a crimson tuxedo shirt and some black velvet tights, that somehow looked great with her Converse high-tops.

Tina gave the man a peck on the cheek. "How you doing, sugarplum?"

Sugarplum turned out to be Tom, the owner of the club. He smirked and shook his head. "I talked Neon Christ into letting you use their kit, so just plug in and go."

"You're a peach!"

"I'm a sucker, is what I am. No idea why I put up with you."

"Because I am your Aphrodite, the siren of your soul and the goddess of all your wet dreams."

He rolled his eyes. "Lord, please, stop. You're scaring me."

Tina and Ruby entered, walked through a small back room and out onto the main floor, carrying their instruments up onto the stage. The stage was only about three feet high. There was a large open space, or pit, in front and an island bar toward the back. Ruby peered out through the haze of cigarette smoke and was disappointed to find only about twenty people in the whole joint, most of them at the bar. But this disappointment was replaced by curiosity as to who these wildly dressed people were.

All of them were decked out to some degree or another, like nothing she'd ever seen in real life; people just didn't dress that way in Enterprise, Alabama. There were a few gals wearing all black, looking like ghouls, with heavy makeup and their hair teased into witchy rat's nests. Sitting next to them were some arty girls, with bleached, two-toned, over-moused hair, wearing groovy jewelry and bright miniskirts. A few typical punks as well, some with shaved heads, others with spiked hair and colorful mohawks. Most of them wearing torn-up jeans and combat boots. Their sleeveless jackets covered in studs and band names like G.B.H and the Exploited. A few long-haired throwbacks were over by themselves, and on the far end, a group of rockabilly kids, decked out in vintage jackets and skirts. One really cute gal had her hair spun up into a beehive that rivaled Kate Pierson's from the B-52's. Ruby guessed it had to be a wig, that there wasn't enough Aqua Net in all of Atlanta to hold that in place. Then just a few other random oddballs here and there that didn't seem to fit into any category.

The thing that surprised Ruby most was how eclectic the crowd was, a real free-for-all. It felt like you could be anything here, express yourself however you chose, and she really dug that. It was everything she'd been starved for back home. A sudden wave of sadness came over her. *If only I'd come to Atlanta earlier,* she thought. *I could've been part of this.*

Tina nudged her. "Wanna show you something." She pointed over to the wall.

Every inch of the walls were covered in graffiti, but next to the stage was a song list in thick black marker.

"You recognize those songs?"

It took Ruby a minute. "Those are Iggy Pop songs."

"Yup."

"Wait . . . are you telling me Iggy played here?"

"You betcha."

Ruby stepped over and touched the wall. "I'm on the same stage that Iggy Pop played on. Oh . . . my . . . God."

"Yeah, and the Ramones, Dead Kennedys, Nick Cave, Fleshtones, Meat Puppets, Siouxsie and the Banshees . . . you want me to keep going?"

Ruby shook her head in disbelief; none of this felt real.

"Stop dicking around!" someone shouted at them, one of the rockabilly guys. "Get this show on the road."

"Oh, lucky us," Tina said. "That's Gary. He can be a real prick when he gets drunk . . . and he's always drunk."

Gary sat on the edge of his stool, leering at them, a beer in one hand, a cigarette in the other, a pip-squeak of a fellow in a red cowboy shirt. He had lips like a fish, but certainly won the award for tallest pompadour in the house.

"Ain't waiting on no train!"

Tina tapped the mic. "Check, check. Checking to see if Gary is still a limp dildo."

"Hey!" Gary hollered. "Bite me!"

"Dildo status . . . *confirmed.*"

This was met with hearty chuckles all around, even Gary grinned.

Tom gave Tina a thumbs up.

"Okey doke," Tina said to Ruby. "I think we're ready. Time to bring in dark and gruesome."

They'd left Vutto in the Cadillac with strict instructions not to get out until they came for him. But when they approached the car, he wasn't there.

"Oh, fuck," Ruby said. "Where'd he go?"

A scream came from around the side of the club. Tina and Ruby exchanged a look and sprinted in that direction.

They found Vutto with blood running down his lips, half a rat in his hand.

The scream had come from a girl, a little mohawk number looking oh-so-tough, decked out in a studded denim jacket. She didn't look oh-so-tough at the moment though, not with a monster eating a live rat in front of her; she looked terrified. Thankfully, Vutto still had on his coat, hat, and shades, but had lost his boa, revealing his scaly skin and large creepy mouth.

Ruby ran up and grabbed Vutto by the arm, tugging him away. "Put that down," she hissed, indicating the uneaten portion of the rat.

Vutto frowned and shoved it into his maw before she could stop him.

"Aw, gross! Yuck!" the girl cried, putting her hand over her mouth and falling back a step. "What in the hell is *wrong* with him?"

"What's *wrong* with you?" Tina shot back, walking up to the girl. "He can't help it. He was born that way. You know, he's not all there upstairs."

"Huh? What?"

"His mom took too much LSD. Now stop staring, it's rude."

"Oh," the girl said, taken aback. "Oh . . . sorry. I didn't know . . . shit, man. That's really sad."

Another woman walked up. She didn't appear to belong to the 688 crowd. Older, late forties maybe, matted blonde hair, hard lines on her face, grime on her jeans and shirt. Whatever her game, she wasn't looking at Vutto, but staring at Ruby. Ruby recognized that look.

Watch that one, Beel said from within. **She smells the taint.**

"Yeah, I see that," Ruby replied, escorting Vutto back around the building. She spotted his boa on the ground, plucked it up, and wrapped it around his neck. Tina had "borrowed" a pair of scruffy boots and a green trench coat from her roommate, completing the disguise. It really wasn't bad, so long as you didn't look too closely. They figured, hoped, that by keeping Vutto behind the drums, they just might get away with having a full-fledged demon in their band.

They were almost to the back door when someone yelled. It was Tom, he was shouting at the blonde woman.

"Get out of here, Lucy! You got ten seconds before I call the cops. I mean it. Get!"

The woman hissed, actually hissed at him. That's when Ruby noticed she was carrying a large screwdriver.

"You want me eat her? Yah?" Vutto asked.

"What? No. Hell no, Vutto!" Ruby snapped. "Don't you dare. You made me a promise. Remember?"

Tina caught up with them. "Was that the woman you were telling me about?"

"Yeah," Tom replied. "Crazy junkie. We've caught her breaking into cars twice now. Swear she's psycho."

The three of them entered the club and hopped onstage, Tina slipping her guitar strap over her head while Ruby led Vutto over to the drums. "Okay, Vutto. Like we said. Keep your head down. Got it?"

He nodded, grinning like a schoolkid.

Ruby picked up the bass and glanced out at the small crowd. Her hands were quivering, palms sweaty, mouth dry. She swallowed hard, wondering how, with her very soul at stake, she could have stage fright. But she'd never played in front of anyone other than a few friends before.

Tina strummed her guitar, getting it in tune, soliciting some curious looks. Ruby was glad to see a few more people now, hoped more would show up soon. It was still early after all.

She noticed mohawk girl sitting on a stool, sipping a beer with three friends, all looking like they shopped at the same punk rock store. They were staring at Vutto.

"You ready?" Tina asked.

Ruby shook her head. "No."

"Hey," Tina said. "You got this, babe. You're voodoo. You've always been."

Ruby forced herself to smile. "Thanks, Tina."

Six preppy kids came in, gawking about like tourists, eyes wide as though they were about to be stabbed or molested at any moment. They couldn't have been more out of place with their perfectly feathered hair and chartreuse or baby blue polo shirts, the kind with little alligators on them. A couple of them had popped up their collars, a clear signal to all that they weren't to be messed with.

"Oh, great," Tina said. "Fucking frat boys. We get a gaggle of 'em dropping in from time to time. It's like some rite of passage for them, a triple dog dare, stepping into a punk club. Y'know, to prove what brave men they are."

"Brave . . . huh?"

"Y'know, because us punks are so gosh darn scary. Or maybe they think being a weirdo is contagious. Anyway, just watch out, these guys never mix well."

The frat crew wandered over to the bar and ordered beers. Gary and his rockabilly pals began smirking and sneering at them. A few of the frat guys were pretty big too, one in particular—a tanned fellow with thick, serious brows. Ruby wondered if he might be a ballplayer. He had his chest puffed out, chin cocked back, like he was just daring someone to say something to him. And of course, it didn't take Gary long to do just that. Ruby couldn't hear what was said, but Gary was definitely mouthing off. The big tanned guy stood up and so did Gary.

Crap, Ruby thought, knowing the last thing they needed was a brawl. "Tina! Shit, I think they're about to start fighting."

"I got this." Tina said, stepping up to the mic. She tapped it. "Hey, all you odious malcontents. Listen up."

Ruby gasped, then let out a nervous snort as everyone in the place turned and gave them a hard look.

"I'm Tina Poontang and this here's my best friend in the whole wide world, Ruby Motherfucker."

Tina banged the strings on her guitar, sending out a bark of reverb.

"And we're the Night Mares."

"You look like a nightmare," Gary shouted back and cackled, his words slurred.

"This first song is called 'Skank Howl.' It's about not giving a shit."

"We don't give a shit," Gary hollered, shaking his cigarette at her. His buddies all laughed.

"Why don't you come over here and say that," Tina called. "You ain't scared of a couple of little girls, are you? How about you guys?" She pointed at the frat boys. "Yeah, I'm talking to you. Talking to all y'all back there. Bunch of pussies hiding behind the bar. Think we're gonna bite? C'mon down . . . dare ya!"

Ruby cut Tina a nervous look, pretty sure this wasn't the best route to get a crowd to sing your song. But Tina appeared fearless, like she was the one looking for a fight.

Gary frowned, hopped up, and headed over, followed by the rest of his pack. A moment later, most everybody else in the club did too, even the frat boys.

Ruby found all eyes on her, and decided she liked it better when they were back in the shadows.

"Shows us your tits," Gary yelled. This was met with hoots from his inebriated pals, and grins from the frat pack. Seemed they'd found something to bond over.

"Tell you what," Tina said, a fierce smile spreading across her face as she pointed to the guys up front. "You boys show me *yours* . . . and I'll show you *mine*."

Every guy in the pit immediately lifted their shirts up to their chins, proudly showing off their nipples.

Then, to Ruby's horror, Tina flashed them. This was met with applause and wild howls of approval.

"Alright dipshits," Tina snarled. "Enough fucking around. Are you ready to hear some teen angst that'll tear your little hearts out?"

They all hefted their drinks and hooted, frat boys too, a jovial sound. They were all in now, ready for a show. Ruby just stared at Tina in awe.

"Alright, hit it," Tina cried, tearing into a riff. Vutto joined right in, not missing a beat. Ruby, however, missed completely, then fumbled through the first few chords.

Tina looped back around to the start, like it was all part of the song. This time Ruby came in at the right point, but her fingers felt stiff and she was having trouble keeping up. Tina gave her a wink and stepped up to the mic. Ruby did the same and they started to sing. Ruby was off-key, off tempo, and kept fumbling chords.

"Shit," she hissed as the song bumped along. She could see people losing interest and it was all on account of her, and after all Tina had done to rev them up.

Get it together, she thought. *Play like your fucking soul is at stake, because it is, dammit.* But knowing that seemed to only make her play worse.

People were talking in each other's ears now, shaking their heads and drifting away.

Thankfully, the song came to an end.

Gary looked right at her, gave her a thumbs-down, and headed back to the bar along with just about everyone else.

Ruby wanted to run off the stage, probably would've if there wasn't so much at stake.

"Let it go," Tina said to her. "Everybody fumbles on their first gig. We need to play the 'Evil in Me' song now, right now. Before we lose everyone."

Ruby felt sure they'd already lost everyone.

"Ready, Vutto?" Tina asked.

Vutto nodded and grinned his creepy grin.

"Ruby?"

Ruby took a deep breath and nodded.

Vutto started with a low beat, tapping his hands on the floor tom. Tina and Ruby began clapping along, then Tina switched the beat to her guitar and Ruby added her bass. Slowly the tempo rose.

Ruby swallowed hard, closed her eyes, and began to sing, trying to remember the voices of the ghosts, their spirit, trying to channel them.

She sang solo through the first verse, diving into the new lyrics.

"'Devil on my hand, Devil in my band. Devil's gonna take me down any way he can.

When the chorus came round, Vutto and Tina joined her.

'Gonna give you all my heart and soul, give you all my heart and soul.
Burnin' like a demon bowl, I give you all my heart and soul.

Ruby felt a faint but familiar tingle, knew the magic, her spell, was there, waiting. She pushed into the next verse.

"'Devil's watchin' me squirm, Devil's watchin' me burn. Devil wants me in his belly like a wiggle worm.

Tina and Vutto again joining her on the chorus, this time Vutto adding both of his voices, creating a lonesome howl.

'Gonna give you all my heart and soul, give you all my heart and soul.
Devil's gonna let you go, I give you all my heart and soul.

They looped back to the first verse, keeping the song going, the magic growing stronger in the air.

When Ruby came round to the chorus again, someone whistled right up front and she opened her eyes.

Gary stood before the stage, nodding and clapping along, a few of his buddies with him. Several more patrons began heading over, lining back up in front, but this time it was different, there was a strange intensity in their eyes, almost a hunger as they stared at her and nodded along.

They hear it, Beel gasped from within. *They feel the magic!*

Ruby let go with newfound confidence, really belting out the next verse. This time when they reached the chorus, Beel joined them, adding his angelic voice to the mix. The song soared, filling the place like a bright light.

More people drifted over, the frat boys, the arty gals. They were nodding, clapping, a few even mouthing the words, but no one was singing. Ruby needed to get them to sing.

Another chorus and the last holdouts shuffled over, drinks left behind at the bar, dreamy looks on their faces.

It is working! Beel exclaimed, sounding stunned. *Do not stop!*

Ruby didn't, she kept looping the song around and Beel brought in his voice below hers, adding a sweet ethereal echo to her words.

"'Gotta gimmie all your heart and soul, gimmie all your heart and soul. Devil's never gonna let me go, unless you give me all your heart and soul.

The chorus came around again, yet still only a few folks were singing. The crowd seemed lost in the song, but it was as though they were waiting for something.

"Okay," Ruby called, keeping her voice low and seductive, talking like a beat poet, while Tina and Vutto kept playing. "Okay, everybody, listen up now. I need your help, need your mojo. Because, see, this ain't just another pretty song. The Devil really has got hold of me . . . and the only way to set me free is for y'all to sing along. So, let's hear it. C'mon, give me your sweet mojo. Put your heart and soul into it. Set me free, baby!"

She shot right back into the first verse and this time, when the chorus came round, Gary began singing, loud and bold. His buddies joined him, the frat boys too.

> *'Gonna give you all my heart and soul, give you all my heart and soul.*
> *Burnin' like a demon bowl, I give you all my heart and soul.*

Yes! Ruby thought as chills rolled up her arms. *Jesus, please.*

The chorus again, and this time, they all joined in, every one of them, even the bartender. They were hers—smiling, nodding, clapping, and swaying to the beat.

> *'Gonna give you all my heart and soul, give you all my heart and soul.*
> *Devil's gonna let you go, I give you all my heart and soul."*

Tina stomped her fuzz box, kicking the song into a sizzling haze of grinding guitar, driving Vutto's wild primitive beat. The magic grew stronger and the song called it to Ruby. Her scar, the symbol on her arm, grew warm, began to glow as the warmth spread into her chest, taking hold of her, then, that sensation of floating.

Now, Beel urged. **The ring!**

The ring! Ruby thought, forcing herself to focus, to push the magic toward the ring, just like at David's house. And just like at David's house, the spell set to the ring.

The ring grew warm, then hot.

Ruby never stopped singing, just let go of the bass and pushed the glove up, exposing the ring. She grabbed it, gave it a tug. The ring twisted a notch.

It moved! Beel exclaimed. ***By the gods, it moved!***

Tina gave Ruby a concerned look, but kept playing, she and Vutto keeping the chorus going.

Ruby tried again, tugging and tugging until she was sure she would tear her finger off, but the ring held tight.

Do not give up! Beel cried.

"It's not moving," she growled.

Harder! Beel cried.

Need more people . . . more magic, Ruby thought. Yet, still she pushed the spell, straining, trying to force it. She felt the magic draining away, fading as though used up. Her vision blurred, the room began to spin. She swooned and fell to her knees.

The song sputtered to an end, leaving everyone staring at each other with dazed and confused looks.

It's me, Richard.

I hit the brakes.

"Whoa," I cried, as I caught the song, Ruby's song. "Hallelujah!" Tears, actual tears, sprung from my eyes. I'd been driving around all day, searching for her, sure I'd lost her, unable to contemplate what I'd do if I had.

I focused, concentrated, again that game of hotter-colder as I drove up and down, round and round different streets and blocks, getting closer and closer, my heart strumming as the song grew stronger.

I drove past a nightclub. She was there, had to be. I could feel the song in my chest now.

I turned around and pulled into the parking lot behind the place and—bingo! I spotted the black Cadillac. I pulled up next to it and—there she was! There . . .

she . . . was! Just leaning against the wall, next to the back door all by herself, like a gift, like a flower waiting to be picked.

My fingers twitched, aching to squeeze her slender neck, crush her windpipe as she tried to scream, tried to beg me to stop.

I glanced around, couldn't believe my luck, couldn't believe there was no one else to be seen.

I cut the engine, reached behind the seat, groping blindly for my bag, afraid to take my eyes off her for even a second. I tugged out the pepper spray and my hammer. Found my cap and sunglasses, put them on.

I stomped the parking brake into place and hopped out, heading right for her.

She seemed drunk, or stoned, or something, staring at the ground, her hands trembling as she took a drag off her cigarette. I hoped the pepper spray would be enough, but had the hammer for backup. Only I needed to be careful. Knocking someone out isn't like in the movies. You're more likely to kill them. Trust me, I learned that one the hard way. And I didn't want to kill her, not yet. Just get her into the van.

I was about thirty feet away when all the sudden a woman with blonde matted hair came running around the corner, heading straight for Ruby. She clutched a large screwdriver, holding it up like she was about to stab someone, and that someone was Ruby.

"Look out!" I shouted, dashing forward.

The woman lunged for Ruby, bringing the screwdriver down with all her might, aiming for her face.

Ruby dodged left, and the screwdriver hit the wall beside her head, taking a chip out of the cinder block. The woman fell onto her, screaming, wailing, clawing, and stabbing over and over.

"No!" I cried and rushed up behind the woman, slamming the hammer against the back of her skull. There came an awful crack, and she went limp. I followed with two more blows.

"Hey!" someone shouted. People were rushing down the hall.

Ruby's face was smeared with blood, but she was alive. I started to hit her with the hammer, some voice deep within me screaming to kill her, kill her now.

"No," I cried. "Not like this!" I wanted more, so much more than simple murder. I wanted to chew her flesh, drink her blood, hear her screams.

I turned and ran, slipping around the corner, melting into the night.

Ruby sat on Tina's couch, her head bandaged. There'd been a lot of blood, but the slashes across her forehead and scalp had ended up not needing stiches. She and Tina were watching the morning edition of CNN Headline News on a thirteen-inch TV and despite the fuzzy picture, the reporter was coming through loud and clear.

"In our ongoing Special Investigation report on the effects of nihilistic music on our youth culture, we feel it's important to bring to your attention an incident that hits close to home for all of us working here, in our Atlanta offices," the reporter stated as the camera rolled across the front of the club. "Last night the Atlanta punk rock club 688 was the scene of a tragic murder." The screen switched to the back of the club, where police and EMT lights were flashing off the walls.

"Christ on a cracker!" Tina cried. "Look! There we are!"

It started as a wide shot of Tina holding Ruby, then zoomed right in on Ruby's face. Even with her new haircut and streaks of blood, Ruby knew she'd be recognizable to anyone back home.

"That's national news, right?"

Tina nodded. "Boy, do we look like trouble."

The reporter continued. "Two women were attacked in the parking lot, one sustaining life-threatening injuries, the other died at the scene due to a traumatic head wound."

"Life-threatening my ass," Tina sneered. "Not my Ruby, she's too *tough* to die."

"The assailant, a white male, no other details at this time, escaped the scene."

"That's not at all what happened," Ruby snapped. "The woman attacked me. It was the guy who saved me."

"Sources have it, one of the victims is the lead singer of a local punk rock band called the Night Mares."

"Hey," Tina said. "We got called out. That's good . . . no, *great*! Folks gonna wanna know more about us."

No, Ruby thought, *not good at all.* She thought of her mother, then of Pam. *God, I need to call Pam.* She grimaced. *Shit. What am I gonna say to her? That I got her father killed by demons?* A wave of sorrow flooded her heart, and in that moment, she felt willing to do about anything to be able to listen to Barbra Streisand albums with Josh again.

"Is this one more incident driven by satanic cults infiltrating our youth?" the reporter asked. "Our sources confirm that much of the music played at this club makes some reference to the occult, as well as murder and self-mutilation."

The camera scanned the crowd, zooming in on some of the more intense-looking punks, while the reporter droned on about how their dangerous lifestyle was fueling drug abuse and violence nationwide. She speculated on drug use as a possible motivator in this incident, how many concerned citizens felt such clubs should be shut down, and on, and on, and on.

"Oh, kiss my ass!" Tina shouted at the TV. "Of course they're gonna pin this on us. Some crazy junkie attacks you and somehow, it's the punks that are the psychopaths. Damn woman wasn't even part of the scene. Hate the stupid news! Bunch of morons." She turned the channel to *Captain Kangaroo* and began pacing.

Ruby dug a cigarette out of her pocket, lit it, and took a long deep drag. And despite everything, found she still had room to hate herself a little for not being able to kick this nasty habit.

"Alright, Ruby dear, let me get this straight. You said it worked. The 'Evil in Me' song. It made magic, or called the magic. Right?"

Ruby nodded. "Yeah."

"Just not *enough* magic."

Ruby shrugged. "That's what it felt like."

"Sounds like we need a larger crowd then. More people, more—" Tina stopped. "Hey! No! No sir!" She stomped over to her bed where Vutto lay curled up beneath the covers. She kicked the mattress. "Hey! Get out of my bed!"

Vutto seemed not to hear her, responding with a deep nasal snore. A string of drool dripped from the side of his mouth right onto Tina's pillow.

"Aw yuck! *Gross!*" She grabbed the end of the blanket and gave it a tug. Vutto, eyes still closed like in a dream, snarled, his face twisting into something dreadful and terrifying.

Tina fell back a step. "Fuck, did you see that?"

"Just . . . just stay away from him," Ruby said.

Vutto's face softened and he resumed snoring.

Look at his scar, Beel said. **It grows ever smaller. He will soon lose control. Do you hear them? The worms?**

Ruby did, faintly.

Lord Sheelbeth is trying to punch through. To get to Vutto. We are running out of time.

Ruby glanced at her gloved hand.

Show me.

Ruby slid the glove down. Her whole hand was black now, but that wasn't what scared her most. It was how thin the film of blood covering the ring had become. Her efforts to dislodge it had only served to scrape off more of the coating.

Tina's right, Ruby said within. *Don't you think? We just need more people? But at least it worked . . . a little. That's something.*

Yes, that is indeed something. I will admit, I am amazed. Perhaps with more people singing, it just might work. Only, how many more? A hundred, two hundred, several thousand? I can only guess. Human magic is so weak.

Tina took a long sip of her coffee, began pacing again. "If we want more people to sing along, we need to get them to our show." She snapped her fingers. "That song is magic, literally. I'm betting if we can get some airplay, we'll have a packed house."

"Another gig?" Ruby mumbled, suddenly finding it hard to keep her eyes open. "Where?"

"Let me handle that. Why don't you take a nap. You look beat-up and worn-out."

Ruby nodded, stubbed out her cigarette, and lay down on the couch. She couldn't remember ever feeling so tired.

Tina draped a blanket over her. "'Night, shug. I'm gonna go make some calls. See what I can make happen."

Ruby felt like she'd only just shut her eyes, when Tina's excited voice woke her back up.

"Hey, Ruby Dooby Doo, got some news for you!"

Ruby sat up, blinking.

"Okay, first, the Metroplex is all over this. Dan caught the news. Turns out getting stabbed by that nutjob wasn't the worst thing that could've happened. He thinks it'll be a hoot having us open for Smuthouse. Did you hear me? Smuthouse! They're gonna bring in a large crowd, a *really* large crowd!"

"When?"

"The gig's tomorrow night, babe. The only problem is, we go on first . . . first of three bands. So, we gotta get folks there early. Y'know how it is at those shows. No one shows up for the first band."

Ruby rubbed her eyes. "How we gonna do that?"

"I've got a friend down at WREK. I'm sure he'll give us a play. But first . . . first we gotta get over to the church and record the song."

"Church?"

"Yeah, Andre's got a recording studio there. He recorded the Battz. I mean it's nothing fancy, but it'll do the trick."

"You wanna take Vutto into a church?"

"What could go wrong?"

"Oh, boy."

"It'll be fine. Just fine. *Trust* me."

Eduardo checked his watch. Martha had the night shift again, but should be on her way home by now.

He went to the bedroom, pulled out his duffel bag, dropped in a combat knife, brass knuckles, pepper spray, two pairs of handcuffs, and finally his hand-gun, a 9mm Glock. He added a box of ammo, started to zip it up, then decided to toss in another, because it was always better to be prepared than not.

When Martha finally pulled in, Eduardo greeted her at the door.

"What is it?" she asked. "Did you hear from Ruby?"

"Sorta."

"What do you mean?"

"I'll show you."

Eduardo led her into the living room and pressed play on the VCR.

The CNN playback jittered onto the screen. He'd caught it that morning, nearly choking on his Pop-Tart when it first came on. When the segment came on again at the top of the hour, he recorded the whole thing, including that annoying commercial with the dancing raisins.

As soon as Ruby came on the screen, he hit pause.

Martha let out a cry. "Oh, baby. Oh, my little girl!" She touched Ruby's face on the screen. "God, look at all that blood!" Martha tugged her keys back out of her purse. "We gotta find her. Did they say which hospital she's at?"

Eduardo caught her by the shoulders. "Martha, hold up. Listen."

Martha pushed past, heading for the door.

"Martha, I called the Atlanta Police."

Martha stopped; he had her full attention.

"She's not hurt."

"What do you mean? Didn't you see all that blood?"

"I mean, she escaped with only minor injuries. She didn't even need to go to the hospital."

Martha let out a loud breath of relief. "Oh, thank God! But we still need to go get her."

No, Eduardo thought. *I* need to go get her, this is *my* big break, *my* big chance.

Eduardo currently worked part-time armed security down at the Coffee County Landfill, which was as close as he could get to law enforcement at the moment. Frankly, it was an embarrassment, but at least he got to carry a piece on the job, which counted toward law enforcement experience. His father had spent his whole life in law enforcement, recently retiring from his position as Captain at the Enterprise Police Department. Eduardo's older brother, Carlos, had been on the force almost fifteen years, something that made Eduardo proud and jealous at the same time, because there wasn't anything Eduardo wanted more than to follow in his family's footsteps. But Eduardo would never be able to join the force, because Eduardo had a felony on his record.

Eduardo decided if he couldn't bring in the crooks as a cop, he'd bring them in as a bounty hunter. But first he needed a license and, again, his felony proved a problem. Only with bounty hunters, there was a work-around—you just needed approval from the county sheriff. Since the Sheriff and Eduardo's father were fishing buddies from way back, Eduardo got his license.

Eduardo soon found out that the fine folks down at Baily's Bonds didn't hire someone just because they had a business card with BOUNTY HUNTER printed on it. No, they were looking for experience, a reputation. Eduardo had neither. But he was pretty sure Ruby was about to change all that for him.

"I agree," he said to Martha. "Someone does need to go get Ruby. But there's more to it." He pulled out a chair. "Here, have a seat. Let me fill you in."

Martha didn't sit, just locked worried eyes on him.

"Like I said, I talked to the police. Made several calls around Atlanta." What Eduardo left out was that the police sergeant wouldn't tell him much of anything, and the only other place he'd called was the 688 Club, and only got an answering machine. "Still following up on a few leads, but I need to tell you, it sure sounds like Ruby has fallen in with a bad crowd. This group could be really dangerous."

"What are we waiting for then? Let's go get her, *now*. Right *now*. Get her the hell out of there!"

"I'm on it. Already packed. But . . . well, Martha, gotta tell you straight. I don't think it'd be good for you to go." What he really wanted to say was he was looking forward to seeing everyone's faces down at the station when *he* brought Ruby in, especially his brother, Carlos. Especially since Ruby had escaped right out from under all their noses. He did *not* want to show up with Martha. God,

EVIL IN ME

he'd never hear the end of it. Eduardo and Martha, the bounty hunting dynamic duo.

"What do you mean?" she asked.

"First we gotta find her," he said. "Could take days, weeks. Can you afford to take two weeks off work right now?" He knew she couldn't.

"I don't care about that. This is my daughter."

"Sure, I understand. But time away ain't the half of it. What I'm leading to is Ruby isn't gonna *want* to come home. You know that. She's a grown woman, *you* can't make her . . . but *I* can." He flashed his bounty hunter license. "There's a warrant out for her arrest, for what she done to that Stacy girl, for breaking probation, leaving the state, and a dozen other things. So, if I can find her, I can bring her in, *legally*. And by force if need be."

Martha shook her head. "Don't feel right, me staying behind. She's *my* daughter."

"These thugs she's hanging out with, they're like a cult or something. Into all kinds of drugs and weird satanic rituals. Like to cut themselves, sniff glue, prostitution and so on. Not trying to scare you," he said, knowing that he was. "But think about all that crazy Charlie Manson shit that went down a while back."

"Charlie Manson?" Martha exclaimed. "What does Manson have to do with anything? What are you even talking about?"

"Where've you been? It's all over the news these days. These kids playing them demonic games, listening to Devil music. It's especially bad in them big cities. Have you had a look around Ruby's room lately?"

Martha put her hand to her mouth.

"Listen," he said. "Let me make it simple. You being there is gonna make things messy. Ratchet everything up emotionally. Can't you see that? Gonna make a volatile situation all the more volatile. If it's just me, I go in fast, flash my badge, grab her and get out, bring her home. Law will be on my side. Anyone get in my way and I deal with them *legally*. You get involved and the law gets muddy."

He could see she didn't like it, could also see he was scaring her, which was good.

"Most of all, I don't want to have to worry about you getting hurt. You're not trained. You being there would put everyone in danger. Might get Ruby, or me, hurt . . . killed even. Is that what you want?"

She shook her head. "Of course not!"

"Okay. Then I take it you're staying here. Right?"

She didn't answer, just clutched her hands together.

He let out a huff. "Just can't let you come along, Martha. I'm sorry. I'd never forgive myself if you got hurt."

She touched the image of Ruby again. "You bring her back and they'll put her in prison this time. You know that."

He did, was counting on it.

"She's gonna hate me," Martha said.

"For a little while. But you're doing what's best. She'll understand that in time. Trust me, it'll sure beat where she's heading now."

"You promise to call me the second you find out anything. I mean *anything*."

"Of course."

"Okay," Martha said.

"Okay?"

She looked at him, tears brimming. "Go get her, Eduardo. Please go get my baby."

Eduardo had to fight not to smile.

"Park over there," Tina said, pointing to a small empty lot. She wanted another cup of coffee, her head still groggy even after a long nap. They'd all napped, even Vutto, sleeping through most of the day, all drained from the chaos of the night before.

Ruby pulled in and parked in front of a sign reading Pet Heaven Memorial Park.

"What's this?" Ruby asked. "Wait, you gotta be kidding me? Is this a cemetery just for pets?"

"Sure is," Tina replied. "Andre asked us to park away from the church." She pointed to a large redbrick building sitting just on the other side of the graveyard, the sign out front read BETHAL AFRICAN METHODIST EPISCOPAL. "It's so his grandfather won't see us. His grandfather's the preacher, and if he finds out what we're up to, then the whole thing's off."

They got out of the car and stretched, then unloaded the guitar and bass from the trunk.

"Okay, Vutto," Ruby said. "C'mon."

Vutto climbed out and Ruby straightened his wig, pulling the hair down to cover most of his face. Ruby had applied some makeup and with the glasses, he almost, *almost,* passed for your run-of-the-mill cretin, as opposed to a servant of Satan. Tina just hoped no one looked too closely.

Vutto grinned at her, revealing his jagged little teeth.

Tina shivered. *Don't touch me,* she thought. *Please, God, do not let it touch me.* She felt sure his touch would spread his vileness, like some kind of satanic disease. An overwhelming compulsion to run came over her, to run away from this creature, to run away from all of this nightmare. This wasn't a game; she'd seen enough to know whatever was going on here was real, sure now that more than just her life was at stake.

Tina closed her eyes. *Indomitable spirit,* she thought. *Indomitable spirit, indomitable spirit.* She visualized the words. It was easy to do, because she'd seen them almost every day of her childhood. They were from a plaque hanging in her father's living room, the five tenets of Tae Kwon Do: courtesy, integrity, perseverance, self-control, and indomitable spirit. She'd never paid much attention to the first four, but that last one had resonated.

Her father often told her she was in control of who she was, how she felt. And if she worked at it, she could not only feel like a success, but be successful at anything she applied herself to. He had added, if you dwell on failure, you will fail. Which sounded cheesy to her now, like some inspiring quote from Confucius. But cheesy or not, it worked, at least for her, maybe not every time, but most times. So, whenever she felt doubt or fear creeping up on her, she would repeat those words, her mantra, her spell of empowerment. Often followed by saying or doing something positive, even if it was as simple as smiling.

"Let's go make some mojo," Tina said, and led them across the cemetery.

"Look at this one," Ruby called, stooping over a gravestone. "*Speck, a loyal friend.* That's so sad."

"Why's it sad? That dog probably had a long, wonderful life."

"Not sad for the dog. Sad for the heartache of those left behind. They miss their furry friend."

The graves became older as they went, they found a mix of dogs, cats, even rabbits and birds.

"Oh, lord, this one," Ruby said. "*Bingo, 1934–1950. Let a little dog into your heart and he will tear it to pieces.* Geesh, that makes me wanna cry."

Tina caught the look of profound sadness on Ruby's face and couldn't help loving her. Here Ruby was, with an actual demon trying to eat her soul, and she still found room to hurt for some long-gone pet owner.

We gotta get you through this, Tina thought. *Whatever it takes, because I can't lose you. You're the only real friend I got . . . only one I've ever had really.* And she wasn't being melodramatic, she'd always been awkward around people—adults, or kids, didn't matter—feeling like an alien, feeling like every word out of her mouth was the wrong word. People just seemed to sense she was odd, making her wonder if maybe she gave off some kind of weirdo scent. She'd like to blame it on folks being prejudice because she was Asian, only even the Korean kids at her church all but shunned her. At some point she'd learned to reject people before they could reject her. One of the many reasons she'd fallen in love with punk—that, and that it helped her to pretend she was socially awkward on purpose. And all of this had a lot to do with why she'd fallen in so tight with Ruby, because weirdos tended to like other weirdos.

There was a little more to it. Ruby had her back, *always* had her back. Tina thought about what Ruby had done to Stacy back in school. Tina's grandmother lived with Tina's family. She'd been making her own kimchi that week, the smell permeating the whole house, including Tina's clothes. Tina and Ruby happened to be standing in line next to Stacy and her pack of friends, when Stacy pinched her nose. "Lord, y'all smell that? Why, *someone* smells like week-old Chinese food." The whole group clamped their noses and started laughing at Tina.

Tina turned on them, but Ruby held her back, told her the bitch wasn't worth getting suspended over. The next day Ruby brought in a small perfume mister, only there wasn't perfume in it, but some horrible mixture of fish oil and minced horseradish juice. During second period PE class, Ruby snuck in and gave a couple of quick squirts inside Stacy's locker, on her clothes and books—not a lot, but enough that for the rest of the day, Stacy smelled like the dumpster behind a fish house. Stacy went home early that day.

Tina found herself smiling as they walked up to the basement door of the church. She knocked lightly. When no one answered, she opened the door, peeked in. Andre sat at a large round table playing a game with five of his friends—four guys and some gal. They all appeared to be in their late teens. Andre was only nineteen himself.

"Psst."

Andre saw her and hopped up. "Y'all can keep playing," he said to his friends. "This shouldn't take too long." He came over and stuck his head out the door. He barely gave Ruby and Vutto a glance, his eyes scanning the parking lot, like he was under surveillance. He quickly ushered them in and Tina made a point of keeping Vutto behind her as they entered, grateful that the basement was so dim.

The basement was one long room with a small kitchen area partitioned off. The place smelled of casseroles and fresh gingerbread. One wall was loaded with photos of the congregation, mostly folks in choir robes, with a few paintings of Jesus in the mix. The other wall held dozens of children's drawings and craft projects, like colorful crosses made from popsicle sticks. Hand-me-down sofas and recliners were lined up below the photos, while several round tables sat in the middle of the room surrounded by folding metal chairs.

"You got the cash?" Andre asked.

"Dang, Andre," Tina said. "Straight to business."

Andre was slim with glasses, his hair trimmed into a tall flattop, which

Tina felt made his large ears look all the larger. His glasses were vintage, like something Buddy Holly would have worn. He looked nerdy, but as though on purpose—a lot of plaid. Tina knew he had good taste in music at least, because he was at most of the same shows she was.

Andre sighed. "You still haven't paid me for the last time."

"Aw, Andre, you know I'm good for it."

"Do I?"

"How much is the session?" Ruby asked.

"Forty."

Ruby tugged out a roll of bills and gave him two twenties.

He gave Ruby a kind smile. "What was your name again?"

"Ruby."

"Thank you, Ruby."

Ruby pulled out two more twenties. "Does this cover Tina's tab?"

"It sure does."

"Ruby," Tina said. "You don't need to—"

"Consider it your birthday present."

Andre slipped the money away. "Happy birthday, Tina."

"My birthday's five months away." She shook her head at Ruby. "Thank you, Ruby. That was sweet."

"Are you kidding?" Ruby rolled her eyes. "I can't even think about how much I owe you right now."

The girl at the table rolled several dice and the whole table let out a groan.

"Looks like your arrow hit the troll, but," the boy checked his sheet, "you only did two points damage."

"Shit!" the girl exclaimed. "We're in deep doo-doo now."

"Oh, heck," Ruby said. "They're playing D&D." She walked over. "Hey, that's *Lair of Blood Spider*. Tina, we played that one, remember?"

"Not sure what you're talking about," Andre said.

"Huh?"

"That's not D&D."

"What? Yeah it is."

"Nope, can't be, because we're not allowed to play D&D down here. Says so right there." He pointed to sign written in marker. The sign read GOD'S HOUSE RULES in bold, below it, a list of don'ts, and there, right under No GAMBLING was No DUNGEON OR DRAGON GAMES. "Only thing going on at this table is Bible studies. Ain't that so?"

"Amen," all five of the kids said at once, one of them thumping the Bible sitting next to his character sheet.

Andre herded them past the game, and Tina caught Ruby's wistful look. They'd spent plenty of long nights in Tina's basement outsmarting necromancers and slaying bands of goblins, usually with her neighbor Shawn, Billy, and sometimes her brother.

They entered the studio—a small setup, partly partitioned off at the far end of the room, the wall and ceiling lined with egg cartons. There was a piano, a drum kit, and several mics set up.

"What's your favorite gospel song?" Andre asked.

"We don't really know any," Ruby said.

"Sure, you do. Have to. You're a gospel band after all."

Ruby looked at Tina confused.

Tina grinned. "We are today, because his grandpa only allows gospel bands to record here."

Andre smirked and pointed back at the sign; the third line down read No ROCKNROLL. "If we move quick, we can get you out of here before he comes down and checks on us."

Tina handed him a tape, while Ruby plugged in. Andre turned the system on and shoved the cassette in the recorder.

Ruby tapped the mic; everything seemed to be working. They strummed out a few chords, loosening up their fingers.

"Let's play a verse for warm-up then just go into it," Tina said. "Andre, just keep everything recording until we're done. I can edit it later, at home."

Andre gave her the thumbs up and hit record.

Tina caught the strain on Ruby's face. "You're kung fu, Ruby Duby. Don't you forget it."

Ruby gave her a weak smile and they started playing. Everything was sounding tight, but just when Ruby hit the vocals a bright red light started flashing from behind a bookcase.

Andre waved for them to stop, a look of panic on his face.

They quit playing and watched as Andre sprinted over and clicked off the flashing light, then over to help the kids as they scrambled to stow away the miniatures and dice. They threw a tablecloth over the game and pulled out Bibles and notebooks.

All eyes went to the walled-off stairs as something began clumping slowly down the steps. The clumping stopped at the bottom and an old man's bearded face peered round at them. He narrowed his eyes.

"Well, hey, Grandpa," Andre called.

"Well, hey, yourself." Andre's grandfather, the preacher, snapped back. He entered the room clutching his cane, a wiry old man with a white head of hair. He wore suspenders over a striped shirt buttoned up to his neck, and tucked into brown plaid pants, leaving Tina to wondered if he and Andre shopped at the same clothing store.

The preacher made his way down the room, his cane punctuating every step. He passed the kids at the table without a look, his eyes—his stern, judging eyes—were on the band. He walked up and pushed his glasses back up on his nose.

Vutto kept his head down.

"Who are *you*?" the preacher asked.

"We're . . . uhm," Tina started.

"That's the Sweet Peas," Andre put in.

"The Sweet Peas, huh? Ain't never heard of 'em. Y'all don't look like no gospel band to me." He gave Vutto a hard stare. "How about y'all playing me one of your songs."

Tina and Ruby exchanged a tense glance.

"Sure . . . thing," Tina said. "How about . . . uh . . . how about . . . 'Amazing Grace'? What do you think, Ruby?"

Ruby looked like a deer in headlights.

"Ruby? 'Amazing Grace'?"

Ruby just nodded.

Tina started the tune, and after a couple of seconds Ruby joined in, bumbling along the best she could, while Vutto timidly tapped the drums. Tina started to sing.

The preacher's face soured. "Good gracious! Stop that! Please stop that racket. Why that's just plain awful!"

"Grandpa, now," Andre said. "Don't be rude. They're just starting out. They're doing their best."

"Well, they need to do better, cause they're gonna scare away the Holy Spirit himself if they keep making that racket."

"Maybe your hearing aid is acting up again."

The old man scrutinized Andre. "If I didn't know better, I'd be suspecting you're recording some of that Devil music again."

"No sir! I'd never record Devil music. Not here, not anywhere."

"Uh-huh. Now, I done told you once, but I'm telling you again. That Devil music is a doorway into your soul. You hear me?"

"Yes, sir! I most certainly do."

"I see you smirking, don't think I don't. You think it's funny now, but that's how he gets you. He sneaks in through your music, your TV, your games, next thing you know . . . he's GOT yah!"

Ruby jumped.

Hang in there, Ruby, Tina thought.

The old preacher turned away, shuffling past the kids as they diligently studied their Bibles. He reached the stairs and stopped. "That's a pretty neat trick, Calvin."

"Sir?" one of the boys replied.

"You being able to read that Bible upside down and all."

Calvin gasped and spun his Bible around.

"Y'all ain't as smart as you all think you is. I done told you, and I'll keep telling you, them Devil games are an invitation to Satan." He let out a final huff and headed back up the stairs.

"Okay," Andre said. "Let's wrap this up."

"We're ready," Ruby said.

He hit record and Tina began to play again, and this time Ruby didn't miss a beat, she fell right in. The song flowed and in short order, Tina felt that familiar tingle in the air, the hair on her arms standing up as that warm, sweet sensation flowed around them. All of them singing together for the chorus.

'Gonna give you all my heart and soul, give you all my heart and soul.
Burnin' like a demon bowl, I give you all my heart and soul.

They finished the song to find Andre and the kids staring at them, mouths agape, tears rolling down their cheeks.

"Quick, one more," Tina said, and started again. "Keep it flowing."

This time when they hit the chorus, the kids joined in. The room swelled with the magical song. Then, somewhere around the second verse, another voice joined them, only it was more of a wail.

Tina spotted a white dog, a collie, by the door, howling. *No,* she thought, *not white . . . pale and wispy.* She saw it had hollow eyes; its mangy fur matted to its skeletal frame.

Oh no! she thought as a chill crawled up her spine.

A moment later another ghostly dog, a dachshund, came trotting in, coming right through the wall, grinning death's grin, followed quickly by a beagle, a German shepherd, and two pugs, filling the room with their long mournful howls.

Tina did her best to keep playing, backing away until her back hit the wall, hoping these ghosts, spirits, whatever they were, kept away from her.

And just when Tina didn't think it could get any weirder, several cats followed, then more dogs, at least a dozen of them, turning the room into a cacophony of yowls and howls and screams—the sound of lost souls.

"What's going on!" someone shouted. The preacher stood at the bottom of the stairs, his eyes ready to pop from his head. He banged his cane atop the table, knocking dice and miniatures all over the floor.

The "Evil in Me" song sputtered out, yet the howls continued, the ghosts drifting and swirling about the room like pale smoke.

"I done *told* you kids!" the preacher yelled, swatting at the ghosts with his cane. "I done *told* you!"

The kids blinked, rubbing their eyes as though awakened from a dream, bewildered looks on their faces. Andre kept backing up until he fell into one of the recliners, clasping his hands to his mouth.

"Look what you done!" the preacher shouted. "The Devil! You done brought the Devil into the house of God. Lord Jesus, help us all!"

Ruby appeared to be in a trance; Tina gave her a shake. "C'mon, let's get out of here!"

Tina grabbed the tape and the three of them dashed out the door, the preacher's booming voice echoing behind them as they sprinted across the lot.

"I done *told* you!"

VUTTO

O kay, be ready in a minute," Tina said, hitting record, dubbing their first take from the church session.

"Hey, Ruby, ask Beel how it is there are dog and cat ghosts? Do they have souls? I mean, I thought only people had souls."

Beel came forward and Ruby allowed him to talk through her. "Of course you thought that. People are arrogant. They believe they are the only creatures that matter."

Tina frowned. "Well, okay, don't need to get all judgy. But, I'm curious, are their souls like ours then? Do they go to doggy heaven when they die?"

"I have possessed many kinds of creatures, and at their core, they are all the same. They just want to live and thrive, they feel love and joy, hate and sorrow. But I will add, animal souls are purer, their desires more honest, they know their hearts better."

"So . . . no doggy heaven?"

"I do not know. Some linger on the earth plane, but most go on to somewhere. I only know I never saw a dog's spirit in Hell."

"That's because all dogs have good souls," Ruby put in.

"Don't know about that," Tina said. "Remember that Doberman, the one near the school? Redd? Redd did *not* have a good soul. Redd wanted to kill and eat anyone who came near his fence."

"Redd had shitty people," Ruby said. "Redd just needed love."

"I like dog," Vutto volunteered. "When I can catch them. They are very tasty."

"Vutto, no," Ruby scolded. "That's not okay."

"So Beel," Tina asked. "What happened then? At the church? You think the ring called all those pets? The taint? The song?"

"All of it perhaps, but especially the song. The manifestation of magic is like a bright light to them."

The tape clicked off. Tina pulled it out of the player and wrote Evil in Me, by the Night Mares on it. She held it up. "Okay, we're ready."

"So, it's a college station?" Ruby asked.

"Yeah, WREK. They're pretty much the only station in town that'll play our kind of music. My friend, Greg, he runs the late show."

"And you really think he's gonna play our song?"

Tina let out a breath. "Well . . . that part's a little complicated."

"Oh, do tell."

"Nothing big, just a minor hiccup."

Ruby waited.

"Greg's not taking my calls anymore."

"Aw, Tina, what did you do?"

"Me? Why do you think it was me?"

Ruby shook her head. "What did you *do,* Tina?"

Tina let out a harsh sigh. "Maybe, just maybe, I threw out his pot."

"Tina! Jesus. You're still doing that? Haven't you learned?"

"Dope's for losers."

"You got a crush."

"What? No, I don't."

"Yeah, you do. Because you only do that to people you really care about."

"Nuh-uh."

"Who are you talking to, here? How many times did you throw out my stash? And your beau, Ricky. What about your brother? Uh-huh. Tell me I'm wrong."

"Don't matter. I got a work-around."

"Oh dear," Ruby groaned.

"We're gonna break into the station."

Ruby rolled her eyes.

"Not as bad as it sounds. I got a key."

"How is it you got a key?"

"Greg gave it to me back when we were hanging out. I used to guest DJ with him sometimes."

Ruby shook her head. "I don't know."

"If you want folks to show up to the gig, we need to get this song out there. Let 'em know when and where we're playing. Folks hear this song and they're *gonna* show up. I know it. Because this song is full of magic."

"We're not gonna be able to play if we're in jail."

"We're not going to jail. It's just a college station. Most of the people know me there. They like me. They're not gonna call the cops. It'll be fine. Just fine. *Trust* me."

The cat hissed and leapt off the porch.

"Leave the kitty alone," Ruby said, grabbing Vutto by his jacket collar. "We don't eat cats."

"*You* don't eat cats," he replied.

"If I catch you near a cat you'll have to leave. You understand?"

Vutto stuck out his lip. "But I am hungry."

"How can you be hungry? You just ate two pounds of raw hamburger meat."

"I am always hungry."

"We'll get you some more meat on the way back. How about that?"

Vutto nodded. "Yah, more wet meat."

"Do you eat anything besides meat? Y'know, bread, or cheese maybe?"

"Yuck, cheese is gross. I like blood. Blood is my favorite."

Ruby shook her head and escorted him to the Cadillac. She opened the door. It was dark out and starting to rain. "Get in. I'm getting wet."

"Do we have to bring him?" Tina asked.

Ruby sighed. "After what happened at the club, yes. Crazies everywhere. This taint is real and he's about the only thing between us and them."

Vutto took a seat in the front.

"No sir," Tina said. "You're not riding next to me. In the back, buster."

Vutto moaned, but climbed over into the back as he was told.

Ruby cranked up the car and drove off, too busy trying to defog the windows to notice the gray van pull out and begin following them. About twenty minutes later they drove on to the Georgia Tech campus.

"Hey, Vutto," Tina said. "Tell me something."

"Yah?"

"Where do demons come from? Huh? Like, are there girl demons and boy demons? Y'all go on dates, get married, or what?"

"Yah."

"Yah?"

"There are every kind of demon."

"Well, what kind are you? Girl kind or boy kind?"

"I am neither kind."

"Well, where do you come from then?"

"I told you, Vutto is good egg. I come from egg."

"So . . . you lay eggs?"

"Yah."

"By yourself? I mean . . . don't you need some help with that?"

"I do not need boyfriend or girlfriend."

"Okay," Tina said. "I'm more confused than ever now."

"I am good egg."

"Yeah, I got that part. Hey, there it is," Tina said, pointing to a large coliseum. "The infamous Thrillerdome. The station is around back."

They drove to a side annex, parking in the back next to a row of dumpsters, and got out. There was only one other car and a semitrailer in the whole lot. The rain had let up, leaving the asphalt glistening under the one flickering sodium lamp.

Ruby scanned the bushes and shadows as they walked up to the building, on the lookout for crazies, relieved to find it so desolate. Other than a gray van driving by, she saw no one.

"Wait here, Vutto," Ruby said. "We should be back shortly." She noticed him sniffing. "What is it? You smell something evil?"

"I smell rats," he said, his lips curling, exposing his needle-like teeth. "Vutto hungry," he hissed, so low that she barely heard him. He closed his eyes for a moment, as though in pain, and rubbed the scar on his forehead.

He's fighting it, Beel said. **Do not turn your back on him.**

Tina tried the door; it was locked. She pulled out the key Greg had given her and opened it.

Vutto's face twisted into something vicious, his eyes turning into red specks of flame. It lasted only a second, but it sent a chill down Ruby's spine. Ruby nudged Tina inside, wanting to get away from the creature, hoping that he wouldn't be waiting to kill them when they returned.

Ruby and Tina entered the building. The place smelled like Pine-Sol. The only light on was at the far end of the hallway. They headed for the stairwell, their steps echoing down the long empty corridor.

"You sure this is okay?" Ruby asked in a whisper.

"It'll be fine."

"And you really think this Greg guy is gonna forgive you? Huh? Not just call the cops on us."

"It's not *if* he's gonna forgive me, it's just how much groveling I gotta do first. He always comes around . . . *eventually.*"

"Wait. Are you saying this isn't the first time you've thrown out his stash?"

"Not saying anything."

Ruby let out a low laugh. "Oh, you really do have the hots for this guy."

Tina grunted. "Let's keep this about the band, okay? Greg really digs helping out new acts. Taking credit for getting them their first airplay and all. It's a point of pride with him. So, I'm gonna leave it to you, to . . . y'know, sell the band and all."

"Me? I don't even know him."

"He's not *mad* at you. And don't worry, he'll like you. Just . . . just don't be afraid to be a little flirty. Y'know, turn on the sex appeal."

"Pffft . . . I don't do flirty. And I certainly don't have any sex appeal."

"Sure, you do."

"No, I don't. I'm a weirdo."

"Look, babe, you've been brainwashed by too many hair spray commercials. Not every guy is into Christie Brinkley. Greg likes weirdos. Just remember, for every weird gal, there's a weird guy out there somewhere."

Ruby wasn't quite sure how to take that, but knew flirting never worked for her. She'd always felt too self-conscious, as though she was coming across like some B-movie hussy.

They found their way to the second floor, then down the hall to a green door covered in band stickers. The whole building seemed empty.

"Shouldn't be anyone around but Greg at this hour," Tina whispered. "But if we do run into someone, just act like we were invited."

Tina opened the door and they entered a small room with a reception desk, the walls covered in band posters. There was no one around. The only light was coming from an adjoining hallway. Tina led them down the hall, to a door with a lighted sign that said ON AIR.

Tina gripped the doorknob, hesitated, sucked in a breath, then opened the door.

The man wearing headphones and sitting behind the console turned out not to be a man at all, but a young woman, a girl really, looking to be around eighteen or nineteen—black curly hair, shaved on the sides, wearing a jean jacket covered in band buttons and pins. She jumped when she noticed them, gave them a perplexed look, then raised a finger to her lips. She leaned into the microphone. "Looks like

I have some unexpected guest. Gonna leave y'all with 'Kiss Off,' by one of my faves . . . the Violent Femmes."

She hit a button on the console and took off her earphones. "Y'all aren't supposed to be in here. You lost or something?"

"No," Tina said. "We're not lost. Greg, he, uh . . . invited us here. We're his guests. Isn't this his shift?"

"Yeah, it is, but we switched out so I could go to the dentist. Sorry, you missed him. Hey, make sure the door is shut all the way on your way out, please. Thanks." She gave them a little wave and put her headphones back on.

"Well, maybe you can help us then?"

The girl slid her headphones back off, looking perturbed. "What?"

"I said, maybe you can help us."

"Y'all need to go."

Tina pulled out the cassette. "I'm Tina and this is Ruby. Our band is—"

"Tape submissions go in that box out front. Now I got to get back to work."

"This isn't a submission. Greg invited us here to play our new song."

"Y'all need to arrange that with Greg."

"We already did. That's what I'm telling you."

"Talk to Greg."

"Look, we're a local band trying to catch a break. Our show's tomorrow night, so it would really help us out if you could just slip this one song into your lineup. What do you say?"

"Put it in the box, please."

Tina came around the console, a big smile on her face. "Hey, forgot to mention I'm on with Greg all the time. Surely you've heard my name around here? Tina Tang? Yeah? Heck, we can even do this together. You and I. Make it a fun thing." Tina walked over to the tape deck.

"Hey!" the girl cried. "What the hell!"

Tina punched the tape deck open and slid in the tape.

"No ma'am!" the girl yelled and grabbed Tina, trying to tug her back while Tina struggled to push play. The two of them landed on the console, then rolled onto the floor. The girl began screaming bloody murder.

"Oh, shit!" Ruby said.

Tina flipped the girl over with one of her fancy martial art moves, and pinned her down in a choke hold.

"Tina!" Ruby cried.

"Push play!" Tina yelled. "Push play!"

Ruby jumped over and hit the button. The tape began to spin, but nothing happened, the Violent Femmes just continued to belt out how much they needed someone to talk to.

"The board!" Tina cried. "Hit the blue switch!"

The girl began gasping, her face turning bright red.

"Oh, fuck!" Ruby cried, straddling the wrestling duo to get to the board. There were at least four blue switches that she could see.

"Which blue switch?"

"The blue one! The blue one!"

The girl's face was purple now, her eyes rolling up in her head.

Ruby started hitting blue switches, managing to cut off the Violent Femmes, but now there was nothing, just dead air.

"Hey!" came a man's deep booming voice.

Ruby spun around to find a large black man in a security uniform glaring at them.

"What the hell is going on here?"

It's me, Richard.

I followed the Cadillac on campus, Ruby's song allowing me to keep a safe distance. It was so strong now I had little fear of losing them.

She parked in a lot near the stadium. I circled around, finding a good spot on a nearby street. There were no lights on the street and a hedge between us, giving me good cover to watch them.

Ruby and some tall Chinese-looking gal got out and walked over to the back door of the annex, the demon trailing along like some mindless pup.

I pulled out my revolver, checked the chamber, wondering for the thousandth time if I could kill that beast, or at least injure it enough to grab Ruby and get away. I had six rounds loaded and a dozen more in my vest pocket. Surely a slug to the cranium would drop that monster. Surely.

Ruby was talking to the demon, like some witch to her familiar. *What are you, Ruby?*

Goose bumps prickled my flesh. Seeing her there, so close, yet unattainable, was maddening. Her song so bright, so sweet. And this brought both joy and pain, as I knew now with certainty, I wasn't the only one who could hear it, not the only one under her spell, not the only one who craved her blood. Where would I be if Ruby was stolen from me? If someone were to murder her before I could? The thought chilled my marrow. How would I ever get over that? Why, it would kill me.

I glanced in the back of the van, at some of my new tools, a blowtorch and a large pair of needle-nose pliers. I had such great plans for her. Just needed to get her, get her before someone else did.

The women entered the building and the moment Ruby left my sight, I felt a wave of panic. *They'll be back,* I consoled myself. Dang it, how easy this all would be if that demon wasn't with them.

The demon paced back and forth, catching bugs out of the air and eating them. After a bit, it started sniffing along the wall, digging around some cinder blocks, picking and scratching in the weeds. God, but the thing gave me the willies. There was a pile of boards and two-by-fours leaning against two trash cans. It flipped over one of the boards and several big rats shot out, racing away toward the hedge. The demon dashed after them, all of them disappearing around the corner of the building.

I held my breath waiting for it to reappear; a minute drifted by, another.

Now! I thought, shoving my gun into my pants and grabbing my handcuffs and pepper spray. I put on my cap, snatched up my bandanna off the dash and tied it around my face. I had no sooner stepped from my van than the back door of the building popped open and the two women came stumbling out. No, they were thrown out, *shoved* to be precise. A large security guard yelling at them and then slamming the door shut behind them.

At that moment, despite being a lifelong atheist, I swore that God was real. Knew he must want me to rid the world of this witch. How else could I explain such luck other than divine intervention? Further, I made a pledge then and there to start attending church every other Sunday.

The pair headed for their car, their backs to me. That's when I moved in, pepper spray in hand, coming up fast along the hedge, intent on blindsiding them.

"See you in church, God."

Beel saw him, the man, and even with his face covered, Beel knew he was one of the evil ones attracted by the taint. The man held a spray can in his hand. He raised it, aiming the nozzle at them.

Ruby! Beel cried, pushing forward, forcing her down.

The man shot a blast of liquid at Ruby, but missed, hitting Tina instead.

Tina screamed and kicked out blindly, striking the man, knocking the spray can from his hand. The man punched her in the side of the head and she collapsed, crashing into the garbage cans, landing on a pile of boards.

Some of the overspray got in Ruby's eyes, stinging them and blurring her vision. Beel tried to push Ruby one way, but Ruby tried to go the other and she tumbled. Before she could get a leg up, the man drove his foot into her stomach, twice, knocking the air from her and doubling her over.

Beel tried to get Ruby up, away, but the blinding pain was overwhelming and all of Ruby's efforts went to coughing and sucking air back into her lungs.

The man grabbed Ruby, began dragging her off. He was surprisingly strong, easily picking her up and tossing her over his shoulder.

Then Beel saw him: Vutto, racing for them on all fours. Never had Beel been so glad to see a demon. Vutto revealed his true form, his blazing red eyes, horns, and gnashing mouth full of teeth.

"Aw, heck!" the man barked, dropping Ruby and tugging a pistol from his belt. A deafening blast followed and a hole opened in Vutto's chest, spinning the creature.

Vutto snarled and came on.

Another blast, another, punching big holes the demon's chest and knocking him backward.

Still, Vutto came on, eyes spurting flames of rage.

"Devil!" the man cried, and shot Vutto two more times.

Vutto made it a couple of more steps before collapsing a few yards away, panting, crawling toward them as black blood oozed from his wounds.

Beel knew there were a thousand kinds of demons, some that could be killed with mortal weapons, some that couldn't. He didn't know for sure with Vutto, but judging by the carnage, he feared Vutto was done.

Vutto tried one more time to get up, fell, and lay gasping.

"It's time to be rid of you," the man said, walking toward Vutto, gun leveled at the demon's head.

No, Ruby whispered, surprising Beel with a sudden rush of rage. She pushed herself to her feet, struggling against the blinding pain, stumbling toward the man from behind.

Yes, Beel thought, letting her rage swim through him, feeding on it, their combined wills giving her a surge of strength. ***Yes, stop him!*** And Beel remembered all the times he'd been a tiger, or lion, or wolf, or bear, what it was to be a predator, to depend on one's claws and teeth. He fed this back to Ruby, the hunger, the savagery.

Together, they pushed her wrecked body through the pain. Together, they rushed the man. Together, they leapt upon his back. Together, they bit into the side of his neck.

The man screamed and the gun went off as Ruby knocked him over Vutto, the three of them tumbling into a heap.

Ruby and Beel didn't let up, their combined fury—their desperation to stop this man before he killed them all, sent them all to Hell—turning Ruby into a savage beast, clawing at the man's face as she chewed into his neck. A hot burst of blood filled Ruby's mouth, feeding their frenzy.

The man brought an elbow up, hard, striking Ruby in the forehead. A second blow knocking her to the asphalt.

The man got to his feet, turned the pistol on Ruby. Ruby had torn away his bandanna and Beel could see the utter horror and confusion on his face. The man clasped his neck, trying to stem the blood running down his shirt. "Witch! Fucking witch!"

Ruby rolled to her hands and feet, crouched like a tiger ready to pounce. Together, Ruby and Beel let out a long, eerie howl.

The man pulled the trigger.

Click.

Nothing.

Click. Click.

The man dug frantically into his pocket, came up with a handful of bullets, backing away as he tried to reload the pistol.

"Fucker!" someone screamed. It was Tina, clutching a broken two-by-four like a ballplayer. She swung it, catching the man on the back of the head. The man stumbled, almost fell, fumbling bullets all over the asphalt.

Tina let out another scream, came at him again. He ducked the blow, turned and ran, darting away into the hedges, disappearing into the shadows.

Tina dashed over to Ruby, helping her to her feet. "C'mon, lets get out of here! Quick, before he reloads that gun."

They were halfway to the car, when Ruby halted. "No, wait. Vutto."

"No, no. We gotta git!"

Ruby glanced back at the demon. He was lying on his back in a pool of black blood, one arm reaching weakly for them. "He saved us," Ruby said. "All of us." She tugged loose from Tina and went to Vutto. She got an arm around him, but was having trouble getting him to his feet. Then Tina was there.

Vutto's eyes flittered open. "I am good egg," he said weakly.

"Yeah, you're a good egg," Tina said, and grabbed the demon's other arm.

Together the two women carried Vutto to the car, put him in the back seat, and drove away.

KNOTS

Eduardo pulled into the back of the 688 Club and turned off his truck. He checked his firearm, then slipped it into his shoulder harness. He kissed his fingertips and touched them to the plastic Jesus dangling from the rear-view, closed his eyes. "Jesus, give me the strength to—"

She came to him in a flash, the woman, the horrible way she was twisted up in the wreckage. Eduardo winced, fighting to push the vision away. Only the harder he strove not to see it, not to think about it, the more it plagued him. He clutched the cross that hung around his neck. "Redemption is a long hard road, but I don't walk it alone. I walk it with you, Jesus." It helped, it always helped, thinking of Jesus, of his love, but most of all his forgiveness.

The accident happened one week after Eduardo had been accepted into the Alabama Police Academy in Montgomery, two days after his twenty-first birthday.

The woman, Wendy Johnson—a single mom, pulling a double shift at the Wally's Waffles—was heading over to her mother's trailer, to pick up her four-year-old daughter. She made the mistake of pulling out in front of Eduardo, forcing Eduardo to brake, which pissed him off. Didn't help that Eduardo was blurry-eyed drunk, so drunk that he'd been cut off by the bartender down at the Red Clay Tavern. Didn't help that Eduardo had gotten tossed out on his ass for chucking his empty glass at the bartender.

Eduardo zipped up on Wendy, riding the tail of her little yellow VW Bug in his big pickup. She was barely going forty in a fifty mph zone. He honked, really laid onto his horn. But instead of speeding up, she actually slowed the fuck down. He could've just gone around her, but he wasn't in a go-around kind of mood.

Eduardo meant to bump her, just tap her bumper, scare her, teach her not to drive like a puss. Contrary to Eduardo's boast that he was a better driver after downing a few, he slammed into the back of her little car, watching in horror as she spun and plummeted off the road, smashing into a ditch.

That night Eduardo learned what someone looked like after being slammed into a windshield while not wearing a seat belt, the way someone screamed after having their cheek bone and cranium cracked, their jaw broken in four places, their eye torn from the socket.

When he was on trial, the prosecution put up a photo of Ms. Wendy Johnson before the accident. Eduardo got to see what a lovely woman Wendy had been. So different from the woman sitting before him now. But it was more than her disfigurement. The prosecutor went on to explain Wendy's struggle to live with debilitating pain, how she could no longer walk without a cane, could no longer lift her own daughter.

Eduardo had broken down and sobbed in the courtroom; probably the only thing that kept him out of prison. The felony went on his record and that's how Eduardo's law enforcement career ended before it even started.

Shortly after his conviction, Eduardo found God in a big way, swore off drinking, hadn't touched liquor since. He floundered around from job to job for a long time, but eventually decided if he couldn't bring in the crooks as a cop, he'd bring them in as a bounty hunter. He wanted to serve the community, wanted, needed that bond with his father and brother.

Eduardo squeezed the cross one more time and got out of his truck. He tried not to look at the horrible scratches Ruby had left down the entire side of his vehicle. "You're gonna pay for that. I'm gonna see to it."

He walked around to the front of the club and knocked on the door. After a moment he heard muffled voices within.

No one came to the door.

He knocked again, this time louder.

"No one's here!" a man yelled back through the closed door.

"I'm looking for my daughter."

"We don't have your daughter," the voice called back, followed by laughter.

Eduardo knocked again, banging loudly.

The door popped open and Eduardo found himself face-to-face with some weaselly looking dude with oily hair, wearing a yellow cowboy shirt. The man squinted into the afternoon sun. "Buddy, your daughter, whoever she is, ain't here."

"Just looking for a little help. My daughter, Ruby." Eduardo held up a picture of Ruby. "She played here a few nights ago. The Night Mares. Caused quite the ruckus. We saw on the news how she got hurt and all. Well, we're real worried about her, especially her mother. Just trying to make sure she's alright. Would you happen to know where she's staying? A phone number? Anything?"

The guy looked Eduardo up and down. "You don't look like her father."

"Stepfather."

"Are you a reporter?"

"I'm not."

"We've had at least a dozen reporters sniffing around here trying to get her address."

"Do I look like a reporter?"

"Is that a gun?" the guy asked, pointing at the bulge beneath Eduardo's jacket.

Eduardo shrugged.

"Wait . . . are you with the police?"

Eduardo thought how good it would feel to drive his fist into this man's smirky little mouth. "Just a phone number. Please."

"Can't help you, man," the guy said and shut the door.

"Prick," Eduardo huffed. He contemplated knocking again, contemplated kicking the damn door down. Instead, he turned around, started for his truck, stopped, turned back around, and stared at the door.

He let out a small laugh. "Right in front of my face." The door was covered in tattered band flyers, and one, a fresh clean one, listed the lineup at a place called the Metroplex. At the bottom of the list was the Night Mares.

"Why, that's tonight," he said, and grinned. Eduardo tore the flyer off, stuffing it in his pocket, and headed for his truck.

"Jesus is showing me the way."

Beel carefully opened Ruby's eyes. Ruby was asleep, and he didn't wish to wake her. They'd returned to Tina's place late in the night, not getting to sleep until just before dawn, no one able to sleep until Vutto passed out; his fitful moans and groans finally settling down.

Beel moved Ruby's eyes so that he could observe Vutto. The demon lay curled up in a blanket beneath the stairs, shivering and sweating. He would survive, Beel was sure of it. The demon appeared to heal much faster than humans. But that wasn't necessarily good, as the scar, the star on his forehead, was almost gone. Beel pondered if they should try and kill the demon, now, while he was weak. Because as soon as the star was gone, Vutto would most certainly kill Ruby. But despite its wounds, Beel wasn't convinced that they *could* kill Vutto; demons were unpredictable things. He had seen one cut in half, only to turn into two demons. He feared trying to kill Vutto might only hasten him falling back under Lord Sheelbeth's control.

How long did they have? So hard to guess.

Beel heard the worms. How could he not? Their song rang in his head now, growing louder as the waxy blood grew thinner upon the ring. Who would get them first, Vutto, or one of the tainted, or Lord Sheelbeth herself? Did it matter? It was all the same in the end. Were they really gambling everything on this show tonight? *By the stars, why?* he asked himself, the answer coming quickly. *There is no other chance. No other choice.*

But there is . . . scrub the ring. Hand myself over to Lord Sheelbeth's mercy.

A twinge of guilt surprised him. *Guilt for Ruby?* he wondered. *No, of course not. What is she to me? Just another greedy human, that is all.* Only he knew that wasn't true, not anymore. They'd joined together, had fought together, had saved one another . . . had drank blood together.

But there was more to his guilt. Something he preferred not to think about. Something that hadn't mattered to him until this very moment. If this ruse *did* work—if Ruby's song was able to remove the ring and he escaped, flew away on some bird—there was still the matter of the taint. He felt certain it would remain on Ruby even with the ring gone, that it would be in her blood, and evil would find her and evil would kill her.

I do not care. There is nothing for it even if I did. Our fates are cast and we must play our roles. When was the last time any human ever cared for me? Never. It was never.

Yet the thought of Ruby running from evil until she could run no more, clawed at his heart.

Stop it. God can look after his chosen children. I have burned, and I am done burning. I must escape regardless of cost.

Ruby let out a whimper, then a small cry. She jerked awake.

"Dad?" she said. "Daddy . . . ?"

It was a dream, Beel said. **A nightmare perhaps.**

Her eyes found Vutto. "No, *this* is the nightmare." She winced, clutched her head. "The worms . . . they're louder now."

Yes. They will break through soon.

She glanced at the clock; it read 4:30 p.m. "The show's soon. We're gonna make it, Beel. We're gonna beat this thing."

Beel wished he shared her optimism.

"We have to." Her eyes drifted back to Vutto and he felt her shudder. "Have

236

to, because I can't take much more of this shit. I mean . . . I drank blood with a demon last night. God, what kind of monster are you turning me into?"

There it was again, she could only see him as a demon, a monster. He was shocked by how much that stung.

A willing one, he said. **You seized on the savagery as though starving for it. It is the same with all you humans. As much as you pretend to be something more, you are all bloodsuckers when your back is against the wall.**

Ruby fell quiet for a spell.

"I miss my daddy. Miss knowing he was there looking out for me."

He felt her sadness; her emotions seeping into him.

"I was eight when he died, so his memory is a bit fuzzy, but he's always so clear in my dreams. I was dreaming about him just now. He was pushing me in a swing . . . laughing, so much laughing. Then he was gone. Just gone. God, how I miss him. How different my life would've been if he'd stayed around."

Her sadness deepened; Beel felt it like a wave. She dug a cigarette out of her pocket. Lit it with a shaky hand and took a drag.

"He was always there for me. Always on my side."

Her sadness turned to anger.

"Can't remember the last time my mom was on my side about anything. Had to be back before Daddy died. Seems like we've been at war ever since." She dabbed at her eye. "I miss my old mom too. The mom before Daddy died. Before she turned into such a bitch. Before that ass-bite, Eduardo, moved in."

Did you not talk to her about this?

"There's no talking to her. She doesn't listen to me. *Ever.*"

Perhaps she feels the same about you. In my experience, humans do not know how to speak from the heart . . . it causes many misunderstandings.

"Look, she thinks I'm mentally ill. Just nags me to take my pills so she doesn't have to deal with me."

Perhaps there is more going on. Maybe she is worried about you. Feels these pills are truly helping you?

"God, you're starting to sound like Dr. Fatass. He's always throwing it all back at me. Well, fuck him and fuck you."

I am only trying to say that there could be misunderstandings. That the truth might be deeper.

"Look, where's this coming from? Why are you defending her? You don't even know her."

But I know you. Maybe better than you do.

"What does that mean?"

I am within. I see what people hide, even from themselves.

"Well, that's creepy as fuck. Why don't keep your nose to yourself."

If only I could. You carry a lot of pain.

"No shit."

You are not the only one. People hide a lot from themselves. Block out the things that scare them . . . the trauma, mistakes, the bad. You would not be the first to create your own reality of who you are.

"What the fuck are you talking about? I know who I am."

It is good to leave the bad behind, to let it go. But sometimes things are shut away before they are delt with. They linger, fester like an infected wound, spreading their poison. Often it is not something intentional, just sometimes a person is born a bit broken . . . unable to deal with life's struggles.

"Oh, and that's me, born broken. Right? Good Lord, you *do* sound just like Dr. Ferguson." She stubbed out her cigarette, grinding it angrily into the ashtray. "Where are you going with this?"

Where am I going with this? Beel wondered, thought he knew. There was once a time when he was more than a tool of murder, when his talents to manipulate the mind did many good things for those whose lives, whose bodies, he inhabited, man and beast alike. How he longed for those days, when his only purpose was to share the many joys of life with those he possessed. So, it was fair to say that if he could once more feel what it is to help someone, then maybe he could convince himself that he wasn't becoming a demon after all. And there was something else. Perhaps Ruby wasn't the only one hiding truths, because maybe, just maybe, this strong-willed woman who drank blood with him was starting to matter. And if he could help her, even a little, on what might be her last hours on earth, then why would he not?

Ruby, it is real. This trouble within you. I can see it. How can I describe it to you? It is like the strings that hold your mind together have become tangled, some even knotted. And these knots . . . they impede your ability to cope, to heal, even to understand yourself. In essence, blinding you to yourself. I am sure your Dr. Fatass has plenty of fancy terms for this, but from where I am, it is simple. Your mind is full of scars.

He felt her temper flare. "You know what I don't need right now? I don't need some *demon* telling me what's wrong with me! That's what!"

I am not a demon.

"Well, you sure as fuck aren't human, 'cause if you were, you wouldn't be laying this bullshit on me."

Her hands began to tremble; he could feel her fighting back her rage. "Here," she snapped. "Let me *tell you* what's wrong with me. My daddy, he came home from Vietnam with his mind messed up. He just needed some love and understanding. You wanna know what he got from my mom? Endless arguments and fights. She was always laying into him. Like he wasn't already dealing with enough crap. But that ain't the half of it. The real kicker, the real kicker is my mom, my dear misunderstood mom, she went off and had an affair with one of Daddy's best friends. Can you believe that? He should've shot the both of them dead. I sure as hell would've. But instead, he killed himself . . . committed suicide. So as far as I'm concerned, she might as well have murdered him."

Ruby pressed her palm against her forehead, groaned. "Now that might make me a little screwed up. But I'm telling you I'm not hiding from it. And I don't have no goddamn knots in my head. I got a fucked-up mother. That's it!"

They both fell quiet, Ruby's sniffles the only sound. Ruby finally got up, got a Kleenex and blew her nose. She picked up the bass and picked softly at it.

"I'm sorry," Ruby said. "You're not a demon. I say mean shit when I get mad. Fuck, why does everything always gotta be this way with me?"

Again, Beel felt her pain, her deeper hurt. *I am going to show you something,* Beel said. *But you will need to trust me.*

Ruby laughed, but it was a bitter sound. "Trust you? Yeah, I'm pretty much all in at this point. Right?"

Lay down, close your eyes.

Ruby kept plucking the bass.

Beel could feel her fatigue, her deep mental exhaustion with all of it. *I would show you something, if you will let me. Now, lay down, close your eyes.*

Ruby sighed. "Sure, okay. Why not?" She set the bass aside and lay down on her sleeping bag. After a moment, she closed her eyes.

Beel gave her time to settle, then withdrew within. *You are in a great sea of night,* he said in a soft, soothing whisper. *You are floating along in a light warm breeze as all the stars of the universe shine above you and below you.*

He did more than say these words, he pushed his visualizations at her, into her, as he slipped deeper within her mind, her soul.

Let yourself go. Let yourself drift away like a flower petal.

He came up against a wall within Ruby's mind, nothing that he could see, just a place he couldn't go.

Let me in, he whispered.

The wall didn't give.

Let me in.

Her breathing slowed as sleep took her. He pressed again, the wall still wouldn't yield, didn't need to, as he slowly became part of it, part of her true self. He was amongst the strings.

A slight moan escaped her lips.

They weren't really strings, but his mind and hers made them so. And here, he could see the knots, so many knots. And even though they weren't real, he could touch them. He strummed a few and felt her body quiver. He gently took one of the knots and untangled it, it only took his touch, then one after another, until he could find no more.

Wake up. Ruby, wake up.

Ruby opened her eyes, unsure where she was. She sat up, blinked, looked around Tina's room, and the weight of it all returned.

Ruby, Beel asked. ***How do you feel?***

She was going to say, *About the same,* only that wasn't true. Somehow, she felt lighter, her head clearer. If not for all the impending doom hanging over her, she would've even said she felt good.

Ruby, brace yourself. I have set your mind, your memories, free. It could come as a shock.

"Memories? What memories? Not sure what you mean."

Ruby, tell me. How was your father the last time you were with him?

"He was sweet . . ." She stopped, the memory she had was of them strolling through the woods, discussing the many birdcalls around them. But as soon as it came to her, another took its place. It was of him arguing with her mother. She had plenty of memories of their fights, of her mother badgering him, but this one felt different. Why?

It was the tone, her mother's tone, she was pleading, not badgering, but begging him to do something. The memory cleared. Her mother was begging him to go to the doctor, for therapy, and he was having none of it.

Of course, Ruby thought. *That's my mom. Always thinking everyone is crazy. Just need the right doctor, the right pill.*

She saw her father dumping his pills down the sink while glaring at her mother. All at once her dad started screaming at her mom, red faced and raging, spittle flying from his lips. He shoved her then, no *slammed* her, into the wall.

Ruby gasped. "No! That's not my dad?" But no sooner had she said it, then another memory came to her, one of him smashing dishes on the floor, another of him punching his fist into the bathroom mirror until it was dripping with his blood, one of him holding a knife to his own throat and screaming at them, threatening to kill them all.

"No," Ruby said. "No way. Stop this, stop it! What have you done to me?"

Hold fast, Ruby. You are whole now. You are strong. Face it. Face yourself.

She clasped her head, fought to stop the memories, but they wouldn't stop. One after another of her father's growing instability, of her mother and her trying to deal with him. And as much as she wanted to believe Beel had vexed her somehow, she knew these memories were true, because they weren't just memories, but missing pieces. And suddenly the puzzle that was her life came crawling together and everything made sense. The chaos of her mind that had plagued her for so long, that had made her feel so crazy, suddenly falling in order.

But it wasn't over; another memory, one that had been buried in the deepest recesses of her mind, came tumbling out of the shadows. "Face it," she told herself, gritting her teeth. She saw her father chasing her through the house with a knife, screaming at her, naked, streaks of blood from where he'd cut himself running down his chest. He cornered her in her room, shrieking and waving the knife. Ruby could still feel the heat of his breath, the crippling terror as she trembled, her back pressed against the wall. And her mother . . . her mother walking right in, even with her father waving that bloody knife about, putting herself between them. Then somehow, calmly telling him that there were no Vietcong coming to get him, that no one here wanted to hurt him. To look, to see that it was his daughter, Ruby, there in front of him. For the love of God, it's Ruby.

Ruby could see the terror on her mother's face, the knowledge that this mad soul before her might murder her at any moment.

How? Ruby wondered. *How could she be that brave?*

Ruby's mother gently, carefully, took the knife from her father.

For me. She was that brave for me. And I can't even remember the last time I told her I love her.

Ruby burst into tears. "God, Mom. I'm so sorry. So fucking sorry."

Ruby's mother, Martha, picked up the phone on the second ring. "Eduardo, that you? Did you hear anything?"

"Mom, it's me."

"Ruby! Oh, thank God! Are you alright?"

"Mom, I need to—"

"Are you in a cult? Eduardo said you're in some kind of satanic cult."

"No, Mom. I'm not in a satanic cult." Ruby glanced at the clock; they needed to leave for the show five minutes ago. "Listen, please, just listen. I only got a minute."

"I'm here."

"These last few days . . . they've really helped me to see things clearly. There's a lot about what we went through with Dad . . . that I . . . well, I put away. You know, like the doctor said, that I suppressed. But I remember now, Mom. All of it. Do you hear me? I remember. The good and the bad . . . all the bad. Especially the bad." Ruby took a deep breath. "I remember what we went through with Dad. What *you* went through. Dealing with his episodes, his trauma, the flashbacks, the tantrums, the violence, the threats. I can't imagine how horrible that must've been for you. Mom, what I'm leading up to, what I really want to say is that . . . is that . . . I haven't been fair to you. Worse, I've been a total shit. And I'm . . . I'm . . . well, I'm just hoping you can forgive me, because—"

"I didn't cheat on him," her mother blurted out. "On your father. I need you to know that. More than anything, I need you to know that. I know it looked bad to the neighbors, him finding me at Todd's house and all. Folks gonna believe what they wanna believe. But I was trying to find us a place to stay until we could get out of town. Todd was helping us, that's all. But your dad . . . he tracked me down. And well . . . and well, you know what happened. Dad assumed the worst and . . . and . . ." She let out a great sob.

"God, Mom, please. You don't need to do this. I know now. I get it."

"He shot himself right there in front of me."

"Aw, Mom. Geesh, God, I'm so sorry. So, so damn sorry. It's not your fault. You know that. You have to know that. You did everything you could for him . . . for all of us. I know that now. Know that you were right about so much. He was sick. He needed help. And . . . and I needed help too."

Her mom was still crying.

Tina walked into the room, tapped her watch.

"Mom, I gotta go."

"Ruby, baby, Eduardo is on his way up to get you. Just tell me where you are and I will have him—"

"Mom, it's too late for that. Listen, please. I know things have been hard between us. That I've put you through a lot of bullshit. We can work through all that later, when I come home. But for now, for now I just need to tell you that I love you. I love you, Mom. You hear me? I love you."

Her mom burst into a fresh round of sobs. "I love you too, baby. You'll always be my baby no matter what. You know that. Please tell me you know that."

"I know that, Mom."

Ruby wiped away her own tears. "Gotta go, Mom. See you soon."

She hung up.

Ruby stared at the phone for a long time, then lifted the receiver. She dialed Pam's number. After the sixth ring, the answering machine picked up.

"This is Pam, please leave a message."

Ruby tried to speak, but couldn't find the words.

She hung up the phone.

They were all quiet as Ruby pulled onto the highway. Vutto had fallen asleep in the back. They'd dressed him up for the show and his hat covered his eyes while he snoozed. The sun was setting and it looked like more rain was on the way.

Ruby pulled out a cigarette and started digging for her lighter. She stopped, realizing that she didn't need a cigarette—more, that she didn't even *want* one. *Beel,* she thought. *You did this.* And for a moment it scared her. *What else did you do to me?* But as she drove, as she listened to herself, her true self, she came to understand that it was more of an undoing. Like the knots in her brain, Beel had undone her dependency, her addiction.

She crumbled up the cigarette.

Ruby glanced over at Tina; Tina appeared lost in her thoughts, absently touching the bruise on the side of her face where that crazy man had hit her. Ruby marveled at how Tina always managed to keep her chin up, no matter what kind of bullshit they were dealing with. It's all about *indomitable spirit,* Tina would say. How many times had Ruby heard that one? But Ruby wondered if it was healthy, the way Tina kept things bottled up, hiding her feelings from everyone. Tina could fool most folks with her never-ending gags and grins, but Ruby could see right through it, and right now she could see the strain and the fear.

Ruby reached over, set a hand on top of hers. "I'm so sorry about all this."

Tina blinked, then her smiled returned. "Sorry about what? This isn't your fault."

"About bringing you into this trouble."

"Trouble is what we do, girl."

That's your indomitable spirit talking, Ruby thought, and sighed. "Tina, you're the best friend anyone could ever have. You know that don't you?"

"Well, yeah . . . that goes without saying, boogerhead." She laughed, and ruffled Ruby's hair, then checked her watch. "Oh, shoot. Greg's show already started. She clicked on the radio, flipped through the fuzz until she came to WREK.

They caught the tail end of a song, and then Greg's cool but somewhat geeky voice came out of the speakers.

"That was 'My City Was Gone,' by the Pretenders. That song always makes me sad. And here's another one for this dreary evening, 'She's Lost Control,' by Joy Division."

Tina turned it up a bit and Vutto suddenly snarled in his sleep, jerking his head back and forth, his claws twitching, his teeth clacking.

Ruby and Tina exchanged a worried look. Ruby had heard of dogs chasing rabbits in their dreams; she wondered what Vutto was chasing.

"Tina, listen to me. I need you to make me a promise."

"Oh?"

"Promise me, no, swear it. If Vutto loses it. If he comes after me . . . you'll run. You'll get the hell out of the way. None of your Tae Kwon Do heroics. Just run as fast and as far away from him as you can get. *Promise* me."

Tina shook her head. "I can't do—"

"No! Don't even. You swear to me right now, that you'll run. If you don't swear it, I'm putting you out right here."

"But—"

"Swear it!"

"Okay, okay, Ruby Duby. I swear."

"Let me see your fingers."

Tina held up both hands; her fingers were crossed.

"Tina!"

"Alright, alright." She uncrossed her fingers. "I swear it."

Ruby checked the rearview again, Vutto was snoring now.

"Hey, listen to me," Tina said. "We're gonna pull this off, babe. Gonna rock the Plex. 'Cause together, we're unstoppable. Don't you forget that."

"I won't forget. I'm counting on it," Ruby said, nodding, trying to sound confident. *And if we bomb,* she thought. *If not enough folks show up. Guess I'm going to Hell. That's all. How about that.*

Greg played several more tunes, breaking in again after the fourth song.

"Okay, wasn't gonna share this, but it's just too good a story not to. Had two crazy women break into the station last night. No, they didn't try to steal anything, just wanted to play their song. I know I shouldn't reward bad behavior, but out of curiosity, I gave the song a listen. And, well, there's something magical about this one. Honestly, can't get it out of my head. So, this is for Tina. Tina, if you're out there, you're a jackass, but I love you anyway." He laughed. "'Evil in Me,' by the Night Mares."

The song started.

"Oh, hot patootie!" Tina shouted, twisting the volume up.

It was the first time Ruby had ever heard herself on the radio, and for a few seconds, she actually forgot about the ring—breaking out in goose bumps at the sound of her own voice coming over the airwaves.

"There's magic in that song," Tina said, and began singing along. Another voice joined, it was Vutto, he began drumming on the back of the seat. And there it was, the tingling. Ruby began to sing with them, letting go, letting the song free her for a few precious moments.

The tingling turned into vibrations, the vibrations surging around them to the tune of the song.

"You feel that?" Ruby asked.

"Oh, yeah," Tina said. "Wow . . . it's the magic, right?"

"Yeah . . . but—" But it wasn't coming from them; it felt like it was flowing *into* the car.

"It's the song!" Tina shouted. "Oh, shit! Folks are singing along. Get it? They're singing along right this second, singing to the radio!"

The magic grew, felt almost like a wind.

Ruby, Beel cried. **Use it! Use the magic. Quick!**

Ruby felt the magic calling to her, the symbol on her arm growing warm, it wanted in. Her eyes fluttered as she fought to keep the car in its lane.

"Watch out!" Tina cried as a truck swerved out of their way, laying on the horn as it flew past.

Ruby jerked the wheel and they bounced over the curb and onto to someone's front lawn, taking out their mailbox.

Ruby slammed on the breaks.

Now! Beel cried.

Ruby closed her eyes, giving herself to the magic. A burst of heat in her chest, then it was fading. *No!* she thought, *Don't go!*

She opened her eyes.

The song was over. It was Greg's voice she heard now. "Wow, just wow! Gets better every time I hear it. The name of the band is the Night Mares and they'll be playing live tonight, at Metroplex, eight p.m. That's tonight, folks, and they're on first. So, if you don't want to miss them, you better hurry on over."

MURDER

*I*t's me, Richard.

I parked in front of the house, the one Ruby was staying at. I knew she wasn't there. Could feel it. Just hoped they'd be back soon. I was having a hard time tracking her. I could still hear her song alright, it was just my head felt like it was about to split in two, making it hard to focus, to follow the song. I'd taken a dozen Tylenol, and that probably wasn't helping either. Not sure what that Chinese bitch had hit me with, but it had certainly messed me up. Hadn't been able to wake up until afternoon. Lord, I probably had a concussion.

I gently touched the wound on the back of my head. Winced. The lump felt as big as a baseball.

I peeked in the rearview at the scratches across my face. My eyes were black and I had a bandage wrapped around my neck. The blood was seeping through again, forming a large red stain.

So much for blending in. And now, on top of all this, I couldn't find Ruby.

I shoved my pistol and combat knife into my belt, got out of the van, and headed toward the house. I crept up onto the porch, on the lookout for tricks and traps, more of her bewitchery. The door was unlocked and I let myself in. It was time to end this, now, tonight, one way or another.

I walked into the living area, not sure what I was seeking. Some clue to where they went, I guess? Someone to interrogate?

That someone was sitting on the couch, watching TV—not a demon or witch, just some stupid-looking kid with bleached hair and a dangly earring, holding a beer.

"Who the hell are you?" he asked.

"Where are they? The witch and her friend?"

"Witch?"

"Ruby. Where is she?"

He burped. "Man, you need to chill out."

I stepped up to him, pulled my knife.

"Oh, Jesus! Hell!" he cried.

"Where are they?"

"Alright, man. No problem. They're off playing a gig."

I set the knife against his neck. "Where?"

"Cool it, man. Just cool it! The Metroplex. Alright?"

"One of them punk rock clubs?"

"Yeah."

"Is it nearby?"

"Not far. Over by Marietta Street, near the projects."

I slid the knife across his throat. Didn't need to really, could've of just tied him up, but I didn't like his stupid earring. He clutched his neck, gagging and gurgling, flopped about on the couch for a few minutes, then died.

I felt nothing.

I found his room, found a well-worn leather trench coat. Put it on and flipped up the collar to hide my bandage. Checked myself out in the mirror. Not enough. I went into the bathroom, found some scissors, and carefully, doing my best to avoid my lump, chopped my thinning hair down to the scalp. That was better—might not stand out like a sore thumb at the freak club if I was a freak too. But there was still a fifty-two-year-old man staring back at me with scratches and black eyes. I found some makeup, pale, ghostly stuff. I wiped it on my face, then applied mascara around my eyes. Now there was a ghoul staring back at me. A weird grin on his face.

"Peachy keen," I said, and left.

Eduardo drove into the parking lot.

"Is this it? Can't be."

He pulled into a parking spot, plucked up the flyer, and even though the name, Metroplex, was written in huge letters along the side of the building, he checked the address again.

"What a dump."

The club—an old two-story industrial building, covered in layers of graffiti—appeared ready to cave in. There were only two entrances, the front and the back. The windows were either boarded up or barred. Luckily, he didn't plan to step foot in the place. From where he was parked—facing out toward the road for a quick getaway—he could keep tabs on people coming and going. The plan was simple, the moment Ruby stepped out of the car, he'd rush up, flash his badge—it was only a bondsman badge, but these dipshits wouldn't know the difference—slap on the cuffs, and cart her off. If anyone got in his way, he'd deal with them appropriately.

He double-checked his firearm, the large can of pepper spray, handcuffs, and his pair of brass knuckles.

The flyer said the show started at eight. He checked his watch, it was seven-thirty.

Where is she? Don't these jokers do sound checks? He thought about how shitty this punk rock crap sounded and figured they didn't.

More cars arrived and people started gathering out front, cutting up, laughing.

"Degenerates," he said, and found himself actually hoping a few of these rejects got in his way, so he could crack some heads.

Eduardo sipped of his coffee, turned on the radio, and began drumming the steering wheel along to Willie Nelson. He was surprised that he was so excited, thought for sure he'd be nervous, even a little scared. But no, he was jacked, ready to go, like a kid about to go out for recess. All he could think about was everyone's faces down at the station when he brought in a wanted fugitive. But more than that, to finally have a story to share with his dad and brother. *God, ain't that gonna feel good. Finally be able to hold my head up again.* Not to mention that he'll be a hero in Martha's eyes. Bringing back her baby and all. Word would get around town, as it always did, folks down at Baily's Bonds be calling him before too long.

He checked his watch again; it was five till eight.

Eduardo clutched his cross, bowed his head. "Lord Jesus, thank you for looking over me, for giving me the chance, the opportunity to better myself. I am your soldier. Please give me the strength I need to save Ruby Tucker, to rescue the misguided woman from the evil that is around her. In Jesus's name, Amen."

Ruby switched lanes, passing the slower traffic as she sped down Ponce de Leon Avenue.

Vutto was awake now, staring out the window, shaking and twitching, snarling at people on the sidewalk. Ruby glanced in the rearview, caught the demon's face twisting into something sinister for a moment. A flash of Vutto tearing Tina's neck open came to her. She bit her lip at the thought of having to see her best friend eaten alive by a demon, just like Josh. One more person she loved dead because of her.

"Beel, the spell that removes the ring, it also removes the taint, right?"

Beel didn't answer.

"Beel?"

I do not know.

"You don't know?"

No. I am sorry. I do not know.

"But there's a chance, right?"

There is a chance, Beel said, but he didn't sound very sure to Ruby.

Ruby's grip tightened on the steering wheel. *I'm never getting out of this.* She glanced again in the mirror at Vutto, caught him staring hungrily at the back of her neck. *I'm just fooling myself. None of this is gonna work.* Her hands began to tremble; she found it harder and harder to breathe.

Stop it, she thought. *Just stop it.*

She concentrated, focused on calming herself, began to breathe again, slow deep breaths, and with each breath she felt more and more centered. Her hands stopped trembling, and for the first time since her father had died, she felt some control over herself. And again, she felt grateful for what Beel had done, or undone, understood that this must be what it feels like to be whole.

Good, Ruby thought. *Good. Hold it together. If you ever want to see your mother again, you* will *hold it together.*

And she *did* want to see her mother again—more, she was looking forward to it, to a second chance at their relationship. She could see now how so many of her troubles, not just with her mother, but plenty of other folks, could've been avoided with just a little bit of empathy and understanding on her part. *God,* she thought. *If I can just get through this, there're so many people I'd like a second chance with.*

A slow, melodic song drifted from the radio, touching the sadness deep within her. Her grief for Josh snuck up on her and she sucked in a deep breath. *I need to talk to Pam. Have to. Can't do this 'til I do.*

She hit her turn signal and pulled into a gas station.

"What're you doing?" Tina asked. "We got plenty of gas."

"Gotta call someone."

"What? No. We already missed sound check. Now c'mon. Whatever it is, it can wait."

"No, it can't," Ruby said, and thought, *because there might not ever be another chance.*

She parked, got out, entered the phonebooth, and dialed. The phone rang and rang. "C'mon, Pam, pick up." Ruby started to hang up when she heard Pam's voice.

"Hello." She sounded slightly out of breath.

Ruby started to reply, found herself without words.

"Hello . . . anyone in there?"

"Pam," Ruby said, in little more than a whisper.

"Hello?"

"Pam," Ruby said a little louder, "I . . . I—"

"Ruby? Ruby is that you?"

"Pam, I didn't mean for it to happen."

"Ruby, where are you? Tell me. I'll come get you straight away."

"Pam, I'm so sorry . . . your dad, he's—"

"He's dead," Pam put in, her voice somber. "The police called me this morning. Told me about the fire."

"I'm so sorry. It's not like it seems. There's this ring. I just—"

"Ruby, stop. Listen to me. This is my fault. Do you hear me? It's my fault. I knew about the ring. Dad had warned me about it for years. I . . . I just didn't *believe* him. Thought it was all nonsense. God, it's such a relief to hear your voice. I was so afraid you'd died in that fire."

"How'd you know I had the ring?"

"Dad left a note. He blamed himself, only himself. You hear me . . . you did *nothing* wrong."

Ruby didn't know what to say.

"The ring . . . is it. . . . did you get it off?"

Ruby didn't answer.

"Where are you, Ruby? I'm coming to get you. We'll get help. Someone has to be able to help you. Just tell me where you are."

"Pam . . . I think I'll be okay. There are some folks helping me. Just needed to tell you about your dad. That's all."

"Ruby, I—"

"Gotta go. I'll be home soon. I know it. We'll work through this together. If you see my momma, tell her I love her."

"Ruby, just—"

Ruby hung up.

Lord Sheelbeth sat on her stone throne, her eye, the one in her head, closed as she concentrated, focused. The worms sang, filling the chamber with their song, with her song, calling to Vutto, trying to break through.

Her eye, the one on the ring, opened. "There," Sheelbeth whispered as blurry light bloomed before her. It took her a moment to realize that the ring was partially covered by a rag or perhaps a glove. When Ruby moved her hand, Sheelbeth could catch quick glimpses of the world above. The blood was so thin now, she could hear the women as though she was in the car with them.

"They will try to use the spell again," Sheelbeth said to her worms. "It is time to put a stop to this madness, to bring Beel home."

When Ruby rested her hand on the side of the seat, Lord Sheelbeth spotted Vutto, could see the scar was almost gone.

"*Vutto,*" she called, trying to reach into his mind.

"*Vutto,*" the worms sang.

"*Kill her, kill Ruby. Her blood, it will cure all your pain. Do it, Vutto. Do it now!*"

The demon groaned, shook his head, and mumbled. "No . . . no, they are my friends. I not kill my friends."

She wondered how this idiot demon could be so stubborn. "*They are not your friends. They hate you. They plan to kill you, Vutto.*"

He shook his head. "No. They are my friends."

"*Kill Ruby,*" she sang, and the worms sang along, sang to the heavens, sang to the hells.

Vutto slowly began to nod along. "Kill Ruby," he whispered. "Kill her."

Lord Sheelbeth smiled and spoke to the worms. "Our nightmare is almost over. The magic book has burned, the last of the Baalei Shem are dead, and soon, very soon, Beel will be ours again. Our time has come at last. We need but gather enough souls and we are free."

She wondered how many souls it would take. A hundred? Five hundred? A thousand perhaps? Did it matter? *No,* she thought. *For I will never quit, not until I am free.*

REDEMPTION

Eduardo watched the black Cadillac turn into the parking lot, spotted Ruby right away. The car pulled into a spot near the back of the building.

"I am a warrior for Jesus," Eduardo said, and touched the plastic crucifix hanging from his rearview before getting out of the truck. He shoved his handgun into its shoulder holster, tugged out his badge, and headed toward Ruby. He had a swagger in his step, like some lone sheriff about to bring in the bandits.

Ruby and another woman, a tall Asian gal with long hair, got out of the car. It took him a moment to realize it was Ruby's friend from school; he thought her name was Tina.

Ruby had her back to Eduardo as he approached. The plan was already going better than he'd hoped; there was almost no one else back here.

"Time to go home, Ruby," he said, with as much gravel as he could muster.

Ruby jerked around and he got his first good look at her, and what he saw shocked him. Gone was the awkward, dorky gal living in her mother's basement, the woman before him appeared hard, intense, ready for a scrap.

Upon seeing him, a look of surprise crossed Ruby's face. Eduardo liked that—intimidate and overwhelm. He expected her surprise to turn to shock and confusion and then fear, but it didn't. Instead, he saw, what . . . anger? No. He saw *confidence*. She was looking at him like he was just some annoying kid and he didn't like it one bit.

"Got a warrant on you, Ruby." He flashed his badge. "Time to go home."

"Not going anywhere with you, fuckhead."

He pulled out his handcuffs. "Easy or hard. You're choice. Either way, you're coming with me."

Ruby didn't run, didn't even flinch, just held his eyes with a steady glare.

Tina stepped up beside her. "Beat it, asshole."

"This is official police business, sweetie. I got the law on my side. You better hear me unless you wanna end up broke in two."

The back door to the Cadillac opened and some creepy-looking kid in sunglasses poked his head out.

"Stay back, Vutto," Ruby commanded.

Eduardo didn't like the way this was going. He couldn't see the kid's hands. Didn't like the look on Ruby's face—like she was the one in charge. Suddenly, Eduardo just wanted to have Ruby in the truck and be on his way. He pulled out his gun, leveled it at the kid in the car. "Like I said, I got the law on my side. Things get out of hand and someone's gonna end up full of holes."

Eduardo tossed the cuffs on the ground in front of Ruby. "Put 'em on."

"And then what, Eduardo?"

"Huh?"

"After you take me home. Then what?"

"Gonna hand you over to the sheriff. Get you some help."

"Yeah, and then what?"

"What the hell are you going on about? Are you drunk . . . on drugs?"

Ruby's eyes burned into him. "I'll tell you how this'll go, Eduardo," she said in a calm, stern voice. "You'll bring me back. I'll go to county for maybe six months, a year tops, but at some point . . . I *will* be released. And where do you think I'll end up when I am?"

He knew, but didn't say.

"Think about it. I'll be coming home to live at my mom's house. The same house *you* live in. The same house *you* sleep in."

He shrugged. "Yeah . . . so."

"You enjoy a good night's sleep, don't you, Eduardo? Sure, you do. Who doesn't? Well, better sleep while you can, because once I'm home, a good night sleep's gonna be a thing of the past."

"If you think I'm scared of you, you got—"

"Something you need to know. I'm in bed with the *Devil*. You hear me? Got a demon in me. He's right here." She thumped her chest and took a step forward.

Without even realizing it, Eduardo stepped back.

"I'm *possessed*." She smiled wickedly. "Do you really want someone possessed by a demon living under the same roof as you?"

There was something about the way she said it that sent a chill down his spine. "Get that out of one of your 'devils and dragons' books?"

"Just trying to warn you, this demon, he makes me do things I don't wanna do. Bad things, Eduardo. Any night, any night at all, he could make me sneak into your room and jab a pair of scissors in your eye."

Eduardo flinched.

"Or maybe put rat poison in your Froot Loops. Throw battery acid in your face. Cut the brake line on your truck. You got eyes in the back of your head? You're gonna wish you had. Because no telling when he might make me sneak up behind you . . . drive a screwdriver into your skull."

"Shut up."

Ruby shrugged. "Won't be able to help myself, because I got *evil* in me. Could be the Devil, or could be I'm just plain psycho. Does it matter? Either way, you'll end up with a pair of scissors in your brain."

Eduardo licked his lips. "Bullshit. Bunch of bullshit. You're off your medication, that's all."

A weird thing happened then. Another voice overlapped hers, a deep eerie voice, creating a warbly echo.

"You're a God-fearing man, Eduardo, Eduardo, Eduardo," their voices said. *"I'm sure the Good Lord will keep you safe, safe, safe."*

Eduardo shook his head side to side, trying to clear away the weird sound.

"The Devil has many friends. You remember the woman in the woods, don't you?"

"She wasn't real. None of that was real." But the nightmares had been real, no matter how much he tried to push the dead woman from his mind, she still plagued his dreams.

"Well, here's another friend. Vutto, show Eduardo your face. Your *true* face."

The kid in the car stood up.

Eduardo jabbed the gun at him. "Careful, asshole!"

The kid took off his sunglasses, his hat and wig, unbuttoned his coat and . . . and Eduardo fell back a step, then another.

The kid was deformed, his skin scaly, and as though that were not horrible enough, he began twisting, right there in front of Eduardo, growing mouths and eyes out of his stomach, sprouting horns. His eyes, all of them, began to smoke, then glow.

Eduardo blinked, rubbed his own eyes, yet the demon, it was still there! The pistol began to shake in his hand. "Stay back! Stay back!"

Ruby picked up the cuffs, held out her wrists. "Okay, Eduardo. You wanna put these on me, so we can get going? Gonna be a long ride home."

Eduardo took a step back, another, then turned and hightailed it back to his truck.

Ruby followed Vutto up the back steps, her encounter with Eduardo leaving her heart drumming, but she was amazed that she wasn't a trembling mess. If anything, she felt invigorated. Not only had she stood up to a bully, she'd stayed in control, not just of herself but of the situation. Something she couldn't have done even a day ago. She'd seen him clearly for the broken man that he was. She wondered how this sad soul could've intimidated her for so long, actually felt sorry for him in a way.

"There you are!" someone called, a thin man with a shaved head and a big smile.

"Oh, hey, Dan," Tina said. "Sorry we're late, man. We're here now and ready to kick up a fuss!"

"Good thing," Dan said, ushering them down the hall. "You got an excited crowd waiting for you in there."

The rumble of the crowd echoed down the narrow hall, and Ruby found their excitement contagious, found she couldn't wait to play, to feel the magic again.

Vutto stumbled and to Ruby's surprise, it was Tina who caught him. "I gotcha, devil boy."

Tina reseated his hat and wig, covering his horns back up. They'd done a good job with Vutto's costume this time, but still, you didn't have to look too close to see he wasn't human. Luckily, it was dark in the hall and Dan wasn't paying attention anyway.

"Y'all wait here," Dan instructed. "Gonna go introduce you."

Tina handed Ruby her guitar and helped Vutto up.

Vutto winced and his eyes flared beneath the sunglasses. The worms, their song was growing louder by the minute. Ruby could see Vutto struggling to hold it together.

Dan's voice echoed down the hall. "Alright folks, they're here and ready to make some noise."

"No!" Vutto snarled, shaking his head. "No! They are my friends! I not kill my friends!"

Tina glanced at Ruby, her face going pale.

Sheelbeth has him, Beel said. **We are out of time.**

"Let's go," Ruby said, and they headed for the stage.

"Hold on, man," Tina said to Vutto, helping him along. "Just a little longer. You're a Night Mare now, you've got the mojo."

Vutto sucked in a deep breath and gave her a weak smile.

"And here they are," Dan announced. "The Night Mares."

The trio climbed onstage and Ruby was relieved to see the place was packed, the main floor and the balcony. There had to be at least triple the people at the previous show, if not more. And she dared to hope that it would be enough if . . . if they could just get playing before Vutto murdered her.

Vutto slid behind the drums while Ruby and Tina plugged in. Tina stummed her guitar and the crowd surged forward.

It's me, Richard.

I found the Metroplex, knew it was the right place because I could feel the witch near, her song so clear, no longer sweet, but cruel—taunting, torturing me. I needed to get my hands about her throat, now that very minute.

I pulled around back, spotted the Cadillac.

"Ruby!" I cried, and hit the brakes. She was there, heading in the back door of the club. I started to jump out, stopped—the demon, it was with them. I froze, terrified, then noticed the creature hobbling, barely able to make it up the steps, realized it was no longer much of a threat. I fumbled for my gun, but it was too late; they'd entered the building.

"Dadgumit! If I'd only been here two minutes earlier."

I pulled into the lot, searching for a spot near the Cadillac, only there weren't any; place was about full. I ended up farther away than I would've liked, but at least I was near the street, which would be good for a quick getaway.

I sat staring at Ruby's car, trying to figure out my plan. Just grab her and run was about all I'd come up with. Only, how was I supposed to do that with the place so full? Can't just drag her off the stage. Yet, waiting felt wrong. I could only guess how many other fine folks were feeling the same draw I was, the same burning desire to taste the witch's blood.

I watched a gaggle of rejects strut by, hooting and hollering, and a chill crawled down my spine. Christ, what if someone else got her first? Can't let that happen . . . no matter what. Be so unfair after all I'd been through. I groaned, knowing my opportunity to play, to have some one-on-one time with Ruby, was over, that I'd have to just shoot her and be done.

I touched the cold metal of my revolver and hoped that shooting Ruby would be enough to satiate this hunger, this craving. I feared it wouldn't.

I gently rubbed the throbbing lump on the back of my head and hoped that Chinese bitch would be there too. Because I wouldn't mind taking her down as well.

I picked up my hunting knife, admired its razor-sharp edge, decided it wouldn't hurt to bring it along, because I still might get the chance to slit Ruby's throat, to feel her warm blood on my hands.

I looked at the duffle bag of tools in the floorboard, at the pliers, drill, the torch. My eyes lingered on the torch and part of me wanted to cry. I'd never used a torch before and it looked like I never would, because I knew, in my gut, I wouldn't be walking away from this—be dead or in jail very soon.

There came the grind of guitars being tuned. I took a long look at the building. The club appeared to have only the front and rear entrance, all the windows being boarded up or barred.

"Fucking firetrap," I said, not wanting to go in there, knowing the place was a disaster waiting to happen. I cocked my head and thought about what I'd just said.

I stuffed the revolver and hunting knife into my belt and crawled into the back of the van. I pulled two empties out of the trash. Grabbed a roll of paper towels and climbed out of the van. I walked around back, to where I kept a five-gallon jerrican mounted next to the spare, unhitched it, and filled both bottles with gasoline. I wadded up a large wick of paper towels and stuffed them tightly into the tops of the bottles, watching as the paper towels soaked up the gas.

"The world starts in flame, the world ends in flame."

I slid a bottle in each pocket of my trench coat, double-checked that I had my lighter, then took a peek in the van's side mirror, nodding approvingly at the insane makeup-covered face smiling back at me.

"Well, I'm certainly not bored," I said and chuckled. "No. Never felt so alive."

I headed for the club, grinning and reeking of gasoline, just another freak going to the freakshow.

Eduardo sat in the front seat of his truck with the doors locked, hands clutched tightly together as though in prayer, trying to stop shaking.

"What was that? What the *fuck* was that?" But he knew, it was exactly what Ruby had said it was. A *demon,* and it had her. Not only had he seen it with his own eyes, he'd felt its evil, almost a thing he could touch. Like that woman, the one in the woods with the dead babies. And that voice coming from Ruby? He tried not to hear it, to force it from his mind. But he couldn't get it out of his head. Was that the very Devil speaking through her?

"God! What kind of wickedness have you got yourself into, Ruby?"

Eduardo let out a weak wail, then a whimper. A pathetic sound, like some terrified child. He glanced at the plastic Jesus hanging from his rearview mirror, then away, too ashamed to meet Jesus's little eyes.

He squeezed his own eyes shut, pressing out tears. "Oh, God. Oh, sweet, Jesus. I done failed you. Failed Martha, failed Ruby, and more than anyone, failed myself." It was his father's face that came to him with a look of utter disappointment, just like when Eduardo had hit that poor woman with his truck. Eduardo let out another whimper. "God, can't go home to them. Not like this. Can't bear it. Help me, Jesus. I'm begging you to help me."

He heard the rumble of guitars tuning up and flinched, stared out through his tears at the club. It was at that moment the little gold string holding the plastic crucifix broke. Just popped loose for no apparent reason. Jesus bounced off the dashboard and landed right on top of Eduardo's praying hands.

Eduardo looked down to find Jesus's little plastic face staring up at him with sad, gentle eyes, and it was as though a hand was placed on Eduardo's shoulder—firm yet full of love, telling him not to be afraid, that he wasn't alone.

All at once, Eduardo understood. This wasn't a test; this was a chance. God was giving him a chance. He saw the woman's face, the one from the accident.

Eduardo's heart sped up. "Redemption," he whispered. "Oh, Lord, I see." He brought the crucifix to his mouth and kissed plastic Jesus on the lips. "Thank you, Jesus."

With tears rolling down his face and snot running out of his nose, Eduardo retied the gold string around his neck, wearing plastic Jesus like a necklace.

"I am a warrior for the Lord."

He stared at the Metroplex, not with fear, but with hard determination.

"Hang on, Ruby. I'm gonna save you."

He shoved the handgun back into his shoulder holster, unlocked his door, and climbed out of the truck, striding boldly toward the front of the club.

"Though I walk through the valley of death, I shall fear no evil. For thou art with me."

"Evil, Evil, Evil!"

Ruby scanned the crowd, surprised to hear so many chanting for the song. She guessed they'd heard it on the radio, then she recognized Gary, the obnoxious rockabilly kid from the 688 show. And not just Gary, but his whole rockabilly crew. She did a double take—there, right next to them, the frat guys, again the same ones from the 688 show, and it appeared they'd brought plenty of friends along with them as well. The arty gals where here too. Ruby realized almost everyone up front was from the 688 show. But this time she sensed no hostility; they were smiling and chanting, rocking back and forth.

They're here for the song, Beel. For the magic. Oh, God, were gonna do it this time. Really gonna do it!

Yes, Beel said. **You are going to do it, Ruby. You are going to set us free. Now, start playing before Vutto kills you.**

Ruby saw the strain on Vutto's face; how he was struggling to hold on. She slipped over to the drums. "Okay, Vutto, let's go. Let's get free of Lord Motherfucker for good! Okay?"

Vutto nodded.

"Hit it, Vutto. Give me a beat!"

Vutto raised his quivering hands above the tom, but seemed unable to start.

"C'mon, Vutto!"

The demon shook his head like he was trying to dislodge an angry bee.

Ruby gave Tina a fretful glance.

Shit, Ruby thought, wondering if they could play the song without Vutto's driving beat. She started plucking at the bass, setting up a slow tempo. Tina joined her, looping the tune, waiting for Vutto.

Vuttos ears perked up, actually wiggled. He gave Ruby a weak smile and nodded. She smiled back and he began to drum.

Ruby grabbed the mic, met the crowd with wild eyes and a fierce grin. "We're the Night Mares and this is 'Evil in Me.' If you wanna feel the mojo, you gotta sing *along.*"

The crowd, especially those up front, let loose a wild howl.

Ruby sang the first verse solo, but this time, when the chorus came round, Ruby didn't have to cajole the crowd to sing with her, they joined right in. At first just those up front, but by the second chorus, almost everyone was singing.

There came the familiar tingling and the magic; it was there, swirling around the whole band. It must've given Vutto a boost, because he bumped up the tempo, banging out his primitive beat. Tina stomped her fuzz box, kicking the song into that wonderful grinding haze of hers. Ruby let loose with her wailing voice, sending the song into a melodic groove.

The crowd surged forward. Kids leaning over the balcony, and this time when the chorus came around, the whole house joined them, all but drowning out the band and Ruby looped around to the beginning.

"Devil on my hand, Devil in my band.

Devil's gonna take me down any way he can.

Only your spell, will keep me out of Hell.

Gotta gimmie all your heart and soul, gimmie all your heart and soul.

Gonna burn like a demon bowl, unless you give me all your heart and soul.

Gonna give you all my heart and soul, give you all my heart and soul.
Burnin' like a demon bowl, I give you all my heart and soul.

Devil's watchin' me squirm, Devil's watchin' me burn.
Devil in my belly like a wiggle worm.
C'mon, set me free, cast out the evil in me.
Gotta gimmie all your heart and soul, gimmie all your heart and soul.
Devil's never gonna let me go, unless you give me all your heart and soul.

Gonna give you all my heart and soul, give you all my heart and soul.
Devil's gonna let you go, I give you all my heart and soul.

Gotta set me free. Gotta set me free. Free all the evil in me,
evil in me, evil in me, evil in me . . ."

Holy fuck, Ruby thought, as goose bumps crawled along her flesh. *We're gonna blow the roof off this place.* The magic grew into a wave, powerful enough this time that Ruby felt it would lift her off her feet, take her wherever she pleased. She found the magic and it found her. It took no effort this time, they knew each other now, her and the spell. The scar, the symbol on her arm, grew warm as the magic entered, spreading into her chest, then, once more, that sensation of floating.

Ruby continued to sing, to howl, to lead the crowd along. The song went round and round, each time they hit the chorus, the crowd joining in, feeding the magic. Ruby could feel it swelling within her, so much stronger this time— she felt fit to burst.

"Gonna give you my all my heart and soul, give you all my heart and soul.
Devil gonna let you go, I give you all my heart and soul."

The ring, Beel called. **Now. Do it now!**

"Yes!" Ruby cried, and focused on the magic, amazed at its vigor, its desire to please. It spoke to her, told her freedom was hers, offering her escape from the ring and so much more.

Eduardo shoved his way through the crowd, pushing toward the stage, trying to keep out of the pit by moving along the wall. But the crowd surged this way and that, and he found no escape from all the sweaty, smelly bodies.

He searched for the demon, had to look twice at the stage before he realized the beast was right there with the band, playing the drums. He could actually see the faint glow of its eyes behind its sunglasses. Eduardo felt a chill, clutched the plastic Jesus. "I am not alone."

Ruby was really wailing now; Eduardo could feel it in his bones. He found himself once more trying to reconcile how this wild, brazen woman howling to the world like she owned it could possibly be the same Ruby that'd been living in her mother's basement just a few days ago.

God, she's howling like . . . like . . . He grimaced. *Like she's possessed.* Eduardo could think of no other way to describe it. He glared at the demon, wondering how Ruby fell into its trap. Then shook his head. He knew, of course he did. He thought of her room, of all the wicked posters, her art, how it was nothing but skulls and bats, and demons, and dragons, laced with symbols of the occult. Her tarot cards and that game, that Demons and Dragons game. And those Weejee, Woji, Oji, whatever-you-called-them boards, the ones with letters all over them. Why, there was just no telling what kind of door she'd opened. Eduardo wondered that it hadn't happened sooner.

He shuddered. *And me and my boy, sleeping in the same house with all that satanic crap.* Eduardo made a promise then and there, the minute he got home, he was going to give Ruby's room an enema, going to take every bit of that wickedness to the dump. Ruby was about to get some hard love, going to get some Jesus in a big way.

The stage was a platform that could be accessed from two sides. A large banner with a neon-green skull spray-painted on it hung down behind the band. The back door was nearest to the right side, so that's where Eduardo wanted to be. He was on a mission from God and there was no way he was going to let her out of his sight, no way he was going to blow this.

The crowd grew denser as he approached, crushing in on him, filling his nose with the smell of Aqua Net, beer, leather, and bad breath. He had to knock some douchey-looking twat out of the way before finding a good spot in the shadows, up against the wall. He wasn't normally claustrophobic, but just knowing there were no fire exits in this tinderbox made it hard to breathe. "For Jesus," he said. "I can do anything for Jesus."

Everyone was singing now. Eduardo wondered what was the deal, what was it about this song that had everyone so lit up? Were they *all* on drugs? And it was then he realized he was tapping his toes, humming along. "Stop it," he snarled at himself. But there was something in the air, hard to put into words, a seductive warmth maybe? He studied the crowd, could see it on their faces, it was more than drugs, they were under his spell . . . *Satan*.

His eyes shot to the demon. Was it looking at him? God, it was. "No, no, you won't get in my head." Eduardo pushed his fingers into his ears, began praying. The prayer clearing his head enough that he realized that this was his chance, now, while everyone was so out of their minds.

There were only two bouncers, neither of them looked like much to Eduardo, and both of them appeared as gone as everyone else. Only the demon then. He touched his handgun through his jacket to reassure himself and pushed forward.

That was when the flaming bottle hit the window and exploded.

There was a slender window on the left side of the stage. There were bars on the window, so the bottle must have hit the bars first, because most of the explosion was outside, but enough broke through to set one of the amps on fire. Someone might've been able put it out in time, but then a second bottle hit and this one came in between the bars, smashing through the old window pane and exploding inside the building. Flaming gas landed on the floor and to the side of the stage, setting another amp and the banner on fire.

The music stopped, there was a moment of almost complete silence, the only sound that of the flames, then someone screamed, then everyone screamed.

"Ruby!" Eduardo cried, leaping for the stage, knowing he had to get her out fast.

A howl went off like a siren, a chilling sound that rose above all the screams. It was the demon, its head thrust back, wailing to the roof. It set blazing eyes on Ruby, snarled, and came for her.

"Ruby!" Tina cried. "Look out!"

Ruby just stood there like she was lost, blinking and swaying as though drunk.

The demon kicked through the kit, sending drums flying everywhere. Tina swung her guitar at the beast. The demon caught the guitar, tore it from her grasp, and smashed it into her head. Tina crumpled to the stage.

Eduardo fumbled for his handgun, started up onstage, only to be knocked back to the floor by one of the bouncers rushing to escape the flames.

Ruby seemed to wake up then, but it was too late, the demon was upon her, jumping on top of her and knocking her down. She kicked at it wildly and it caught her foot in its mouth, sinking its teeth into her ankle. There came an awful crunch and Ruby screamed.

Eduardo made the stage, leapt over, and drove his boot into the demon's side—a scoring punt in any game, but it barely knocked the creature back. But barely was all Eduardo needed. He leveled his handgun and fired, four hollow-point rounds into the thing's chest, and four more directly into its head, blowing flesh and bone all across the stage.

The demon clutched what was left of its head and stumbled back, howling and flailing. The beast tumbled into the burning banner, tugging the banner down on top of it in a flaming, tangled heap.

There came a bright burst of flame, followed by a green plume of foul-smelling smoke. One final screech and the thing crumbled to ash right before Eduardo's eyes.

Eduardo pulled Ruby to her feet. She let out a painful cry and collapsed, clutching her ankle where the demon had bit her. He could see it was twisted at an odd angle, was probably broken.

Smoke was rapidly filling the room. Eduardo started to pick her up and carry her, but to where? Both exists were blocked by the crowds of panicking people. He knew they'd never make it out, that those people were doomed.

"Jesus help us!" he cried, coughing on the smoke as he searched for any other way. There was another window on the right side of the stage. Eduardo hefted one of the amps and ran it into the window. The glass shattered, and a wave of fresh air came into the room, but the amp was stopped by the bars.

"No!" he cried, then noticed the amp had knocked the lower hinges loose on the bars. "Oh, Lord Jesus. Thank you!" He tugged the amp back out, and with a mighty groan, hefted it over his head and threw it with all his worth into the bars.

This time the amp smashed through.

He let out a triumphant shout and grabbed Ruby, carrying her to the window. But to his surprise, she grabbed the broken bars and wouldn't let go.

"Tina!" she cried. "We gotta get Tina!"

"Let go!" he yelled at her.

"No! We can't leave Tina!"

"Okay, I'll get her. I swear. Just let go!"

She let loose and he helped her slide down the short drop to the parking lot. She landed on her good foot, then fell over onto the gravel. Eduardo had a moment's hesitation, afraid he'd lose her, but looking at her ankle, he felt sure she wasn't going anywhere.

Eduardo fumbled his way back through the smoke, found Tina on her knees, clutching her head. He grabbed her and pulled her over to the window, then helped her down.

He started to follow, then stopped, hearing all the screams, really hearing them. He couldn't see much through the smoke, but knew they must be packed like sardines trying to escape. People would be dying soon, suffocating under the crush of bodies.

"No, I can't help them," he said, when a woman stumbled past. He grabbed her without even thinking, because he knew he *could* help her. "This way," he yelled, leading her to the window.

He spotted other shadowy figures nearby. "No," he said, yet he went for them, guiding two more kids over. He went back again, to the tangle of people this time, coughing and choking as smoke burned his eyes, wrangled a few more kids free.

"Jesus, what am I doing? I'm gonna die in here." And it was then that he understood what was going on. God had put him here, in this burning building, for this very purpose, to save these stupid kids. *This! This is all part of my redemption.*

The flames were burning themselves out, which was good, but it made for more of the black choking smoke. And Eduardo knew it was this deadly smoke and the crush of the crowd that was going to get him killed, yet he continued guiding people out, must've led three dozen people to safety before the fire trucks finally showed up.

Eduardo climbed down out of the window, collapsed onto the gravel, gasping and heaving up a gutful of black sooty snot and bile.

The fire crews began knocking out windows and entering the building.

Eduardo pushed himself up to his feet, looking for Ruby. She was gone. So was her friend.

"Oh no," he said. "No!"

He headed toward the Cadillac, hoping to catch them before they got away. But the car was still there.

He saw Tina. She looked frantic. He grabbed her. "Where's Ruby?"

"Some guy, some weirdo . . . he took her! I don't know—"

"Took her?" Eduardo scanned the parking lot—all was chaos, lights and sirens, a few ambulances had arrived and people were running every which way.

He let Tina go and headed up toward the road, heard a woman yelling. He slipped past a truck and spotted Ruby. She was handcuffed and some freak job with his face painted white, was trying to force her into a van. The guy punched her in the stomach, doubling her over, then shoved her in the back.

"No!" Eduardo growled and sprinted for the van, coming up fast on the creep, hitting him from behind, slamming the guy into the side of the van. The man bounced off the door and landed on the ground. Eduardo put a knee in his back.

"You're not going anywhere, asshole!" Eduardo shouted.

"Eduardo," Ruby gasped, trying to tell him something.

That's when Eduardo heard the blast, felt the slug go into his gut.

Eduardo fell back against the van, clutching his stomach.

The creep crawled to his feet, a gun in his hand. He wiped the blood off his mouth, spat, then shot Eduardo three more times.

Eduardo slid to the ground, lay there groaning with tears streaming from his eyes as he watched the van drive away. The world was growing dim. He reached for the plastic Jesus around his neck. Kissed it.

"Redemption," he whispered, and his world went dark.

ICE PICK

R uby jolted awake, glanced around the inside of the van, moaned. It wasn't a nightmare, she was still here, still tied up. This was really happening.

She was pretty sure they'd been driving the whole night, but it was hard to tell, as she'd nodded off a few times, exhausted from terror. But she knew they must be hundreds of miles from Atlanta by now, that they could be anywhere, that no one would even be looking for them this far away.

They'd stopped only once that she could remember, not too long ago, sometime after leaving the highway. That was when he'd stripped her down to her underwear and strapped her to the ties in the rear of the van. One side of her face was swollen and hot from where he'd slapped and punched her when she'd tried to resist.

She sat now on a small bed, her back against the paneled doors, her hands cuffed to either wall, her ankles bound together at the base of the bed.

The van slowed and hit a bump, then another. Ruby couldn't see the driver because there was a panel between them, but she could see a little out of the front, enough to tell it was morning and they were on a dirt road in the woods somewhere.

Beel, are you there?

I am here.

God . . . I'm so scared.

I am here.

The van stopped, backed up, pulled forward, straightened. The man cut the engine and popped his head around the panel, studied Ruby. His makeup was smeared and he looked like a melting ghoul.

"Have to relieve the old bladder," he said and grinned. "Be right back, gumdrop. Don't you go nowhere."

Beel, please. Do something.

He didn't reply.

Beel?

I am here, Ruby. I . . . I do not know.

Ruby began to tremble. And even through the terror, the knowledge that she was about to die horribly, that she was going to Hell, whatever that meant, an overwhelming sadness took her. It was her mother, it was knowing she'd never see her again, would never be able to hug her and tell her in person, that she loved her. "Mom . . . I love you, Mom."

The side door slid open and the man climbed in, shutting it behind him.

"Goodness gracious, that felt good. Not healthy holding it in that long, y'know." He took a seat on the short bench next to Ruby.

"Hi, I'm Richard, but most folks call me Dick. I don't like being called Dick. Don't know who does, really. So, Richard, okay? That sound good?"

Ruby said nothing.

Dick unbuttoned his shirt and tugged it off, followed by his pants, stripping down to his dingy briefs and socks. He scratched his flabby belly, then grabbed the handle of a duffel bag and slid it over. There came a metal clang that chilled

Ruby's teeth. He unzipped the bag and began removing tools, setting them on the small table beside him.

"Please," Ruby pleaded. "Please, don't do this."

He stopped and looked at her for a long moment. "Well, okay then. If you really don't want me to, I won't." He started putting the tools back into the bag, a screwdriver, pliers, ice pick. He stopped and smiled at her. "Just kidding." He let out a big laugh and pulled the tools back out. He laughed again. "That would've been funny though, huh?"

"Listen," Ruby said. "You kill me and you're gonna release it. The demon. It'll come for you. Gonna take you straight to Hell."

Dick paused, seemed to be contemplating this. "No . . . I don't think so. I mean, I might've bought into that a few days ago. But I've come to see things differently of late."

"You're doing Satan's bidding. Playing right into his hands."

Dick plucked up the ice pick. "See, I'm thinking just the opposite . . . that I'm doing God's bidding here. Which is a pretty funny thing, considering that I was an atheist up until yesterday. But, man, oh man, it just seems that God, the Good Lord Jesus, has been there for me every step of the way. He practically handed you to me out of that fire last night. I mean, it was biblical. Still haven't got over that. And . . ." He tapped his head. "This song, this sweet, terrible song. It's like angels are singing to me . . . leading me right to you. If that isn't enough to convince a man that God exists, I don't know what is."

"It's the demon singing to you. Can't you see that?"

"No . . . I don't think so. The way I see it is, you're some sort of servant of Satan, a witch perhaps. I mean, heck, you had a demon following you around, protecting you. Like to see you explain that one."

He waited. "Yeah, that's about what I thought." He tapped her nose with the ice pick. "Well, whatever you are. God wants you dead."

He jabbed the tool into her shoulder. Ruby fought not to scream, but couldn't help it as he twisted the tool around; the pain overwhelming.

Dick watched mesmerized as the blood rolled down her arm, then he pulled the tool free and started lapping the blood, licking his way up to the wound, then sucking on it, slurping loudly.

Ruby struggled to tug her hands free, the cuffs biting into her wrists. She struggled to breathe, her whole body shivering and shaking. She was on the verge of fainting, hoping she would, anything to escape the pain, the horror.

After a minute he leaned back. Blood was smeared into his makeup. He smacked his lips. "God, that's amazing." He burped. "Really, it's the cat's pajamas. But, y'know, it's somewhat troubling. Want to know why?"

Ruby didn't, all she wanted was to be as far away from this man as she could get.

"Because this isn't who I am." One of his eyes began to twitch. "It brings everything into question. I don't even know if I'm evil anymore. You see, this used to all be horrible to me. Something I had to force myself to do. I would cry right along with my victim. But I'm not crying now. No, because I *want* to do this. No, I *need* to do this, *have* to. And that's all wrong. It's more of a compulsion then, right? Are you following? How is this act evil, if I can't control it? Or worse, if it controls me? How am I morally culpable? It's a real conundrum."

He squinted at her. "Hey, are you listening? You look like you're thinking about something else." Dick tapped the ice pick against his teeth. "Boy, I sure got a lot to unpack here . . . a lot to mull over. But I can work it out later, because right now, right now, all that matters is that I've never felt more alive."

He stabbed Ruby in the belly.

Tina tapped the glass of the WREK broadcast room.

Greg looked up from the board, gave her a small smile, and waved her in; he'd been expecting her.

"Here's one of my all-time favorite bands, X, to put a little pep in your morning commute," he said, speaking into the mic. He pushed play on one of the cassettes, tugged off his headphones, and stood up.

"Greg, I'm . . . I'm sorry about . . . I shouldn't of . . ." Tina started, but didn't know where to go from there. She'd been up all night and was exhausted, hadn't even had a chance to change out of her smoke-stained stage dress.

"Hey, no. We're not gonna worry about any of that. Not now. Besides, seems I'm in the habit of rewarding bad behavior."

She gave him a weak smirk and shook her head.

He came around the desk and gave her a hug. "Any word? Anything about your friend?"

Tina fought back tears. "No. I mean a lot of folks saw the van. Got the license plate and all. The police are looking everywhere. But it's like the van just disappeared."

"Okay, I got the tape queued up. You sure you're up for this? I can do it if not."

"I got it," Tina said, taking a long sip of Greg's coffee. "Anything for Ruby."

Greg put his headphones back on and handed a pair to Tina.

The current song wound down and Greg clicked on his mic.

"Good morning, WREK listeners. I hate to have to share such sad news with you, but for those who haven't heard, there was a terrible fire at the Metroplex club last night. According to eyewitnesses, a man wearing bizarre face paint threw two firebombs into the building. Four people suffocated during the panic to escape, and a fifth died from smoke inhalation. Dozen more are still being treated. Thankfully, the fire department was able to extinguish the flames before more lives were lost.

"But that's only part of the story. Apparently, the same suspect that set the blaze also shot and killed a man in the parking lot. The shooting taking place as that man tried to stop the suspect from kidnapping a woman."

Greg sighed. "The woman that was abducted was Ruby Tucker, the lead singer of the Night Mares, the band playing during the attack. This morning, I have Tina Tang, the guitarist for the Night Mares, joining us. She has something she'd like to share with everyone."

Greg nodded to Tina and she leaned into the mic. "I watched a man kidnap my best friend last night. I've never felt so helpless in my life. But I'm not giving up on her. Never gonna give up on her, because she's not only my best friend, she's also a bright light in the world . . . there's a spark of magic in everything she does. Like her song, 'Evil in Me.' Ruby believed that this song was a spell, that it would free her from the many demons in her life. That all she needed was for folks to sing along, that their voices, their spirits, would lift her up and set her free. So, I'm gonna play her song this morning and I'm hoping every one of you out there will lend Ruby your voice and a bit of your heart. Hoping that maybe, just maybe, we can send some magic her way. Enough to set her loose of this terrible man."

"So, here it is, folks. 'Evil in Me,' by Ruby Tucker and the Night Mares."

Greg clicked play and the song began, Ruby's voice drifting out over the airways, sending a chill down Tina's spine. When the chorus came around, Tina and Greg joined in. Tina hoping and praying everyone out there did too. Greg once told her that WREK reached upward of sixty thousand listeners on any given morning. Tina figured if even half of them were to sing, something would happen, something big.

"Beel," a distant voice called. *"Beel,"* this time a little clearer. It was Lord Sheelbeth. *"It is over. It is done. The girl will be dead soon. I am sorry it has come to this."*

Beel knew it was over; the worms' song ringing loudly in his ears. **Do not kill her,** he pleaded. **There is no need to kill her now. You have me.**

"It is too late, Beel. You have made your choice."

Spare her . . . make the man stop. You can do that.

"You are not hearing me. The woman is mortally wounded. She is dying."

Beel could feel Ruby's diminishing heartbeat, could plainly see she'd lost too much blood.

The man, this Dick, was slurping at Ruby's neck. He released her, leaned back against the wall of the van and gasped—Ruby's blood dripping from his lips, his chin, all down his bare chest, staining his underwear red. The man pulled the ice pick out of Ruby's neck and laid it on the table. He must've stuck Ruby a dozen times with that ice pick, all over her body, drinking from each fresh wound like some ghoulish vampire.

"Wow," he burped and wiped his mouth. "That was . . . *sublime*. The bee's knees, I'm telling you. Never felt anything like it."

"*Beel,*" Lord Sheelbeth called. "*Finish it . . . wipe the ring and come home. There is no need for you to share her pain any longer.*"

Beel knew there was nothing left that he could do for Ruby, it was only a waiting game at this point.

Beel set Ruby's thumb to the ring, started to wipe it clean.

Ruby moaned.

Just a little longer, Beel pleaded with Sheelbeth. **Please. I do not wish to leave her to die alone with this madman.**

"*No!*" Lord Sheelbeth said sternly, her voice growing sharp. "*You must do it now, right now!*" Beel detected a touch of panic. Why? What did Lord Sheelbeth possibly have to worry about at this point?

"*Beel, quick, wipe the ring. This is your last chance, or the flame!*"

Beel felt it then, a tingling in the air. **Ruby,** Beel called. **Ruby, do you feel that?**

Ruby didn't respond.

It was all around them, growing stronger.

Dick sat up, looked furtively about. "What's that?"

The curtains ruffled as though from a light breeze, only there was none.

The magic, Beel thought. *By all the stars, it is the magic!*

Dick pushed aside the curtain, peered out into the morning light. "I don't like this. Not one bit." He picked up a long knife and glared at Ruby. "This is more of your witchy voodoo. Isn't it?"

Beel could hear it now, or rather feel it—vibrations in the air. The vibrations moved to the tune of Ruby's song, "Evil in Me," growing stronger by the second. He didn't know how or why, didn't care. **Ruby, do you not feel it?**

Ruby didn't respond.

Ruby, your magic . . . it's here! Ruby, call it. Ruby!

Nothing from Ruby; he could no longer sense her heartbeat.

Her song grew louder, pushing away that of the worms.

Ruby! Beel cried, going deeper within, into her subconsciousness, trying to find her, trying to bring her back. **Ruby!**

Beel?

Your magic, it is here!

"Stop this!" Lord Sheelbeth cried.

Let it in, Ruby, Beel cried. **Let the magic in!**

The magic, it seemed to lift her and for a moment, Ruby was with him. *That's my song.* She smiled.

Let it in!

"Beel!" Lord Sheelbeth screamed. *"What are you doing? You will ruin every-thing!"*

"Yes," Ruby whispered to the magic. "Come to me. Please come to me." The scar on her arm heated up, the symbol glowing golden along her arm.

"What the fuck?" Dick cried.

"Stop this!" Lord Sheelbeth shouted.

The magic entered the scar, so much magic, flooding into her, filling her up, her whole body quivered.

The spell, Ruby, now the spell! Set us free!

"Free . . . fre . . . f . . ." Ruby was trying to speak, trying to steer the spell, drifting in and out of consciousness. *Beel . . . I can't. Please . . . help.* And in that moment, she gave herself over to him, completely, heart and soul. Her head lolled, she tried to say something else, then her chin fell to her chest.

Ruby! Ruby! Beel cried. She was still there, barely, but so weak. He came forward, becoming one with her and her magic. He felt the power of the spell as he'd never before, the potency, the promise, all his to command. "Freedom," he whispered through Ruby's lips, and took her thumb and pushed the ring. It slid over the knuckle.

"So much magic!" Lord Sheelbeth said, all at once sounding more amazed than anything else. *"Beel, do you know what this means?"*

It means I am free.

"If you leave now, the woman will die. She will be in Hell with me. Is that what you want?"

I do not care, Beel said, only he did, and he hated that he did. He hesitated.

"I can save her. I am a healer, a savior, you know this. How many have you seen

me save? Use this power to free me of my prison, to free us all, and I swear on my soul to you that I will save her life."

Beel wondered if it would work. If he really could free the lord. It was a freedom spell. But even if so, why would he? That would be madness. **And then what? For us to be your slaves, serving you for eternity?**

"Hear me, Beel. I Lord Sheelbeth swear on my soul before all the gods living and dead, that I will heal this woman, that I will set her free, that I will set you free from me forever. I swear it a thousand times. There, you have my vow. Now do it, Beel. Save her life, save her soul!"

No, no, there is too much at stake!

"Beel, you are letting your hate blind you. We can all win. You owe me this, Beel. You owe me!"

No, Beel said. **I cannot . . . I—**

"Witch!" Dick screamed, raising the knife and stabbing Ruby in the chest.

No! Beel cried, and pushed the spell into the ring, willing it to free Lord Sheelbeth, and found, in that moment, saving Ruby was the only thing that mattered. He felt the magic shooting into the ring, down into Hell itself.

The ring began to throb, the eye opened wide, began to glow.

Beel felt the magic connect with Sheelbeth, felt it tearing, tugging, struggling to free her from Hell's unforgiving grasp. **What have I done?**

Dick yanked the knife out, started to stab Ruby again, when a loud hiss came from the ring, followed a moment later by twisting smoke spewing from out of the eye. The smell of sulfur filled the van.

"Stop it!" Dick cried.

Beel steered the spell to Ruby and the handcuffs crumbled, the straps holding her legs snapped. Ruby collapsed onto her side, on the mattress.

Dick's eyes bulged as the funnel of smoke rolled around him to the front of the van, as it began to boil and thicken, to take on the shape of a person.

Dick grabbed Ruby by the throat and held the knife over her face. "Send it back! Send it back now, or die!"

Beel reached for the tools on the table, his hand, Ruby's hand, landing on the ice pick. With a tremendous effort, he grabbed it and jabbed it into Dick's side.

"Mother of God!" Dick cried, fumbling the knife as he clutched the ice pick, groaning as he slid it out.

Laughter came from behind Dick. He spun round, and there, squatting between the front bucket seats, was Lord Sheelbeth, nude, the worms squirming in her gut—every one of them glaring and screaming at Dick.

Dick screamed back.

"I am free!" Lord Sheelbeth shouted and laughed again, loud and bold. "By all the damned angels in Hell, I am free!"

Dick pointed the ice pick at Sheelbeth.

Lord Sheelbeth cocked her head, studied the quivering man. "I am hungry," she said, and slapped the ice pick away. She grabbed Dick by the neck and shoved him face-first into her gut, into the mass of screaming worms. "Feast!" she cried, and the hundreds of tiny mouths did, devouring the man inch by inch, grinding him away in a short minute.

"What have I done?" Beel moaned, from Ruby's throat.

Lord Sheelbeth set her single eye on Ruby, on the ring. She extended her hand. "To me," she said, and the ring sprouted legs, hopped off Ruby's finger and onto Lord Sheelbeth's. Lord Sheelbeth brought the ring to her lips and kissed it.

"Save her," Beel said, barely able to make Ruby's lips move. "Save Ruby. You promised."

"I did, Beel. I did. And I have never broken such a vow in my life. But maybe this is a new chapter for me. Maybe honor is just another trap. Maybe you need a lesson." He saw it then, the fury beneath her smile. "How Beel, how could you betray me so? My heart is broken."

"That is between us, not Ruby."

Lord Sheelbeth studied Ruby for a long minute, as though weighing Beel's words. Finally, she knelt next to Ruby, taking her hand, examining the black lines twisting up her wrist. The symbol on her arm was no longer glowing, once more just a scar.

"Her magic . . . it is all used up," Sheelbeth let out a long sigh. "Perhaps I owe her something."

Lord Sheelbeth clasped Ruby's hand between both of hers, and just as Beel had seen on the battlefield an age ago, when Sheelbeth healed the wounded and dying, she began to sing to Ruby. A moment later the worms, all of them, joined in.

A warmth slid up Ruby's arm, spread through her body, burning into each and every wound.

The wounds began to heal.

Ruby let out a loud gasp and then a moan, coughed loudly. She stared up at Lord Sheelbeth. "Beel? Am I dead?"

Lord Sheelbeth fiddled with the van door handle, couldn't seem to figure it out. Ruby sat up, waited a moment for her head to stop spinning, then lifted the handle and slid the door open for the lord.

Soft morning light streamed in, along with the fresh forest air, the smell of pine needles and dew filling the van. Ruby heard birdcalls and the sound of water trickling nearby.

Sheelbeth hopped from the van with catlike grace and stood in a ray of sunlight, utterly shameless in her nakedness. She was too intense to be beautiful— her face all hard angles, her single eye blazing, but there was a regalness to her that created its own beauty. Her body was thin and sinewy, muscles rippling like taut ropes beneath her pale ashen flesh. The gaping wound, the worms' lair, slowly closed, sealing off its squirming denizens, forming a tight-lipped slit that looked like some aquatic gill running from her sternum to her pubic mound.

The lord strolled a few steps, stopping at the edge of a sandy creek. She began to shake, then suddenly dropped to her knees. She dug her hands into the soft earth, bringing two fistfuls of soil to her face. She sucked in their scent then kissed the dirt. She let out a sob. "I am free. By the sun, by the moon, by all the heavens, I am free. Never again shall I let down my guard." She sat staring at the soil in her hands while the honeybees buzzed around her. A butterfly flittered along, landing on her arm and she stood, studying it with a small smile on her face.

Ruby slid out of the van, almost fell, steadying herself against the vehicle. She had on only her bra and underwear and the morning air felt cold against her bloodstained skin. Her ankle where Vutto had bitten her still throbbed a bit, but it, along with her other wounds, seemed to be all but healed.

Lord Sheelbeth walked back to her, held out her hand. "Come with me. We have unfinished dealings, you and I."

Ruby looked at her, unsure. *What does she want, Beel?*

I believe it is okay, Beel replied.

Believe? That's not very reassuring.

Ruby took Lord Sheelbeth's hand and the lord helped her walk down the short embankment to the edge of the creek, to a spot where the water ran dark and deep.

"Remove your rags, girl, and let us go into the water."

"Ma'am?"

"To cleanse your soul."

Beel! What the hell is she talking about?

Sheelbeth laughed. "The taint. I would cleanse you of it. Unless, of course, you prefer to have every wicked soul chasing you until the end of your days."

"Oh . . . no, ma'am, I don't."

"Then follow me."

Ruby removed her underwear and followed the strange woman into the creek. "Ah, heck, it's freezing!"

"I have known nothing but the kiss of flame for centuries," Lord Sheelbeth said. "How good it is to feel the breath of cold once more." Sheelbeth waded in to chest level. "Come to me, child."

Again, Ruby hesitated.

"I will not eat you, not this day, maybe another time, but not this day." She grinned.

Ruby came to her and she slid in behind Ruby, wrapping her arms around Ruby's waist and pressing her belly against Ruby's back. Ruby felt the pulsing scar, shuddered.

"Are you ready?"

No, Ruby thought, but nodded.

Lord Sheelbeth tugged her under and they sank into the murky depths.

Ruby had a moment's panic, sure she would drown, then a song came to her, vibrating through the water, eerie and full of echoes. It was Lord Sheelbeth of course. The worms joined in, filling the deep with their song. Ruby felt them squirming against her back, yet no longer felt any dread. A sort of warm sleep stole over her and it was as though she no longer needed to breathe, all she needed was this song.

Ruby awoke, lying on the sandy bank, Lord Sheelbeth sitting beside her, watching the water bugs skimming along the surface of the creek.

"It is done," Lord Sheelbeth said.

"It is?"

Lord Sheelbeth stood, offered Ruby her hand, helping her to her feet. Only Ruby realized she didn't need help, that she felt, what? Renewed, yes, and so much more. She felt the forest around her as though it were a living, breathing thing, every cricket's chirp, every bird's call, and she was a part of it all. She sucked in a deep lungful of air, marveled at its sweetness, then noticed that every wound on her body, even the scar from the spell, was completely gone, not even a trace.

"It is time for me to disappear," Lord Sheelbeth said. "The angels have become complacent in this age. But we opened a door here, and they might very well investigate. I do not wish to be here if they do."

She touched Ruby's shoulder, pushed the wet bangs from Ruby's brows, and looked deep into her eyes, into her soul. "Beel, I hope you find the joy you are seeking in this new world. And perhaps, one day, if you can let go of the hate in your heart, you will seek me out. There are not many of our age left, we might very well be the last. And sometimes it is good to share the past with one who has lived it with you. I hope there might come a time when you will once more enjoy my company. I know I would enjoy yours."

With that she headed away, vanishing into the woods.

I will never seek her company, Beel said. *I am done with lords, and gods, and devils.*

"Yeah, me too."

Ruby, it is time I go.

Ruby was surprised to feel a wave of sadness steal over her. "Now? You gotta go now?"

Why, Ruby, if I did not know better, I would say you are in no hurry to be rid of me.

She grinned. "Well, you're pretty okay for a demon."

He laughed. *And you, Ruby, are pretty okay for a human. But we both know I must go.*

Loud squawks came from all around, and Beel pushed Ruby's head up so they could both see the flock of crows hopping around in the pines above them.

"You're gonna fly away, aren't you?"

I am. It is time to live with the wild things . . . at least for now. Life is so much less complicated amongst the wild. To go where each day leads me. Nothing more.

"Y'know, on one hand I'm jealous. For so long there was nothing I wanted more than to just leave it all behind. But I've got a lot of fixing to do, and I'm grateful I'm gonna get the chance to set some things right. Especially with the folks I might've hurt." She knew she'd most likely be serving a bit of time as well, wasn't looking forward to it, but felt after all she'd been through she could deal with anything. "You've given me that second chance, Beel. Thank you."

One of the crows landed on a nearby limb.

Yes, a second chance. You have set me free in so many ways, Ruby. Goodbye, Ruby.

She felt a sensation like wind passing through her skin and saw him then, a wispy, ghostly form drifting upward toward the bird. He glanced down at her, gave her a nod, then it was as though he were sucked into the bird.

The crow let out a startled squawk, leapt in the air and flew away, disappearing into the woods in the opposite direction that Lord Sheelbeth had gone.

"Goodbye, Beel," Ruby said, as a wave of loneliness like she had never known fell over her.

My name is . . . my name . . . heck, what is it?

Oh, yeah, Richard, my name is Richard.

But most people call me Dick. I used to hate being called Dick. Doesn't matter a lick of spit to me anymore. Nothing matters really, but Lord Sheelbeth. She's the bee's knees, the cat's pajamas, my sun and moon, the icing on my cupcake. I've never been much of a singer, but by Jove, I live to sing now. Her songs . . . her wonderful, terrible songs . . . any and all of them. God, I hate them, God, I love them. There's nothing better than squirming around in all this hot worm spunk with my brethren, singing our little wormy heads off. Happy as clams in butter sauce we are. Hoping and praying it never ends. My name is . . . my name is . . . ah, hell, can't remember. And know what? I don't care. Not a lick of spit, because it doesn't matter . . . nothing matters, not anymore . . . nothing but Lord Sheelbeth.

ACKNOWLEDGMENTS

First and foremost, a huge thank-you to my editor, Kelly Lonesome. For her intuition of story and character, and for helping me find the tale I truly wanted to tell. Kelly, you are voodoo.

I would like to express my gratitude to all the souls at Tor Nightfire for their hard work making this book happen. Thank you, Kristin Temple, Michael Dudding, Valeria Castorena, Jocelyn Bright, Esther Kim, Jeff LaSala, Greg Collins, Sarah Walker, Jessica Warren, Susan Cummins.

Additional round of appreciation goes to my beta readers, Ivy Brom, AJ Grey, and Laurie Brom. All three of you made a tremendous impact on this story.

A special thank-you to AJ Grey and the Maxines for their role in bringing the "Evil in Me" song to life. To hear their haunting rendition, please visit them on Instagram: @themaxinesband.

And always, a big thank-you to Julie Kane-Ritsch, for her friendship and guidance.

ABOUT THE AUTHOR

Over the past few decades, acclaimed dark fantasy author and artist **BROM** has lent his distinctive vision to all facets of the creative industries, from novels and games to comics and film. He is the *USA Today* bestselling author of *Slewfoot, The Child Thief, Krampus, Lost Gods,* and the award-winning, illustrated horror novels *The Plucker* and *The Devil's Rose.* Brom is currently kept in a dank cellar just outside Savannah.

bromart.com
Facebook.com/Brom.Artist
Instagram: @geraldbrom
Twitter: @GeraldBrom